Frank Lean

Nine Lives

ARROW

Reprinted by Arrow Books in 2004

1 3 5 7 9 10 8 6 4 2

Copyright © Frank Lean 1995

First published in the United Kingdom in 1995 by Mandarin Paperbacks

Arrow Books
The Random House Group Limited
20 Vauxhall Bridge Road, London, SW1V 2SA

Random House Australia (Pty) Limited
20 Alfred Street, Milsons Point, Sydney,
New South Wales 2061, Australia

Random House New Zealand Limited
18 Poland Road, Glenfield
Auckland 10, New Zealand

Random House (Pty) Limited
Endulini, 5a Jubilee Road, Parktown 2193, South Africa

The Random House Group Limited Reg. No. 954009

www.randomhouse.co.uk

A CIP catalogue record for this book
is available from the British Library

MIX
Paper from
responsible sources
FSC® C018072

ISBN 0 74 931679 9

The Random House Group Limited supports The Forest Stewardship
Council® (FSC®), the leading international forest-certification organisation.
Our books carrying the FSC label are printed on FSC®-certified paper.
FSC is the only forest-certification scheme supported by the leading
environmental organisations, including Greenpeace. Our
paper procurement policy can be found at
www.randomhouse.co.uk/environment

Printed and bound in Great Britain by Clays Ltd, St Ives plc

For my parents
May and Jack L. and
my son John Robert.

Prologue

Spring 1994

These days anyone who has a brush with one of life's grimmer aspects can get counselling. Not me, though. A counsellor would run screaming once they heard my story: corpses, assassination attempts, unjust incarceration, mayhem . . . If ever I tried confiding in anyone I'd end up doing five years for manslaughter at the very least.

When I study my face in the shaving mirror I can't understand how such an honest-looking, friendly, open character as me could have landed in such a quagmire. My dear father Paddy Cunane, a retired detective superintendent in the Manchester Police Force, thinks I have a congenital disposition when it comes to landing myself in the brown stuff. He may be right.

As usual, I'd jumped in with both feet. It was Kath Headlam's simple little commission to recover a lost briefcase that landed me in the untreated effluent in the first place. How could anyone, even someone as farseeing as my father, have known what that simple commission would lead to?

1

Wednesday before Christmas. 22nd December 1993

The place where it all began was unlikely: a travellers' camp in Salford.

Searching a tinker encampment for a stolen car hadn't seemed like a good idea even at the time and I wouldn't have been there if it hadn't been for the letter from Miss Attleigh at the Polar Building Society. She was going to 'put matters in the hands of the Society's solicitors' if I didn't cough up some of the arrears on my mortgage. Her letter had arrived the day before. Business had been terrible recently; stock leakage in the supermarkets was down – the public were too poor to go out and steal – and no one wanted to hire a private investigator. Of course I'd made things worse by telling Charlie Sims, Happyways Supermarkets' security boss, where to go when he offered to take me onto his payroll full time.

Now the price of my pride was a trawl round the slums of Salford, a city whose record for casual violence makes Manchester look like a kiddies' playground. It was a freezing day, too, with heavy mist in the air and a ground frost glistening on all surfaces.

Chasing up missing cars isn't my usual line of work, but having turned my back on what few openings existed in the retail trade I had to take work wherever I could find it. A lady calling herself Kath Headlam, a total stranger to me, but apparently a well-known figure down at the studios of Alhambra TV – Manchester's number two commercial station and rival of Granada and the BBC – had telephoned me at Pimpernel Investigations this morning. My former boozing partner, Ted

Blake, now a rising star in the media world himself, had recommended me, so she claimed.

She told me her car had been nicked from the studio car park last night. Amazingly enough, the police had promptly located it abandoned on a street in Broughton. She wanted me to go and collect it, but I soon realised that the car wasn't her main concern. She was more worried about the loss of a briefcase containing all her personal papers, journals and diaries, which she had left in the car. The police reported that they could find nothing on the front passenger seat, where she'd left it. She was sure it had been nicked and could I trace the car thieves and get it back? In her own words the Filofax alone was 'an irreplaceable treasure containing years of painstakingly gleaned contact addresses, not to mention my diaries'.

She'd made it clear that the £500 she was prepared to pay as reward, on top of my fee, was nothing to a woman with her resources. The patronising tone she'd employed when discussing the financial arrangements made me all the more anxious to get my hands on some of her money. If she was trying to convey the impression that there was something infinitely grubby about private detectives she'd certainly succeeded. But being patronised's an occupational hazard and I must have made the right noises because I'd got the job.

It couldn't have been more routine, but I played things by the book. I even did a perfunctory telephone check on Headlam with Ted Blake to find out if she was who she said she was. Ted assured me that she was a bona fide client, 'A highly intelligent tart pulling down seventy grand a year. Not your sort at all – a really classy number with cast-iron pants,' was his comment, which only went to show that the woman must have had the sense to spurn his rough and ready seduction tactics. Ted was

3

going up in the media world: he now had his own late-night TV show – 'Bang to Rights' – a sort of cod investigative piece which is only transmitted in the North West. It mainly consists of Ted harassing some harmless citizen. He's good at that.

His researchers find a local half-wit who's been separated from his cash by some dodgy double-glazing firm or time-share salesman or what not. Ted extracts the maximum mileage from the aggrieved idiot, showing him up as a prize turkey, before setting off in heavy-handed pursuit of the alleged villain – Ted Blake, the knight errant of the media.

He was very definite about me doing anything I could to assist Headlam. 'Just the sort of career move you need, Dave . . . She can do us both a bit of good . . . Snotty-nosed piece but she's very well placed. It'll get you out from behind those everlasting supermarket shelves and you never know, she might need you for other things.' His hint fell on deaf ears. 'When she asked me where she could get hold of a private detective I gave you a really good boost, stressed your probity, credit worthiness, bloodhound-like determination etc, etc. I gave her my personal guarantee that she can trust you, so don't let me down, Dave.'

Ted's always trying to make me feel under an obligation to him. But he must have done the business because when I called at the television studios later that morning, although I didn't get to lay eyes on the fabled Headlam, a bespectacled, black-booted research assistant, wearing a miniskirt no bigger than a wide belt, handed over an envelope containing £500 without any fuss at all.

A nice little earner, if I could handle it.

I took a taxi to the Broughton district of Salford and cruised up and down the street where Ms Headlam's car was supposed to be. There was no sign of it. It looked as if my journey had been a waste of time, but for £500 I was ready to do a lot of looking. No one would have been less surprised than me if the car had been stolen a second time – police only visited Broughton by the van load. If it *had* been stolen again, at least there was a chance that the contents, including the precious brief-case, were still intact, and the car hadn't suffered the usual fate of vehicles abandoned around here – to be stripped and then burnt out.

A housewife from the nearby flats gleefully informed me that I was too late ... Youths from the travellers' camp had cleared off with the vehicle an hour or two since. My taxi had already left in a hurry, the driver wasn't keen on hanging around the district, so I debated spreading a little cash around the locals in exchange for news of the briefcase; they certainly looked as if they could use it. But I decided I'd better find the car first. My grinning informant gave me directions to the travel-lers' camp and with the courage of ignorance I set off in pursuit, on foot. The Building Society had a lot to answer for. Conscious of the amount of cash I was carrying, my own as well as Headlam's, I was hoping that the early hour and the freezing weather would persuade the local muggers to keep their greasy heads tucked up under their dope-stained duvets. My thin-soled shoes offered little insulation from the frozen ground. I hadn't gone far before I began to regret my decision to walk.

It didn't take me long to find the encampment. It was signposted by flatbed trailers and new lorries parked on the crumbling pavements. These were definitely not 'New Age' travellers. There wasn't a broken-down bus in sight, only shiny chrome trailers and newish vehicles.

I stood on the broken pavement outside the camp, debating procedure. I knew enough about travelling people to realise that just asking the odd question round and about was likely to result in me being chased down the road by an angry mob – at the least. On the other hand if I stood still much longer my feet were going to get frost-bite. So it was a stroke of luck when a tinker lady wearing her entire wardrobe of outer garments hove into view, and took matters into her own hands.

'You're not from the police, are you?' she asked me before answering her own question. 'No, they only come up here in big groups and you're too nice looking to be one of them anyway. Well, as you're a good-looking fella, I'll give you some advice: don't go any further.' A big woman, she spoke with an Irish country accent.

'I've got to, love,' I replied, trading familiarity for familiarity.

'Just you be careful, we don't like strangers coming poking their noses round here, and all.' She waved her arm vaguely to encompass the whole camp and environs.

'Believe me, it's the last thing I want to do!' I said. 'I'm here looking for a stolen car, you wouldn't know anything about that sort of thing would you?'

'Dear God! I'm not the one you should be talking to about cars. It's my cousin Mickey Joyce who lives in that big trailer over there that knows all about them. There now, I've said enough to get us both into trouble.'

As I looked into the trailer camp I could see that we were being observed from several windows. The trailer she had indicated was the largest on the site, a lot longer than the usual thirty-foot, with a heap of car hub-caps piled up at the door alongside the stainless-steel water churns. Its curtains were drawn.

'What do you mean, trouble?' I said anxiously, 'I've only asked you a couple of simple questions.'

'The lads don't like strangers talking to their womenfolk, not even to a broken-down old wreck like me,' she

6

explained. I thought she was exaggerating, both about her own appearance and about the situation, but even as she spoke nine or ten feral-looking youths were gathering outside the caravans and giving me hostile glances. I stood my ground, partly because my feet and legs were so numbed by the cold that flight was out of the question and partly from a fleeting hope that they would confine their attentions to hostile stares.

'You don't look like an old wreck,' I said pleasantly. Flattery's never wasted in my line of work. Her bulky and shapeless appearance might well have been due to the fact that she was wearing at least two coats, a stained white Burberry over a tattered Barbour, like a refugee kitted out in cast-offs from the Cheshire County Show. Her feet were protected from the freezing ground by a pair of brown suede boots. I couldn't see much more of her face than the tip of her nose; a flat cap, pulled well down, obscured her eyes. She was certainly equipped for the weather.

'Aren't you the charmer?' she said, laughing again. I noticed that her teeth were crooked. 'What did you say your name was?'

'I didn't, but it's Dave Cunane.' I'd hardly got the words out of my mouth before the pack of youths were loping forwards to surround us.

'Is the long bollocks bothering you, Mary? Do you owe him money?' asked a dark, thick-necked youth with close-set, squinting eyes who seemed to be their spokesperson. He gave me a hard push on the right shoulder. It could only be a matter of seconds before other parts of my body than my feet were in contact with the frozen ground.

Mary came to my rescue once more.

'Leave him alone, Declan! Is this the way you treat my relatives? He's my cousin Maisie Cunane's son and

Mickey won't be pleased if you start kicking his relatives around. Just back off and give the man some space.'

The mention of 'Mickey' was enough. Squinting Declan retreated but not before he had showed his followers what a hard man he was by issuing a general threat against visitors to their camp. This was probably the bunch that had twocced Headlam's car: they could certainly have been up and active at the relevant time and their hostile attitude was another clue. But I wasn't crazy enough to question them directly even if they really had accepted Mary's spur-of-the-moment tale that I was a remote relative of their chieftain.

I thanked Mary and asked her if she'd any idea how I could get the stolen car back.

'I shouldn't be standing here talking to you like this,' she answered rapidly. 'I've got my three fatherless children to think of even if I don't care about my own safety. I can't help you with the car. If that lot have it, nothing I could say will make them give it up. It's probably already on its way to a customer. They don't like me, and I don't like them. The only thing I can do for you is to walk you over to Mickey's trailer, then you're on your own. If you offer him money he'll bite your arm off.'

'Thanks, Mary,' I said when she paused for breath. 'What's your other name? I'd like to give you something for your trouble.'

'Don't be a bloody idiot!' she snapped as I reached into my jacket for my wallet. 'Put it back for God's sake! Mother of God! Do you want to leave me with no reputation at all? Taking money from a man in the street when I'm on my own! I could only take money off you if I had a baby with me! Look, I'll walk you over there, and leave you at his door like I said. I can't do any more

8

than that. Tell Mickey that Mary Wood sent you.' She grasped my arm firmly.

'Lovely spot, isn't it?' she said grimly as we set off into the encampment.

Tethered piebald and skewbald ponies scraped listlessly at the frozen grass some distance behind the trailers. There was a cloud of condensed breath rising from them, and nearer at hand dirty-faced children peered at me from behind a pile of scrap. The pungent smell of excrement hanging over the whole site wasn't diminished by the smoke from several open fires.

We weren't three miles from the centre of Manchester, and close to the luxury development of Salford Quays. Mercifully, the heavy frost had anchored all the loose bricks and stones to the ground, so nothing was thrown at me.

Mary Wood cast me adrift as she had promised and I knocked politely at the door of Joyce's 'van. Nothing happened. I could hear giggling from the children behind me and I braced myself for the onslaught of stones. I knocked again. Still no answer.

'Hey, Mister, he's deaf. He'll not come out unless you bang louder,' one of the bolder kids shouted.

I banged on the door with my fist and suddenly it flew open. A furious-looking, unshaven man I judged to be in his mid forties stood framed in the doorway pulling his braces over his shoulders.

'Hey, Mickey! It's your cousin ... Dirty Dicky from City Cow Titty,' shouted one the wags. Joyce glared at them blankly, then focused on me.

'What in Christ's name do you want? Can't a respectable man have a drink in peace round here?' he bellowed to the world. A pigeon fluttered into the air and the derisive kids began to scatter.

He was a cliff of a man, built like the North Face of

the Eiger – tall, mean and pitted looking. His position in the narrow caravan doorway, four feet above the ground, made him look even more imposing. His flattened and thickened features lacked definition: his exceptionally broad face looked as if it had been crushed when he was a baby.

I stared at him.

'What are you gawping at?' he shouted down at me.

'Mary Wood sent me to see you,' I quavered, fear lending inspiration, 'and I never said I was your cousin.'

His weather-beaten face creased slightly. 'Well, you'd better come in from the cold then, you daft sod, before they start pitching dog shit at you.' He waved both his arms at the kids like the sails of a windmill and they dispersed to the destructive tasks they'd been at before my arrival.

Mickey's lair was warm and welcoming. The interior of the caravan couldn't have been in greater contrast to the squalor outside. The standard of tidiness was 'museum quality' – all surfaces were shining, hardly a pin out of place and everything stowed away in compartments. There were two separate sinks, one for cooking and one for washing. Heat was provided by an expensive Calor gas fire. The whole place was painted in vivid colours and there were cut-glass mirrors and ornamental horse brasses on most flat surfaces. I'd taken his earlier reference to drink as meaning tea but there was no sign of any teapot. I detected no sign of feminine influence either.

'Sit down. Why don't you?' my host invited, pulling on a long brown knitted pullover which reached to just above his denim-clad knees.

It looked like the sort of homespun rig-out a medieval peasant might have worn and didn't match the gleaming, ultra-modern caravan interior. Perhaps he was wearing
10

it to please a relative; the stains down its front gave any number of clues to his diet. He noticed me looking but didn't seem to mind. Now that he'd had the chance to get over being roused by a stranger just after 9 a.m. he looked friendly enough. He could smell the money I was carrying.

The warm reception inside the caravan put me off my guard fractionally, as did the discovery that Joyce, like myself, was a tidiness freak. I explained my mission, hoping to keep him guessing about whether it was the car or the briefcase that I was interested in most, but he soon worked out what I was really after. The word 'reward' clinched it. Although the car had only been moved to his campsite half an hour ago, Joyce blustered that it would be impossible to recover it now.

'The thieving gets who took it will have passed it on by now,' he claimed. 'Not that I know who they are, of course, but I know their ways.'

I could see the cunning in his hazel-coloured eyes as he spun me this unlikely yarn. He'd get plenty for the car, a brand-new Mazda, but the reward for the briefcase would be the icing on the cake, the only drawback being that he'd have to admit involvement.

'I keep my ear to the ground and I hear things,' he conceded. 'I'll see if I can recover some of the lady's bits and pieces for you. I know the lads, you see. It's terrible, but what else is there for them to do? They have us penned up here like caged animals.' His voice held a touch of authentic Celtic melancholy and self-pity. 'Won't you have a drop with me?'

He took a medicine bottle and two small glasses out of the cupboard and put them on the table. I was puzzled. Was I expected to share his cough medicine?

'It's weather-proofing. I take a sample before I go out to face the world, especially on a bitter morning like this.

Take a drop, it'll put a lining on you. It's the poteen, won't you try it? It keeps the damp out of a man's chest.' He raised his glass to his lips and knocked it back. The glass looked no bigger than a thimble in his hand.

Drinking the brew seemed a small sacrifice in return for his cooperation. I took a preparatory sip of the clear liquid. It tasted like baby's gripe water – harmless – so I imitated my host and swigged it down.

Seconds later, I felt as if someone had bashed me over the back of the head with a hammer. I could hear a clear ringing note bouncing around inside my skull. I felt dazed. Yet I knew what I must do next. I started the bargaining and offered him £20 for the briefcase. It was strenuous work and I could feel the deal slipping away from me. I had intended to go no higher than £50. After all, what was an old red leather case and a few books worth to him? But he was crafty. Years of trading had honed his instincts. If I didn't make the deal he still had the car, while I had nothing. He asked for £300 and we settled on £180.

'Will you be paying me now?' he asked innocently, while pouring us another dose of the medicine.

'Payment on sight of the goods only,' I managed to mutter.

'Ah, well. Wise man, you are. "Put your horse in the middle of the market for all to see and take the best price in the morning," was what my old dad said to me, and it's a wise man that doesn't buy a pig in a poke.'

My head was swimming. With his horses, pigs in pokes, doses of medicine, and cunning bargaining he'd got me exactly where he wanted me.

'You sit there, sir,' said Joyce, totally unaffected by his own dose, 'I'll go and have a look round.' He pulled on his jacket and exited without another word.

I didn't stir from my seat. The bell-like tones in my

head gradually died away, and after about fifteen minutes he returned, shoving the briefcase under my nose but keeping a tight grip on the handle.

'Any news of the car?' I asked hopefully, but unsatisfied.

'Ah, it's long gone, Sir. Your lady can claim on the insurance, can't she?'

I didn't feel like arguing. He was too big, and anyway my client had made it clear that the briefcase was worth a lot more to her than the car. Losing the car was an inconvenience, but loss of her Filofax and all her carefully gathered contacts was potentially ruinous. As for the diaries, they must be of sentimental value. I cautiously took out my wallet, trying to shield its contents from Joyce's gaze.

'You wouldn't consider a cheque?' I asked.

Mickey's hearty laugh rocked the caravan.

'You know what we say: "East, West – cash is best!" '

I counted out £180 in twenties, which he carefully pocketed but not before he'd checked each note for forgery. I wasn't happy about giving him so much but there was nothing I could do. The way he assumed I was a partner in crime was starting to annoy me.

'It's cold enough to freeze the balls off a bishop. It's a raw day out there, sure enough,' he said genially. 'Won't you have another sample with me?' He was still clutching the briefcase, which bore the name Headlam embossed in faded gold letters on the red Moroccan leather.

On the principle of when in Rome, I accepted his offer as politely as I could.

'The second never goes down as bad as the first. That first shot of the day takes the lining off the throat and the next one puts it back,' he said, pronouncing throat

13

as 'troat', as he measured out the medicine. 'This is the real McCoy, straight from my cousin Tom in Westport.'

I drained the glass. Another hammer blow hit the back of my head. Snatching the briefcase out of his fingers I struggled to my feet. I could just about get my legs under me. I lurched to the door with my prize.

'You're not going yet, are you? You mammy's boy! Come on back, and have another. It'll put hairs on your chest.' When these blandishments had no effect Joyce changed his tone and raised his voice. 'Just what you'd expect from an Englishman,' he said contemptuously, 'no manners at all and can't hold his drink.'

At the caravan door the cold air hit me like a slap on the face as I staggered down the steep steps and headed for the main road, weaving my way through the scrap piles.

When I reached the main road I looked over my shoulder: no sign of any inhabitants. The site looked as tranquil as it had when I'd stood talking to Mary Wood. All I needed now was transport. I patted my jacket to reassure myself that my wallet was there for the taxi fare.

It wasn't.

No wonder Mickey Joyce hadn't haggled much over the briefcase.

As I stood on the broken pavement waiting for my head to clear I wondered what they made poteen from anyway. I must have been so stupefied that I hadn't felt him lifting my wallet. It was my own fault for coming here without my 'apprentice', Jay Anderson. As soon as I heard where Kath Headlam's car had been found, I should have phoned for Jay.

Jay Anderson is a nineteen-year-old Afro-Caribbean youth from Moss Side. His mother, Lovena, is a midwife and general public agony aunt in the area to whom I owe a great deal one way and another. She helped to keep me sane when my wife Elenki, a young African medical student, died a few years ago. Jay has his problems; working with him is not easy, he seems to need a lot of sleep for one thing, and he can be very touchy and easily upset, but he has his uses. If I had taken the trouble to rouse him from his slumbers before setting out for Salford, he could have brought my car and looked after it while I sorted Mickey Joyce out.

I certainly could have used him now, but by the time I'd phoned for him, and he'd arrived to back me up, my cash and the culprits would be long gone. It might just be fine for a rich media type like Kath Headlam to stand the loss of a brand new Mazda but I was damned if I was going to hand over my wallet while the thief sat snugly in his caravan not a hundred yards away. That was my last thought before the backlash from the poteen hit me and I blacked out.

I hit the ground face first still clutching Kath Headlam's briefcase. There was no sensation of motion or pain. I now knew why poteen drinkers have flattened faces. When I came to, I found myself in another warm and lighted space. I didn't want to move, just to curl up where I was. Consciousness repeatedly faded and returned like a wonky radio drifting on and off station. I was vaguely aware of someone trying to force coffee down my throat and daylight filtering through a caravan window. It hurt. When I shut my eyes the outlines of the windows remained printed on my retinas. I tried to sit up, which was a bad mistake. My head felt loose, as if my neck had been replaced by string. I groaned loudly.

Mary, for it was her caravan, was making coffee. She'd removed the layers of clothing in which she'd been swathed earlier and was now looking presentable in a

15

new green Adidas tracksuit. She was far from shapeless.

'What day is it?' I managed to croak.

'Wouldn't it be Wednesday afternoon?' she replied, as if perfectly agreeable to it being Thursday or Friday if I wished. 'It's one o'clock. You've slept three hours. You were *palatic* earlier. I had to take you in. That cousin of mine's poisoned you with a drop of bad stuff, the bastard. I suppose you'll be wanting to go now? Well, I've got your wallet for you.'

She drew back the curtain, and I felt a wave of pain break over me as stronger light hit me.

'You'll not be right for days yet,' she said consolingly. 'But haven't you got the pair of shoulders on you? You're nearly as big as Mickey. I almost crippled myself heaving you in here, and not one of them would give me a hand. You'll have to sweat the poteen out of your system, but your car's here. Look.' She pointed through the small window to a red Nissan Bluebird which was even now being slowly driven over the uneven ground towards her caravan. To my horror, I saw that it was none other than Delise Delaney at the wheel. 'I got the number of your office from the wallet,' Mary explained. 'The woman who answered wasn't very polite when I told her you were *palatic*.'

I looked inside the wallet she thrust into my hands. There was no cash in it, but the credit cards and cheque book were intact. My shoes were still on my feet. The cash I'd stuffed into the thin-soled moccasins as insulation was still there, the remaining £300 of Headlam's reward in the right shoe and all my own Christmas spends, amounting to slightly more, in the left. I might be able to make a big enough dent in my mortgage arrears to hold off Miss Attleigh and the Polar Building Society after all.

When I came to again, Jay was fussing over me while

Delise counted my money. She was exchanging harsh words with Mary but I couldn't follow what she was saying except that it was unpleasant.

Delise Delaney is my secretary and lover. Along with Jay's mum Lovena, she was responsible for saving me from the whisky bottle following my wife's death. Delise is a beauty; young, athletic, capable of immense charm. Her skin has a lovely honey-bronze bloom, product of mixed Jamaican and Irish parentage. I could spend all day looking at her, but now she was casting a very tight-lipped stare in my direction. She flashed me an indignant glance. I swear I could see sparks of static electricity crackling in her wavy, dark-brown hair. She had Kath Headlam's briefcase tucked very tightly under her arm.

She and Jay dragged me out to the car. Their mutual concern for my health wasn't enough to stop Jay re-tuning the radio to his favourite monotonous ragga music. Why did he need to turn the car into a ghetto blaster on wheels? The noise caused me real pain but I wasn't strong enough to protest. A nightmarish journey back to central Manchester with the heavy beat battering my ears was interrupted by several stops while I parted company with the contents of my stomach.

The harsh chemical after-taste of the poteen was stabbing through my taste-buds like a sharp knife. I was too sick to explain myself to Delise, but I wasn't so oiled that I couldn't sense the waves of resentment.

After an hour back at Pimpernel Investigations, pouring more black coffee down my throat and stumbling up and down the narrow landing outside my office draped over Jay's shoulder, I was beginning to recover sensation in parts of my body below the ears.

I realised that normal services were being resumed when I found myself noticing what Jay was wearing.

Jay's obsession with clothing was one of those little

17

failings that Delise and I were working on. There had been a time when he was almost ready to start up as a drug dealer in order to lay his hands on the price of a pair of fancy trainers. That episode was in the past, I hoped, but the partial reformation didn't include many concessions towards a more normal life style.

Today he was wearing a paisley-patterned, dark-coloured headscarf tight round his skull, fastened with a single knot at the back, pirate style, a single large gold ear-ring in his right ear and massive gold rings on six of his fingers. A tan-coloured, suede bomber jacket, black jeans and brown 'Timberland' moccasins completed his ensemble. The outfit must have set him back several hundred quid.

'What are you posing as now, Jay?' I managed to croak at him as I took in his gear.

The sound of my voice roused Delise from her lair. I realised that the repetitive sound I'd been listening to with half an ear was the noise of the photocopier carrier. She stood in the doorway.

'Don't you start on him, Dave Cunane. You're the one who has to explain himself. How the hell did you get yourself in such a state so early in the day? You only went out to look for a stolen car. Next thing, we find you with your clothes hanging round your ankles, bidding a fond farewell to some gypsy fortune teller and blind drunk into the bargain!'

Delise's peroration ended on a rising note and I knew that I would have to come up with something good. I told the tale of my visit to the traveller encampment as coherently as I could in my enfeebled state, stressing my skill in preserving our reserves of cash. I had to get it right because Delise had often made it plain enough that saving me from the bottle was a once-only job. She didn't plan to spend the rest of her life repeating the experience.

18

If she thought I was back on the sauce it would be 'Goodbye, Dave' from her.

Standing in the corridor, with Jay holding me upright, I must have made a pathetic spectacle as I stumbled through my story. 'The swine's deliberately given me alcoholic poisoning,' I concluded lamely.

'Well, in that case we'd better get you down to Manchester Royal Infirmary and have your stomach pumped out,' Delise said briskly and unsympathetically. 'Can you drag him to the lift and get him back into the car, Jay? The sooner we get him there the better, there's quite a queue for the stomach pumps at this time of year.' She was in an uncompromising mood.

'No, I'm sure I can manage. I must have got rid of most of it by now, please let me back in the office,' I pleaded.

Taking me at my word, Jay withdrew his support. I made it through the outer office to the armchairs in my own room. Things were still spinning but I didn't feel quite so sick. Relenting slightly, Delise came in with yet another cup of black coffee.

'You're an awful fool, Dave. Why didn't you take Sinbad the Sailor here with you?' she said, gesturing to Jay, who stood against the filing cabinets. He had removed his turban and was now running his ring-bedecked fingers through his 'funky dred' do. He did this by the hour and I knew it drove Delise wild. Sure enough she followed my glance and turned her attention onto him.

'Get that turban back on or I swear I'll cut your locks off myself,' she barked at him. Poor Jay jumped and guiltily replaced his makeshift headgear.

'I faxed Kath Headlam at Alhambra and let her know that we'd managed to recover her briefcase but not the car and this came back almost at once,' Delise said, handing me a flimsy sheet of fax paper.

I had trouble focusing on it, the letters seemed very blurred.

'Oh give it to me, Poteen-head!' she snapped. She was lovely when she was in a temper. Her eyes glowed like sparks out of a fire.

> 'Dear Pimpernel Investigations,
>
> I'm not bothered about the car. Well, not as much as about the briefcase, but I will need statements for insurance purposes. The briefcase is really <u>urgent</u>. Can you return it tonight? I must have the briefcase put in my hands by you <u>in person</u>. Unfortunately I won't be free to see you till this evening after nine as we're casting for a new series. Come to the studio Christmas party and meet me there. This fax will admit you and a guest. I would like to speak to you about another matter at the same time, and introduce you to Simon Rishton.
>
> I will tell Reception to expect you. Please <u>respect my confidentiality</u>. I don't want anyone here to know that I had to hire a detective to find my briefcase. I'm always mislaying things, it's an office joke.
>
> Kath Headlam'

I could sense Delise's excitement. Kath Headlam's message was a lot more friendly in tone than her earlier phone call. I started to revise my opinion of her. Attached to the fax was a separate postscript:

Admit Mr David Cunane and partner to the party in studio nine . . . authorised by Kath Headlam. Deputy Director of Drama. 22.12.93.

'You know who Simon Rishton is?' Delise asked breathlessly. 'Mr Big down at Alhambra.' I'd heard of him. How could anyone not know about Simon Rishton, a man who'd used his position at Alhambra Television to trumpet his own importance for the last thirty years.

'I've already typed out a statement for you to sign,' Delise said. 'The insurance company won't make any trouble when they hear from the police that the car disappeared in Broughton. This looks like a really big break for us, a chance to get work with a TV company, and actually meet Simon Rishton in person! And what do you do? Turn up drunk!'

I looked at her. I could see that she was only limbering up for some really heavy-duty stuff. She's the world's leading authority on the defects of David Cunane, just ahead of my father. My performance as a detective and as a lover would be next on her list. I had to do something. I overcame my woes sufficiently to give her a faint smile. Even in her super-efficient, businesswoman guise she was beautiful and as desirable as ever. She's both more ambitious and more easily impressed by people's positions than I am. I knew she thought there was a chance that a meeting with the great and famous Simon Rishton might launch her into a glamorous career in a soap opera. I'd seen the glint in her eye at the mention of Alhambra Studios when we'd taken the commission from Headlam this morning. Putting that precious diary back into Miss Headlam's hands just might be her passport to fame and fortune.

I decided a spot of exercise might be the answer to my hangover and so after a stop in Moss Side while Jay picked up his bike and cycling gear we made our way back to flat 4, Thornleigh Court, Chorlton. Jay did the driving. I didn't need to go upstairs to change. My helmet, gloves and cycle clips were with my bike in the garage. The clothes I was wearing – leather jacket, thick green cord slacks and scarf weren't going to get any

21

dirtier than they already were after my crawl round the tinker camp.

There was a dense white mist hanging over the Mersey Valley. It was fading into dark grey rapidly, as the poor light failed. Once on two wheels I kept my balance well enough. I lurched down the familiar trails with Jay following me, crossing the river at the Jackson's Boat bridge and then climbing up the slope towards the motorway. The bitter cold froze the teeth in my face, I lost sensation in my fingers but we pedalled on. Two gallons of black coffee meant I had to stop and look for a convenient bush every few minutes.

It was Jay who called a halt to our efforts on the third circuit of my 'short' training route – round Sale Water Park, and back again via the railway bridge.

'Look, Boss, it's getting too dark to see where we're going. Let's call it a day and turn back.' Jay didn't like to overdo the exercise. We must have done about fifteen miles and I was beginning to get a buzz from the old endorphins. Still, I was ready to call it a day.

After putting the bikes in the garage I let him take the Nissan; he promised it would be safe for the night. I knew he had a good relationship with most of the local teenage car thieves in his area and anyway I was too drained to care.

My progress up the stairs must have been noisy because Finbar Salway met me on the landing outside his floor. I might have known that he would be there. Finbar rarely misses a chance to intervene in my life, sometimes with beneficial results, sometimes not. He shares the flat below mine with his twin sister Fiona. She actually owns the flat. Although he's over sixty now, as a former officer in the 17/21st Lancers, Finbar looks on me as an opportunity for him to continue his 'Action Man' life style. Others in his position might take up service with the National Trust, or become a bursar at a private school, but the abortive Suez Landing was the highlight of Finbar's Army career and to make up for that disappointing affair he seems to have decided that my rather erratic life style is the means for him to get some more action in. Fortunately, Fiona is usually on hand to restrain him. She's a former infant-school teacher and has had a lifetime of experience in calming excitable boys.

Finbar blocked my way. There was no sign of his minder.

'My God, Cunane, you're glassy eyed! You look as if you've seen a ghost,' he said in a friendly tone. In the state I was in, half way between exhaustion and nausea, I could have done without his comments, however well meant, so I gave a non-committal grunt as reply.

'Like that, is it? Been drinking before the sun goes over the yard-arm, eh?' I could see that there was to be no escape from Finbar, I was too fond of him to snub him however ill I felt. I explained my situation to him. As usual he had a solution.

'The same thing happened to me once out in the Middle East, touch of manky arrack. I know just the cure for you, a colour sergeant in the Green Jackets showed it to me. I've always made sure I have all the ingredients . . . have you right as rain in no time.' Protests were useless, he led me into his flat.

'You take this first,' he said five minutes later, offering me a tumbler of black liquid, 'and then this one when your stomach's settled.' The way he spoke, so knowledgeable in his precise Army officer's tones, made it difficult to dispute anything or even to ask for an explanation. I took the glasses nervously, my hands were shaking slightly. I expected that Finbar would force me to knock them back on the spot but to my surprise he

23

made no objections to me using them in my own flat. 'Station yourself near the bathroom,' he said solicitously 'and don't forget, black first – yellow later.'

Back in the haven of my own flat, I could feel life returning as I defrosted. Like Socrates knocking back his hemlock, I drained Finbar's black draught. It was bitter.

The effect was as dramatic as he had implied. For a while I thought that I was going to die with my head rammed down the porcelain. 'What a vulgar and typically Mancunian way to go!' I thought, 'kneeling before the shrine of Twyford.' The undertaker was going to need an angle-grinder to free my head. But then, just as things seemed to be at their worst, the muzzy, partly drugged feeling left me. I was weak, but I was whole.

I staggered back into the living room and drained the second half of Finbar's cure – the yellow draught. I felt as if my internal organs had been switched back on. I could feel sensation and life returning to my body.

Returning to the bathroom I ran a full bath with the water as hot as I could stand it, stripped and got in.

Afterwards, feeling better by the minute, I set the alarm for 7.30 and stretched out for two hours' sleep on the double bed I occasionally share with Delise. There was a hint of her perfume on the pillow.

The insistent ringing of the phone woke me from a dreamless sleep at 6.45. It was Finbar checking to see if I was still alive. I thanked him for his 'cure' without enquiring as to the ingredients. Then, as I couldn't get back to sleep, I dressed in a tracksuit and went into the kitchen.

As always when my self-confidence was shaken I needed to perform a familiar domestic ritual to restore my sanity.

There was nothing to do. Everything was gleaming. The sink and the cooker didn't harbour the slightest stains, even microscopic ones. I washed the inside of the pedal bin and put in a new liner, but that didn't take long. I even thought of taking the cans out of the larder and cleaning them, but then I noticed a faint line of black between the paint of the window frame and the glass. It was some sort of bacterial growth caused by condensation. I happily set to work removing it and eventually, I felt completely normal again. It struck me that I needed someone to come and mess things up so I could indulge my hobby of tidying. I needed a careless woman like Delise about the place all the time.

I went into the bathroom and shaved carefully, then chose my clothes: black Oxford shoes, a white dress shirt with a red and white spotted bow tie; and a single-breasted dinner jacket which I had only worn twice previously. I'd bought it years ago to wear to dinners given by the Police Benevolent Association when I was still in good enough odour with the fuzz to get the invitation. It still fitted perfectly. The red spotted bow tie I'd chosen brought out the traces of colour in my corpse-hued features. I studied myself in the wardrobe mirror. As I stuffed a red silk handkerchief into my top pocket and put on a pair of gold cuff-links I thought I looked less like a freshly resuscitated corpse and more like the young, upwardly mobile businessman of my imagination.

2

The Alhambra Studios. Evening of Wednesday 22nd December 1993

When Delise buzzed my door bell I was as ready for my foray into the tinsel world of mass entertainment as I was ever going to be. I went straight down. Outside it was clear and freezing and Delise was sitting in the 2CV. She was dressed to kill, or maybe she had the casting couch in mind. She certainly wasn't too warmly clad under her black leather jacket. The heater in the 2CV would take ten years to defrost a frozen chicken so I let Delise drive to take her mind off her chattering teeth. The car didn't match the image I was cultivating but we could claim that we were ecologically friendly, or try to laugh the car off as a fashion accessory.

Delise didn't say much as we drove to the Alhambra headquarters in Dock Street just off Deansgate but at least there was more warmth in her smile than I was getting out of the 2CV's heater. The building, designed as a statement of the station's commitment to the new and the modern, had been completed just two years before, bang on time for the recession and collapse of the company's advertising revenue. It's a glass and steel monstrosity with an oddly curved structure attached to the whole length of the roof, like a flattened letter S, or the twisted deck of an aircraft carrier that has somehow run aground in Central Manchester. It has won major architectural prizes for its French architect, but the rumour in town is that the £60 million pound building is proving to be a bit of an albatross round the neck of Alhambra.

In striving to establish its corporate 'identity', always

in danger of being stifled by the massively successful Granada operation only a block away, not to speak of the all-embracing BBC, one of whose many tentacles was on Oxford Road, Alhambra had virtually bankrupted itself.

We parked the car in the studio car park across the street from the brand-new ziggurat and made a dash through the freezing night air to the imposing marble-lined entrance. Despite traces of queasiness, I felt confident and brash. Whoever else turned up at this studio bash, I knew there would be nobody there to match Delise in looks or charm. I could see that she was psyching herself up, too, she really thought there was a chance that she'd be 'spotted', as we bounded up the steps to the entrance, in orthodox film-star style. Move over, Richard Gere, I thought. What had he got that I hadn't, apart from a few million dollars? Lights were shining in our faces and red-nosed, shivering children and teenagers were standing around clutching autograph books in blue fingers. None approached us for a signature, but we did get one or two hopeful glances. Suddenly I felt more 'Christmassy' than I'd done since I was a kid myself.

In the event, expectations exceeded reality by a margin as wide as the smiles on the doormen's faces. The squad of smartly dressed bouncers at the top of the steps let us through when I waved our 'invitation' but the uniformed commissionaire turned us back when I presented him with the faxed flimsy.

The commissionaire examined our faxed party invitation with scrupulous care, his eyes flickering from the paper to us and then back again. For some reason he wasn't as impressed by us as we were by him. The badges on his cap and shoulders were small and discreet but he still had all his stripes up on his sleeves. He looked hard, mean and tanned by exposure, as if he'd just completed ten years outdoors on the Brecon Beacons with the SAS, eating unmentionable things as well as fornicating with them.

'We had this invitation from Ms Headlam today,' Delise explained urgently. Her voice sounded louder than she intended, I guessed.

'I've had strict instructions from senior management . . . No one's going in here without a proper invitation, which this ain't,' he said, handing the sheet of paper back to Delise. 'Ms Headlam knows all about the ruling. She's no right to go faxing invitations to all and sundry. There's such a thing as security. I'm sure you've not been vetted,' he concluded with a dismissive air. Then he turned away from us and switched on a sickly smile for the mink-swathed Lucy Longstaff as she swept in, towing her latest toy-boy behind her. She rewarded him with a one milli-second glimpse of her pearly teeth. Unlike Delise, Longstaff had her place in the scheme of things at Alhambra. She plays the part of a kind-hearted night-club proprietress in the studio's never-ending story about everyday Northern folk.

I considered pressing on regardless and crashing the party but the commissionaire followed my speculative glance into the atrium with a cold-eyed look.

'Don't even think it, Sunshine!' he warned. 'You won't get past the first door.'

I was very annoyed with Headlam. We were being treated like a pair of gatecrashers caught trying to mingle with the 'stars' of the studio's turgid soap operas. My impulse was to leave and try to salvage the evening somewhere else, but Delise wasn't so easily discouraged.

'Is it possible for you to ask Ms Headlam to come to the door to meet us?' she asked politely. 'We've got something for her which she wanted urgently.'

28

Without bothering to reply directly, the stormtrooper looked up Headlam's number and dialled on the desk phone. He took his time about it and he turned his back while he spoke. I felt my temper rising, but Delise looked at me and put her finger to her lips.

'You're in luck,' he said passing the phone to me and ignoring Delise, 'she's in and she'll speak to you. She says she doesn't know anything about the female.'

'What a bitch this Headlam must be,' I thought as I looked at Delise. She was clearly bitterly disappointed. I put my hand over the mouthpiece of the phone and whispered in Delise's ear, 'That bloody briefcase is going into the Ship Canal if she doesn't let us in.'

'Ms Headlam, David Cunane here,' I said, oozing charm. 'I'm with my partner, Delise Delaney. You sent me a fax this morning. It quite definitely says it will admit me and a guest to the studio party. I didn't ask for the invitation. I came to return a valuable piece of property belonging to you and I certainly didn't expect to be insulted by this jumped-up lollipop-man on the desk down here.' The commissionaire stiffened.

There was a pause and then an irritated voice said, 'I've already left the clearest possible message at the desk to say that you were expected. Do they want me to carve it on a six-foot-high block of stone? Put the doorman on!' She sounded genuinely indignant. Her accent was purest Benenden or Roedean, the clack of hockey sticks always in the background. I handed the phone back to the commissionaire who was scrutinising my features carefully, as if he wanted to commit my face to memory.

'Yes, ma'am . . . John Poulter . . . No, ma'am, I've had strict instructions from the top floor . . . No extra guests allowed . . . It doesn't matter if you do come down in person, only Mr Trevose can approve . . . Very well, yes, that's all right . . . I'll get someone to escort them.'

He put the phone down and looked at us through narrowed eyes. 'You're not getting into the party, but you can go up to Miss Headlam's office.' He seemed pleased with the outcome.

I wasn't done with him yet. 'Mr Poulter, let me put you straight about something. You called me "Sunshine", which I take to be a term of racist abuse to myself and my partner. I'm going to see that your precious senior management hear how guests are received at Alhambra.'

'Take it how you like it, sport. Anyway, what are you on about? You're as white as I am. I call everybody Sunshine, not just . . .' Poulter then looked coolly at Delise, rich skin glowing under the powerful lights. 'I wasn't speaking to the woman,' he said roughly. 'You shouldn't be so cocky, mate. If you want an apology from me you'll be waiting a bloody long time.'

Delise gave me a withering look as if the snub over the invitation and the quarrel were *my* fault. Despite her Irish/Caribbean ancestry she's British enough to loathe any kind of 'scene'. We followed a porter as he led us into the marble-lined loggia where the celebs were waiting for the lifts to take them to the studio party. Massive crystal chandeliers dominated the space, and piped music rippled soothingly through the air. 'At least we get to rub shoulders with the famous for a few minutes,' I murmured to Delise as we waited in line behind a soap star and a news announcer. Four floors up, we were led along a winding corridor towards Headlam's office. The walls were lined with modern paintings whose clashing colours and oppressive scale in the confined space, coupled with the maze-like twists and turns, revived the dizzy feeling I'd been struggling to overcome all day. No expense had been spared in fitting the place out. Everything was of non-standard type – even the door frames were of an oddly curved design. It all added up to a look I found vaguely repulsive. With the coloured guidelines on the floor, piped music whispering round us, and the massive artworks everywhere, the place had the ambience of a luxurious private psychiatric hospital.

I was pleasantly surprised by the woman waiting to greet us at the door of her office. There was nothing repulsive about her. She made a very pleasant sight standing against the curved door frame. 'Oh, I'm so embarrassed about all this,' she cooed in her private-school accent, 'I'm afraid somebody's decided it's time to play executive power games again. It happens from time to time here – at least it relieves the monotony of our existence.' She didn't look embarrassed.

I realised that my preconceptions, formed from Ted Blake's thumbnail sketch, were completely false. He'd given the impression that she was a hard-nosed harpy with her claws firmly fixed on the levers of power. The vibes reaching me were quite different.

Of medium height, she was slightly built with sandy hair and blue eyes. Her face was marred by slightly obtrusive teeth, nothing too horse-like but noticeably prominent. She closed her mouth firmly by pressing her lips together with a motion that creased her whole face into a friendly smile. It was the odd double action that drew my attention: her lips met, then her cheeks creased. It took me a moment to work out that this was her way of reducing the visual impact of her teeth.

She was elegantly dressed in a duck-egg blue fitted jacket, over a cream vest with wide trousers. I was favourably impressed, and I think Delise sensed that I was; I felt her drawing back in a way that contradicted her earlier eagerness to penetrate into the heart of the TV world.

'Do come in,' Kath Headlam said, giving us a glimpse of her teeth. We entered a spacious and ultra-modern

31

office furnished with high-tech, neo-brutalist armchairs on which we were invited to crouch. They weren't designed to accommodate the human frame. From my perch I was reduced to peering up at Headlam from between my knees.

'Those awful men down on the doors now, they really are like the Gestapo.'

Headlam paused in remonstrance to give us another short-sighted smile, moving all the muscles in her face. Everything's well connected up, I thought, and smiled back at her.

'I can't apologise enough if those brutes were unpleasant,' she continued, interrupting our mutual dental admiration. 'Since those horrible financial people put Lance Trevose in to run this place we have to account for every thumb-tack and paper clip. I ask you, how can anyone produce creative work in these circumstances? Trevose's only previous management experience has been in running a huge wholesale butchery business! Anyway, I can see you've done awfully well and have recovered my briefcase.' She paused. There was something faintly donnish and academic about her manner, certainly nothing at all aggressive.

I turned to Delise, expecting her to turn the briefcase over now that Headlam had at least explained the mix-up at the door but Delise didn't seem willing to let her off so easily. She continued to hang onto the red leather case, awkwardly balancing it on her knees.

'Well we wanted to discuss that . . .' said Delise hesitantly. I looked at her in surprise.

'Oh! I do understand,' cut in Headlam. 'Too silly of me! Would £500 be all right? I realise Mr Cunane had an awful time getting my case back but after all, he didn't manage to get down to Broughton in time to recover my car, did he?' Then speaking in clipped tones and holding her hand out to me, she said, 'Your fax said you only spent £200 of the £500 my personal assistant gave you.'

So there it was: the authentic iron hand in the velvet glove. I handed over the £300 that I'd hidden in my sock that morning.

'It was £180, actually. The tinkers stole the extra £20,' I explained.

By this time she had her cheque book out and was already scribbling the cheque. Delise was still hanging onto the briefcase.

'There was the statement for your insurance company about the car, that had to be typed out and witnessed. We normally charge £50 for that,' Delise interjected.

'Well, shall we say £600 just to keep everything friendly?' Headlam said in dove-like tones. 'So, deducting the £180 you paid if I give you back this £300 in cash, and a cheque for £70 we're all square. That is right, isn't it?' Her tone ensured I understood her question was meant rhetorically; at the same time she zapped me with her short-sighted smile and I had the chance to see all her molars in vivid Technicolor.

I realised why she was earning £70,000 a year as a TV executive. She bargained as well as any Irish tinker.

She had promised a £500 reward on top of my fee and I didn't see why I should split the reward with Mickey Joyce. His £180 was down to expenses. We hadn't even mentioned my fee yet. She'd arbitrarily decided that the value of my morning's work amounted to nil.

I angrily cleared my throat to speak, but Delise gave me a sharp kick on the ankle. She could read my mind.

'Oh, great!' I thought, 'Delise is going to hit the roof and refuse to hand over the case for anything less than a grand.'

'Yes, that sounds right,' was Delise's cool reply. I almost

33

fell off the seat. Delise handed the briefcase over in exchange for the cheque and cash. I saw hopes of avoiding a visit from the Polar Building Society's bailiffs fading.

'Before we go, Ms Headlam, you mentioned that there was another matter in which you might require our services.' I was determined to salvage what I could from my second, bruising bargaining session of the day. There might still be a chance to rustle up some cash.

'Yes, that's why it's so inconvenient not being able to get you into the party. It concerns my friend Simon Rishton, he needs some help but he has to be at the party to see that none of the cast of "Slatheredge Pit" damage themselves. That's why I wanted you to come to the party, so that you could meet him.'

I laughed out loud. Headlam had a sense of humour.

'You might well laugh, but you've no idea. We call it "Lathered Up Pits" among ourselves. There are so many members of the cast who want to have a go at each other that we have to have an executive constantly on duty especially when the drink's flowing. It's worse than a school playground.'

I felt myself warming to her more and more, then Delise kicked me again. Her psychic powers were really switched on tonight. 'So what was this other matter then, Ms Headlam?'

'Well, Simon and I need some help in a personal matter. Oh, I do wish he was here to explain! It concerns his ex-wife ... No, that's not right. Gloria's still Simon's wife in the eyes of the law, but they're estranged ...'

'They're getting divorced and I take it that you're the third party,' butted in Delise, daughter of a deserted mother herself. 'They used to call the wife the "wronged woman" in cases like that.'

'Golly, your partner's awfully direct isn't she? She should be on "Bang to Rights" with Ted Blake,' said

34

Kath Headlam, addressing me and blinking several times; either her contact lenses were irritating her or she was trying to signal something. 'At any rate, you did awfully well in getting the briefcase back so promptly. So Simon and I feel we can trust you to sort out something very personal for us. In fact, the situation on the personal relationship front isn't quite as black and white as Ms Delaney has just stated. Simon and I knew each other long before he met Gloria in 1989. We had an open relationship, then he met Gloria . . . Almost before I was aware of her, he'd upped and married her, you could say "overnight". He can be impetuous at times . . . That's what makes working with him so exciting,' she gushed girlishly, before carrying on.

'She's his fourth wife, and I think she rather swept him off his feet. She's awfully glamorous, but she's not got too much going for her upstairs, poor thing. And Simon can be quite susceptible to a certain sort of woman.' Headlam favoured Delise with a pointed glance.

I could almost visualise the scene when Rishton had told Headlam she'd lost out on the star role as the fourth Mrs Rishton. Rishton must be a brave man. Still, like a real trouper Headlam had hung in there and now here she was, centre stage again.

'Life with a high-powered TV executive seems very desirable to some of these young girls, they've no idea what they're letting themselves in for . . .' Kath continued, pausing to look directly at Delise again. 'But to cut a long story short, Simon and I got back together this summer. He's moved in with me. He's had all kinds of scenes with Gloria, but over the last couple of months there's just been a dead silence. She doesn't return calls and hasn't been in touch at all . . .'

'We don't handle "matrimonials",' I intervened. 'You'll have to go somewhere else for help.'

'Just hold on a minute, Dave... You mean we don't *normally* handle matrimonials,' cut in Delise firmly. Anticipating another kick, I moved my foot.

'No, we don't need *that sort* of help,' Headlam said quickly. 'You've got the wrong idea, Mr Cunane. Spying on one's spouse is hardly necessary these days, is it? Simon and I just wanted someone to go and see that Gloria's all right. We couldn't enjoy Christmas together if we were worrying about the poor old thing. Simon's really got a very soft centre under the tough exterior. We thought if you were to just pop down there and see how she was, perhaps let us know if she's found someone else. It's the sort of thing you might get a relative to do but we're both so tied up with work, you see how it is...'

I saw very well how it was, and felt no keener than before to do this charming lady's dirty work for her.

'Of course, Simon will want to see you and tell you himself exactly what to say to Gloria. He may ask you to take something personal to her, or collect something from her. She is still his wife legally, after all.'

'We'd have to charge you our full daily rate, and we'd have to send two operatives, always have to in cases like this, and you'd also be charged for any incidental expenses.' Delise sounded conciliatory now. It was hard to keep up with her twists and turns.

Weariness was now setting in as far as I was concerned. Between them, Delise Delaney and Kath Headlam were grinding me up. The prospect of a third female, Gloria Rishton, being given the opportunity to throw her handful of grit into my workings was becoming less appealing by the second. I was half hoping that Headlam would take Delise's statement of her terms as a refusal on the part of Pimpernel Investigations to help her, but not a bit of it.

'Oh, that's no problem. Simon gets paid as a freelance and a lot of his expenses are tax deductible, and anyway I'm sure your rates are very reasonable.'

In no time at all Kath was giving Delise Gloria's address. She said she would phone me first thing in the morning to arrange the meet with Rishton. As I watched her I had the impression that Delise knew more about the Headlam/Rishton situation than she was letting on – there could have been an item in the gossip-column of one the papers I'd missed. Delise spends hours poring over such trivia, especially anything concerning the goings-on down at Alhambra, or Granada. She owns all the yearbooks put out by the TV companies.

Finally, still smiling and bobbing her head up and down, Headlam ushered us out of her office, apologising again for the mix-up over the party. She handed us over to the Gestapo, patiently waiting outside the door.

Our ejection from the precincts of Alhambra took far less time than did our entry.

'Well, are you going to give me a lift home?' I asked Delise as we crossed the street. She hadn't spoken since leaving Headlam's office. I could see she was buzzing.

'You don't deserve it. After the way you were ogling that woman in there I ought to make you get a taxi,' she snapped. 'It was embarrassing.'

'Oh, I should have known it was all my fault that you didn't get a part in "Slatheredge Pit". You don't seem to care that we've come away with £370, and no fee, when we were promised £500 on top of our fee,' I said in my most aggrieved tones. 'My Christmas spending money.'

'Dave, you can be so stupid at times. This is a chance for us to break into a completely different line of work. It was worth taking a loss.'

'And you aren't interested in a career in TV, I suppose,

Delise?' I said sarcastically. 'You nearly blew it yourself when you told her that Gloria was a wronged woman.'

'Well, I was disappointed that we weren't going to be working at the studios. Anyway, if you're so worried about money why did you hand her that £300 back? She'd never have known the difference if you'd said the tinkers had had it all. I'm keeping Headlam's £300, plus what I found in your shoe this morning, to cover arrears on my wages and as a Christmas bonus. You can put her cheque into your account.'

She looked at me closely after saying all this very rapidly. This was definitely one of those times when silence was golden. It was far too cold to risk walking home and I hadn't even the price of a taxi on me. I kept my face neutral and made no further response. Delise carried on lashing into Kath Headlam until we reached the car. With the weird mixture of grandeur and parsimony that marked all of Alhambra's productions the car park across the road from their new multi-million-pound headquarters was a rough and unpaved patch of waste ground. The 2CV was completely iced over, inside and out, and we had to postpone further discussion until we got the wheezing, air-cooled engine running. The heater was too feeble to melt the ice off the inside of the screen, so we scraped it clear and then had to drive with the windows open to stop our breath fogging it up again.

'Would you like to go to a club?' I asked half-heartedly. There was still plenty of traffic heading into the centre as we drove along Chester Road in the direction of Chorlton. The day's activities had left me feeling slightly unravelled but if it would put Delise in a better mood I was ready enough to go back into town and hit the clubs. After all, she was the one with the money. It was still early, only just after ten.

'Why don't you drive over to the travellers' camp for

some more poteen? That's more your style,' Delise replied grumpily.

'Well, we could go to the Yew Tree Arms for an hour if you like. Your mother's not likely to be around, it's one of her animal rights nights, isn't it?'

Delise's mother, nicknamed the 'Killer Whale', frequents the pubs along Willows Road in Chorlton Village. I go to some lengths to avoid Molly Delaney. She has an irrational aversion towards me.

Even chance encounters with her often end in harsh words and deeds. Thanks to her habit of concluding arguments with a head butt most of the pubs in Chorlton have barred her. The Yew Tree, one of the cosiest pubs in Chorlton, was one of the few that still let her in.

But rather than putting the world to rights in the lounge bar, Molly, I knew, would be nursing sick cats and tortoises at the animal shelter this evening.

We clattered down Willows Road in our rattle-trap vehicle, which actually belonged to Molly, found a space in one of the side streets, and then plunged into the warmth of the pub. It's all tricked out like a Victorian squire's parlour with fake bookshelves and cupboards suspended from the ceiling. Even on a Wednesday evening in the depth of winter it was packed. A local quiz team called the 'Wayne Bobbitt Sewing Circle' were noisily celebrating their victory in the Christmas quiz. Delise slipped me some cash and I got myself a fruit juice and a double Bacardi and coke for her. We managed to wedge ourselves onto two stools at the far end of the lounge.

Delise's nose had turned grey with the chill and my own felt similarly frozen. We sat in silence for a few minutes until we stopped shivering and Delise slipped off the soft black leather bomber jacket. Her costume, or rather lack of it, attracted most male eyes in our direction.

39

Delise was wearing a bra top with chiffon sleeves and flared cuffs, black and white polka dot tights and seventies style platform shoes. Her hair was clipped up and she had a chain belt fastened with a large gold disc round her waist. It had all been part of her master plan to make an impression down at Alhambra. Although it hadn't worked there, it was working in the Yew Tree.

'You're looking great,' I said.

'Flattery will get you everywhere with me, Dave Cunane,' Delise said, flashing her perfect teeth.

'Did you notice the way Headlam's mouth opened,' I said shamelessly. 'I thought her face was going to split open. Her lips go right round the front of her head.'

Delise looked mollified. 'All that crap about Gloria Rishton, I expect what they really want is for you to catch her in bed with the new man in her life. Still if they want to pay us for a trip to Macclesfield, why should we object?'

Later, round at my flat, we completed our reconciliation in a more suitable setting. Before she fell asleep Delise promised to hand over some of my cash if I swore not to spend it on drink.

3

Thornleigh Court, Chorlton. Thursday 23rd December

I woke up early with a thick head. Whether it was the result of poteen poisoning or of driving round in an open car in the depth of winter I couldn't say. I felt that strenuous exercise was the only way to fight back. Leaving Delise tucked up under the duvet, I slipped into my tracksuit and running shoes, and let myself out quietly.

After running for about five miles along the main roads I was beginning to feel loose and fit again. It took me about twenty minutes to get back to the flat by the shortest route and into the shower.

Delise was up by the time I returned and she'd prepared a breakfast of muesli and skimmed milk with a glass of grapefruit juice to wash it down. She barred the way to the fridge door when I headed for the bacon. It was these little domestic touches which made me realise that we had a serious relationship.

'You're not my wife, you know, Delise,' I commented as I swallowed a mouthful of Swiss cattle food. 'You don't have to worry about my diet.'

'That's the one job I'm not applying for, Dave. I suppose I take after my mother and looking after dumb animals runs in the family,' she said, putting me in my place. 'I don't think I'll come in to work today. I've not finished my Christmas shopping. Do you think you and Jay will be able to mind the business?'

'I thought employees were supposed to ask the boss before taking a day off work.'

'Don't be so stuffy, Dave,' she pouted. 'There's nothing

to do in the office anyway. It'll be New Year before business picks up.

'OK,' I conceded, 'but can't you give me a lift into town? Jay's got my car.'

'No, I'm going to Stockport with my mum. You'll just have to catch the bus.' Before she went I made sure that she tipped up £200 towards my bus fare.

The tram tracks of Manchester's new rapid transit system haven't yet reached Chorlton so I had a bus ride into Central Manchester. I sat in front of two girls who were effing and blinding like a pair of drunken paratroopers as they loudly discussed their boyfriends' sexual skills for the benefit of other passengers. Fortunately my attention was distracted by the sight of the immense heaps of rubble in Hulme. Crescents and deck access flats, which I vividly remembered being built against all objections from the locals, were now themselves laid low. For no apparent reason I felt an uneasy sense of foreboding.

I wasn't pleased at where life had brought me so far. Here I was, rushing in to the office on the off chance that Kath Headlam might phone with what my father would rightly call 'some tuppenny ha'penny job', while my partner was out spending my last bean.

I wasn't in a very good mood when I reached the Atwood Building, right in the middle of the jumble of streets between the Rochdale Canal and the Institute of Science and Technology. Economic recession has brought more occupants to the crumbling old listed building. I have a tiny partitioned office on the top floor of the wedge-shaped structure. The Atwood, part of the history of Cottonopolis, is distinguished by having one enormous, sloping wall of glass, six storeys high; a relic of the days when textile buyers needed to see cloth samples in natural light. Small businesses looking for cheaper offices as part of their survival strategy have re-located themselves there and nowadays I rub shoulders with people in all sorts of businesses. The old days of sneaking downstairs to use someone else's photocopier have gone for ever.

As I emerged on the top floor to walk to my own cramped little space I was startled to see the bundled-up shape of Mary Wood, the traveller who'd rescued me yesterday. Her ample shape was blocking the narrow corridor. A faint aroma of wood smoke accompanied her.

My heart sank. I'd been hoping to draw a line under yesterday's alcohol-soaked exploits.

'What do you want?' I demanded, a touch aggressively.

I was expecting her to name the amount of the reward due for the 'rescue' she'd performed yesterday, always assuming that she hadn't already taken the missing £20 out of my wallet as payment for her 'Christmas present'. You had to hand it to this bunch, their scam was highly productive. They'd got it off to a fine art: first poison you and rob you, then claim the reward for rescuing you from the result of their crime.

'Oh, *wisha*! Don't take on like that! You're up and on your hind legs, so a few drops of the hard stuff can't have had all that much effect on you!'

'Cut out all the "Come back to Erin, Mavourneen" crap with me, Mary. Just say your piece and go. I'm busy, I've got a job to do if you haven't.'

'Aren't you the ungrateful one? You'd not have done much of your job yesterday if it hadn't been for me,' she said. 'If I'd left you on your own, that Declan would have had the clothes off your back, never mind just your wallet. He'd have had all that money you hid in your shoes too, if I hadn't pulled him off you. First place they look, the shoes.'

Feeling neither humble nor grateful, I fumbled

43

through my pockets for the office key, opened the door and let her in without further argument. She made no move to remove her outer covering and I didn't ask her to. The sooner she said whatever it was she wanted, the quicker she'd be out of here.

Looking closely at Mary in my well-lit office I realised that she didn't look as old as I'd thought yesterday in the fog and gloom of Salford. Her skin was worn and lined but there was still a suggestion of youthfulness about her complexion. Some might have regarded her as reasonable-looking with the sun shining from the right direction, but I was unimpressed. The memory of yesterday's experience had a depressing effect on my ever-active libido.

'Get on with it,' I said coldly. 'I'm expecting an important phone call.'

'I found your address from this business card you left in my trailer, and I got to thinking last night about something that I've been meaning to do for a long time. It says here that you offer a private investigation service,' she said, holding up the card.

I nodded, wondering just what kind of services she was after.

'Take a good look at my face,' she ordered. 'Don't I remind you of someone?'

I looked closely.

Her cheek-bones were prominent and the shape of her face was well rounded and fleshy. There was nothing that would make you pick her out as a typical 'colleen' from a bus queue in Didsbury, nothing specially 'Irish looking' about her. Her chin was firm and well formed but slightly receding, and her eyes were a very pale blue. The skin colour was fair, beneath the wind-scoured complexion, matching the dark golden hair; and her nose was straight and broad with wide nostrils. Her lips were full, round a fairly wide mouth and fairly terrible teeth, and her eyelids were heavy with the eyefolds slightly drooping at the corners. A lifetime of lugging water-churns had ensured that she'd never need to wear shoulder padding, and her figure was full. I decided that staring at her was no hardship.

I couldn't imagine whom she thought she resembled, though. If I hadn't known anything about her background I might have said that she had some Jewish ancestry from her features, or German forefathers from her heavy gold hair and broad squarish-shaped head.

'All right then, I'll give you a *fecking* clue. My great-grandfather was King George V,' she said proudly.

I nearly fell off my seat, as I burst out laughing. I knew the travelling people were notorious for claiming descent from the ancient Kings of Ireland, but claiming a connection to such a recent King of England was a new one on me. What kind of a con-trick was she trying to pull now? Was she going to sell me shares in the Manchester Ship Canal, or was it going to be some long-lost royal heirloom?

She didn't smile and was not amused by my evident hilarity. As she looked at me sternly with her lips set, I could suddenly see a resemblance. She was a dead ringer for Queen Victoria! The same full bosom, the hands folded on the lap! I struggled to assume a properly respectful demeanour.

'Come on, Mary. Tell me you're joking.'

But she was serious. It was no con.

'It's no *fecking* joke to me! My grandfather was that idiot King Edward VIII! That bastard put my granny up the spout when she was in service at Windsor in the early 1930s . . .'

I waved her to silence.

'Look Mary, have you any idea how many people

45

claim royal descent in this country? They've whole wards full of people in the psychiatric hospitals claiming to be Windsors and lots of mad people on the outside claiming it, too.

I realised that I had to humour her. She wasn't here for money, but the poor woman had fixed on me as the person who could clothe her obsession in some sort of reality. That was just my bad luck. I had to coax her along until I could get her through the door without a scene. She'd probably been recently released for 'Care in the Community' from some institution so my reference to psychiatric establishments was poorly chosen.

'Just what was it that you thought I could do for you?' I extricated myself from behind the desk and went over to the window to reassure myself that I wasn't dreaming. I wasn't. The dirty red brick warehouses and offices of Chinatown and Piccadilly were still there.

'Well, I've always known what I've told you. My daddy told me about it when I was a child, but we had to keep it quiet. It wasn't the sort of thing you'd go bragging about among the travelling people in the West of Ireland, but he had papers which proved that what he said was true. He had his mother's and Prince Edward's marriage certificate. He often showed it to me. He said it proved he wasn't a *fecking* bastard. It didn't seem so important to me at the time, then he died when I was fourteen and I got married soon after.' The way she said Edward, it sounded like 'Et-wort'.

I smiled reassuringly at her. It was essential that I kept on the right side of her until she'd finished. She was a solidly built woman and she was sitting between me and the only exit. There wasn't room enough to swing a cat in here, let alone dodge my way past a furious royal pretender unscathed.

'What happened next, then, Mary?' I asked sympath-etically.

'As I say, I got married young; it's the way of the travelling people. I had my daddy's papers but everything else belonging to him was burned when he died . . .'

At this she must have detected the sceptical expression on my face because she exploded angrily, 'I can see you don't believe a *fecking* word I'm saying, just like that *fecking* husband of mine when I told him. But I can pay you well, and I've got something that you want . . . I managed to get back that lady's car that you were looking for. It's outside and you can have the keys just as soon as you say that you're going to help me.'

It was my turn to act unamused now. 'You got the car back? Your dear cousin said it was on its way to a buyer yesterday, so what's happened? You said yourself that Declan and his pals steal cars to order.'

'That's right. They do, but the fellow over in Bolton that they pass them on to was arrested yesterday. Declan and Sean drove over there just after you fell on your face. They came back in one hell of a hurry,'

I noticed that her language had improved. I wasn't sure what that meant, perhaps she just swore in casual conversation.

'Are you going to help me?' she demanded.

'I'm thinking about it but I need more information about who I'm dealing with. You'll have to tell me the lot,' I said.

'I don't approve of what they're doing, if that's what you think. My daddy made an honest living collecting scrap metal and as a roof repairer. Maybe he did have the lead off a church roof, now and then, but only when he was sure there was no one using it. He was very religious was Daddy,' she said self-righteously.

'Fine, I'm sure he was as honest as the day is long,

47

but just tell me about the car,' I interrupted impatiently. I knew well enough that declarations of honesty usually precede admission of some appalling crime and while I was happy enough to get Kath Headlam's car back for her I didn't want any come-back if it had been used for some bank robbery, or any other villainy that Mickey Joyce and his relatives might have been up to.

'The car's clean. You'll not get in trouble. The boys were going to take it back to Broughton last night and set fire to it but I gave them a couple of hundred and they let me have it instead. They thought it was a great joke.' She placed the keys of Headlam's car on my desk.

'I'm ready to help you but you haven't told me what it is that you want me to do,' I said in a reasonable way, moving back to sit behind the desk rather than poising myself for a dash through the door. Returning Headlam's car unexpectedly would be a nice stroke. It would even help to restore my credit with Delise after last night's fiasco at the TV studios.

'Well, when I was younger I couldn't read much, but my husband Dermot could. He'd read anything – newspapers, formbooks, anything. He read my daddy's papers. He made a big joke of it, said they were fakes. Then when we moved to England fifteen years ago to do the tarmac he began suffering with his lungs . . . You know, the fumes, he couldn't do much work.

'He showed the papers to one of his workmates on the road crews, his foreman James Clarke. Clarke said he ought to be able to raise some cash on them, that the papers would pay plenty for any dirt about the Royals. Anyway, Clarke took the papers and he must have got something for them because Dermot had money for a while before he died, and he'd never told me where from. All I want you to do is to find this Clarke, make him tell you what he did with the papers, and get them back.'

'You don't want much, do you? Have you any idea how much I charge for an investigation? It's fine that you've brought the car back, but that doesn't count as payment; I've already been paid for that job. Do you know where this Clarke is now?' I was still humouring her.

'I heard he was working on the M5 near Birmingham. He moves around a lot. When Dermot knew him he was a foreman for Strachan-Dalgetty, the road-building firm, and I think he's still with them. I sometimes hear the men mention his name when they talk about where to find work. And don't worry about me being able to pay you. I won the jackpot on the Tote "Ten to Follow" competition.'

I must have looked mystified.

'You enter this competition and pick ten National Hunt horses. Every time they race you get so many points if they win or get a place. At the end of the season the punter with the most points wins a £150,000 jackpot. I won the *fecking* jackpot,' she said in the same matter-of-fact way that she'd announced her royal connection.

I stood up again, perhaps I'd better be ready for rapid movement after all. 'Mary,' I said, as calmly as I could manage, 'you're just full of surprises. First you tell me you're of royal blood, then you tell me you're loaded. You're doing my head in, I just can't cope with any more. You're not going to tell me that you've had an illegitimate son by an Irish bishop, are you?'

She blushed and retorted angrily, 'Indeed I am not! The very idea!' Then she smiled again. 'But it's true I've got money and I can pay you.'

She opened the plastic Happyways carrier bag she'd

49

been hugging to her chest, took out a thick bundle of £50 notes and laid them on the desk.

I could feel my eyes popping out. Perhaps there was something regal about her, after all.

'You haven't been raiding Mickey's piggy bank, have you?' I asked quietly.

'I have not! It's my own money and here's the receipt for it,' she said heatedly, taking out a crumpled-up piece of paper that she had tucked up in her cleavage. Sure enough, it was a receipt for the £150,000 from the Tote, signed with a crudely drawn cross and her name printed underneath.

'I'm sorry, Mary, I apologise for doubting you but would you like to tell me why you're still living in a caravan and going round dressed like an Oxfam model when you've got so much money?' I asked.

A cunning expression crossed her face. 'I've told no one about my luck. You're the first one to know. You've an honest face and when I saw you lying yesterday on the same bed where poor Dermot used to lay his old head, I knew I could trust you. If I let anyone back at the camp know, they'd have the money, you see it's clean money – not like Mickey's. No, I thought I'd hold on to it and find out about my family, and then perhaps move into a house later on, when it suits. You will help me, won't you? I'll pay you the same as any other *fecker* would.

I opened the desk drawer, took out a standard contract form printed on self-duplicating paper and pushed it towards her. Pimpernel Investigations was in existence to supply a service to the public and the £1735.28 I needed to avoid eviction from my flat was within my grasp. If she was willing and able to pay for that service, why should I stand in her way?

'I can't be doing with reading them *fecking* things, I

haven't got my glasses with me,' she said. 'You tell me what it's about.'

'It's just a standard contract,' I said. 'It makes everything clear and legal between us. I agree to work for you, and you agree to pay me £400 a day. I'll try to trace this Clarke and get your documents back but that's it. There's no way I'm going to try to prove that you're the rightful Queen of England.'

'Oh, that's *fecking* great Mr Cunane! Shall I pay you in advance?' she said with pathetic eagerness. 'I don't mind paying you, just as long as there's enough left for a house. That was always what me and Dermot wanted, God rest his soul. All he could get was tarmacking and that did for him.'

I felt guilty in a way, but if I did an honest week's work in trying to track down this Clarke character and found her papers, whatever they might be, if they existed at all, then I might be able to persuade her to relinquish her daft obsession. There couldn't be any genuine legal papers proving a marriage between her granny and the former Prince of Wales, so by taking her money I was really undertaking to prove a negative and cure her of her fixation. If it only took me two days to find Clarke I could always give her a refund.

'Yes, that would be a good idea because I'm not going to call on you at that blasted camp. I don't want to meet your cousin Mickey again. Why don't you get out of there?' I asked.

'It's hard for a traveller to give up the road, all the people I know live in camps but I'm thinking about it,' she said slowly, then in a more practical vein asked, 'How much do you want?'

'If you pay me for a week in advance that'll get me started, and you'll have to pay any incidental expenses.' I spoke bluntly, maybe when she had to hand over actual cash she'd think twice about employing me. 'It'll be £2000, plus VAT.'

Mary gave me a cool look. 'You don't come cheap, Mr Cunane, but I suppose the best never does. I was impressed by the way you weren't going to let my cousin get the better of yous yesterday.' She counted out forty of the notes from her parcel and laid them on the desk. Then she tidily moved Kath Headlam's car keys next to the pile. 'Do we have to bother about the VAT?' she asked. She might be thinking of giving up the travelling life but some tinker habits obviously died hard.

She wasn't as green as she looked.

'If you're not coming out to my trailer, how will you get in touch with me?' she asked, still concerned with practicalities.

'Where are you moving to?'

'I won't know until I get there. They don't tell me, but probably out Agecroft way.'

'You aren't on the phone?' I asked with a smile.

She shook her head.

'You could afford a portable phone.'

'And how do you think I would explain that to my cousin? Anyway I couldn't be messing with them things,' she said scornfully.

'I'll put an advert in the personal column of the *Banner* saying "M.W. get in touch with D.C.".'

'No, there's a problem there,' she replied, looking at me sheepishly, 'I never really learned my letters very well. It took me hours just to read your card.'

'Well, we'll have to meet then but not here,' I said reluctantly. 'I don't want Delise to know I'm taking this on. She thinks I'm investigating something else and life's complicated enough already. Now just sign the contract here and take your copy.'

She laboriously printed out M. WOOD in capital letters

52

at the bottom of the page and I took the top sheet and gave her the pink copy. She smiled very warmly but I felt uncomfortable; was I ripping off the 'intellectually challenged'?

Still, if it was an elaborate con-trick at least I was starting off on the right side of the deal. As if she could read my thoughts, Mary said, 'Don't think I'm a fool, Mr Cunane. Everyone's entitled to know the truth about themselves. Even when I could do nothing about all this I used to lie awake at night and wonder about what my daddy told me. When I got the money, I thought I'd try to find the proof again as a sort of present to myself.'

'What did you say your daddy was called?'

She blushed furiously. 'I've already told you – Windsor, that was his name and he had as much right to use it as anyone else . . . "Et-wort" Windsor, the same as his father,' she said with every sign of real indignation. 'Of course, he didn't use the name, the family wasn't exactly popular in the West of Ireland when he was a kid, so he called himself Castle instead or maybe they nicknamed him that. Anyway before I got married I was known as Mary Cassells, it sounded more Irish than Castle.

'Now I've got the money I thought I owed it to Daddy and myself to find out the truth, but I just couldn't think how to get started. Then you turned up. I don't want to find out so I can claim anything, I just need to know.'

'All right. I'll do what I can. It's coming up to Christmas and New Year and I'll need a full working week to get this sorted so can we arrange to meet on the first Saturday in January? You give me a ring on this number,' I said, giving her the office number, 'and I'll let you know how I'm getting on.'

She gave a disappointed little grunt.

'Look,' I said, 'you've waited so long, a little longer won't hurt. And don't go getting your hopes up, remember it was you who said that Clarke had sold the papers, so even if I find him he might not have them, and if he hasn't sold them he might have lost them. It's seven years since your husband died, isn't it? So if Clarke's travelling on the tarmac he might have lost them.'

'That bastard of a ganger Clarke would never throw away anything he thought might be worth money,' Mary said fiercely, clutching her carrier bag of cash to her well-rounded bosom as I drew her chair back and escorted her to the door.

Back in the office I picked up the pile of money she'd left and examined the notes. They seemed genuine.

Just out of interest I pulled a copy of the *Encyclopaedia Britannica* out of the shelf over my head and looked up previous imposters and pretenders to the English throne. Lambert Simnel and Perkin Warbeck had claimed membership of the royal family. Bonny Prince Charlie had been trying to uphold a recognised claim. All three had received help from the Irish. Lambert had even been crowned King in Dublin Cathedral.

The only serious pretender this century had been Anna Anderson who claimed she was Anastasia, the last Tsar's youngest daughter. Her story had never been conclusively disproved, even now. Looking at the photo of the unlucky Tsar Nicholas II with his wife and children, I was struck by the resemblance of the oldest girl to Mary – they had the same squarish face and heavy-lidded eyes – but then if what Mary said was true, they were related.

4

While I was thinking about what Mary Wood could hope
to gain by claiming membership of the Royal Family I
heard the outer door to the office open and Jay Anderson
arrived. He was late as usual. Timekeeping wasn't his
strong point but on this occasion I was grateful.

'Come in, Jay,' I shouted. 'Don't bother taking your
coat off, we're paying a visit to Alhambra Studios.'

He put his head round my door, muttered a 'Morning,
Boss' and withdrew his head. He didn't seem pleased to
see me.

'Come right in, Jay and let me look at you,' I urged.
He didn't seem to want to be inspected. I could hear him
whispering. He either had someone with him or he was
talking to himself. Reticence was not one of Jay's usual
qualities, he was generally only too anxious to strut his
stuff. He must be up to no good.

'Get your butt in here, Anderson! Don't make me
come out there, old buddy-boy,' I drawled. I wanted to
check he hadn't been on the crack again as well as
inspect his latest wardrobe variation.

He re-emerged in front of me wearing an outsized
navy-blue bomber jacket with heavily padded shoulders,
black leather trousers and red boots. Behind him, to my
amazement, stood a small mixed-race boy of about ten
years old, also in red boots, but clad in a bright-blue
fleecy jacket and a red cap with the ear flaps down.

He only lacked a little white beard to double as a
garden gnome.

Jay got his word in first, before I could make a

comment: 'Wow! Boss, have you crapped in here?' he said, flapping his hands. 'It smells like it. Real hot scheiss, man!'

My previous visitor must have left a stronger aroma than I'd thought, unless I was developing a personal body odour problem. Now Jay mentioned it, there was a noticeable smell of unwashed clothing in the small room.

'Open the window, then! What do you expect? Air conditioning? You get these smells in old buildings.'

Jay sloped lethargically towards the window, still fanning a breeze with his hands.

'Who's your friend, then?' I asked. 'Aren't you going to introduce us?'

'This is Liberty Walker, Boss. I brought him with me to play on the computer,' my assistant said in an apologetic tone.

Liberty looked me over, his little sharp bright eyes missing nothing. His face held a quizzical, cheeky expression on it as he looked up at me intently, as much as to say 'Who does this old fart think he is?' He was small for his age and his eyes, which were blue in contrast to his light-brown skin, gave an impression of alertness and intelligence. 'I just want to play on your computer, I've got Lemmings 2,' he said forcefully as if it was the most natural thing in the world for him to play on a perfect stranger's office equipment. He spoke with a strong Glasgow accent and his voice sounded shrill to my ears.

I looked at Jay. In my experience, the role of friend and mentor to the young was a new one for him. He had never showed much concern for his brothers. Why was he inflicting this scourge on me?

'OK, show the kid how to play on the computer, then come in here,' I responded gruffly. 'I need a word.'

'You can say what you like in front of Liberty, he's deaf. He can only lip read, so he can't tell what you're saying as long as you're in front of the window. Can't make out your lips, you see.'

'He can't be completely deaf, I can see a mark on the side of his head where his hearing aid sits,' I said curtly. 'We're supposed to be a private investigation agency, not a bunch of child-minders.'

'It's the background noise,' piped up Liberty. 'It picks up too much background noise, I'm better off without it.'

'Well, I'm glad to hear that, but I need to talk to Jay so why don't you go next door and have a look at the computer?' I spoke slowly, mouthing my words for him.

He pulled a face and reluctantly retreated towards the outer office. Before leaving me alone with my employee, he leapt into the air, gripped the narrow ledge above the other side of the door and swung himself through. This was all done so nimbly that I didn't have time to speak. It was possibly the neatest ever exit from my office.

'Look, Jay, I don't want to tell you off or anything,' I took a reasonable tone with him. I didn't want him throwing a wobbler and storming out of the office mouthing insults about oppressive white men, 'but it seems like I'm the last person to be told what everyone's plans are.'

His face remained impassive as he listened to my mild complaint. I never know exactly what's going on inside Jay's head. He has a temperament which gives an unusual quality of unpredictability to the boss/employee relationship. I once read a management text book. It had a lot of jargon about 'span of control'. With Jay and Delise as my employees, neither of whom can be counted on to do what I want more than fifty per cent of the time, my 'span of control' is pretty feeble.

'Anyway, I hope you haven't made any plans tonight

because we've got a job on in Macclesfield. We've to go and deliver something to a young woman there. Then something else has come up. I've managed to get back the car that I went looking for yesterday. We'll have to take that back. Why don't you and Liberty go and check the car out? You know what you're looking for, don't you, a new silver Mazda RX7?' I tossed him the keys. He caught them eagerly. After new trainers and clothes, cars are the major interest in Jay's life. Sex comes a long way behind display and transport on his personal agenda.

When he and his gnome-like Scottish friend had left I decided to phone Alhambra to give Kath Headlam the good news. Returning the car might jog her memory – it was now 10.30 and she still hadn't phoned to fill me in properly on the Gloria Rishton job. Before I called her, I decided to try and find out something more about Simon Rishton.

Delise has a full set of yearbooks from Alhambra TV in her cubby hole and I spent twenty minutes leafing through them to glean what I could. One thing was certain, Rishton had a genius for self-publicity. There was hardly a mention of Kath Headlam in any of the annuals, but Rishton featured prominently in each one.

The lives and times of TV personalities are a closed book to me. I was vaguely aware of Rishton from the occasional glimpse of him on TV, but I knew nothing in particular about him. It looked to me that he was one of those people who were famous for being famous.

Skimming through various articles, I gathered he had started his meteoric rise to fame as an all-purpose presenter and compere in the early days of Alhambra. According to the hype in the yearbooks, Rishton had shown a genius for coming up with new ideas for shows and had moved smoothly and swiftly from performing in front of the camera to presiding over the fortunes of the company behind it – he was a sort of poor man's David Attenborough, except that the animal species that Rishton seemed to have specialised in over the years was that section of the human race that's female, under twenty-five and with outsized chest development.

I was at a loss really. There seemed to be a lot of pictures of Rishton standing on the sets of TV shows that didn't seem to tax the public's mental faculties much, with page three look-alikes.

To get the dirt on him I really needed my mate Ted Blake. He can remember every TV programme he's ever watched since the days of 'Joe 90' and the 'Beverly Hillbillies'. But when I tried Blake's number there was no reply.

As I sat racking my brain over what else I'd ever heard about Rishton it came to me: he was one of my mother's 'bêtes noires'. *That's* why his face was familiar; whenever it appeared she would give a groan and insist on a pro- gramme change. Throughout my adolescence my dear mother, Eileen Cunane, that noted moralist, had cen- sored the guy out of my consciousness.

What had he done to incur her wrath? In the dim recesses of my mind vague memories stirred. Hadn't there been a messy divorce from his first wife, a pretty co-presenter? Hadn't he been the second or third man to use the f-word on British TV? Quite enough to turn my mother against him.

More came back to me. During the recent sale of TV franchises he had been Alhambra's leading champion. A sort of 'stage Northerner' they had wheeled out to show that the company had strong local connections.

I have an out-of-date copy of *Who's Who* bought at a car-boot sale. I looked him up. Yes, there he was . . . *'Born Harrogate 1932 . . . educ. Oundle, Trin. Coll. Cambs., . . . married twice . . . Producer of a long list of TV shows. Director*

of Programmes Alhambra TV... etc, etc. Recreations...
mainly horizontal.'

I had found out as much about Rishton as I was going to without leaving my desk so I phoned Headlam to give her the glad tidings about her car. She wasn't in but I was able to coax her secretary into trying to connect me to Simon Rishton. I didn't manage to reach the great man in person but one of his assistants relayed my message to him. She reported that he was delighted about the car and invited me to bring it out to the studios a.s.a.p.

As I put the phone down, Jay and Liberty returned.

'Wicked, man, that mother's just wicked!' Jay enthused. He looked happier than I'd seen him for weeks. 'It's got everything: alloy wheels, silver metal paint, tinted glass windows.'

'Yeah, it's pure!' squeaked his friend in his reedy Glaswegian voice. 'It's even got a message written on the number plate!'

I noted the look of surprise on Jay's face.

'Your mate's got sharp eyes, hasn't he,' I commented. 'I'll have to take him on as a detective.'

'He's closer to the ground than me,' Jay explained.

'It says "To Kath with love from Simon",' chanted Liberty in his sing-song accent. 'It's just in small writing below the number.'

'He's a good reader, isn't he? I'm glad to see your friend hasn't been missing his lessons but are you sure he's not playing truant now?' I asked Jay. I was determined not to legitimise Liberty's presence by taking too much notice of him.

'Leave it out, Boss!' Jay snarled. 'The schools aren't open at Christmas!' He changed the subject. 'Can't I go for a run down the M56? That's one great set of wheels. When does it have to be back?'

'Right away, so forget it,' I answered.

'Go on, nobody'll know,' said Liberty, adding his small weight to Jay's plea.

I could see I was facing a revolt so I softened a little and beat a tactical retreat. There was no point in making a big issue out of it. Rishton and his lady friend wouldn't notice if we put a bit more mileage on the clock, and anyway, they were lucky to be getting the car back at all. So what the hell, I needed to keep Jay happy.

'Oh, all right. We can take it back by a long diversion and if Rishton complains we can always say we're testing it, but there's no way you're driving. If the fuzz see you behind a fancy set of wheels like that, they'll pull us over right away.'

The car was a dream. The rotary engine was so quiet and smooth that there was a warning buzzer to tell you when to change gear. There was a multiple CD player and wrap-around sound. We zoomed down the Parkway and onto the M56, keeping the speed down until we were well away from the spy-cameras. There wasn't much traffic and when I passed the turn-off for the airport I put my foot down. We surged forward and reached the M6 in record time.

When the police Range Rover shot in front of me and flashed me to a halt at the turn-off I was glad I'd told Jay to bring the documentation on Headlam with us. I was approaching the M6 roundabout to point the car back towards Manchester when they stopped me. They'd nabbed me just on the off chance that a fancy car containing two young blacks and a white man might be stolen. I explained that the registered owner was our customer and that we weren't 'twoccers' – car thieves. That was my first mistake. The car was registered to Rishton – one of his tax-free expenses, no doubt.

They had to phone Rishton to confirm my story before reluctantly releasing us with a caution.

When they'd gone Jay crowed: 'Better let me drive back to the studios, Boss. Them Dibbles are more used to seeing a black guy driving a set of hot wheels like this than one of your lot!'

I let him drive us back and he kept to a sedate speed the whole way despite being urged to do the ton again by his little Scottish confederate.

I was half expecting a temper tantrum from Rishton, or at least a liberal use of the f-word that he was so fond of, when I saw him waiting by the entrance to the studio car park with Poulter . . . the same security man who'd been so officious last night. I feared the worst for a moment. Rishton might be going to have me done for taking without owner's consent. At the very least he would want to know why I was heading towards London in his girlfriend's car instead of bringing it straight back as promised.

'It's in great shape, Mr Rishton, no damage at all,' I said as he and the hatchet-faced security man strode towards us. Rishton seemed small and slightly built, almost fragile, alongside the heavy-set security man, like a child with a much older brother. He was wearing a heavy black overcoat with the collar turned up and from what I could see of his expression he didn't seem too pleased. His face looked pinched and pained, perhaps due to the cold. It appeared to be much thinner, the long nose more prominent and pointed than when seen framed on the TV screen and his wispy hair blew about in the wind. He bounced along beside Poulter, moving like a much younger man than his *Who's Who* entry stated he was.

To my relief, he switched into celeb mode, just like turning on a light. He gave us all the full benefit of his smile, grabbed my hand and said, 'It's wonderful. How did you manage to get it back? Kath will be ecstatic.

Trade secret, I suppose! I can see you've got your contacts with the underworld,' this said as Jay and Liberty emerged from the Mazda. 'Everything all right for this evening? . . . Kath briefed you? . . . This is fabulous. How about something to eat? . . . Oh, don't be alarmed. Mr Poulter's just here to identify you . . .'

There was no stopping him. He spoke in choppy little sentences and the effect was totally different from the very few occasions I'd seen him doing one of his 'turns' on the telly. Then he spoke in connected sentences like a wise elder statesman. The difference between the reality of the man and my expectation left me feeling uneasy. He seemed like a completely different person, not that I could claim a very profound acquaintance with his public face.

On and on he effervesced. I realised that he must be well aware of the effect he had on people.

'Kath'll be over the moon . . . Birthday present, you know . . . Met Poulter before? . . . Oh yes, 'course you have . . . Gave you a sharp elbow . . . Sorry about that. Kath was upset . . . Cutbacks from on high . . . Free and easy days over here, aren't they, Poulter?'

The black-uniformed security man nodded and left without comment, but not before taking a careful look at the three of us. His departure didn't stem Rishton's flow for a second.

It crossed my mind that nothing short of physical violence would get Rishton to belt up for a second. A smack on the gob seemed like the only way. If only my mother was here with her remote control, she could turn him off.

'Can't stand him . . . Kath can't either . . . New man . . . Part of the Trevose regime . . . Anyone else would have let you in . . . Asked questions later . . . Must make it up . . . This your kiddy?' indicating Liberty but not pausing for an answer. 'Need to talk to you . . . Kath's out spending money . . . Doesn't know everything about Gloria, really . . . Like to tell you why I'm sending you to see her . . . Real surprise for Kath . . .'

It was Liberty who put an end to Rishton's overwhelming flow. Apparently his mother and mine had similar feelings.

'You're on the telly, aren't you? My mammy says you're rubbish,' he bawled very loudly while peering intently at Rishton's face.

There was a dead silence while Rishton contemplated the unamiable Scottish child.

'He's not with me,' I said hastily. However truthful Liberty's remark might be, a commission was still a commission. 'Today's the first time I've ever laid eyes on him. Why don't you walk him back to the office, Jay? . . . and shove a sesame seed bun, or several, down his throat at McDonald's on your way.'

Rishton gave me a sceptical look.

Mercifully, Jay removed Liberty without any argument and they set off back on foot. 'Is he your gopher, then?' Rishton asked as we watched Jay lead Liberty away.

'Hardly. If I want anything done it's quicker to do it myself, but he does have his uses and I owe him a favour. He's supposed to be my trainee,' I answered.

'Come on, I know somewhere where they do a really good steak,' Rishton commanded, taking me by the arm in a strangely gentle grasp and press-ganging me back into the Mazda. 'You don't have the look of a vegetarian, Dave. Don't be stuffy, call me Simon. As I said before, I'd like to tell you more about your mission for this evening. I don't think Kath quite understands why I want someone to go and see Gloria.'

He was speaking at a steadier pace than previously but

I got the impression it wouldn't be long before he revved right back up to his racing speed.

'I don't quite understand why you can't just telephone her yourself,' I said.

'Absolutely fatal! Out of the question! I'll tell all when we get to the restaurant, Dave, old cock.' He concentrated on his driving, accelerating sharply down Deansgate, and weaving his way cheekily through the traffic. While he drove I examined him out of the corner of my eye.

He lived up to one of the clichés about media folk by being a lot smaller in the flesh than he seemed on screen. Everything humanly possible was being done to hold back the processes of physical decay which must have set in by now – he was nudging bus-pass age. He was only about five foot five or six in height and looked as if every square inch of his surface area had been worked over by teams of fastidious craftsmen. He radiated that feeling of wealth and luxury an old master painting gives when it's on the wall of a private room rather than in a public gallery – a rare object, lovingly cherished. There was no suggestion that his self-proclaimed 'horizontal' recreation was wearing him out. Perhaps all that meant was that he slept a lot.

There were one or two grey streaks in his hair, as a minor concession to reality, but the predominant shade was an unnatural looking light brown. It was either dyed or he was wearing a very well fitted toupee.

His face was equally fresh and youthful, with a high colour now he had recovered from exposure to the cold; the skin still appearing young and elastic. There weren't even any tell-tale crow's feet under the eyes. There was a faint silver line at the base of his left cheek; he obviously didn't share his plastic surgeon with Kath Headlam, who looked far more in need of one than he did.

His left hand, resting on the steering wheel, wore a wedding ring, a wide gold band, and I noticed a large ring on the little finger of his right. The oval-shaped cabochon was of some brownish-coloured semi-precious stone. A bit over the top for my taste, whatever it was.

Our destination turned out to be a large pub-cum-restaurant in the heart of the Quays, the Dock House restaurant. The lower floor was a fancy pub where local yuppies who'd survived the recession sipped their Mexican beers, while the upper storey was a comfortable restaurant done up in Olde Englishe gentleman's club style.

Rishton's celebrity status served us well because, although the place was packed with diners starting their pre-Christmas festivities, and there were many waiting, the manager found us a table immediately, making it clear that we were special customers.

As soon as he was comfortably seated Rishton's flow of chat resumed. He quickly scanned the menu through his half-moon glasses. 'I'll have my usual, George,' he snapped to the manager, a grovelling and humble Scot, who was waiting on us personally.

I hastily selected my own meal and settled down to listen.

'It's the old story with me, Dave. Marry in haste . . . repent at leisure. Married her in 1989 . . . Gloria's my fourth wife. You'd think I'd learn . . . but no. Can't do without it . . . got to have it twice a day . . . get headaches otherwise. Sexual energy, you see . . . close to creative energy.'

As he spoke, his beautifully manicured hands were roving all over the table top, straightening cutlery, fidgeting with the bread rolls and butter cartons.

I sat on the edge of my seat to await his next revelation. I could see why he made interesting programmes. He had a natural gift for self-dramatisation.

The arrival of a waiter with a huge piece of barely cooked rump steak for Rishton delayed the narrative. 'Yours will be a little longer, sir,' the waiter apologised.

Seeing me eyeing his bleeding piece of meat suspiciously, Rishton said, 'Best Angus steak . . . get it in for me specially. Cook it just the way I like it . . . start when they see me coming. Should eat yours like this . . . more energy.'

Rishton's litany, in which he made all the responses to his own recitative, was starting to wear me out. I found my head nodding forward in time to the beat of his two-part statements.

'I'm not short of energy. I've never had any complaints in that department,' I butted in defensively.

'Still young yet, though. Look at you . . . jerking up and down on your seat. Look like a trainee rabbi saying his prayers. No staying power. Bet the girlfriend's feeding you energy-sapping foods . . . Muesli eh! Pitta bread, hmm, cottage cheese eh! . . . Gave my second wife, Arabella, the boot when she started that. "Muesli . . . or me," I said. Well,' he sighed, ' . . . she stuck with the muesli and took a nice fat settlement.'

Although his comment was made in a self-deprecating way, Rishton didn't laugh or smile. The man was totally serious about everything concerning himself. His vanity completely armoured him against any suggestion of ridicule.

I took the opportunity of him cramming a piece of raw steak into his mouth to steer the conversation back to my mission.

'Simon, could you fill me in on tonight? Miss Headlam didn't make it quite clear what it is you want,' I said.

'Yes, took me four marriages to realise that . . . a kept

woman's far cheaper than a wife in the long run. Starts mucking about with muesli . . . she's out on her arse and know's it! Good girl, Kath, though . . . always had her in reserve . . . like a fine old brandy waiting for a rainy day. Top of the First Division . . . fine when things go wrong in the Premier League!'

My own well-grilled steak arrived before I could guide him back to the subject of tonight's job. Rishton was swilling red wine by now, a fine dry Lambrusco, and his tongue showed no sign of going into a lower gear.

Filled with raw steak, he started patting his chest and then the pockets of his trousers. 'Must do something,' he muttered, pushing back his chair. 'You haven't got a large denomination banknote on you by any chance, have you?'

I thought for a moment that he was asking me to pay for his meal. Then I understood. The old sleaze bag wanted a snort.

'Just need it for a moment, give it you back in a jiff.'

I took out the bundle of £50 notes I'd received earlier from Mary Wood and peeled one off. They were all new notes.

'Christ, you're loaded, aren't you, old lad? Never carry the stuff myself. Just off to the powder room for a minute,' he said and hurried off towards the loo, leaving me to catch up with his super-fast eating methods and consume my own steak in peace.

When he returned he handed me back the note.

His eyes looked even brighter than before and he had carelessly left a trace of snow under his right nostril. He noticed me looking and grinned knowingly as he wiped it off.

'You know what they say about cocaine – it's God's way of telling you that you've got too much money . . . I can let you have a line if you want . . . find it aids the

68

digestion,' he said in a slower and more relaxed way than earlier.

'No, no. I don't use it,' I said hastily.

'More into crack then, are you? Does your young gopher find it for you?'

This carefully preserved relic of the sixties was rapidly becoming a pain in the butt. Not only did he think I was a dealer, but he was also trumpeting his suspicions all over the restaurant.

'No, he doesn't. He's a youth trainee and I'm trying to keep him away from that sort of thing!' I said self-righteously. I knew I sounded pious, but in the circles Jay and I moved in, drug dealing wasn't something you joked about.

'All right, chuckie! Calm down. Just seeing you with such a large roll of money made me think you might be connected. No offence intended.'

His dazzling white smile was brought to bear at point-blank range, and I subsided back into my seat. The halo of celebrity round Rishton's carefully coiffured head had the effect of causing a lesser mortal, such as myself, to forgive him for mistaking me for a dealer where normally I would have kicked the table over and broken someone of lesser import's limbs.

'Mr Rishton, as far as I'm concerned I'm here to discuss arrangements for a visit to your wife which your friend Kath Headlam asked me to make. If there's something else on the agenda I'm not interested,' I said coldly.

'Great, Dave! You look just like Al Pacino in *Godfather II*. Those eyes! Have you ever considered a career in TV? No, I suppose not . . . look, Dave, don't take me seriously, my friends don't. I'm just a playful child . . .' he said, making his right hand into a fist and smacking it into his left.

There was certainly something childlike and endearing about his performance. I smiled.

'OK, Simon!' I said emphatically, 'but you must tell me exactly what I'm supposed to do tonight or I'm leaving now.'

'Oh, I like it, I like it. Well, I don't want you to put the frighteners on Gloria or anything like that! If that's what you're worried about let me put your mind at rest once and for all.'

'Simon, do you mind turning the volume down a few degrees? You've got half of Manchester tuned in to you here,' I said. I was beginning to get used to him but I didn't see why everyone around us should know our business.

He had the half-moon glasses on top of his head now and he leaned forward and spoke in a more conspiratorial tone. 'All I want is for you to check that she'll be all right over the festive season and to give her this envelope . . . It contains some cash. It's too open to misinterpretation for me to go and give it to her myself, and I'll only get involved in another emotional scene . . . Call it conscience money if you like. Kath's an old softy . . . Doesn't like to think of Gloria on her own at Christmas.' He pushed a heavily taped-up envelope across the table.

I left it where it was. The man had spent twenty minutes shouting his head off about drugs and here he was handing me a large packet in full view of about thirty people. For all I knew the Drug Squad would pounce the minute I picked up the envelope.

Rishton must have read my thoughts.

'Oh no! Silly boy! It's just money.'

'Is it?' I asked. 'Why would you trust me, a total stranger, with your money? Why not send it to her recorded delivery? And by the way, Simon, I must tell you that my mother always switches off any programme that you appear in.'

For the first time since I'd met him he appeared slightly disconcerted. He laughed uneasily, not sure whether to take me seriously or not.

'Can't win 'em all, I suppose,' he said finally. 'I have that effect on some women. . . . It is just money. The thing is, if Gloria's lawyers get hold of this, they'll claim I pay her lump sums as maintenance on a regular basis. I want you to be a "deniable" cut-out. That's why I can't use the post or someone well known to either Gloria or myself. Please take the money and deliver it to Gloria as I ask. The envelope doesn't contain anything but cash.'

It was put-up or shut-up time.

I put the envelope into the inside pocket of my leather jacket, a thick bundle of notes. I'd no idea how much, but even if it was all in £5 notes, there had to be plenty. The bundle was so securely taped that I'd have needed to use a knife on it to check the contents. If Declan and Sean from the tinkers' camp caught me sleeping on the ground again they'd think they'd won the Tote.

'Yes, you just give her that,' Rishton said.

I started fumbling round in my pockets for a contract form to give him as a receipt but I hadn't got one. I picked up an unused napkin off the table and started writing one on that but Rishton snatched it away and crumpled it up. 'I don't want anything written down or receipts or anything or her lawyers'll start whinging,' he said. His expression was guarded and hard to read.

I wasn't exactly thrilled with the assignment. If I hadn't been getting hostile glances every time I went in my bank to plead for an extension of the overdraft I'd have thrown the money back in his smug face, but he'd judged me well. To get a fat fee and tide myself over into the New Year I was ready to do anything that could remotely pass as legal. Still, this job stunk like the breeze from a fish-finger factory. Rishton claimed to be shy about

71

delivering cash to his estranged wife yet he'd made the arrangements for me to do it in the middle of a crowded restaurant. All the event lacked was a flashing neon sign or one of those day-glo motorway jackets for me with the words 'The Go-Between' stencilled across the back.

'How much is there in the envelope, Mr Rishton?' I asked.

'There's ten big ones in there, my son,' he replied from behind his smoke-screen. 'You see, I really do trust you. Tell me, Dave, exactly what is it that your mother objects to about me?' He looked uneasy.

I carefully composed my own face before replying, 'Simon, I was only joking. She loves your programmes, never misses them.'

The look of relief on his face was palpable. I didn't doubt for a moment that he believed me.

He was speaking much more confidentially now. He'd switched the loudspeaker off. It seemed he wanted to tell all. 'The thing is . . . things are rather sticky down at Alhambra at the moment . . .' He paused long enough for me to wonder whether Lucy Longstaff had done some mischief to her rival in love last night. 'The old management, of which I was a key player, rather over-extended themselves . . . Too much marble . . . too much glass . . . too bloody lavish all round in fact . . . The long and short of it is they want to say "Farewell" to yours truly without even the benefit of a golden handshake and retirement plan.' He suddenly banged the table, making the cups rattle and causing his spectators to avert their eyes quickly in case they found themselves becoming involved.

'God! I dragged that studio up from nothing with my bare hands.' He was back at full volume again. 'You can't imagine the difficulties there were in the early days . . . the lack of vision. But, some of my opponents, one of them in particular actually, are well connected with the national media.' His complexion had turned purple.

'Not that effing little rat Trevose, he's just the goddamned office boy! It's that other bastard . . . Christ! Do you know they only want to dump "Slatheredge Pit"!' . . . There was a long pause after this revelation, obviously I was supposed to be very shocked.

When I made no response he continued, 'Sorry. I'm straying from the point . . . there are people not a million miles from the tabloid press who'd be delighted to pay the lovely Gloria for all the lurid details of our love life she can muster and then splash them all over the newsstands . . . So I want you to give the money to Gloria, tell her it's just a refresher . . . there'll be lots more if she keeps shtum, but if she talks – zilch! She'll be hawking her pretty little behind round the national press and not living at my expense in Prestbury! Got it?'

'Simon! Calm down, you're going to burst a blood vessel,' I said hastily. He looked quite insane.

I didn't believe a word he'd said. What could the press possibly print about Rishton that they hadn't already? Gloria must have got some pretty hot stuff on him if he was about to send her £10,000 through an intermediary he'd never met before.

'Do you mind getting a taxi back into town,' he said as he strolled to the car, 'all this talk about sex : . . I think I'll call in at a place I know for some refreshment before I get back to work. Care to join me?'

I cut the farewells short. I was delighted to get a taxi and refuse his offer. He shot out of the car park at such high speed that I thought that he'd end up in the Dock under thirty feet of polluted water if he wasn't careful. But no, there was a final gleam from the pinkie ring as he waved farewell and then the silver car moved at speed towards the main road, swiftly merging into the fog.

5

Manchester. Thursday Afternoon

Standing on the Quays in the fog I shivered; not from the cold, though it was cold enough, but from the feeling that my quest for cash to keep PI Ltd afloat was leading me into strange waters.

Despite the rawness of the day, I decided against getting a taxi and set off walking towards Trafford Bar to catch the MetroLink tram into town – a confident decision in view of the amount of cash I was carrying. It wasn't quite as bitter as yesterday and I needed to think for a while without anyone pestering me. Rishton had aroused my inherited puritan instincts with his gung-ho attitude towards the opposite sex. But the feeling of revulsion was balanced by a sneaking admiration. He certainly squeezed the juice out of every available moment, and look at what he'd achieved . . . all those programmes he'd fronted . . . fame and wealth . . . instant recognition wherever he went . . .

He'd been through four wives, entertained himself with mistresses and resorted to prostitutes as if sex was going to be rationed at any moment. You had to admire his stamina, if not his selectivity. Nothing was allowed to come between him and instant self-gratification. I reflected for a moment on my own sex life. My tryst of last night with Delise had been a brief enough encounter.

I soon realised that I'd picked the wrong time and the wrong place to go for a walk. Residents driving back to their flats were gawping through their windscreens at me in alarm as I trotted briskly along the dockside. This area was definitely one of those places where all the respectable folk were motorised. It was also extremely cold, now that the illusion of warmth bestowed by Rishton's brandy had dissipated. I started to run down the road past the Copthorne Hotel, and the bitter wind from the docks pursued me like a bad conscience.

When I got to the office, Jay and his friend were concentrating on the computer and barely acknowledged my arrival. I went into my own room and treated myself to a slug of Scotch. Jay loped in. 'That car was double top, Boss. Why don't you swap the Nissan?'

'I'm happy with the old Bluebird, Jay; blends in wherever you go. By the way, did you bring it in all right?'

"Course I did. What do you take me for? No one round my way would rip me off anyway,' he bragged. 'Your car's probably safer with me than it is parked outside your flat in Chorlton.'

I didn't feel like arguing.

'OK, I only asked, don't get excited. What's the story with this Liberty, I know it's Christmas but you're not usually known to bring in waifs and strays.'

'It's complicated, Boss . . .'

'I've got all afternoon.'

Jay made a sort of twisting motion with his wrists, rotating his hands. I took this to mean that it would be uncool to pry further but I was feeling persistent. I am an investigator, after all. If I had to let Rishton impose his life style on me, or at least put up with him while I earned the money to pay my mortgage and keep the firm afloat, there was no reason why I should put up with Jay doing the same.

'Come on Jay. Spill the beans,' I ordered.

'Kid's in danger, boss. You know I said he was deaf? Well, he is, but he's very clever, he's wicked at lip reading – he can even guess what people are saying by the way they move when they're talking when he can't see their

75

lips. It's wicked, Boss! He can read a conversation a hundred yards away!'

'Well, what's so wrong with that?'

'It's going to get his head blown off for him, is what's wrong! He's taken to wagging school and following the youth round the streets. He keeps bunking off from home, too. His mother got the police onto him but when they brought him home he told them about a very interesting conversation he'd overheard in the street. The Dibbles got interested, some of them detectives would be very pleased to have him telling them who's saying what to whom. He has a social worker who's supposed to keep an eye on him, but the guy's on holiday and anyway short of chaining Liberty up, no one can control him.'

I laughed.

'It's serious, Boss! If the youth think he's grassing them up, some paranoid crack-head is going to freak out and take a shotgun to him.'

'That's all very interesting, Jay, but what's your involvement in all this?' Underneath the banter, I was now annoyed. My little firm had done more than its share to remedy the deficiencies of the educational and police services by taking on Jay Anderson, without him going round recruiting other social casualties. That was the way these things worked, I thought sourly . . . take on one passenger and before long you have a bus full. I couldn't say that Delise hadn't warned me often enough.

Jay looked embarrassed. He sensed the sudden chill in the atmosphere and knew it wasn't due to the poor heating. He looked at his hands, rotating them again, and gave me a sulky grin. 'It's family, Boss,' he muttered. 'I'm related to the kid. When my father went into prison for the first time, my mum wouldn't have nothing to do with him when he came out. So he moved in with Liberty's mum, a white girl from Glasgow. Liberty's her kid. Mum thinks his name was meant as some kind of joke against her, but I don't know.'

'So he's your half brother?'

'I suppose so,' Jay said moodily.

'Well, is he, or isn't he?' I pressed.

'He is, and I've been lumbered with looking after him.'

'Wrong,' I said breezily. 'Social Services are just going to have to get off their rear ends and do something about him.'

Jay didn't seem too delighted.

'It won't work out like that. They won't have him in school. All he wants to do is to play on computers or bang his drums. I'm going to get stuck with him.'

'Can't Lovena do anything to help?' I asked. Jay's mother, Lovena Anderson, is a pillar of the community.

'No, she won't even have the kid in the house. Says it's between me and my father, and you know where he is – in the special wing at Barlinnie, doing life.'

I could see that it would cramp Jay's cool-dude style to have to tow a ten-year-old around with him. I was surprised at Lovena's attitude, though. She was normally so generous with her time, but I suppose it figured. She'd brought up three kids on her own without male assistance, so why should she take in Jay Senior's by-blows? – Particularly as Liberty's mother was still on the scene.

What was wrong with *her*? Why wasn't she looking after Liberty?

Looking at Jay's intent and worried expression I relented. Acting on an impulse, I gave him £50 and said 'Take Liberty out now to Laserquest or the bowling alley. Tell him it's his Christmas treat and you'll treat him again if he gives you his word he'll stop wandering the streets. Go on now Jay, take the car, drop him at home when you've had your fun and then get back here by five o'clock. Make sure the car's tanked up.'

Jay brightened up a bit. 'Yo, mon! I'll give it a whirl.'

I wasn't in the Boy Scouts for nothing, or was it that the day's events had left me with a bad taste in my mouth? I'd no idea what a child psychologist would think about my methods but it was better than giving the kid a belt in the face. Anyway, I could always stick the money on Rishton's bill as an incidental expense.

After Jay left, I put my feet up on the desk and fell asleep reading my forensic medicine textbook. I didn't feel guilty about not starting Mary Wood's investigation, nothing was going to be happening two days before Christmas.

I was wakened by a call from Kath Headlam, she sounded very business-like – 'I'd like to thank you for getting the car back, but that's not the only reason I'm phoning. Something's come up and I need to see you right away. Do you think you can come over to Alhambra?'

I struggled to get my head together, it's never a good idea to sleep during office hours. If she and Rishton wanted to cancel my trip to Prestbury and Gloria that was just fine by me – they'd still have to pay me for the day.

'It's just after four now, Ms Headlam, and as I'm setting off for Prestbury at five, I'm going to find it hard to fit you in. Can't you tell me about it over the phone.'

'It's your visit to Prestbury that I want to talk to you about. You'll have lots of time. Gloria never leaves work until 5.30. There's something important I need to discuss with you.' She was speaking in a more brusque tone than previously and I didn't like it much.

'If you want to call the whole thing off, that's OK,' I said. 'I can put the £10,000 in a secure container and send it round to you by motorcycle courier. You could have it within half an hour.'

There was an audible gasp at the mention of '£10,000' but she quickly recovered. 'That makes it even more important that we talk . . . If you can stop being so bloody macho for a moment. I want to talk the whole thing through with Simon and I want you there when I do. Don't worry, you'll be paid for your time whatever happens, but just get yourself round here Mr Cunane . . . please?'

In the circumstances I could hardly refuse her so I set out again into the bleak midwinter. Before leaving I phoned Jay on the car phone and told him to meet me outside Alhambra as soon after five as he could manage.

The Alhambra building loomed up through the midwinter murk with its port holes, decks here and there, missing walls, and weirdly curved roof – looking at it was a strain on the eyes. Unusually, the place seemed deserted. When I arrived at the scene of last night's humiliation, the odious Poulter was on duty at reception on his own.

He stared at me, with a look as cold as the weather. 'Go straight on up to Ms Headlam's office, she's expecting you and you know the way,' he said.

I had no trouble finding my way, the ugly but memorable pictures on the walls made signposts unnecessary. Once again, I was conscious of the absence of activity in the building.

Only Headlam and Rishton were present in her office. Rishton's small figure was tucked so far back on the low sofa that he looked like a realistic soft toy someone had placed there, perhaps a piece of modern art. Headlam was behind her desk. There was a strained atmosphere in the room, neither of them was speaking. Headlam invited me to sit on a matching low armchair opposite

Rishton but I took one look at the expression on his face and declined. There was a steel-and-leather chair shaped like a small radar dish in the corner, so I sat on that. It groaned in protest but supported me. It put me on a level with Kath Headlam, with Rishton sprawled on the sofa in front of the pair of us.

'We were just wondering if it would be entirely wise for you to go to see Gloria,' Kath began tentatively.

'You mean *you* were!' Rishton spat out. 'I was perfectly happy with the arrangements.'

Knowing Rishton's stated views about feminine interference with his plans I wasn't confident in Headlam's future as his partner. She could at least expect to be demoted back to the Reserves, if not relegated to the Third Division. So far I'd played it very gently with these two. Delise had done most of the talking last night, and I'd been a passive audience for Rishton at lunch-time. I'd had enough.

I stood up, took out the envelope with the £10,000 in and dropped it in Rishton's lap. 'I'm off. If you sort something out give me a call after New Year if you still need my assistance.'

Rishton bounded up off the sofa like a terrier. 'Sit down and shut up. We're trying to come to an important decision here!' he yelped at me. His face was purple and his dark-brown eyes were blazing. I was frightened that if he wound up his temper just one more notch he'd vanish in a puff of smoke, leaving his elegant Wannabe mock croc loafers behind on the carpet.

This was an ace performance – Rishton in creative mode – and I was privileged to watch it. After his efforts at lunchtime, not to mention his visit to the brothel, given his age it was remarkable that he was still upright. He made a visible effort to control himself.

'Kath's worried that Gloria might get the wrong idea

if we send a stranger to see her. She might think we're trying strong-arm tactics. I told her you'd have a calming effect on Gloria, but she had her doubts . . .'

'I do have doubts. For one thing I can't see how you can possibly afford £10,000 as a sweetener for Gloria what with all this hassle you've been having from Lloyd's,' Kath interrupted.

'You didn't complain when I bought you the Mazda for your birthday,' he snapped back.

'That was before your syndicate collapsed and before Trevose and you-know-who started putting the heat on.'

'Okey-dokey! Let's pay her less then, but don't blame me if we end up reading all about ourselves in the *News of the World*,' Rishton said, and slashing open the envelope with a paper-knife he began counting out £50 notes. 'There, that's £5000 then,' he said handing the cash to me.

I took the cash and sat quietly for a moment. Then I took out a standard contract form from my pocket to provide Rishton with a receipt and myself with evidence that I'd come by his cash honestly.

'Oh, no,' he said, pushing the contract back into my hand. 'We'd rather not bother with all that. I thought I made that clear at the restaurant. We trust you and we'd like to keep this little expedition "sub rosa", as it were.'

I suddenly realised, looking at this obnoxious little man, why Kath Headlam was getting strain lines under her eyes. Rishton was wearing her out, she hadn't got much lolly left on her stick.

Moving decisively again, he grabbed the phone and began dialling. 'She's at work till 5.30. I'll give her a call and tell her to expect you.'

While he performed with the phone, Headlam got up and poured me a cup of coffee from a dispenser in the opposite corner. She smiled at me and arched her eyebrows as we listened to Rishton feeding Gloria an elaborate explanation of his intentions. I noticed that she was wearing a turquoise, ethnic-print, flouncy skirt and a white blouse from Monsoon, with sturdy shoes. Shopping expeditions with Delise have sensitised me to the liberated female's tastes.

She looked quite fetching in her own way. I could get to like the fascinating variations in the way she folded her lips over those teeth. It was different every time. She took a packet of Camels cigarettes out of her desk drawer and offered me one. I refused, and she lit up. Rishton was tying himself in verbal knots on the phone but eventually he concluded his negotiations.

'There you are,' he said brightly. 'Nothing to stand in your way now.'

'But do I really need to go all the way to Prestbury?' I asked. 'Why don't I just meet her when she finishes work?'

'Ah, well, there was just this last thing . . . We'd like you to cast your keenly trained eyes over the place. Your friend Ted Blake said you don't miss much . . . er . . . in the detection line . . . and we rather thought if Gloria had found herself some consolation . . . er . . . you know, if she's sharing her bunk with someone else . . . you'd spot it and tell us. It can make quite a difference to the bank balance – especially as I've been having a spot of bother with Lloyd's. Makes it quite difficult to maintain all my ladies in the style they've come to expect.'

I nodded understandingly. He didn't need to say any more. 'Is there anything else?'

He looked at me searchingly. 'There is one final thing . . . Christmas post as it were . . . Gloria will give you a folder . . . don't look at it, just bring it to me tonight. I'll be here . . . ring up from reception when you arrive . . . I'll come down to you.' He kept his eyes on mine the whole time he was speaking, and I noticed that his voice had reverted to the jerky syncopation that he'd used when I first met him. I deduced that this 'final thing' must be of major importance to him so I smiled reassuringly. He was trusting me with £5000, and as far as I was concerned that earned him quite a lot of trust in return.

'Well, that seems to be that then. If everyone's satisfied,' he said holding out his hand to me.

'Just hold on a minute, Mr Cunane,' interjected Kath breathlessly. 'As usual, Simon's left out all the most important details. Look, I don't want to be rude but we're hiring you because you've got a reputation for keeping your mouth shut. If Gloria goes to the press anyway, and says we sent round a heavy to frighten her and buy her silence, you're to say nothing. We will deny all knowledge of you. Is that clear?'

It was perfectly clear. They were hiring me to act as a cut-out. It seemed like a fair enough bargain for what they were paying me. I nodded my agreement.

I disentangled myself from the ultra-modern chair, shook hands with them both, and left. As I made my way to the exit through a deserted building and passed the sullen Poulter at his desk, I asked where everyone was. It was 5.40 p.m. 'Staff party tonight, they've all gone home early,' he croaked in a hoarse voice. 'There's practically only you and your friends in the building.'

Jay was outside in the Bluebird. He had his headphones on and was chewing gum strenuously. I jumped in beside him and he threaded his way into the abnormally heavy traffic.

'You took your time, didn't you, Boss? I've been cruising for a bruising here. Them wardens are just desperate to give out their stupid tickets,' he said grumpily.

'Did you get rid of the kid?' I asked, ignoring his mood.

I didn't want Jay to get in the habit of thinking that I was answerable to him for my movements.

'Yeah,' he growled, replacing his gum and his headphones in one economical movement.

The car phone rang almost as soon as I'd finished fastening my seat belt. It was Delise.

'How did you get on?' she asked casually. 'Had a nice lazy day?'

'I got us a new customer who paid more than £2000 in cash up front for an interesting genealogical investigation. Then I recovered Kath Headlam's car intact and returned it. And then I had lunch with Simon Rishton at his favourite restaurant, and I sorted out Jay's problems with his unexpected relative, so you might say I had a productive day. How about you?' I knew I couldn't do without Delise but for the sake of my own self-esteem I occasionally had to let her know that she wasn't entirely indispensable.

'You didn't go to see Rishton without me?' she responded angrily. 'How could you? You did it on purpose. What did he say? What was he like? Why didn't you get in touch with me? Are you going to see him again?'

'I'm sorry, but how could I get in touch with you? You were shopping with your mum in Stockport. Anyway, he wasn't at all like he is on the box.' I paused for a moment, and then decided it was worth trying to disillusion her. 'He asked me if I wanted to accompany him on a visit to his local brothel.' I knew that would get her going.

'You didn't go, did you?' she asked quickly.

I spared a glance for my driver before speaking. Jay was completely oblivious to what I was saying, moving his head in time to the beat, just barely audible to me, on his tape.

'No, there are some limits to what I'll do for trade or the Polar Building Society. Anyway, why would I go trailing after a disgusting old shit like him when I already have the fittest girl in Manchester as my partner?' I hesitated a moment, then plunged on. 'I think we both need a rest from your mum, Delise. She's getting worse. Why don't you move in with me permanently? I'm getting tired of having to coax you into my bed on the nights when I can be sure she won't come barging in between us.'

There was a moment's silence. Then, 'Dave, that would be lovely. I've been thinking the same, especially after last night. Why don't we visit the jewellers' shops tomorrow. Now you're so flush you can buy me one of those little round things that begin with "r" and then Mum will have to accept that she can't change things between us.'

It was my turn to pause and think for a moment. Delise had never suggested putting our relationship on that permanent a basis before, if that's what she was suggesting now.

'You're not very romantic, are you?' Delise broke in. 'You've never once said that you love me. Just that you want me more conveniently to hand.'

It seemed to be decision-making time on the car phone.

'Of course I love you, Delise. If you don't know what I'm like by now, then heaven help you. If buying a ring is what we need to make your mother accept we're a couple, then I'm ready for that and all that goes with it. We'll go tomorrow,' I said firmly. 'How does that grab you, then?'

It was clear that the price of saying goodbye to evenings in the company of the Killer Whale was going to be high: I was prepared to pay it, but I wondered how my own parents would react to becoming in-laws of Molly Delaney.

'You're so resolute, Dave. Hurry to Prestbury and then get on back to your flat and we'll celebrate in style. I'll get some champagne in.'

I put Delise's sudden change of heart down to the season, or maybe one of her friends had been getting at her. Still if this was the way she wanted to play it I had no objections. I've nothing against marriage, except that the only marriage I'd had so far hadn't lasted long enough.

It was quite a wrench to realise that I was sitting in rush-hour traffic crawling out of Manchester along the Parkway, bound for the prosperous southern suburbs in Cheshire with my assistant Jay still plugged into his sound system.

Our progress was slow.

Once over the Cheshire boundary startling signs of prosperity began to appear. I had plenty of time to take it all in.

On both sides of the road stylish new buildings began to intrude among the suburban homes; new offices for database companies with adverts for systems analysts posted up outside, handily sized blocks in fresh brown brick with bright red window frames and huge overhanging eaves, then BMW salerooms, ultra-modern manufacturing facilities, fashion shops and garden centres.

Was there room here for a well-established private investigation service, I wondered? Delise and I ought to discuss relocating ourselves to the prosperous suburbs. There must be lots of interesting crime here.

We didn't want to get to Gloria's house too early, so we stopped at the Bull's Head in suburban Handforth for a bar snack. The service wasn't too welcoming. I must try to get Jay into a suit, he looked too much like the caricature of a drug dealer for comfort and people probably took me for his minder. The locals kept their distance and we were in and out in five minutes.

Simon Rishton had said that his wife's house was actually in Prestbury – allegedly one of the most exclusive suburbs in Britain, situated on the border of Macclesfield – and that the house was best approached by driving to the town of Alderley Edge, then over the steep escarpment of the Edge, through to Prestbury village. According to Rishton, Prestbury is very much a movable feast, its location a conspiracy by estate agents. It was true that nearly every road to the west of Macclesfield was signposted 'Prestbury', even ones leading in opposite directions.

We drove up the steep hill past the famous beauty spot, its beech woods shrouded in darkness and fog, and the Wizard pub, bearing right along the road and ignoring misleading signposts to Prestbury on our left. Here and there, the Christmas lights outside some mega-rich soccer star or pornography retailer's home gleamed in the darkness. As directed by Rishton, we soon found the ugly council flats to our right, then the tall block of town houses where Gloria Rishton lived.

I got out while Jay parked.

This wasn't going to take long. I had half a mind to ask Gloria bluntly who she was having it off with. That would settle the matter! As I rang the door bell I looked at my watch. It was exactly 7.10 p.m.

There was no answer. I rang again. Still no answer. There was a light on in the first-floor living room, so somebody must be here.

The whole place was absolutely quiet. The block of town houses was set back slightly from the road on a small cul-de-sac. There were only garage doors and

87

entrance doors on the street level, no one to overlook us.

'She must be back from work now. She finishes at 5.30,' I said to Jay.

'Maybe the bell's bust,' he said, 'or she might be in the bathroom, it's two storeys up.'

We knocked and tried the bell again. There was only a profound silence from the house. I considered my next move. Should I sit in the car and stake the place out until she decided to turn up? She might have decided to ignore Rishton's request. She might be at an office party or staying with a friend for the night. Then I thought about Delise and the promise of a warm welcome back at the flat. What was I doing here, freezing my backside off in the wilds of Cheshire? The neighbouring houses were in darkness, not even a fairy light showing. Should I just shove Rishton's packet through the letter box and clear off, leaving him to sort out his own problems?

In the end I decided to wait at least an hour, but before going back to the car I tried the front door. It was unlocked and swung open at my touch.

Puzzled, I entered the premises and shouted, 'Mrs Rishton, are you there?' Still no reply. It was possible, as Jay had suggested, that she might be in the bathroom at the top of the house, so I advanced up the stairs to the living room on the first floor. I knocked on the door and repeated my call. Nothing. Jay had come up behind me.

'She's not here. Shall I get it sorted, Boss? Shall I check upstairs?'

I nodded. He bounded up the stairs. A minute later he reappeared. 'You'd better come and have a look at this, Boss.' He looked strangely pale.

There was an ugly reddish-brown stain on the ceiling above the stair well. It looked like blood and it seemed to be fresh. I felt as if someone had put their hand inside my chest and was squeezing my heart. There was absolutely no reason to suspect foul play I told myself, but sick pessimism had a hold on me.

Jay pointed to the lever for pulling the attic stairs down. He and I are very familiar with the inside of lofts.

I think I stopped breathing when he shoved his head into the loft, but it was only for a second. 'She's got a leak in her cold-water tank, Boss, that's what's caused the stain. It's just rusty water,' he said cheerily. 'Shall I turn the stop-cock off?'

'No, leave it. None of our business, we're not plumbers,' I said with relief. 'Let's get out of here. Shove that ladder back up.' I took a quick glance in the bedroom. She wasn't in there either, nor was there any sign of a male occupant, no underpants or socks scattered about. 'Tough luck, Rishton,' I thought.

On the way out, I debated locking the front door but decided to leave it as I found it. Gloria may have just gone out for a moment and be coming back shortly.

'Shall I check the garage, Boss? See if her car's here?' Jay asked obligingly.

'Might as well,' I said, pleased that he was being so helpful.

He grasped the handle in the centre of the garage door and pulled. The door slid upwards, he changed his grip and pushed it fully open.

'Oh Christ!' he gasped, turned back towards the pavement and vomited violently onto the kerb.

Crouched in the centre of the garage floor there was a figure, kneeling and facing the rear wall. The arms were pinioned behind, the head and shoulders fully resting on the concrete. By the dim gleam of the sodium lamps from the street it was possible to see that there were two large holes at the base of the skull and an even larger one where the forehead should have been. I turned the

89

light on. Dark blood and brains were mingled with the long blonde hair on the oily floor. If this was Gloria Rishton she was very, very dead. Death had been instantaneous; she'd not moved from the kneeling posture her killer had directed her to take.

It was an execution.

My brain continued to work in spite of what my eyes were telling me. I bent over the corpse and touched the carotid artery with my fingers. The body was warm. I jerked my hand away with a shiver. There was still a sharp smell of burning nitrocellulose. The bullets had only been fired minutes ago. If we hadn't stopped at that pub in Handforth we might have been in time to save her.

My attention focused on a small detail, perhaps so I could take my eyes away from that ruined head. That's the way these things take me. I think they call it displacement. Some people want to run about screaming and waving their hands in the air when they see a corpse. I want to find out what's happened.

To the right of the body there were two brass cartridge cases. They looked like .357 Magnums or possibly .38s. It was difficult to tell whether they were rimmed, semi-rimmed or rimless; from a revolver or an automatic. To the left of the corpse there were two more similar cartridges but they were placed neatly together, side by side, on their bases. They couldn't have been ejected from an automatic like that. I fixed my eyes on those cartridge cases.

Racking coughs from Jay brought me back to reality and I retraced my steps towards the kerb. He looked up at me with an expression of utter horror on his face. 'Boss, let's get out of here quick!' he said in panic. He moved towards the car. I grabbed him by the shoulder, anger and fear swiftly replacing shock. 'Stay where you are. If we run now, that's as good as an admission of guilt. We've got to be the ones who report this.'

I got the car phone out and summoned the Cheshire Constabulary. The woman officer who received my call calmly took down all the details including my name, address and telephone number. There was no going back now. I could see that Jay was still fighting his natural impulse to do a runner.

'We've nothing to be frightened of. We're innocent,' I said, more to reassure him than because I believed it. 'You're just the driver, you know nothing about what we're doing here except that we were paid to call on Gloria Rishton. Just tell them what happened when we got here. If they start asking funny questions about me, say you know nothing and that's the truth. Refer them to me if they start asking difficult questions. Be polite to them whatever they say to you.'

The police response times for Prestbury must be amongst the best in the country. It seemed like no time at all before we heard the wail of a police siren approaching. I went to the main road and flagged the patrol car down, determined to be as cooperative as humanly possible.

A heavily built constable in a day-glo jacket and flat cap strode towards me. His partner remained cautiously behind the wheel of the car.

'In there,' I indicated the corpse.

He strode right into the garage. I placed a hand on his arm to restrain him. 'Excuse me, shouldn't you wait for the scene of crime boys?' I asked. He brushed me aside. 'Mind your own bloody business,' he snarled. It was on the tip of my tongue to say that if I had minded my own bloody business he wouldn't be here, but he was obviously a dickhead. I shut up.

There was a tinkling sound like tiny bells as his boot

connected accidentally with the two upright cartridge cases and kicked them to one side.

He heard the noise too and stepped out of the garage but he didn't say anything. He studied the pair of us intently and spoke into his communicator. 'Definitely violent death . . . Yes, the individual who reported it is standing by . . .' Then to me, 'You are David Cunane, aren't you?' I nodded.

It was 7.45 when the tapes round the crime scene went up. Jay and I were corralled to one side. We weren't cuffed or anything but the hostile attitude of the first officer to arrive was relayed from officer to officer by a kind of osmosis. Burly figures in tight clothing kept coming up and giving us both angry stares while we stood and shivered.

Eventually at about 7.55 Jay and I were taken to Macclesfield police station in separate cars to make a statement.

Somewhere in my consciousness a little dull ache of self-pity sneaked in along with the cold and the chilly night air. Why did this have to happen to me?

I was ushered into a grim windowless interview room with dirty white glazed tiles extending two thirds of the way up the walls. I felt nervous away from Manchester. At least with the Manchester Police I had some background knowledge of whom I was dealing with. Here, I was like a fish out of water.

I was handed over to two senior detectives in suits. The older one was a baldy, a quite large, portly individual wearing a poorly fitting, double-breasted brown suit. I instinctively distrusted him for wearing the brown suit.

He certainly reciprocated my dislike. Even when I told him my address I could see the hostility in his eyes. I told him Chorlton, Manchester but I could see that he was mentally transposing my words into 'Drugsville, Hell

City' as I spoke. His face was fleshy, rather greasy, with a bad dose of razor burn on his bristly blue-black jowls. He looked as if he'd grilled many a little old lady for shoplifting in his time. He had shrewd little piggy eyes, and I guessed that he would be the hard cop if it came to a game of 'Good Cop, Bad Cop'. The other detective was younger, altogether more up to date with his grey suit, and nondescript looking.

The senior man told me he was Jim Jerrold or Gerald James, I couldn't take it in immediately. I was so tense from trying to look relaxed that the name passed me by. I felt like an early Christian in the arena waiting for the lions to pounce.

I think I must have been in delayed shock. I should have insisted on legal representation and at least twenty-four hours to recover from the trauma before speaking at all.

I don't blame the police for what happened. It's the system. The interrogation was hostile and abrasive from the start. Jerrold and his partner arrived in that room with all their prejudices honed to razor sharpness. For all I know, they'd spent the previous week with vicious child-abusers, rapists or armed robbers dripping lie after cunning lie into their ears.

Whatever the reason, it was obvious from the start that I wasn't just clearing up a few points for information purposes. The question of guilt lay heavy in the air. The older man, Jerrold, seemed to think that the fact that I was a private detective from Manchester meant that there was a sufficient case to answer in itself. What was I doing in Prestbury with a black Moss Side resident? He had a technique I'd not met before. He'd ask me a 'When did you last stop beating your wife' type incriminating question while glaring right into my face, sweat gleaming on his greasy nose. When I replied, he put his head

93

down so I couldn't see his face. This flummoxed me more than slightly, because I come out sounding too flippant unless I can see the effect of what I'm saying. I've never been good on the phone for that reason.

The questioning went on and on until finally Jerrold said he was not satisfied with my story and that I was to be detained in custody while further enquiries were made. I was allowed a phone call and spoke to Delise, not to a lawyer. I was so exhausted that I was only able to give her the bare outline of what had happened and took little notice of her reaction.

It was a struggle to remain polite and reasonable. I could see that Jerrold was having trouble reining in his prejudices. His body language said it all. He kept turning away without listening to my answers and his constant disbelief created a tight sensation in my chest. I knew he wanted to panic me. I had to control the flow of information. I started pausing before answering and varying the pace of my replies. All without effect. I began to feel a strong need to smack the great bald dome of his head every time he lowered it to the desk. Whatever else the man was, he was pig ignorant. He was also a very effective interrogator.

He asked why was I carrying such a large sum of money in cash and I explained and added that ACC Sinclair of the Greater Manchester Police would tell him that I often carried large sums for clients. After playing bat and ball like this for what seemed like hours it finally dawned on me that he probably thought that all the coppers in his neighbouring police force were corrupt as hell anyway.

Questioning resumed after a short break for a cup of milky tea. This time the grey blur took the lead. What had I done with the gun? I might as well tell them because they had thirty men scouring the area for it and it was only a matter of time before it was found. On and on he droned, but being bored was better than having every answer ignored. His technique was not as aggressive as Jerrold's, he seemed to think he could wear me down by repetition, and by trying to catch me out in a slip. He kept hammering away at my connection with Kath Headlam. How had I come to meet her? How much had she paid me? I tried to bring him back to Rishton, but he wasn't interested.

After two hours of this his voice developed an edge and finally, he came to a dead stop. I looked over the table at him as calmly and innocently as I could. This provoked Jerrold beyond endurance, which goes to show that you should never underestimate a man in a brown suit. I could see what was coming next. He lost his rag completely. Without saying a word he leaned over the table and took a swing at me. Resisting the temptation to grab his arm and pull him over the table I dodged the clumsy blow, fell off the chair and banged my head against the hard tiles of the wall. I was dazed but not unconscious.

Jerrold spoke into the tape recorder. 'Let the record show that Mr Cunane has deliberately banged his head into the wall to avoid answering any more questions,' he said and switched the machine off before I could say anything. Well, I suppose the blow served me right for not insisting on having a solicitor present, but in a way the fact that they were prepared to try violence was a good sign. They must be hard pressed for evidence. Jerrold gave me a withering look and left the room, taking his blur with him. An extra uniformed officer replaced them.

I picked myself off the floor and one of the two constables brought me a wet tea towel to put on my head. I could feel a lump rising above my left ear.

I spent most of Friday, Christmas Eve, counting the tiles in the cell walls, presumably while Jerrold was out trying to drum up some hard evidence against me. It gave me plenty of time to think. If Jerrold was baffled, so was I.

If Kath Headlam and Simon Rishton had set me up, how could they have known that I'd be there at the relevant time, that is, *after*, not before, the killing of the unfortunate Gloria; or even that I'd go there at all, or hang around after finding the corpse?

I can be as paranoid as the next man, and if I thought that Headlam and Rishton had intended me to be arrested for murder in their place I'd have been singing to Jerrold loud and clear; *fortissimo*, in fact. But it just didn't make sense.

I'd left them in Central Manchester at 5.40 and gone straight to Prestbury by the most direct roads with only a five-minute stop en route. They'd never have had time to dispose of Gloria themselves.

In any case, why involve a third party at all? Why arrange for me to go blundering about down there? If they wanted me to take the blame, then they must have also calculated that they'd be accused of hiring me. There were plenty of witnesses to connect us. If the police thought I was guilty, that would immediately throw Headlam and Rishton into the limelight. Rishton had discussed my mission at the top of his voice in a crowded restaurant. Has anyone in human history ever hired a hitman under such circumstances?

I didn't sleep for long that night. I woke after dozing for about an hour. I felt disoriented – groggy and baffled. What scared me was my lack of knowledge, and lack of control. How did I know what incriminating evidence was being cooked up against me either by the police, or by Headlam and Rishton, or by the real killer?

Further sleep was out of the question. Cell doors were slamming, rowdy scenes and fights taking place after Christmas Eve revelry and throwing-out time. None were sent to join me, though. The 'murdering bastard' was left to himself. I knew I was holding up my end in the interrogation well enough, but for how long? On Boxing Day, I decided, I'd have to get a solicitor. I knew that holding me after tomorrow, without charging me, would be illegal, but right now I was feeling too dazed to do anything about it. I convinced myself that he would charge me with murder in the morning.

What a Christmas present that was going to be!

6

Macclesfield Police Station. Christmas Morning.
Saturday 25th December 1993

I lay on the hard mattress, listening to the early morning
sounds of the cop shop. Someone was sweeping out the
adjoining cells. Whoever the sweeper was, he or she was
cheerful – the rattling and banging was accompanied by
the strains of 'O Come All Ye Faithful' in a high-pitched
whistle. The sweeper came up to my door but then went
away, leaving me to my morose imaginings.

Not long before 10 a.m. I was roused from my cell by
the custody sergeant. A sour-looking type, he was backed
up by a constable in case I cut up rough. As he marched
me to his desk I felt like a condemned man taking his
last walk down Death Row.

'This is it, Cunane,' I thought. 'A murder charge.' I
kept a bold face but it was one of those moments when
time seems to stand still, my blood drained into my legs.
But then, to my amazement, instead of charging me the
sergeant began handing me back my belongings, still
without a word.

'What's going on?'

'You're being released, you're not required for further
questioning,' he mumbled, looking down at his paper-
work. He pushed over a receipt for me to sign.

'The bloody hell I am! What's going on? What about
Jerrold? Has he nothing to say? Fourteen solid hours of
questioning just for reporting a crime!' I could feel the
veins standing out in my neck, anger had swiftly replaced
fear as my dominant emotion.

'Calm down, *sir*. It's all been a mix-up. You're free to
go. Your thirty-six hours in custody are over. Your friend
98

will tell you all about it,' he said. I shook my head. It was still sore.

'A *mix*-up?' I repeated incredulously. 'A *mix*-up? What about the injuries I sustained in custody? What about the lump on the side of my head where one of the interrogating officers tried to assault me?'

'I'm sorry about that, *sir*. It's not our fault, it's the press, they've stirred up a lot of interest in the case. There's always unpleasant incidents with these kind of cases, *sir*. Our understanding is that your injury was self-inflicted, *sir*. You can take it up with the Police Complaints Commission if you wish. You may be required to sign a statement later on, *sir*.' The prune-faced geek seemed to be getting maximum job satisfaction.

But even as I stood there, my momentary spurt of anger against him and the police began to evaporate. Haven't I had a lifetime's training in seeing things from the police's point of view from my father? It was myself I blamed. No one had forced me to take on Rishton's commission.

The custody sergeant handed me my money in a separate envelope. The full £2350 was there. There was a note saying that the £5000 belonging to Simon Rishton was required as evidence. So, for now, they were accepting that part of my story.

I tried to show my scorn by turning on my heels without a further word. But I wasn't allowed the satisfaction of a contemptuous exit. My feet came adrift from the unlaced shoes, and I stumbled.

'Well, a Happy Christmas to you too, sir,' the sergeant said and I could hear his mate sniggering. I stepped out of the shoes, picked them up with one hand, and, holding the bag of clothes in the other hand, passed out of the detention area in my stocking-feet.

When I pushed my way through the swinging doors,

still bitterly angry with myself and still in the police overall, I spotted Delise sitting on a bench. She did a double take when she saw me and hesitated slightly before standing to greet me. I must have looked sinister with two days of stubble on my chin and an expression on my face fierce enough to make a small child cry. Fortunately, she didn't make any adverse comments; so I struggled to raise a smile.

'Dave, it's you, I can't believe it! If you only knew how long I've been here trying to get them to let you go! I've brought you some things, they wouldn't let me send them in to you.' She kissed me and I held on to her. I needed some reassurance. We didn't prolong the clinch. Practical as ever, she pulled away and pushed the carrier bag back into my hands.

'Go in there and freshen up,' she said, indicating a toilet. 'Your battery razor's in the bag; give yourself a shave, your chin's like sandpaper.'

The facilities in the washroom had been reduced to basics by the efforts of generations of vandals – a chipped sink and a broken mirror. I managed to raise a thin trickle of cold water and tried to wash the grime of two days off my face with the piece of red carbolic soap provided. There was no plug. I dried myself with the shreds of the police overall and changed my underwear and shirt gratefully.

'What about Jay?' I asked when I emerged.

'Don't worry about him, they let him out yesterday morning. Think about yourself now. There are at least a hundred press and television reporters waiting outside here. They're not waiting for you. The police are bringing Rishton and Headlam in at the front and they're going to let us out the back way just to be on the safe side, so hurry up.' She turned and led me away.

Coming out of prison, even after only a couple of

days, is like being resurrected from the grave, I thought. Especially as I'd feared my visit could be the start of something more permanent.

'I've got your car tucked away down a side street. We'll have to walk for a couple of hundred yards.'

Delise slowed her progress through the police station and linked arms with me. 'I haven't told Mum about what we agreed the other day. You know, about the ring. I don't think that would be a very good idea in the circumstances, do you? I told Mum to expect us for Christmas dinner, if I managed to get you out. We can break it to her gradually.'

Christmas dinner with the Killer Whale hadn't been high on my agenda for post-release activities but Delise had certainly picked her moment well; caught between prison and press, and with her offering the only escape route, I could hardly stamp my foot and start an argument.

When we got outside there was no sign of the press and the weather had improved since the last time I'd seen daylight. It was a crisp and bright day. The mists and frosts of the last few days had cleared up. Church bells were ringing and people were scurrying up and down the hilly streets of the old silk-weaving town.

'Don't look like that, Dave! You're going to have to get used to her. She is my mother, after all,' said Delise, mistaking my smile for a scowl.

'That's all right. A few hours with your mother can't be worse than what I've just been through,' I replied.

We turned the corner into the street where Delise had left the Bluebird and standing beside it was the familiar figure of Ted Blake, the friend and mentor who had given my name to Kath Headlam in the first place. His bulky body was swathed in a tight-fitting brown leather overcoat with the belt fastened, which made him look more like a badly done-up parcel than usual. Quite a number of cows had gone into making the coat, which had all kinds of flaps and appendages attached to it. There was a smile on his big, square, red face.

'Now, be pleasant to him, Dave. He's been very helpful,' Delise warned. I hadn't exactly fallen out with Ted but there were fewer occasions since he'd made it as a telly celeb when he needed either a boozing partner or someone to rescue him from some sleazy shebeen. As we walked towards him, I told myself he couldn't have known what a poisoned pill the commission would turn out to be. At least, I hoped he couldn't.

'It's great to see you emerging from durance vile, Dave. Has Delise filled you in on what's happening?' he asked. 'Simon Rishton and Kath Headlam have just been arrested for the murder of Gloria Rishton, and Delise here is the reason the police have decided to charge them and not you.' I looked at Delise and she gave me a thin and expectant smile as if she was waiting for more praise from both of us. I didn't know what he was on about. What could Delise have possibly known to bring this about?

I favoured Ted with a thin smile, and he continued . . . 'The idea is that I'm coming back to Manchester with you. You can tell me everything that's gone on. The rest of the press are hanging about round the front of the police station but I know you've got the real story.'

I should have known that Ted wasn't here just to see me. His instincts for a story, honed by years working as a stringer for the national press, hadn't deserted him now that he had his own late-night TV show.

There didn't seem much point in further arguing. It had all been arranged without me. Delise opened the car and I climbed into the back with Ted. The Bluebird's springs creaked ominously. So far my loving reunion with Delise had lasted ten minutes, of which we'd been alone for five. Delise didn't seem to mind, and two days of doing what I was told had reduced my powers of resistance.

'How come they've arrested Rishton and Headlam?' I asked wearily. 'It doesn't make sense. I'm supposed to be their hitman and the police have just released me.'

Delise piped up from the front, 'It's the diary that cooked their goose.'

'Just run that one by me, Delise?'

'Yes, you know – Headlam's diary. It was in the brief-case, there was her filofax and her diaries right back to 1988. One of them had this sentence in about Gloria: *"I can see that Simon + Gloria is going to be a problem. If only I could work out some way to subtract her from the equation. But how?"* When the police got hold of that they began to lose interest in you and Jay.'

'But how *did* the police get hold of it?' I asked patiently but I was beginning to feel sick. I had a feeling I already knew the answer. Delise had had the diaries all to herself for almost the whole day on Wednesday. I remembered the sound of the photocopier when I was trying to sober up outside the office.

'I told them about it,' she said defiantly.

I was livid. 'Delise, she's a client. How many times have I told you that we don't grass our own clients up. We're like priests or lawyers. We keep shtum and let the police get on with it.'

'Don't be so stupid, Dave. Was I supposed to let you go down for life to protect a client's confidentiality? Particularly one who was trying to frame you for murder. Get real! I just took a few photocopies to safeguard the firm and look how well it's turned out. Where would you be now if I hadn't?'

'She has a point you know, my old china,' chimed in

103

Blake. 'After all, you're breaching their confidentiality yourself now, aren't you?'

I wasn't having this. Being told that Delise routinely made copies of anything remotely confidential was bad enough without my own integrity being challenged. She'd copied the diary entry about Gloria long before she could possibly have known that it was going to do me any good.

'Crap!' I said. 'All I've told you are the bare facts which are a matter of public record. I don't suppose it's occurred to you that I've just spent thirty-six hours trying to prove to the police that neither Headlam, nor Rishton, nor myself could have possibly killed Gloria.'

Ted shifted uncomfortably in his seat. 'Someone must have done it. Gloria didn't kill herself. You're not saying that someone just walked in off the street with an automatic pistol and executed a perfectly innocent woman for kicks, are you? Because no one's going to believe that. Rishton had the motive and the opportunity. He must know something about it. They must have wanted you there to give them an alibi and to establish that she was missing and it was pure chance that your assistant opened the garage door, and found what they'd done before they had time to dispose of the body.'

I ran the idea over in my mind. Even if I accepted that Rishton had tricked me, it just wasn't possible for him to have done the job in the time available. 'But the taxi driver dropped her off at seven and they weren't there when Jay and I arrived at 7.10. There just wasn't time for them to have done it.'

'That just proves it – they were in a desperate hurry and so they forgot to lock the garage,' he replied. 'They must have meant to raise the alarm themselves when they were well clear. Look, Dave, the interest in this killing is phenomenal; it isn't every day that a man like

Rishton, a big-wheel TV executive responsible for a major national soap, starts acting out his fantasies in the real world. What would you say to me signing you up for an interview? You could fill in the "Who, what, when and wherefores". If we did it now, before they've been charged, we'd be allowed to broadcast it. It's not *sub judice* until they've actually been charged.'

I said nothing. Ted's wheedling, joined with Delise's flexible attitude about protecting our clients, were strengthening my mood of post-incarceration trauma.

'It would be really good publicity for my show,' he said, getting down to the nitty-gritty at last. 'You know I'm going independent. It's not as if I was asking you to tell lies, just answer a few questions and let the public make up its own mind.'

'In other words, trial by television,' I said.

'I'm just supplying the public with the unvarnished facts. No one ever went wrong by overestimating the public's appetite for a dose of honest smut. In any case, there's good money in it for you, Dave, and you owe me one after the strokes you've pulled on me over the years.'

I couldn't see how I owed Ted anything since the story I'd fed him in the last case I'd followed up had established him as an 'ace crime investigator', but I kept quiet.

'It isn't as if we're doing so well that we can turn away trade,' chipped in Delise, 'and, anyway just because *you* think they're innocent, it doesn't mean they are.'

'I don't know. I need time to think,' I temporised. What I *did* know for certain was that if I appeared on TV discussing a client, I could kiss goodbye to being a *private* investigator.

I had a resentful feeling that maybe this *was* Delise's very aim. She'd never been as wedded to Pimpernel Investigations as I was. At the back of her mind she must have some scheme for me to work as an errand boy for

Ted – I would do the legwork for him, out in the hinterland digging up dodgy traders for him to defend the public from. No doubt, Delise would be in the studio helping him to present the show.

I thought again about the murder. The police had a statement from Gloria's regular taxi driver that he'd dropped her off at home at seven, the same as usual. Even if Rishton had been waiting for her, how could he have got her in that position in the garage? It was a professional execution. No wife would have walked to that garage and knelt, knowing her husband or his lover intended to kill her. She'd have struggled.

Gloria's killer had to have been male and a stranger to her. He must have surprised her almost as soon as the taxi drew away from her door, pushed a gun in her face. Terrified, hoping against hope that if she obeyed his orders he'd leave her alone, she'd walked into the garage and knelt on the cold concrete. Perhaps her last frantic thoughts had been that he intended to rob her or rape her.

But the bastard had killed for maximum effect. It takes real cold-blooded calculation to blow the top off someone's head like that. He'd used two bullets, probably Magnums, judging by the result. Then he'd ejected the spent shells and carefully placed two more to the left of the body. Obviously that was meant as a warning, but to whom? and why?

Delise was negotiating her way through Stockport while all this was going through my head. Ted kept giving me hopeful glances but I kept my mouth shut. He'd had Delise's story, but I wasn't going to corroborate it for him. When we dropped Ted off at his flat in Didsbury he said, 'Let me know one way or the other this afternoon, Dave.'

I wished him a Happy Christmas as he departed for

his lonely feast. Ted's wife had taken the two children with her when she decamped with a sports reporter from the *Banner* and I knew that he'd never seen them since. His unexpected success hadn't softened her attitude. Real life isn't like a soap opera despite Ted's attempts to make it into one.

I didn't want to end up like Ted: an increasingly eccentric and lonely figure, an embarrassment to my friends. Whatever Delise was up to I'd have to keep on smiling.

It was a relief to find myself back in the tangled streets of Chorlton again, even if the destination we were heading for wasn't the one I would have preferred. Delise didn't say much but I could see from the set of her mouth that she was going to make sure that I would be doing the interview with Ted. I was equally determined that I wasn't.

The terraced street that Molly lived on faced a little park mainly used as an animal toilet, and even on Christmas Day there were a fair number of man's best friends trotting about. A huge, brindled German Shepherd cross had parked itself on Molly's doorstep. Delise walked up to the front door, past the dog and let herself in. When I followed her it bared its teeth and growled. It seemed to be at home on Molly's doorstep so I guessed it must belong to her.

It followed me in to the lounge-dining room. Delise had already gone through to the kitchen where I caught a glimpse of Molly's burly shoulders rising like the foothills of the Himalayas through clouds of steam. I stood hesitantly, still not sure of my welcome. Last time I'd entered these premises I'd had to leave in a hurry when Molly tried to assault me. Like a recurring nightmare, she emerged at full speed from the steamy kitchen with a frying pan raised to strike. I cowered back to dodge

107

her blow, but she rushed past me and chased the German Shepherd out into the street.

'Did you let that bloody bitch in here?' she demanded. 'The damn thing is always pissing round my doorstep. I don't want it in here. This is a new carpet.'

'Sorry, Mrs Delaney,' I said.

'Don't start that now! You know damn well I'm not Mrs anything,' she growled. She was swinging the pan from hand to hand.

'Sorry again, Molly, I thought it belonged to you.'

She peered at me suspiciously to see if I was trying to wind her up. Her fierce blue eyes were narrowed to small points in her fleshy, scowling face. I marvelled at the wonders of nature, how could this be the mother of Delise? Then she relaxed, although she remained distinctly under-joyed at the sight of me. She seemed to have come to a decision.

'Right, well let's forget about that,' she said briskly. 'A Happy Christmas to you. If you're ready to let bygones be bygones, then I am too. Delise seems to be attached to you, though God knows why. Anyway, come in and make yourself at home.'

The Christmas meal passed off peacefully. Feta cheese in a filo pastry basket, vegetables and Christmas pudding made with vegetable suet. It made a contrast to the traditional Christmas meal.

When the meal was over Molly retired to bed for her siesta and Delise and I retired to the sofa for ours. Specially constructed to support the Killer Whale's sturdy frame it was more than adequate for what I had in mind. I could hear Molly's snores echoing round the bedroom upstairs. I'd only been 'inside' for two days but I saw no reason to deprive myself of the released prisoner's traditional consolation. Delise was more than willing to oblige.

"Have you filled in that hole in her bedroom floor?' I asked cautiously, as she slipped her blouse off.

'Just listen to her,' she said with a laugh. 'I gave her enough Bushmills to knock her out until Boxing Day.'

Finally, as the afternoon slipped away, Delise asked me the question I knew was on her mind. 'Are you going to give Ted Blake a call, Dave?'

I shook my head.

She twisted her fingers in my hair and gave it a sharp pull. 'Oooh you are the most infuriating man alive, Dave Cunane! Do you want to stay in a dead-end job all your life? . . .'

There was an interruption in the volcanic snoring from above that had formed the background noise to our reunion so far. The snoring faltered, then resumed. Delise and I started to pull on our clothes.

When she was dressed, Delise started clearing the table banging and clattering the dishes together. The frequency and volume of the snores from above changed again. I scuttled round the table and joined her in gathering up the pots.

'At least phone him, Dave,' she said. 'Tell him why you're turning down the chance to make a decent living. You might tell me at the same time.'

'Delise, Ted Blake will promise anything to get a story. But when it comes to delivery it'll be an entirely different kettle of fish. I've known him for years.'

Delise stomped into the kitchen and began rattling the dirty pans together so loudly that even had Molly been under anaesthetic she couldn't have remained oblivious. This was the ultimate weapon in Delise's armoury. I would have to face the wrath of Molly Delaney.

Sure enough the little terraced house was soon shaking to the sound of her heavy footfall on the stairs. I stood my ground, determined to remain cool, calm and collected in the face of the temperamental Delaney women, but when Molly staggered in she didn't notice anything unusual.

'Oh, I've not missed the Queen's speech, have I?' she asked, lowering herself onto the sofa, and straightening the cushions.

'You're not telling me you're a closet monarchist, are you, Molly?' I asked.

'Ah well, maybe I am and maybe I'm not, but I always like to see the Christmas broadcast,' she said cautiously. 'Come away out of that kitchen, Delise,' she ordered. 'Leave the bloody washing-up until tomorrow, and let's have another drink.'

It was after midnight when I got home. I ran a bath and soaked for two hours and then went to bed and slept the clock round until lunch-time on Boxing Day. I had the rest of the holiday to myself now Delise was in a sulk. I could have joined my own parents but my brother and sister and their families would be there. I found their sympathy over the death of my wife hard to put up with, and I was tired of playing the role of unattached member of the family. Finbar and Fiona Salway were also away, spending Christmas with their nephew's family.

It never even crossed my mind to phone Ted Blake. I'd nothing to say to him.

That afternoon I took the bike along the Mersey Valley as far as the Bridgewater Canal. I pedalled until I was exhausted and as usual the exercise helped me to think. I was certain that I was right, and that Headlam and Rishton could not have been directly responsible for Gloria's death. They had certainly been aware that the mission involved danger, which must be why they had sent me to collect the mysterious folder, but as for killing her themselves . . .

They just weren't the types. Anyway, Rishton had divorced three wives before Gloria. He discarded women. He didn't blow them away.

As I was exonerating the TV execs of culpability an ugly thought occurred to me. If Gloria hadn't known the man who killed her, and if Rishton had previously phoned her to tell her to expect a visit from me, had she thought the man who led her out into the garage was Dave Cunane? Did she open her door to a man she believed was Dave Cunane, sent by her husband as part of whatever secret dealing was going on? The idea drained the light out of my day.

I was so absorbed by this gloomy conviction that I nearly rode the bike into the dark waters of the canal. There were plenty of people about, mostly fishermen and couples taking their narrowboats for a cruise round the Cheshire Circle. The fine weather had lingered on and it was warm for late December. I got as far as Dunham Massey before I stopped and looked across the fields to the country house and park. There were throngs of people walking among the massive oak trees of the deer park. I thought that if I was in DCI Jerrold's cramped and no doubt smelly boots, I would be trying to find out if Gloria Rishton had any criminal connections, and also if Simon Rishton had any enemies who would want to punish him through his wife. I would be questioning Rishton closely but certainly wouldn't arrest him at this stage.

When I got home I had a shower and changed before turning the TV on for the news. It led with the story that Rishton and Headlam had been remanded in custody, both charged with the murder of Gloria. So much for my theories! Obviously the police must have more information than I had. They, and the Crown Prosecution Service, would never have charged a man like Rishton

111

with such a serious crime without being sure of their ground: either that, or they were prepared to let the Appeal Court sort things out yet again.

When I got into the office on Tuesday morning neither Delise nor I made any comment about personal events, but we had lots of other things to think about. The papers were full of Headlam and Rishton. In the *Star* the headline was 'OUR GUILTY SECRET' above a picture of them together. In the *Mirror* there was a big picture of Gloria Rishton above the headline 'KILLED FOR LOVE'. Even the heavy papers showed little inclination to give them the benefit of the doubt; the *Guardian*, despite its name, had a wedding picture of the Rishtons accompanied by an account of Simon's career obviously extracted from his obituary file.

None of the papers carried any statement challenging the police version of events. At best Gloria's death was portrayed as a wicked crime of passion, the killing of a lovely young woman just before Christmas. There was no mention of me anywhere, the victim had just been 'discovered', but surprisingly Poulter, the man from the reception desk at the Alhambra Studios, was mentioned. He had also spent several nights being questioned by the police. They'd held him over the Christmas holiday.

I went through into the outer office and put the copy of the *Sun* down on Delise's desk. 'Have you seen this? How can anyone expect a fair trial after this?' I asked.

'Dave, don't go on . . .' She gave me a wistful smile. 'I'm sorry I tried to make you do that interview, I know you have strong feelings about your job but anyone can see that the two of them must be guilty. They wouldn't have all this in the papers if they weren't. Look here,' she pointed to a paragraph. 'It says a man and woman answering to Headlam and Rishton's description were
112

seen entering the house at 6 p.m. They must have found some way of getting themselves to Prestbury that you don't know about.'

I reread the passage. There was something badly wrong.

'There's no way they could have been in Prestbury by six, even if they'd had a Harrier jump jet waiting on the roof of the Alhambra building to take them. I didn't leave them until 5.40. Gloria didn't arrive until 7.00 and she must have been killed by 7.05 or Jay and I would have walked in on the murder.'

Delise made a face.

'I can't let this rest,' I told her. 'I'm going down to Alhambra to see what's being done about providing them with a defence. They need a good lawyer. Whatever it says in the papers, I'm certain the police are making a mistake.'

'Dave, grow up, will you? There's no way we can do anything about something like this. The police must think they have an open-and-shut case,' she said.

I knew it was useless to argue. Her voice had that 'more in sorrow than in anger tone' that she used when all else failed. And she was right in a way. There was nothing I could do until I knew exactly what the case against Rishton and Headlam was. Then I could offer my evidence to their defence lawyer.

When I made no further move to rebut her argument Delise gave me one of her warmest smiles. 'There you go, Dave, you need me to keep you straight.'

I thought it would be cruel to disillusion her and unnecessary to start an argument so I decided to change the subject. 'What do you know about the Royal Family, Delise?' I asked.

'Only what I read in the papers. I did ancient history and archaeology for my degree, not modern history.

113

You're changing the subject, aren't you, Dave? What are you up to?'

'I'm just getting on with the job,' I said indignantly. 'I told you we were being paid for genealogical work and as you're the closest thing to a genealogist on the staff of Pimpernel Investigations I'd like you to handle it. I'd like you to dig up everything you can about the late Duke of Windsor.'

She nearly fell out of her chair laughing when I told her who the client was.

'Oh Dave!' she laughed. 'And she actually paid you £2000! We're not going to have a posse of people round from Social Services demanding the money back, are we? . . .'

'Very funny, Delise,' I said dourly, 'but talking of Social Services, where's Jay? He should have been here by now.'

Delise promised to go to the Central Reference Library as soon as Jay came in to mind the store. I had to leave the office myself to pay off my mortgage arrears at the Polar Building Society. That was an even more urgent task than rescuing Headlam and Rishton. I drove down to the Polar's sale branch and paid off all arrears in cash, then went straight from there to Alhambra TV.

My reception was not at all what I was expecting. I thought I'd have to wrangle for hours before getting a hearing from some underling but not at all. I was whisked straight up to the office of the chief executive, Lancelot Trevose, as soon as I had stated my business. I felt that Rishton and Headlam needed friends and this was where I might find them.

Trevose's office made a complete contrast to Kath Headlam's, the only other one I'd seen in this building. It had dark linen fold panelling on all the walls and was furnished in solid oak. No doubt it was intended to recreate the air of financial probity appropriate to a nineteenth-century banker's parlour. If the splendid panorama from the window hadn't been of Salford, with the Pennine hills in the background, the room could have been the headquarters of some ancient government ministry in London rather than a TV mogul's office in an ultra-modern block in Manchester.

All I knew of Trevose was what Kath Headlam had told me in her few jaundiced references to him – that he had been a big wheel in the wholesale meat trade, and was careful with the pennies. Neither of these pieces of information prejudiced me against him. A man of about forty-five, rather tall and stooping, he was wearing a well-tailored pin-stripe and fitted the office as well as the suit fitted him. That is to say, not very well. He looked more like a struggling undertaker than a TV mogul.

His most prominent feature was a large Adam's apple which seemed to have a life of its own and was matched by a pendulous, wet-looking lower lip and a nose that came in a large, economy-sized packet above it. Looking at him I was reminded of the Easter Island statues in one of Delise's archaeology tracts.

I immediately felt suspicious.

He sprang from behind his wide antique desk to shake my hand, and held onto it so long that I began to wonder what his intentions were as he led me towards an alcove. Such a cordial reception from the man they called the 'Knacker', due to his previous incarnation in the whole-sale meat trade, was very unwelcome to me.

As he led me forward I realised that we were not alone in the room; there was an enormous bald head projecting above the back of one of the armchairs.

I recognised its owner immediately. It was Jake Gordon. I was certainly moving in exalted circles now.

I, along with most people who weren't blind, deaf or under twenty-five, knew something about him. He had first achieved fame, or at least prominence, in the late seventies in the 'Winter of Discontent' during the closing days of the Callaghan Government. He had been fairly small time then, running his own heating fuel distribution network from a base in Runcorn, and his fame or notoriety, depending on your politics, had arisen when he fired his entire labour force and replaced them with non-union drivers and delivery men on lower wages. His base had been besieged by pickets for months and Gordon had been on the television almost nightly arguing his case against all comers. The Tories reckoned he'd won them thousands of votes. In the end the unions had had to back down, and he'd subsequently expanded from heating fuel to his own service stations.

When the Tories won the election in 1979 he'd enjoyed a brief period of national acclaim, egging the Prime Minister on to some of her worst excesses and he'd been seen coming out of 10 Downing Street so often people thought he was starting a franchise operation there. Soon afterwards he'd been dropped. No one had ever really known why, but there'd been plenty of speculation. He was still well known in these parts, though: he always seemed to emerge when some well-loved local institution was about to go belly up. Whatever it was, a football club, a newspaper, or even the 'Ferry across the Mersey', Jake Gordon would be on hand with a 'rescue package'.

He had been married to a well-known model, Sandra Torkington, for a while but she'd ditched him in favour of a minor American film star. I had Delise to thank for that little nugget of information.

His packages usually turned out to be a complicated game of 'pass the parcel' where Jake ended up with the goodies and some other unfortunate was left with all the debts, but he was currently in fairly good odour with the public – the memory of his union-bashing days had now faded into the past, he was certainly rolling in cash and his businesses had continued to flourish. He had his own chain of petrol stations, bearing his company logo: a circular Union Jack surrounding the letters JG.

Gordon had presence. He was very much younger than I'd thought, about the same age as Trevose and alongside him Trevose looked like a glove puppet. The only hairy feature on Gordon's whole expanse of skin were his eyebrows: they were thick, jet-black and very startling. I speculated on how he went about dyeing them. He probably used special little eyebaths.

'Hello, Mr Cunane,' he boomed in his famous fruity voice. 'Nice of you to pop round. We were just discussing whether we should ask you to pay us a visit and now here you are. That shows real initiative on your part. Lance and I have been lucky enough to receive an extended visit from that pompous policeman, Jerrold. Take the weight off your feet and join us ... Get the man something to drink, Trevose! For God's sake, man! Don't stand there hovering like a blue-arsed butler in a whore's boudoir!'

So I sat down. I was slightly stunned. I had come to Alhambra to see how the land lay with regard to Rishton's problems and now here I was hobnobbing with Jake Gordon while he treated the chief executive of Alhambra TV like an office boy.

'I'll just have a coffee, please,' I said in a meek voice. Gordon would have none of this.

'Give the man some of that special twenty-year-old malt, Trevose. DCI Jerrold told us you're a whisky drinker, Cunane! Get some of this down your neck, it's

117

all on the company, isn't it, Trevose?' Trevose hastily poured out three big tumblers of malt whisky.

Gordon's proprietorial behaviour in the inner sanctum of Alhambra TV confirmed the rumours I'd heard: the company must be strapped for cash. Like one of the old-time Cornish wreckers, Gordon only showed up when a ship was heading for the rocks.

I realised I was being subjected to the famous 'Gordon treatment' often talked of in the press and claimed to be the reason for Gordon's success in taking over so many companies with so little cash.

But I thought there was something very menacing about him. He was already having a compressive effect on Trevose and myself. When I got home I'd have to wring the personality out of my clothes.

'Take a cigar, Cunane,' he said, pushing a huge tobacco torpedo into my hand.

I realised that apart from the extravagant greeting as he led me into the room, Trevose hadn't spoken at all so far. We were both waiting for Gordon's next utterance.

'I really came to see Mr Trevose, to find out what's being done for Mr Rishton and Ms Headlam. You see, I was very surprised to hear they'd been arrested and I wondered if someone here could put me in touch with their defence lawyers. I might be able to help them.' My voice sounded squeaky to my ears.

'That's very helpful of you. We were just saying that we thought you might be a useful witness, weren't we, Lance?' Gordon boomed. 'That bloody copper needs taking down a peg or two. Too bloody bumptious by half for my liking. Still, the subversive little git's got Simon Rishton and his fancy piece just where he wants them. They've both got their pinnies caught in the mangle, like my old granny used to say. He wouldn't even hear of bail. Cold-blooded, premeditated murder, so he reckons.

118

Ambushed the poor bitch he claims . . . the pair of them. Waiting for her, but didn't count on you being so punctual, Cunane, eh?'

'Just a minute,' I interrupted. 'Is this the eyewitness who saw them in Prestbury at six o'clock? That can't be right. They were here in this building at 5.40. I was with them.'

'Happen, you're a few minutes out,' Gordon said pointedly, and started ravelling both his eyebrows strenuously with both hands.

'Look, I'm not saying they're innocent, but I know they couldn't have done the murder in the way that the police say,' I said.

There was a sound like a cement lorry dumping its load as Gordon cleared his throat, then he spat the end of his cigar onto the carpet. 'You know that, do you? Well, I know that we've got due process of law in this country, young Mr Private Detective and I am convinced that they have been lawfully charged. That Jerrold may be a conceited little prick, just like yourself Cunane, but I've every confidence in the police.' He spoke as if addressing a very large public meeting.

'Well, you might have, but I've not,' I said cheekily. 'I know that there's no way they could have left this building in time. Your man Poulter can confirm that. I spoke to him as I left just after 5.40.'

Gordon and Trevose exchanged glances, but it was Trevose who replied. 'There must be some mistake. Mr Poulter has told the police that you left at 4.30 p.m., a moment or two before Kath Headlam and Simon. There's even an entry in his log book to that effect. Mr Poulter's a very reliable man, with a good service record. I'm afraid the police view his evidence as unimpeachable. It looks very bad for Simon and Kath. We were hoping that as you were the last person to see them before this dreadful

119

event you might be able to shed some light on their state of mind which might help to put them in the clear. Mitigating circumstances . . . er provocation . . . er . . . as it were.'

There didn't seem to be much point in contradicting him. I could see that I was on the road to Nowheresville. Gordon was still wringing his eyebrows, they looked like two caterpillars stranded on a rock.

'All right, who knows? You may be right, I may have thought it was 5.40 when it was actually 4.30, but I'd still like to give their lawyer the chance to hear my evidence. You must know they're being crucified in the press,' I said.

Gordon sighed. 'I like what you're saying. I really like it. I understand it and admire you for saying it, but please allow me to tell you how naive you are being.' He really was overwhelming, that fruity voice was like a musical instrument; now charming, now threatening. 'Powerful men like Rishton would never even *see* the inside of a court if it wasn't for the opinions expressed in papers like the *Sun* and the *Mirror* keeping the police and judiciary up to the mark. The powers that be are far too deferential to types like Rishton. I'm a great believer in the freedom of the press.' He smiled unctuously at Trevose, the man who was busy replacing his own station's current-affairs output with vapid chat shows.

'So you think there's nothing to be done?' I asked him. It was now very clear what the official line of Rishton's own employer was. He was on his own.

'I believe Rishton has been very foolish indeed,' Trevose replied, echoing Gordon slavishly. 'Not that I'm surprised. I hear he's lost a fortune at Lloyd's, like a lot more of the self-serving, so-called creative, élite who think they're entitled to more consideration from the legal system than the average *Sun* or *Mirror* reader. He'll not be the first that's resorted to desperate measures and gone to pieces when faced with financial ruin – '

I interrupted him. 'He wasn't ruined at all. He had plenty of money. He'd given me five thousand to take to his wife. That's on record. The police have the money.'

Gordon made a smoothing movement with his hands, as if wiping my remarks to Trevose off an invisible blackboard, and carried on as if I hadn't spoken. 'No, Cunane, in your place you'd do better to let the processes take their natural course and refrain from any further involvement in this sorry business. Rishton and his mistress are entitled to legal aid like anyone else, let the law look after them.' It was obvious that this phase of the discussion was over. Gordon was still smiling in a genial way, like a great white shark thinking about its next meal. Trevose was tense, he was compressing his lips nervously. They were now giving each other significant glances to such an extent that I wondered whether they'd been trained in non-verbal means of communication. They looked like a pair of tic-tac men or a comic double act with their nods and winks to each other. 'I was wondering if Alhambra Television might be able to put some work your way, Mr Cunane,' Lancelot Trevose said finally.

I didn't reply.

'Come along, Cunane,' joined in Gordon. 'We're all businessmen here. We know the recession is biting into you little chaps. Mr Trevose is making you a splendid offer. A little bird tells me you're having trouble keeping up with your mortgage payments. A sensible man knows when to cut his losses.'

I was so surprised I nearly choked on the whisky I was sipping. What had my mortgage to do with him? That must have been another piece of information I'd let slip to Jerrold.

'You mean a rat knows when to abandon the sinking ship,' I said angrily, when I'd recovered my breath. I put the whisky down on the massive oak coffee table.

'Talking of rats, Cunane, name your price to take your long snout out of this affair,' rumbled Gordon. 'We'll double whatever Rishton owes you, but that'll be an end to it. Trevose and I aren't so green that we don't know what brought you sniffing round here in the first place. You think a bit of media attention will do wonders for your firm, don't you? Well, you'll get none. At this particular time we don't want anyone muddying the waters at the company's expense.'

'I didn't come here for either money or business,' I said. 'You've become too used to letting your cheque book do your persuading for you, Mr Gordon. You can stick your readies. I'm not going to change my story because you dangle some cash in front of me.'

Trevose went to the intercom on his desk.

'Don't bother having him thrown out, Lance. I expect he'll come crawling round here again in a couple of days, when he's had time to see things in a different light,' Gordon said. I thought he sounded a bit rattled. 'We'll just have to try and make him see reason by other means.'

I stood up to leave, but it was not to be. 'I think we'd better have security in here,' said Trevose, possibly in a last, feeble attempt to assert his independence. 'This man's a drunk and is noted for his violence.' He flicked the switch on his intercom and spoke the words 'Security Six' into it. Immediately the room was flooded with black-coated security guards. They must have been lying in wait. At a nod from Trevose they flung me to the ground and then six of them picked me up face down. I didn't struggle. The last thing I heard was Gordon's booming laugh as I was carted bodily out of the office.

7

Alhambra Building. 11 a.m. Tuesday 28th December 1993

Although it was only eleven o'clock in the morning, my ejection from the Alhambra building created a scene worthy of the dramatic tradition of the company. My enforced departure coincided with the arrival of Lucy Longstaff of 'Slatheredge Pit' and her entourage. At least I guessed it was her familiar voice saying 'Eeeeah ... never mind love, there's a lot more going to be getting the bum's rush round here besides you. Been cheeking Mr Trevose, has he? It's getting like a real knacker's yard round here.' But it's hard to be certain when you're being carried face down by six men.

My bearers got me out of the building and paused at the top of the six steps leading to the pavement. I braced myself for a bone-crunching landing, but then heard another familiar voice ... 'What are you doing with him? He's a friend of mine. Put him down gently.'

They let me go and I was able to land safely on my hands and feet. Maybe they wouldn't have thrown me down six steps, but perhaps they would – this town's getting more and more like South America every day. Ted Blake helped me up.

'Been making yourself unpopular again, Dave, you crazy bugger?' Behind him the security staff now formed a solid phalanx in front of the main entrance. I was so angry that I was ready to fight my way back up to the top floor for another confrontation with Gordon and Trevose but Ted held me back, and I slowly calmed down. There didn't seem much point in shouting abuse from the street.

There was the usual crowd of curious onlookers gathered on the Alambra steps and 'Slatheredge Pit' actors were arriving all the time. For some reason, possibly my personal safety but probably Alhambra's public relations, Ted was anxious to get me out of the way. He led me across the road to the car park and opened the passenger door of a huge green Mitsubishi Shogun. His name was painted on the door. 'Get in, Dave, and calm down. This is just like old times, except then it was usually me getting thrown out, and you coming to the rescue.'

There was something reassuring and solid about Ted after my recent encounter with the slime in the executive office. Greedy for a story though he was, there was nothing treacherous or sadistic about him, and nothing wrong with him that a few cracks over the head with a cricket bat wouldn't put right. He was clad in an expensive tweed suit which did nothing for him. He looked like an extra from a romantic serial set in Scotland in 1920; all he lacked was a deerstalker hat.

The car seemed to drive itself, moving through a corridor of its own creation and rolling down Deansgate in stately and unimpeded progress. Ted was heading for the Throstle's Nest, a pub we'd used a lot at one time. I could see that it had been renovated since our last visit and I didn't like it. All the interesting old decor had been ripped out and it had been tarted up in 'airport lounge' style with a few art nouveau touches. But it would serve its purpose.

I ordered a single brandy for myself and Ted had a double vodka and a packet of cheese and onion crisps to take the smell of alcohol off his breath. We sat in an alcove at the rear of the barn-like lounge bar.

I gave Ted a brief account of the morning's events.

When I'd finished he sat quietly for a moment thinking and then turned to me with a very earnest expression.

'Listen, Dave, I'm considering setting up an independent production company to put out a programme of my own. I'm tired of just having a late-night spot at Alhambra that doesn't get national networking. What you say makes me believe that now might be the time to go for it. I've had an offer from Heart of England Television to reformat my present show and take it to Birmingham.'

'Treachery, Ted! You can't desert Manchester! Brummagen? What are you thinking of? Can't you sell your programme to the BBC? They've gone down market lately.'

'You may laugh, but seriously, Dave, Gordon's issued more redundancy notices in his time than the Coal Board. You didn't find out what he was up to at Alhambra, did you?' he asked.

What Ted was saying wasn't news to me. The issue about whether Gordon was a genuine 'white knight', or a scavenging vulture, had been debated more than once in the financial pages of all the heavy Sundays, but I was surprised that Ted was so concerned about it. The name 'Gordon' seemed to really upset him.

He took a long drink from his glass and munched a handful of crisps, then began stabbing the air with his podgy fingers. 'You know, it's all that bloody fool Rishton's fault. If he hadn't persuaded the management to spend millions on a prestige headquarters they'd never have had this gaping hole in their balance sheet. They'd never have had to bring the knacker Trevose in to set things straight and he'd never have had to bring in Gordon Gecko to refinance the company. I ask you!' Ted was getting a touch emotional about the whole thing.

'But where does Gordon get his money from?' I asked mildly.

'Where have you been, Dave? The guy claims he's

providing the nation with cheap petrol due to his special relationship with the Al Sabahs.'

I must have looked blank because he explained, 'You know, Kuwait. They let him have a soft deal on his oil, either that or he's very clever at manipulating the Rotterdam spot market, but mostly he gets his money from banks. They lend him the money so he can make a nice fat profit for them. He owns dozens of oil tankers bobbing up and down in Liverpool Bay. He can always dispose of a few supertanker loads if he needs to meet an interest payment.'

It hardly seemed fair that such a man should be taking an interest in my financial affairs. There must have been some more pressing reason for Gordon's behaviour than Ted had suggested. I told Ted what Gordon had said about my mortgage repayments. He gave me a funny look and then said, 'You should feel flattered, mate. You've been given the Gordon Treatment. He must really want Rishton out of the way if he's going to such lengths to put a little fish like you back in your box, Dave.'

Ted went and bought himself another packet of crisps while I washed the taste of whisky out of my mouth with a beer. There was so much I didn't know. Why had Rishton really sent me to Prestbury? Why had Gordon tried so hard to get me on side? Why had Lance Trevose suddenly turned into a mere lackey of Gordon's? Was there something going on between those three that had led to the killing of Gloria Rishton?

'I can see you've got that fanatical gleam in your eye again, Dave. Forget it!' Ted warned. 'Gordon's too big for you to tackle. He's already rapped your knuckles. Stay away from him. You don't owe Simon Rishton or Kath Headlam anything.' He sounded quite angry. 'There are things going on in this town that you don't know about . . .' Ted's attempt to fill me in on how little I knew

126

about the Manchester crime scene was a heartfelt one, and his interest in my welfare was almost touching.

Contrary to what he thought, I felt strongly motivated to heed his advice. The gleam in my eye was induced by fear and alcohol. The irritating thing about this whole saga was the way my credibility seemed to be on the line. It really burned me up. They were so anxious to get a conviction that they were willing to ignore vital evidence. Obviously, when I faced Rishton's prosecutors in the witness box they'd try to establish that I was a lush and that I suffered from memory lapses, as Jake Gordon claimed. Just let them try!

Ted drove me back into town. Fortunately I'd left my car in a multi-storey at Gartside Street, behind the law courts, so I didn't need to go near the Alhambra building again.

I used the car phone to get in touch with my office. To my surprise it was Delise who answered, not Jay . . . 'He's not turned in for work, so I haven't been able to start your royal research yet. Would you like to go and find him? He's probably still in bed or combing his hair,' she said pointedly.

I agreed to go and round up my errant employee so that Delise could get on with her assignment and drove out of the car park in the direction of Jay's neighbour- hood. Jay still lived with his mother and brother in a little close near the Manchester City football ground. I'd promised his mother that I'd try to keep him on the straight and narrow and if I failed at everything else I could at least try to succeed in that one commission. The streets were still quiet. It would be after 1 p.m. before many of the young stirred from their beds and got out and about on their mountain bikes.

Jay's mother, Lovena, wasn't home but her other son Douglas, on holiday from school, let me in. I always get

127

on well with Douglas. He's cheerful and free of the hang-ups which can make Jay so unpredictable and difficult. As usual, he made a great ceremony of greeting me, always coming up with some new formula. 'Good to see ya, wouldn't want to be ya!' was his latest effort.

'That's nice, I must say! I hope you don't say that to everyone.'

'No, it's just a joke.'

'Where's Jay? Is he still in bed?'

'He went out hours ago looking for that Liberty Walker. Liberty's mother phoned to say he was on his way over here but when he never arrived Jay went to look for him. That was about nine o'clock.'

'Weren't you worried?' I asked.

Douglas's expression was now more concerned. I knew he was well aware of his brother's previous record. 'I thought he might have gone into town after, he said he was working today.'

Douglas put his jacket on and we began driving round the streets, taking it slowly. There was no visible police presence on the estate and the awkward layout of the streets made it difficult to check everywhere. They were designed to enhance communal feelings and had in reality achieved all the antique charm of a medieval rookery. They certainly weren't designed for the age of mass transport. Jay might be lying injured in any of a hundred ginnels or doorways.

Then I spotted Liberty, no great feat as he was still wearing his red cap, red boots and blue fleecy jacket. He was clinging to the fence peering round the corner into Clarence Road and seemed to be playing hide and seek. I stopped the car, got out and crept up behind him. Douglas came with me. It's not hard to creep up on a deaf person, especially when, as in Liberty's case, he was intent on something that was happening round the corner but I grabbed his arm just to be sure that he wouldn't run. As soon as my fingers closed round his pitifully thin forearm I knew I'd made a mistake. This boy needed somebody to give him three squares a day, not to creep up behind him. He turned and spoke in his quick reflexive way before I could release him.

'Oh, it's the cool dude,' he said. 'Get your hands off me, I'm not going to run.' His expressive blue eyes looked really frightened, his features were drawn. 'It's Jay. Look, they're troubling him, Boss . . .' I stepped forward but he pulled me back with surprising strength. 'Be careful, it's the youth.' I cautiously poked my head round the corner.

Sure enough, there was Jay standing on the wide grass verge where the road followed the curve of the park fence. He was not alone. He was standing in the middle of a group of youths, some of whom were on mountain bikes. Most of them were wearing dark anoraks with the hoods up. The group was about one hundred yards away from us.

Douglas took a peep. 'He's in trouble, he's in bad trouble. I can't tell what they're saying but it looks bad,' he said.

'I can tell you what they're saying,' chipped in Liberty. 'That tall one, he's called Luther. He's saying that Jay has been hanging around on their pitch. He's working the others up, they're going to shoot Jay in the leg. He says Jay is going to get a shot lickin' so he won't forget whose patch he's on. You'd better do something, they've got guns.'

I looked again. There were too many for me to tackle on my own even if I'd been carrying a gun. They'd just shoot Jay and then scatter if they were disturbed. There were no police in sight, and even if I summoned them on the car phone they would be too late to help Jay. While I tried to think of some plan I was aware of Liberty

129

pulling my arm. 'You'd better do something, they say they're going to take him down a side street and do the job on him – shoot him in both legs.'

I scooted back to the car with Douglas and Liberty, gunned the engine and took a racing turn round the corner into Clarence Road. The only thing I could think of was to mount the pavement, drive right at the group and hope that Jay could seize his opportunity to make a break for it.

I didn't need to mount any pavements. Jay's luck was in; when I raced round the corner they had already started to cross the road towards the estate. With drug-induced arrogance, they affected to take no notice of a car coming towards them. Jay was right in the middle of the bunch. I knew he would recognise the car. I sounded the horn, and then did a handbrake turn right into them. That scattered them all right. The back end of the car made several solid thumps, only into bikes I hoped, then in the fraction of time we were stationary Jay hurled himself through the door opened by Douglas and we roared away in the direction of Victoria Road with his legs sticking out of the window. We were round the bend in the road and away from them in seconds.

'Awesome, man,' was Liberty Walker's comment. He thought he was taking part in a video specially laid on for his benefit. The poor kid was in a world of his own. The rest of us were silent. Jay was trembling, and his lips were moving but he couldn't bring himself to speak.

I drove back to Lovena's house. A red Nissan wasn't easily identifiable so I was prepared to leave it outside Jay's house for a few minutes, but I knew how dangerous it was for Jay to stay in the area. The gang who claimed he was spying, or trying to muscle in on their territory, knew where he lived. I told Jay to grab a few clothes and leave a note for his mother, but I should have known better. Jay had such an extensive wardrobe that he needed a couple of trunks to move even a small selection from it. Trying to choose something paralysed him, or maybe it was delayed shock from his narrow escape. Douglas saved the situation by cramming a few of Jay's most necessary items into a sports bag.

In the end I had to drag Jay out of the house and into the car and we drove around while I tried to work out the next move. Jay's recent experience had made him less resistant than he usually was to direction from me. If he disappeared for a while, maybe the youth would forget him. All I needed now was a suitable bolt-hole for him until the heat died down. There was only one possible place.

'Right,' I said, 'we'd better drop Liberty off at his own home. His mother will have to take care of him. We can't have him roaming the district on his own.'

'Oh, no. Please, mister, don't take me home. My mother won't be in. There's only her boyfriend there,' piped up Liberty in his shrill Glasgow accent. So far he'd been enjoying everything but the suggestion he might be better off at home clearly terrified him. He was sitting in the back and I hadn't realised that he could tell what I was saying, but he was watching my lips in the driving mirror. 'Don't take me back there, he'll give me a good hiding.' I wasn't used to children but his distress seemed to be genuine.

'It's no good taking him home until his mother's back. She won't be in until after five,' Jay explained. He was beside me in the front seat of the car. I could tell he was upset by more than his recent experience. He leaned across and whispered to me, 'Don't make a big thing about taking him home. Don't hassle him, Boss.' As this was the closest Jay had ever come to asking me for something I could only agree.

'All right, Jay, but I'm taking you to stay with my parents for a week or so. You need to be out of circulation for a while or somebody's going to let some air into you,' I said.

'That's right, they're going to ventilate him,' chipped in Liberty gleefully, lip reading me again. He obviously thought all this was funny and I could understand now why Jay had been so worried before Christmas. This kid was a danger to himself. It was a miracle that he'd survived so far.

I turned round briefly to Douglas. 'See if you can talk some sense into his silly head, Douglas,' I asked. Jay had relapsed into silence. I think if I'd suggested putting him on the first plane for the Caribbean he wouldn't have objected. He was very frightened. Douglas maintained a sympathetic silence, but Liberty kept up a continuous stream of chat and questions throughout the journey.

I drove to Stretford and took the motorway to Bolton. It wasn't the first time I'd used my parents' remote moorland home as a safehouse. As we travelled on northwards the weather became bleaker and colder despite brilliant sunshine. There were patches of snow on the hills and piles of dirty slush on the roadside. My parents live in a village on the moors above Bolton and at eight hundred feet above sea level it's close to the upper altitude limit for human habitation in Britain, as I often remind them. Other people retire to Bournemouth or Torquay but not my parents.

When we arrived at their tumbledown farm, the snow-ploughs had carved a narrow track down to the house, not for my parents' convenience but so the farmers could get the milk through to the tanker on the main road. We slid down the steep slope to the house, through the semi-derelict farmyard and parked in the little arbour outside. It was as cold as a dead man's nose.

At the doorstep Liberty provided an interesting little diversion by jumping up and swinging Tarzan style from the lintel as he entered the house. I apologised to my mother for his unconventional entrance into her home. My mother is short and plump and deceptively benign looking in her granny glasses, like a character out of an advert for brown bread, but I could see the unreconstructed primary school teacher in her rising to the surface. She hasn't spent half her life controlling classes of up to fifty frisky kids without developing certain forceful habits, as I knew only too well. I hastily explained that it was the sober-looking Jay that I wanted to leave with them, not the wild child.

Neither Paddy nor Eileen raised any objections to having a house guest for a few days, nor to the sudden visitation. They were getting philosophical about my odd ways. Still, there weren't many people of their age who would have been flexible enough to agree to take in a young man as unfamiliar as Jay at such short notice. I think they get lonely up there in winter, maybe a new face helps to stave off cabin fever.

'Got yourself in a pickle again, have you?' said Paddy when he'd manoeuvred me into the kitchen on my own. My heart missed a beat. I looked at his face, so like my own, searchingly. He wore his habitual suspicious frown, a hangover from his days with the Manchester Police Force. 'You're turning this place into a counselling centre for victims of crime,' he said. 'Your mother doesn't mind, gives her something to do, but you'll have to keep her straight financially. We've only got our pensions and that lad looks as if he can tuck plenty of food away.'

'Of course,' I said, only too glad he was talking about cash and not enquiring as to my whereabouts over the festive season. 'I didn't expect you to be out of pocket. It might only be for a few days, until I find him somewhere else to stay. He won't give you any trouble. I think he's in shock.' I gave my father £150 in £50 notes and he pocketed them swiftly.

I knew they weren't badly off. The pair of them have always been keen savers, a talent they haven't passed on to me.

'Hmmm, will this lad be wanting special food?' he asked. I shook my head. Paddy looked me straight in the eye, there was a very speculative expression on his face. This was an unusually long chat for him. Did he know more than he was letting on, I wondered?

Douglas and Liberty were both ready to get their feet under the table but I had other ideas. I wanted to get back to the office. Jay was very subdued. It took the efforts of all of us to get the car back up onto the main road, the snow was piled three or four feet deep at either side of the narrow cart track.

Before we finally got away Paddy put in another appearance, heavily bundled up against the cold. He gestured to me to get out of the car. I gave a weary sigh.

'I just wanted another word in private before you go, David. Your mother was quite upset that you didn't feel like spending Christmas with us again, but of course I know the reason for that.'

'Oh, I see,' I replied weakly. It had been too much to hope that I would escape without some heavy-handed parental guidance. I felt about seven years old again.

'You didn't think you could keep something like this quiet, did you? Half the retired Manchester Police Force have phoned me to tell me all about you being locked up. There's nothing some of those simple-minded moralists enjoy more than a fellow copper's son coming to grief. Are you all right?' I stared back at him, conscious of the melting snow working its way into my socks. He gave me another piercing look. 'Don't admit anything and don't sign anything until your lawyer has read it first, and look after yourself.' He raised his arm in a gesture that was half threatening admonition, half a wave of farewell. Just when I think he's finally got over me not going into the police force, he says something which shows it still rankles.

Jay stood in the road waving goodbye until we turned the bend in the road, a sad figure against the snowy background of the West Pennine Moors.

It took me about forty minutes to get back to Manchester. I hadn't much option but to bring Douglas and Liberty to the office with me.

'This is happening too often, Dave,' Delise said in welcome. 'I ask you to go for Jay to relieve me here and you return with two new waifs and strays. You're going to have to decide whether Pimpernel Investigations is a branch of Social Services or a profit-making business.'

'We are a business, Delise. Now I asked you to dig up something about the Wood case. You could have left the answerphone on. We can't afford to have someone sitting in here all day long on the off chance that the phone's going to ring.' The tone of my voice surprised me, it came out nastier than I'd intended.

Liberty sat quietly for once, keeping a beady eye fixed on the computer. I knew he would be only too happy to stay. I scrabbled through my pockets and managed to come up with £12 in loose change, which I thrust into Douglas's hands. 'Get him something to eat, Douglas, and then take him to see a film. Don't let him go home before five o'clock and for God's sake don't leave him to ramble round Moss Side on his own. Can you do that, Douglas?' I could see that he was no more pleased than Delise, or anyone else, at the prospect of looking after Liberty but he agreed to take him.

I knew that Delise was perfectly right, we couldn't

afford any more diversions. I apologised for speaking to her harshly but her response was cool. She left the office for the library and I decided to use the rest of the day in renewing my contacts in the construction trade. I wanted to see if I could track down the foreman James Clarke, who Mary Wood believed had her documents. Delise and I had agreed to meet back at the office at 5.30 to compare notes and after my early liquid lunch with Ted I didn't feel hungry so I skipped a refreshment stop.

At various times in my career I've worked on building sites and I occasionally bump into former workmates in the pubs of Chorlton. I knew that tracing Clarke might not be all that easy. In any case, it was seven years since Mary's late husband, Dermot, had given or sold her papers to Clarke and in that time Clarke might have died himself, or returned to Ireland. There was also the possibility that he might have changed his name several times for tax avoidance purposes. If he had, it would make it doubly hard to find him. His friends, assuming he had any, would be more likely to give me a thump in the mouth than give me his address.

As I expected, enquiries in the usual pubs led nowhere. I bought the occasional packet of crisps and glass of tonic water to keep myself going. Recent campaigns by the DSS against benefit fraud made even those who knew me wary about giving out any information about Clarke to someone who didn't have the right accent.

Finally, I struck lucky in a pub in Levenshulme when I spotted Barney Beasley drinking on his own. Barney's a forbidding-looking character who works in motorway maintenance and wears suits to show that he's not labouring on the tarmac any more. 'Hello Dave,' he said in his thick Kilkenny accent. 'What brings you here?' It is claimed by some that the inhabitants of Kilkenny speak pure Elizabethan English with the same pronunciation

136

as Shakespeare. I explained my mission and he agreed to make a few enquiries, for the sake of our long acquaintance, but not from the pub. 'There were too many ears flapping in there,' he explained as we left. Barney had a big 'Paddy Wagon' van belonging to Strachan-Dalgetty in the car park.

I drove in convoy behind the van to his home in a side street not far from the big Dale supermarket in the centre of Levenshulme. It took us five minutes to find somewhere to park in the narrow street, which was jammed with vehicles belonging to market traders, and Barney led me into his house and sat me down in the cluttered front room. Barney has five children, all of whom wear very large boots and lots of clothes, which they shed wherever they happen to be. It took us some time to clear a space on the sofa. He told me that he'd been forced to give up subcontracting because of tax problems and the recession and now worked directly for Strachan-Dalgetty. He collected a bunch of men every morning and drove them out to sites on the motorways within range of Manchester.

It only took him one phone call to establish that James Clarke was still working for the firm. He was currently at a site on the M25 near the M40 junction. 'You want to be careful of him,' Barney warned me as I left. 'That guy's connected with the wrong people.'

'I know he's connections with the travellers,' I said innocently.

'No, it's not them I'm talking about.' Barney lowered his voice. 'It's the Provos, I mean, PIRA. He comes from one of these Republican families. His great-uncle posed for the statue of the Volunteer in Athlone Market-place.'

'What volunteer? What are you on about, Barney?' I asked. I guessed that he knew a lot more about Clarke than he was letting on. For all his easygoing ways Barney was as cute as a cageful of monkeys.

'He's mixed up in the wrong sort of politics, that's all,' he said as I struggled to decipher his thick accent. 'Just be careful how you approach him, and for God's sake don't tell him I gave you his address.'

A chill ran down my spine. Who would be more likely than a bunch of Republicans to pay good money for material that might be hostile to the monarchy?

Barney must have caught the change in my expression. 'There's something, isn't there? I can tell,' he said, looking at me astutely. 'Leave it, why don't you? These fellows don't sort things out with their fists and boots, you know. They won't just follow you out of a pub and give you a black eye in some back alley. They don't believe in leaving anyone around to tell a tale.'

'I'll have to follow through,' I said fatalistically. 'I've taken the money for this job and it's already spent.'

'Well, take care then,' he said.

When I got back to the Atwood Building it was just 5.30 and Delise seemed to be in a happier mood after her time in the library. I decided not to tell her anything about the less pleasant aspects of my day. Getting pitched out of the Alhambra Studios by a platoon of security men was hardly likely to endear me to her in her present frame of mind.

'You'll have to give this Wood person her money back, Dave,' she said pleasantly.

This was not music to my ears. 'Why should we?'

'She can't possibly be Edward VIII's granddaughter, that's why.' Delise smiled sweetly and I waited for the rest.

'Orchitis,' she said. 'He had orchitis. He was able to copulate . . . He was even able to abdicate . . . but he couldn't inseminate!' Delise laughed at her own joke; she was enjoying this. When I gave her a stern look she went on to explain. 'In February 1911 there was an outbreak of measles and mumps at the Naval Academy where both Edward and his brother, Prince Albert – the future King George VI – were training to be naval officers.'

'So what?' I asked impatiently.

'So, orchitis is one of the complications of mumps, it affects the testicles and lowers the fertility of those men suffering from it. Some are left completely sterile.'

'Oh, I see,' I said. This news, if true, put the tin lid on Mary Wood's claims. 'You don't need to sound so pleased, Delise.' The note of glee in Delise's voice grated on me.

'Come on, Dave! You didn't really expect to find that Edward VIII had been littering the Irish countryside with illegitimate offspring, did you? He was no Louis XIV or Charles II; no one has ever claimed descent from him before. It seems that the idea of royal bastards became unpopular during the later Victorian era, hardly any of the European Royals produced children by their mistresses, at least not on the scale that their ancestors did and when they did have an illegitimate kid the child wasn't acknowledged or given a title or anything.'

'So if Edward VIII did have a child it might well have been hushed up,' I said hopefully.

'Likely, but then it's unlikely that he could ever have fathered a child in the first place.'

I reluctantly agreed. At least Pimpernel Investigations had sorted out one mystery. Mary Wood was not Edward VIII's granddaughter. But then I'd never believed that she was and this confirmation didn't mean that I wouldn't still try to recover her 'papers' from Clarke.

Delise was smiling. I could never keep up with her rapid mood swings.

'Dave, why don't you come round to my place tonight? Mum's not in, she's gone to a vegetarian rally at Folkestone. She'll not be back until tomorrow. Have you ever seen her bed? She's got a lovely antique brass bed.'

'Great, Delise. But what's wrong with my place? You've never objected to it before,' I asked.

Delise looked at me sharply. 'It's a strain just being in your flat. I keep thinking I have to perform to a certain standard,' she said.

'I didn't know you felt like that,' I said pensively. What she'd left unsaid was that the flat wasn't a bachelor flat, it had once been my marital home, and there were reminders of Elenki, my dead wife, in every room. I was a fool. I felt very remorseful all of a sudden and we left the Atwood Building holding hands like a pair of teenagers.

I still had £200 of the money Mary Wood had paid me, so without telling Delise where we were going I drove round to the G-Mex car park and took her to the Holiday Inn-Crowne Plaza bar for a treat. There were other men there accompanied by younger women so I felt quite at home and several of the bar staff gave me knowing glances. We had an expensive 'tapas' meal, a dull selection of squid, chorizo, meatballs and mushrooms, which left me feeling hungrier than when I'd started, then left at about 8.30 ready for an early rendezvous with Molly Delaney's brass bed.

When we came out it was raining, not heavily, but with that penetrating Manchester light rain that can soak you to the skin in minutes. We drove back to Chorlton and just to reassure myself that the events of the morning hadn't rattled my nerves as much as they had Jay's I took the route past the battered Moss Side Precinct and up Withington Road. As usual all was quiet in the reputed Bronx of Britain and the sodium lights gleamed through the drizzle on empty streets.

We decided to go via my flat at Thornleigh Court first, so I could pick up a change of clothes.

When we reached my landing I held the fire door open for Delise to go through first but it wouldn't open fully, there was furniture piled along the corridor. I felt as if someone was gripping my throat. It was *my* furniture, every stick of it. Exchanging a glance with Delise, I squeezed my way to my front door. The locks had been changed and the Polar Building Society had left a notice sellotaped to the door saying that the flat had been repossessed due to non-payment of the mortgage.

I began to beat my head against the door, hard.

Delise grabbed me and pulled me back. 'Dave! Stop! I didn't know you were in such a mess. You never said.'

'I'm not in a mess. Look!' I pulled out my mortgage repayment card and thrust it under her nose. 'I paid off all arrears this morning. The swine only sent me their threatening letter last week and I paid every penny I owed them this morning.' I could feel the pulse pounding in my neck and I wanted to do violence to somebody.

'It must be a mistake. It must be a computer error, Dave,' Delise said, trying to calm me. 'What are we going to do with all this stuff? At least they haven't thrown it on the street.'

I surveyed the pile. The jumble of possessions filled the whole of the corridor as far as the window at the end. I tried to consider what my next move should be. I needed a van and at least two strong men to help me. A fresh wave of rage swept over me as I realised how impractical that was at this time of night. But she was right, there was no point in beating my head against the door.

As always, the Salway twins had a solution to my problems although they were both away at the moment. Their flat is directly below mine and in their absence I look after it by performing the usual anti-burglar routines with lights and curtains. They do the same for me. Fiona is a little obsessive about it. So I had their key, and all I had to do was hump everything downstairs to their flat and make a space for it. When I explained to Delise, we decided that I'd better phone them at their cousins' house first. Fortunately I had the number. Fiona had insisted.

Finbar wanted to return immediately when I told him the problem. He was eager to help, but luckily he was in Ramsgate so he couldn't. I think if I'd asked his permission to stable an elephant in his sister's flat he'd have agreed. He was on duty as babysitter and Fiona was out, but my need was too urgent to wait for her permission. Finbar said he wasn't due back in Manchester until Thursday afternoon so that gave me a day and a half to get things sorted.

Delise drove off to Moss Side to recruit Douglas Anderson as an assistant furniture remover while I started work.

Delise returned accompanied by Douglas and Liberty. I didn't make any objections and soon we had everything apart from the bed and the sofa and armchairs stowed away. Liberty was a major pest, rummaging through my belongings, looking for food and anything else that interested him. Every time I arrived back in the room with another load he had moved on to investigate some different layer of my past. Annoyance and anger gave way to amusement while I watched his eager little face lighting up as he found each item of interest.

'My mammy had to move like this, when we couldn't pay the poll tax. We had to get out before the bailiffs came round,' he volunteered. Delise gave him a dirty look but I didn't say anything. There was a similarity in our situation, after all.

It didn't take long to shift my stuff and we stopped off at the drive-in McDonald's in Chorlton to satisfy Liberty's insatiable hunger before dropping him and Douglas at their homes. It was just as well that Delise was with me because I felt quite capable of driving to the Poynton headquarters of the Polar Building Society and setting fire to it. The vision of building society offices in flames kept intruding on my thoughts as we drove back to Chorlton.

'Dave? You are coming back with me?' Delise asked as we turned into the turd-littered lane her mother called home.

'Are you willing to take one of the homeless in?' I asked bitterly.

'Oh, come on! Lighten up, Dave!' Delise said. 'It's probably just a computer error and you'll be able to straighten it out in the morning. Come in and have a drink with me, where else have you got to go?'

8

Molly Delaney's house, off Willows Road,
Chorlton.
6 a.m. Wednesday 29th December 1993

My sleep was interrupted by a terrific crash which shook
the whole house as the front door was flung open and I
felt Delise's body tense as if a thousand volts had shot
through her. She sat up, instantly awake. She knew what
the noise heralded.

'Mother! It must be mother.' She was out of the bed
in a flash and gathering up the clothes strewn around
the bedroom. I wasn't in any hurry to get up.

'Well, so what?' I said lazily. 'She knows you're over
twenty-one.'

Delise shot out of the bedroom on tiptoes and dumped
all the clothes she'd gathered into her own bedroom.
When she returned she abruptly pulled the duvet off the
bed.

'Get up quick, and get into my room before she comes
up here. She'll have the balls off you if she finds out
what we've been up to in her bed. Mum only takes her
liberalism so far.'

This threat was sufficient to cool my passions and get
me moving towards Delise's own cramped little bedroom.
I listened for further sounds from below. There was a
very faint buzz of voices for a while. The quietest one
must have been Delise speaking in her reasonable tones,
then Molly's louder voice. She seemed to drone on for
ever, only rarely interrupted by Delise and I had plenty
of time to think about my own plight. Why should the
Polar Building Society be in such a hurry to evict me?
Why just at this precise moment? There were bound to

be lots of people who hadn't replied to their threatening letters immediately. It was Christmas after all. Besides I wasn't even six months in arrears.

'Well, this is a fine thing, I must say,' Molly began portentously when I finally summoned up the courage to venture downstairs. There was a look of concentrated malevolence on her face, which suggested that despite her daily study of the *Guardian*, the frontiers of sexual morality had not shifted as far as she was concerned.

'Don't start, Mum. Remember what I told you. Why don't you go and make us all a cup of tea?'

Molly slammed the tea things down on the table with such violence that I knew I was pushing my luck to hang around here much longer. I managed to scald my lips with the hot tea and then to the general relief announced my departure on urgent business. Delise bustled out after me.

There were four squirrels running along the park fence when I got out into the street quite undeterred by the steady rain now falling, and dripping off the overhanging trees. They stopped and looked at me cheekily. All kinds of animals got their rights in this street, I just hoped that they left a few rights for male humans, I reflected gloomily, remembering that I'd now joined the ranks of the homeless.

'What are you going to do, Dave?' Delise asked as she used the car mirror to touch her lipstick up.

'I'm going to Poynton to sort out these maniacs at the Polar Building Society,' I told her. Then I felt a stab of guilt. I'd taken Mary Wood's money but so far hadn't produced much in the way of a result. 'You'd better carry on with your enquiries into the Wood case. Produce a folder of photocopies, get all the family pictures you can. See if you can put together some sort of dossier on what

145

Edward was up to in the early thirties. It'll make a good souvenir for Mary if nothing else.'

Delise made it clear by her waspish expression that she thought the whole thing a waste of time.

I drove her into town and she gave me a reluctant kiss as we parted outside the office.

As I drove towards Poynton, I could feel the rage I had experienced last night surfacing again. It wasn't so much directed at the Polar Building Society as at the people who were trying to manipulate me. The eviction must be connected somehow to the murder of Gloria Rishton. I remembered reading somewhere that MI5 had once used similar methods to rid themselves of Soviet agents. When they found an undercover agent busily extracting useless information from some Ministry, they didn't necessarily want to cause a diplomatic incident by booting him out. They had just quietly cut off the spy's gas, water, phone and electricity; made sure that all his cheques bounced, and that no post was delivered. No fuss, no mess.

I'd always understood you were supposed to receive all sorts of warnings and counselling before a building society foreclosed. That must be public relations crap because I'd only been four months in arrears and was now fully paid up.

I felt nervous as I took the roundabout way to Poynton along Moor Road and past the Woodford Aerospace factory. There were 'For Sale' signs on dozens of houses en route. Poynton is a pleasant dormitory town which has grown up round an old mining village and the centre retains a village atmosphere only marred by the grotesquely ugly building which houses the offices of the Polar Building Society. Erected in the eighties by a megalomaniac speculator now in Ford Prison for fraud, this neo-Toytown structure well merited the attentions of an arsonist, but I'd already decided to leave the petrol in my tank.

Anyway, when I located the visitors' car park and entered the building, I was posing as a humble seeker of assistance rather than as a vengeful fury. I'd decided it would probably get me further.

I was shown up to Ms Attleigh's office after a short wait and she turned out to be an attractive, well-set-up blonde in her thirties. It seemed like a good omen.

'I've come about the eviction,' I started politely.

'Wrong terminology!' she interrupted briskly. 'We don't evict people, we repossess properties where the client has failed to keep the terms of the mortgage agreement.' Her attitude was distinctly frosty as I stared into her cow-like blue eyes, trying to exert every ounce of charm, a little boy lost in the complexities of modern life.

'That's just it,' I countered. 'I've kept to the terms of mine. Here, you can look at my mortgage payment book. It's fully up to date. Payment was a little belated but that's no cause for a rift between friends.'

She took my payment book suspiciously, as if expecting it to bite her and compared the number with that in my file, which she had open in front of her; she ran her finger down the list of payments and I could feel my heart thumping painfully. Then she frowned and looked again with incredulity dawning, and held it up to the light as if the numbers might vanish.

'There seems to be an irregularity here,' she murmured.

'I got your letter just before Christmas, and as you can see I paid at the earliest opportunity after the holiday,' I said in a slightly victimised tone.

'Well, you do seem to be up to date, but the thing is there is no record here,' she said, indicating her file, 'that you have paid. It's just possible that there's been an error

147

at this end. I'll have to take this payment book and get it verified.'

Humble though I might seemingly be, I had no intention of letting her walk out of the room with the only available record of my cash payment. I leaned over the desk and took the book out of her hand, smiling pleasantly as I did it.

Her expression was neutral now, rather than hostile.

'I see you don't trust us. There's a copier in the next office. I can make a copy and take it up to Mr Harrison, if you'd like to come with me. I'm sure we can sort this out.' She stood up quickly and strode out, made the copy and then marched decisively towards the lift, leaving me to sit on a bench in the corridor outside her office.

Time passed slowly, and it was at least half an hour before she returned. All the cool efficiency seemed to have been knocked out of her, she looked flustered and nervous, no longer the hard-faced executive. She ushered me back into her office. I could tell the news wasn't good.

'There was no mistake. We got your money but we're not accepting it as payment and we're going to hold onto it because we have been informed by an unimpeachable source that you obtained the mortgage in the first place by fraudulent or criminal deception. Legal action is being prepared against you. We're holding your money against our legal costs.'

I held onto the chair firmly, trying not to come unzipped. I've taken some stick from bank managers in my time but there'd never been anything to match this.

'You can't do this,' I managed to croak.

'We can. It's in the Society's rules which you agreed to when you took out the mortgage.'

'I demand to know who made the allegation against me,' I said.

148

'Mr Harrison has instructed me to refuse to inform you.'

'Well, how was my original application fraudulent? In what way? Surely I have the right to know?'

'Mr Harrison says not.'

'Can I see Mr Harrison, then?' I asked.

'Direct meetings are not in line with company policy in cases like this,' she replied.

I seemed to detect a faint trace of disapproval directed at Mr Harrison's actions in her tone as I looked at her. At least she gave no sign that she was enjoying her role.

'Have you a family?' she asked. I shook my head. I should have stuck to my original plan, hijacked a petrol tanker and run it into the building. There was nothing to be gained by being soft with these administrative swine. Go in hard and come out fast like Mr Harrison did, that was the way to play it.

Miss Attleigh coughed to get my attention. 'Between you, me, and the gate post, I think you're getting a very raw deal.'

'Fine, but your sympathy doesn't put the roof back over my head,' I said.

'Look, I can see you're angry and disappointed and I think you've every right to be but just listen. I came into this job to serve the public, not to victimise it. I'm going to go out of the room for a glass of water in a moment and if you should happen to accidentally pass your eye over the papers on my desk you might get a clearer idea of what's happening to you. Don't take the papers away or I'll lose my job.'

With this she stood up and strode out of the room looking as impressive as Boadicea on her chariot. What a woman! And I'd thought she was cow-like! I had been unfair to bureaucrats and bovines alike! I rushed round her desk to look at the open file. It was mostly records of payments and copies of letters but the relevant item lay in the form of a memo at the bottom of the pile.

It riveted me to the spot.

'Following information received from Mr Gordon it has been decided to proceed with foreclosure of property belonging to D. Cunane, Membership No. 436,789, on the grounds of fraudulent submission. Action immediate, B. Harrison.'

It was signed and dated yesterday. There was even a receipt attached for the fresh lock on my door. I was to be charged for that as well. I had no idea that Gordon had such clout.

There was a tap on the door and I swiftly moved back round the desk as Attleigh reappeared with a determined expression on her face. There was something about her posture and the way she stood waiting for me to pass her in the narrow space that suggested that further personal consolation from her might not be out of the question. I think if I'd been able to manage a few tears she might have put her arms round me.

I brushed past her close enough to catch a whiff of her perfume but restrained myself from making any overt move beyond a smile, and a twitch of my right eye that didn't really amount to a wink, in return. I noticed that she wasn't wearing a ring; still, even if I wasn't planning to remain deeply faithful to Delise I just hadn't got the time to take things further.

As I drove away it occurred to me that the Polar Building Society was on dubious legal ground. They'd confiscated my payment and foreclosed on the mortgage just on the say-so of one individual. When I'd bought the flat back in 1988, I'd had to get an audited statement of my earnings for the previous two years before they granted the mortgage and the firm of accountants I'd used had been a well-known Manchester firm the Polar had recommended themselves. There might be every chance that the Society would have to pay substantial compensation for its mistake.

Cheered by this thought, I was just negotiating a difficult curving slip-road to join the end of the M56 when the phone rang. Holding the receiver with one hand and hoping that I wasn't spotted using the phone at the heavily policed intersection, I took the call. It was Delise.

'Dave, I've just had Jake Gordon on the phone asking for you!' she said breathlessly. She might have had the Queen or the Pope or even Michael Jackson on the line, judging by her awed tone. 'He says he's very anxious to talk to you about a business proposition and will you call him back right away. He'll be in the Manchester area for the next few days and is very anxious to retain your services.'

Gordon's methods were certainly direct. This was how he'd got to the top of British industry; pressure and charm, charm and pressure. Well, it wasn't going to work with me. The Building Society must have told him that I'd been round and now he wanted me to grovel.

'You return the call, Delise. Tell him I'm on my way to London to follow a line of enquiry and that I'm fully booked up at the moment. Be nice about it but make it clear that I'm already working on something.'

There was dead silence from the other end. I heard my lover clearing her throat for an onslaught.

'You're turning down one the richest men in the country, who's gone to the trouble to make a personal call asking for your services, Dave! Have you fallen out of your pram completely!'

'I'm not turning him down. I already have a client. I'm going to London to find this character who has Mary Wood's papers, and by the way I thought I told you to go out and research on her ancestry.'

'Dave, there's nothing at all in the published record to

151

show that Edward VIII had a son and you know it. I got some books out of the Central Ref. but I'm not going to waste my time trying to read every word that was ever written about him.'

'All I wanted was some background on the Palace staff, his recreational activities etc.' I had turned off the end of the motorway as I said this and parked on Barlow Moor Road opposite the corner of the Southern Cemetery. I'd had no intention of going to London when I set off this morning but now it seemed like a good idea.

'Very masterful, aren't you?' commented Delise. 'How did you get on with the Building Society?'

'Very, very badly. In fact, if you still want to do me a favour you could go out and buy me a camp bed and a sleeping bag because it looks as if I'm going to be sleeping in the office for the time being, seeing as Molly won't let me sling up a hammock at your place.'

'Oh, God, Dave! Why? I thought you said you'd straighten things out easily enough.'

'It's complicated, Delise. I'll explain later. Expect me to be back about nine. I'll meet you in the Woodstock. Now be a good girl and phone Gordon back.'

I waited until there was a gap in the traffic, did a u-turn and headed back towards London. As I followed the M6 and then the M40 the long drive gave me plenty of time to ruminate about my position. I hadn't a clue how to approach Clarke. Mary Wood had referred to him as a 'ganger', which was uncomfortably like 'gangster', and he sounded like an awkward customer. But I was only going to ask him a few simple questions after all. Really, he only had to say 'No' to every question and my conscience would be perfectly satisfied. I wouldn't be able to return all of Wood's money right away, but perhaps she'd be satisfied with instalments if I promised to pay interest.

152

Once out of Manchester the rain stopped. The weather was bright and clear all the way through the Midlands. I called at Keele Services for a greaseburger and chips washed down with two cups of tepid coffee. There was little traffic on the road, hardly any heavy lorries at all. I'd been going for over two hours and was just past the turn-off for Stratford on Avon when the phone rang. It was Delise again.

'Dave, I'm frightened. It took me ages to get through to Gordon and when I did he couldn't seem to take it in that you weren't going to go round straight away. I told him you were pursuing enquiries in London and he went crazy. He was cursing and swearing down the phone. I've never heard anything like it. I thought he was going to send someone round to the office so I left. I'm phoning from home. Dave, what are we going to do? It was him who put you out of your flat, wasn't it?'

'You didn't tell him where I was going in London, or what I was doing, did you?' I asked in as calm a voice as I could. Delise sounded really upset and I knew it took more than a bit of bad language to rattle her.

'No, I just told him what you said, "enquiries in London". He doesn't believe you're going to London at all. He thinks you're going to Runcorn to check out his headquarters or something. He said he would have a warm welcome ready for you if you went snooping anywhere near his business.'

'Listen, Delise, no one's paying me to investigate him. He must be paranoid or something. Don't let him frighten you.'

'You sound pretty cool, I must say. All right, I'll get the camp bed and bag from the Army and Navy store in Chorlton. See you later.'

The thought of annoying such a powerful figure as Gordon, even if it was only because he was jumping to

153

the wrong conclusions, did wonders for my ego, and I drove on in a much better mood. The road was so quiet that I began to wonder if the building workers would still be at the M25/M40 junction. Perhaps they'd all stayed on holiday after the Christmas break. Isolated in my little speeding cocoon, it was easy to imagine that I was the only person in the country going about his business.

Perhaps Mary Wood would turn out to be the heir to the throne after all, and James Clarke was just waiting for someone to relieve him of his awesome burden. Fame and fortune might lie round the next bend in the road.

When I reached the M25 I immediately realised that I was on the wrong side of the motorway for the building works. They were spread along the northbound carriage-way, right up to the actual M40 interchange. I went on to junction 15 and turned back, driving in a clockwise direction on the M25, with the great despond of Slough on my left. Fortunately there was a speed reduction policed by cameras, so I could go slowly until I came to the first sign saying 'Works Entrance Only' and pull off the motorway into the building site.

It was as desolate as the far side of the moon. Massive ruts filled with pools of grey liquid threatened to sub-merge the Nissan with its low wheel base, so when I saw cars parked off to the left I pulled in amongst them. Leaving the car proved to be a mistake. The temperature was just above freezing and my navy-blue business suit did little to keep me warm. I was soon shivering, and the going on foot was even rougher than driving the car down the rutted track. I tried to hop from one dry island to the next with little success. It was my own fault for visiting a road-works site in winter without proper gear. Cursing steadily, as grey mud encroached onto my trousers, I made my way forward, dodging round huge stationary machines. I spotted a yellow Portakabin labelled 'Site Office' but it was deserted.

The site seemed to stretch on for miles. I'd been doing 60 when I passed it in the opposite direction and it was much bigger than I'd thought. To go back for the car would be as tedious as going on. I rolled my trousers up, tucked them into my socks and went on a little further.

There was a battered-looking collection of mobile homes jammed into a narrow space at one side of the site, their tyres inflated and their hitching bars sticking out into the track. They must belong to the itinerant workers on the site. When I got closer I could see that they had crudely lettered name cards stuck in their windows. Hope resurged as I saw that one of them said 'Jas. Clarke'. It was certainly an unlikely looking spot to come searching for information about the sexual activities of a member of the House of Windsor. Nevertheless, Windsor Castle and Sunningdale were only a few miles away as the crow flew. I reflected that it would be a strange coincidence were I to find the keeper of the alleged royal documents in just this particular corner of England.

I knocked and my luck was in. The door was opened at once by a man of about fifty. He seemed friendly, as he gave me a quizzical smile and he struck a posture in his doorway, fists on hips and elbows stuck out. He gazed at me intensely from very bright blue eyes, his brow wrinkled in concentration. His skin was very fair, with a red, almost livid, complexion, deeply folded and creased, and there was a paler band round his forehead marked by freckles, where he wore his cap. He still had all his hair, faded carroty red in colour, and set in close waves like the late Tyrone Power's.

As phoney as a £9 note, I thought, though he might fool the uninitiated. I introduced myself and explained

155

that I was trying to track down some information about someone he might have known.

'You're not from the Department of Employment or the DSS, are you?' was his first question, and 'Are you from UCATT, then?' his second. I assured him I was not connected to the Government or any trade union. He seemed unsure how to respond but invited me in and I was met by a strong reek of stale bacon fat. There was nowhere to wipe my feet and the floor seemed to be coated with a thick layer of grey mud. I carefully avoided letting my distaste for his domestic squalor show.

He spoke in a curious sort of strangled non-regional accent. If I hadn't already known that he was Irish, I might not have detected the faint Irish intonation given to about one word in seven.

'I'm a private detective,' I said, taking out the fancy identification documents that I'd concocted for myself a while back.

He relaxed a little as he studied them closely, and then handed them back but I noticed that he was still drumming his heels, as if uneasy.

'I'm acting for Mary Wood, a lady who lives in a caravan in the Manchester area,' I said. 'She claims that her deceased husband, Dermot, left some documents with you for safe keeping. She wants them back and is willing to pay for their return.'

The mention of Wood's name had an immediate effect. I'd expected to be met with incomprehension, but Clarke obviously knew all about Mary and Dermot Wood. In an unconscious movement he broke eye contact and looked over his shoulder at a sort of chintz-covered wardrobe, that stood against the wall in the middle of the cramped caravan, just to the right of the door.

'How do I know you're not from the Social, trying to trap me into some sort of admission?' he said suspiciously, with his eyes narrowed. He wiped his greasy hands on his thighs.

'You've got me there, Mr Clarke,' I said with a laugh, trying to lighten the heavy atmosphere. 'Mary can hardly read, can't write at all, and I doubt a mobile phone is on her shopping list, so it's hard to get in touch with her. You don't fancy a trip up the M40, do you? She could tell you herself, then.'

'And why the hell would I be doing that?' he demanded angrily. 'I hardly know the bloody woman.'

'Ah, so you do *know* her, then? What if I brought her here?' I cajoled. 'She'd be willing to pay you well for any trouble she put you to.'

'Now I know you're not from Mary Wood. She's never had two ha'pennies to rub together,' he said triumphantly. He gave the chintz-covered wardrobe another surreptitious glance. It drew his gaze like a magnet. When he saw me watching him he hastily looked away.

'Come on, Mr Clarke,' I coaxed. 'Give me a break. I've come a long way. There's no way I can prove that I'm from Mary. Suppose I tell you what I want and then you can think about it?'

He gave a non-committal grunt.

'Mary claims that Dermot gave or sold you certificates and papers proving that her father, Edward Cassells, was actually the son of the Duke of Windsor . . .'

'Ha! That bloody idle tinker, Dermot Wood. He only worked about one day in three,' he said before I could give further explanation. 'All right. I got a mate who happens to be on the site. He'll tell you all about Dermot Wood and his royal wife, if you just hang on here for a few minutes.'

'So there are documents?' I said hopefully.

'Ah well, you may be getting a bit too previous with

157

yourself there. I wouldn't be saying that,' he said tantalisingly.

The thought crossed my mind that I might have to repossess Mary's papers without giving him the option of making a bargain, as it were.

The same thought had evidently occurred to him because he got up suddenly and went to the door.

'Look, I'll have to go and get my friend. He knows more about Dermot Wood than I do. Wait here for a while. I'll be back in a few minutes,' he said before making a quick exit.

In a pig's ear, 'wait', I thought. He'll be back in a minute with his mates. The prospect of an interview with them didn't delight, but having come so far, I had to take the risk of giving Clarke's trailer a quick once-over. I hastily locked the door and turned to the interior of the trailer. I didn't have far to look. The chintz wardrobe turned out to be a couple of filing cabinets, stuffed to capacity with official-looking papers. It would take me hours to go through them.

At that moment I heard an engine revving. I looked out and saw Clarke returning, at the wheel of a big Transit. He had lots of company by the sound of the voices. They were making that curious noise – never forgotten by those who've heard it as I have – of the labouring classes baying for broken teeth. It was the second time in less than a week that a mob had gathered round the door of a trailer with the sole intention of kicking the liver and lights out of me. I slid open the offside window and squeezed myself through, landing silently in thick mud at the side of the caravan. There was a narrow clearance between the side of the trailer and the ground, just sufficient space for me to get underneath Clarke's trailer.

I heard Clarke shouting over the roar of the engine,

'Spread out and look for the bastard. There's £50 for the man that brings him back.' He spoke with a broad Irish accent now. Obviously, he was a man of parts. After a few moments the sounds of pursuit receded. I couldn't see any of the proceedings, but it was reasonable to suppose that Clarke had cleared off with the rest to muster the search. I got ready to make a dash for my car, but just as I was about to squirm out from under the trailer I heard its door opening and several men tramping overhead.

'Who do you reckon he might be, James, the Branch, MI5, or the Department of Employment?' someone asked. The accent this time was not Irish but eastern European.

'How the hell do I know?' Clarke's voice snarled a reply. 'But he's been in here. He knows where the files are and he knows all about that bastard Dermot Wood. We'll have to fix him. We should have shut that bloody tinker's mouth up sooner.'

As I listened to my future being discussed in this charming fashion, I was aware that I was slowly sinking deeper into the chilly grey mud. I had a sudden overwhelming fear that the extra weight above would press the trailer down and smother me in the mud. I had no intention of leaving my corpse to improve the fertility of the soil of the Home Counties: despite having Rupert Brooke drummed into me as a child, this particular 'corner of a foreign field' was not going to conceal my dust. I got a hold on the side of the caravan and hauled myself clear. It took all my strength to break the grip of the clinging grey mud.

The movement must have alerted Clarke because I got a glimpse of his angry face at the window as I ran off. There were no fancy detours made around pools of mud this time, I ran as hard and fast as I could towards the perimeter in the opposite direction from the motorway. Looking back over my shoulder I saw Clarke emerge round the back of his trailer and start firing a gun at me. I could see the flashes. God knows what I had stumbled on, but Clarke wasn't playing games. He must be a bad-tempered bugger. I hit the orange plastic perimeter fence at speed, rolled over its top and down a bank into a ruined field.

Camouflage and concealment are the main rules of evasion. My roll in the freezing mud under Clarke's caravan had taken care of the first. What about concealment? I flung myself into one of the deeper ruts left by the digging machines and submerged myself so that only my mouth and nose were above water. The shock of the cold water was terrible, I could only stick this for a few minutes before I froze. In my favour, the light was fading rapidly and even the keenest eyes would hardly make out my shape in the muddy water. I could feel the heat draining out of my body and I tried to think of warm things, about being snugly wrapped up in Delise's bed.

Then I heard a faint squelching sound nearby, and one of Clarke's men put his booted foot down hard on my chest and stood for a moment. He swivelled his foot round to get a firmer stance but didn't realise he was standing on his quarry. My face was forced completely under the water. He passed on. He hadn't seen me. I cautiously raised my head. Silhouetted against the fading light was a ragged picket line of searchers. They were moving rapidly away from me, shouting hoarsely to each other as they tried to keep in line. This was my chance. I crawled out of the pool, and being careful not to raise myself above tussock level, shimmied on my hands and knees towards the bank.

There were lights and movement in the direction of

my car and Clarke's trailer was brightly lit up. If I ran for the car I would be spotted.

When I reached the back of the trailers I stood up behind one of them to try and assess my chances of making a break for it and as I peered round the corner towards Clarke's front door, I found myself looking straight into the barrel of his gun. He must have heard me slithering along behind his trailer and waited to surprise me.

Whether my reactions were just a little quicker than his, or his gun misfired, I'll never know but desperation gave me speed. I punched him on the forehead, feeling the bones in my fist crunch out of place as I struck home and he dropped the gun. There was nowhere to run to. It could only be seconds before he retrieved his weapon from the mud and finished me. Running like a hare I leapt up into the cab of the Transit van that he'd driven up in earlier. My life depended on the key being in the ignition. It was.

I gunned the motor and raced forward towards the corner of the site where it abutted the motorway. I couldn't see an exit in this direction but I wasn't going back. There was a pile of gravel which I crunched through and a thin plastic fence, then I was on to the 'Works Vehicles Only' lane of the motorway. It ran parallel to the two enclosed narrow lanes which were all that was left of the M25 at this point. There was plenty of traffic heading north for the M40 and M1. I could see the end of the 'Works Only' lane coming up fast and I veered sharply right onto the motorway. Horns blared, but I didn't hit anything and pursuit by the police was the least of my worries.

There were signs every hundred yards saying 50 mph. The traffic in front was moving slowly, obedient to the police signs. I was in an agony of frustration. I knew

161

Clarke must be organising pursuit. Then, to my relief, the M40 interchange came up. I took it and put my foot down. Once I was on the motorway heading for Manchester I realised that I'd made a mistake. If I'd wanted to hide I should have stuck with the M25 and lost myself in the myriad of streets in London. Now it was Manchester or bust.

I inspected the vehicle I was driving. The main thing was that it had a full tank. I could drive all the way home without stopping. It had been a great day. I'd lost my home in the morning and my car in the evening, and now I was driving back to Manchester looking like a Papuan mud man. Another suit of clothes ruined into the bargain. To think I'd been worried that I wouldn't be able to give Mary Wood full value for money.

Where had all those men suddenly sprung from? The site had seemed practically deserted. Had I stumbled on a meeting of the local coven of the IRA? I knew from my own experience that it had once been common practice to have collections for the 'Cause' on building sites, but not nowadays surely?

I'd have to change my image. This wasn't the first time that I'd been taken for a heavy from the security services. When I got back to Manchester I'd have to make an anonymous call to the Anti-Terrorist Squad.

Every mile I travelled was a mile nearer safety. I'd already passed High Wycombe and was climbing up the long slope to the ridge of the Chilterns when the bullet shattered the side window and whistled through the hair on the top of my head. I distinctly heard the droning sound as it passed through the skin of the van just above my face.

I heaved the wheel to the left in panic and drove onto the hard shoulder still doing 80. I hadn't seen a thing.

Clarke must have been quicker in organising a pursuit than I had thought possible. It could only be him.

The driver of the massive container lorry I was now driving alongside started flashing his lights, and sounding his horn. As far as I was concerned he could do what he liked as long as his leviathan continued to shelter me. Then I realised that it wasn't me that he was signalling. I pulled slightly forward for a look and saw him hanging out of the window and shaking his fist at something to his right rear side. I surmised that he was all that stood between me and my pursuers. Maybe they'd put a bullet into the side of his lorry, trying for another shot at me. The driver must have thought he was being hijacked. There'd been quite a number of highway robberies on the roads out of London recently.

I got a quick vision of what was going to happen next; the juggernaut driver stamped on his brakes for an emergency stop, swerving left onto the hard shoulder as he did so and I shot forward to avoid him, just missing impact.

I was now fully exposed to my antagonists again, in an identical Strachan-Dalgetty van to the one I was driving. I could make out several faces. The fatal bullet could only be seconds away now. Like the lorry driver I stamped on my brakes; they swerved violently into the slow lane to cut me off, then lost control and spun right off the road onto the steeply sloping bank of the motorway. Their van went over on its side but didn't burst into flames like they always do on television.

I kept going. If Clarke was in that van, then in the natural course of events he had every right to be dead. It had turned over twice.

I was expecting to be flagged down at a police checkpoint every mile of the way from then on, but nothing else happened. I drove into South Manchester at 8.45

and parked on Mersey Road outside the Woodstock a quarter of an hour early for my rendezvous with Delise. I noted listlessly that it was still raining just as steadily as it had been when I left Manchester this morning. My nerves were fairly shredded, particularly when I examined the trajectory of the bullet that had missed me.

The marksman's aim had been perfect, too. He couldn't have known that he was aiming at the mud-plastered hair sticking up in front of my head, not at my skull. If I had leaned forward slightly at the crucial moment my skull would have been as irretrievably shattered as poor Gloria Rishton's had been only a few days ago.

9

The arrival of Delise in her mother's battered old 2CV brought me back to reality. I watched as she swiftly parked the car in a narrow space and got out. There was something admirably competent about Delise's most trivial actions. Stirring myself, I jumped out of the van and ran forward. I didn't want her to go into the pub, I could hardly follow in the state I was in.

She cowered back in fear when she saw me, drawing in breath ready to scream 'rape' at the top of her lungs. I stopped in my tracks, waved my arms and spoke in a whisper. 'It's only me, Delise.'

She exhaled slowly, still looking at me very suspiciously.

'You've been hitting the sauce, haven't you? Look at you.' She took a few steps forward. 'You look like two red eyes peering out of a ball of shit. Christ, Dave! Did you even go anywhere near London? I should have known . . .'

'Delise, will you shut up and let me get a word in? I've been to the building site near London but I don't want to discuss it in the street, with you shouting the odds all over Didsbury.'

'You're not coming in my car like that,' she shot back, practical as ever.

'Calm down. I've got transport. Just follow me down to Thornleigh Court and I'll tell you what's happened.'

'Where's your car? I can't see the Nissan. It's not here.'

'I'm in that van! Just get in your car and follow it and stop fussing.' Without waiting to see what she was doing

165

I turned and got back in the van. I'd been through too much today to be able to tolerate any temperament from Delise and the day was far from over yet as far as I was concerned. I drove slowly to Thornleigh Court, she followed.

Having already imposed on the absent Salway twins once, I proposed to do so again by making use of their shower. I had to wait a few minutes to check that there was no one coming out before sneaking into the building and up to their first-floor flat. It felt strange to be an intruder where once I had been a resident. Delise followed me up and stood by to watch me emerge from my mud chrysalis.

Having extracted anything of value from the pockets, I dumped all the clothes I was wearing straight into a bin-liner and took a shower while Delise packed all my clothes into suitcases. I had enough clean and ironed shirts and underwear to last me for two weeks. There must have been twenty pounds of grey mud clinging to me. I hope it did wonders for my complexion, there was no crevice of my body it hadn't penetrated.

As I dried off I mentally ticked off my problems in order of priority: I had to get my Nissan Bluebird back from the motorway work, and quickly at that.

I'd noticed that the van I was driving had a towing attachment on the back. What was to stop me driving back to the building site, hitching up Clarke's trailer and making off? Then I could study his filing cabinets at my leisure. If I took Delise she could pick up the Nissan at the same time.

I couldn't see any snags. Clarke wasn't likely to be around. He was either lying on a slab by now with a tag on his big toe, or hiding out somewhere else. If I struck now I would have all the advantages; the longer I left it the stickier everything would become.

166

For once in my life everything seemed to slot into place. Delise listened to my plan with a resigned, fatalistic expression on her face like I imagined one of my grandfather's fellow soldiers in the Great War might have looked at being told he was to go over the top. But she agreed to go with me straight away. Perhaps she was past caring. The only condition she imposed was that we get some food on the way, so we called in at McDonald's and I consumed my second burger of the day. I didn't tell Delise about the shooting at the site or about someone parting my hair with a bullet on the way home, I just left her with the impression that there'd been a mild difference of opinion.

We were on the M6 heading back to London by 10 p.m. I didn't have much to say for myself and Delise was unusually quiet. The only thing worth discussing was the question of my sanity and I didn't want to start on that. Delise didn't spot the bullet hole in the roof – I'd plugged it up with chewing gum.

When we reached the road-works site just after 1 a.m. everything went like a dream. My car was where I'd left it, undamaged, and Delise drove it back to the slip-road to wait for me while I backed the big van down the muddy track and hitched up Clarke's trailer. Brute force and ignorance shifted the stabilisers from the mud, then I towed it off down the track to join Delise without disturbing a soul.

We took the M1 north because I needed to stop for fuel. The only indication that I'd joined the ranks of the 'New Age Travellers' in the eyes of the world came when the pump attendant at Watford Gap rushed out and made me pay for the fuel before I filled up. I didn't check the trailer out at the service station and hadn't been on the road again for more than ten minutes when Delise, who was following me, began flashing her lights. I thought perhaps the wheels were coming loose and carefully pulled onto the hard shoulder just in time to see a figure clad in a long white night shirt emerge from the door of the trailer and run screaming into the night. He was quickly lost in the darkness. I stood open-mouthed. Before moving again I quickly looked to see if we had any more passengers. There was nobody else, but the bed was warm and there was a half-empty bottle of whisky lying on it.

Clarke, if it was him, must have woken from his drunken slumbers to find himself cruising down the M1 at 60. His odd craving for old-fashioned clothes apparently extended to his choice of night attire; I could swear he had been wearing a night cap as well as the night shirt.

My little convoy resumed its progress northwards through the dark and no one stopped us or questioned us. People who complain about police interference in this country don't know what they're talking about. I didn't see a single police vehicle on either of my round trips.

Dawn was conveniently breaking when we reached the West Pennine Moors above Bolton. The weather had improved and it was bitterly cold but dry. Two days ago I'd brought my parents an unexpected guest, now I was bringing them some unexpected sleeping accommodation. I couldn't think of anywhere else to park the trailer that would avoid all sorts of questions. Well, I'd be subject to all sorts of questions from my father, but he wouldn't be phoning the fuzz.

In reality his objections were surprisingly few when I told him I wanted to park the trailer on his lawn. He was up, of course, in his dressing gown when I arrived. He must have some kind of internal radar that warns him to get up when I'm in his vicinity. I've never yet caught him in bed.

'Turned gypsy then, have you, David?' he said, taking in the different licence plates on the trailer and van. 'Are the police after you again? You haven't got any New Agers in there, have you? I expect there's an alert out that there's a mass movement of travellers heading for the West Pennines.'

He welcomed the weary Delise into the house and went to get dressed. When he returned he was accompanied by Jay Anderson who didn't seem any the worse for wear. For once he was delighted to see me, slapping my hand and laughing.

'No time for all that,' Paddy said to him gruffly. 'Put your wellingtons on, young man, and help us get this eyesore David's brought under cover.' Jay, in wellingtons?

We unloaded the chintz-covered filing cabinets into the Strachan-Dalgetty van, then towed the trailer a short way down the lane to a semi-derelict barn belonging to a local doctor. Paddy said he wouldn't mind us leaving it there. Walking back down the muddy lane, I couldn't help noticing how well Jay seemed to be getting on with my father. Paddy was bossing him about and he was lapping it up.

Mum was up making tea when we got back and Delise was asleep in an armchair. It saved her from having to make conversation, at least.

'Quite an interesting vehicle, David. American Army surplus by the look of it. Still a lot of life in it. Good chassis on it. Should be quite easy to renovate if you were interested. Does it belong to you?' Paddy was far more interested in the trailer than in my recent adventures.

'He's like a kid with a new toy,' Eileen said as she poured out the tea. 'He'll not rest until you let him play with it.' She sounded sharper than usual; Paddy can be

169

very wearing when he's not got some major rebuilding project in hand. He recently finished yet another extension to the kitchen; if he lives to be two hundred the place will have as many rooms as the Palace of Versailles.

'It belongs to me in the same way that America belongs to the Americans or Australia to the Australians. I took it and the former owner won't be asking for it back,' I said optimistically.

'Fair enough,' the former policeman agreed eagerly, his hawk-like eyes gleaming. 'Right of eminent domain, possession nine tenths of the law.'

Now I had the filing cabinets containing Mary Wood's papers, I had no thought of taking the trailer for keeps but I wasn't too concerned about Clarke's rights. The events of the past few hours began to catch up with me and I hardly had the strength to hold onto the teacup. 'Do what you want with the trailer, Paddy. I was only going to dump it somewhere,' I said. I glanced over at Delise, and saw she was still sound asleep in the armchair, snoring slightly. I only needed Liberty here to make my little family complete, but fortunately the little munchkin was with his mother.

My own mother smiled. 'This is just like when you were little, David. You'd come home exhausted and curl up for a few hours. Stretch out on the settee if you want. Paddy won't disturb you, he'll not be back for hours now.'

It was half twelve when I was reluctantly woken by Delise shaking my arm.

'Wake up, Dave. Your mother's made you an old-fashioned Lancashire hotpot for your dinner. It's your favourite, so she says.' I detected the hint of sarcasm in her voice. Eileen had set the table in her extended kitchen and Jay and Paddy were already in from the barn and Jay's nose was blue from the cold. Paddy's was bright red.

It *was* a favourite meal and never better cooked with masses of red cabbage, and a thick piece of doughy crust. Despite her sneer, Delise tucked in as well as anyone.

'This is what you need to survive in this climate. Ballast, lad,' said Paddy to Jay. 'None of this nonsense about "Soul Food", not that it isn't all right in its place, but you need solid victuals inside you to survive at this altitude.'

'I don't eat much soul food, man. Dumplin's is mi favourite,' Jay replied.

Paddy turned his attention to me. 'Look what we found stuck in a wall cavity. "Cash is the oxygen of the private detective", eh?' he said, handing me a bundle of notes tied up with an elastic band. 'There's at least a £1000 in Irish punts there. I haven't counted it. You can have this lot but if I find any more I'm using it to buy materials. Finders keepers.'

'Jay, I don't think it's a good idea you staying with my father. He's going to corrupt you.'

'Nonsense. I'm trying to persuade the lad to join the police and get a proper training in detective work instead of hanging about with you.'

'Poach my labour force, would you! They'd make him cut his locks off to get the helmet on. You'd never become a ball-head, would you, Jay?'

'I don't know about that, man,' Jay said seriously. 'I'm getting sort of tired 'bout them locks. Skin is in, man! Paddy mi laddy, here, says that a lot of them Dibbles smoke ganja to relax when they's off duty. It don't sound so bad, my man. I might give it a whirl.'

This was a long speech from Jay and I realised that he was serious. The incident in Clarence Road might have had something to do with his change of attitude.

I hadn't said anything to Paddy about the filing cabinets and he knew better than to ask. After the meal I cracked the whip and got everyone moving in the right direction. We could drop the files off at the office and then use the van to move some of my furniture from the Salways' living room to the basement of the Atwood Building.

I didn't manage to make my getaway without the usual little parental lecture from Paddy. He trapped me in a corner of the garage.

'I had a call from Jock Sinclair yesterday,' he said. Sinclair was the most senior serving policeman in the GMP, and still a close friend of Paddy's. He'd been a junior officer on Paddy's squad.

'He wants a meeting with you. Call him on this number.' He handed me a slip of paper. 'I spoke to him about your friend, Jay. He's a fine young man.'

'I don't think you should encourage him to join the police, you know his father's doing life in Barlinnie.'

'So he told me, but Sinclair doesn't think it should be any obstacle as long as Jay keeps his nose clean. He doesn't use his father's name, does he? So you make sure he stays out of trouble.'

'All right, I'll send him back here tonight in the van. He should keep away from home for a few more days.'

I was getting annoyed but there was worse to come. 'Another thing, David. Jock says this evidence about what time you left the Alhambra building on 23rd December is critical?' He looked at me questioningly. I nodded.

'Well, don't count on young Jay as a witness. He's very vague. Can't fix the time you left to within half an hour. A good brief would make mincemeat of him.'

'Paddy, you don't know what you're talking about,' I said.

'Oh yes, I do. I'm talking about you ruining yourself

for your stupid pride. You're only doing this to prove this DCI Jerrold is wrong, aren't you? Listen and get this into your thick head, the Chief Inspector rank is due to be abolished if these blasted so-called reforms go ahead and this Jerrold must be desperate for promotion. Just try and see things from his point of view.'

'Fine, Paddy, I suppose the next thing you'll be telling me is that he's got six kids,' I retorted.

'Four actually, and his wife's an invalid,' he said.

I let him have the last word. He was partly right, as usual. But I wasn't just acting out of pride.

As I drove away in the stolen van on my own, Jay following in the Nissan to safeguard his reputation, I couldn't help smiling at the thought of Paddy and the trailer. He had looked quite at home in it; the old bugger, he'd end up selling clothes pegs yet.

That was the last pleasant thought I had that day.

We cleared my stuff out of the Salways' flat and stowed some bulky items in the garage at Thornleigh Court, then carted the rest across town to the Atwood Building, which would now provide a roof over my head, as well as cheap office accommodation. Then, when I'd sent Jay back across the moors to Paddy in the stolen van, I was ready to phone Sinclair.

I was in no great hurry to answer Sinclair's summons. He was now the Assistant Chief Constable of the GMP, still not in the top chair, but a hell of a lot closer to it than he'd been before. He'd weathered the fall of Chief Constable Benson without any bother, being the only copper in the GMP to glean any credit at all as a lone voice in the wilderness calling for 'up front' policing during the brief Benson regime. He could claim that he hadn't spent all his time sitting on his hands, unlike some.

He hadn't felt the need to show any gratitude to me for my, by no means small, part in his continuing upward progress, but there hadn't been any overt hostility either, so I wasn't complaining. I felt I could survive without him. Dropping his name during the interrogation in Macclesfield hadn't done me much good.

By the time I phoned it was 5 p.m. I called from the car outside the office rather than within earshot of Delise. If I was going to get a bollocking I'd rather she didn't witness my discomfiture. It was one of those very heavy, dark evenings when you feel like going to bed about six o'clock to shut the grim, chilly world out of your thoughts. No such luck for me, I thought self-pityingly.

'Is that you, laddie?' came the familiar, 'refeened', Edinburgh accent, when I finally got through to Sinclair on his private line. 'You took your time, as usual. I was contemplating sending someone out to fetch you in a wee while.'

'Well, I'm phoning now. What is it you want?' I said rudely.

'David, laddie! Is that any way to speak to me? I'm practically your uncle,' he said, exaggerating wildly. 'I only wanted to give you a bit of advice for your own good, but in the circumstances I can hardly invite you round to Chester House.'

I didn't respond.

'I need to speak to you before you get yourself in deeper trouble than you are already.' It was hard to believe, but I thought I detected a very slight pleading note in Sinclair's tone. 'Wait in your car at the Barlow Moor Road end of Burton Road. At exactly eighteen hundred hours, that's six o'clock to you, start driving slowly up Burton Road. You will be contacted. Have you got that, David? And keep this to yourself. I don't want that young lady of yours involved at all. Is that clear?'

I strode back to the Atwood, butting my way through the freezing evening air like a boxer on a training run.

In the office, Delise was taking a leisurely look through the files we'd just acquired.

'Put those away, love. I'll look at them myself later,' I ordered. 'I've got to meet er . . . a friend at er . . . somewhere in Didsbury and I'd better drop you off at your mother's.'

'Fine by me, massa. You've been a real slave driver today. I'm covered in sweat. Tote that sideboard, lift that bed. By the way, you know you can't stop at my place now that Mum's put her foot down.'

'That fact had just about penetrated my dim wits, Delise.' She had bought me a camp bed and sleeping bag so I intended to spend the night back in the office. All my clothes and personal gear were there. I dropped her off and headed for my rendezvous with the law.

I had nothing on my conscience that the Manchester Police could be interested in. There was no way Sinclair could know about events on the M40.

It was all a bit different from a visit to GMP headquarters at Chester House, I thought, as I waited on the corner of Burton Road opposite the mosque, tuned to Radio 4 for the six o'clock time signal.

I set off on the final pip and hadn't gone forty yards before I saw a Rover 600 coming towards me, flashing its lights. It stopped in the middle of the road so I did the same alongside. The rear passenger window of the Rover wound down automatically and there was Sinclair, in person. I looked in my mirror. There was no traffic queuing behind me as yet.

'A bit public for a meeting isn't it, Mr Sinclair?' I asked.

'Not at all, laddie. I find it encourages brevity. Far more private than anywhere else we could go, and even an audio expert such as yourself would find it hard to get much of a recording of what I say over the traffic.' He was right. I had to crane my head out of the window to catch his reply as it was.

'You're in a wee spot of bother again, laddie,' he drawled. 'Just the tiniest wee spot.'

'All that about Gloria Rishton's been sorted . . .' My lie was punctuated by the blare of a horn as an impatient motorist behind showed his disapproval of our conference location. Another one, behind Sinclair's car, joined in. Sinclair's burly driver got out and leaned against the bonnet of the Rover. He blew on his knuckles and turned the collar of his jacket up. The horn blowing stopped.

'I know you had nothing to do with that. Not your style at all, eh? You're far too sensible to leave corpses lying about for people to stumble across, aren't you, David?' He revealed his teeth in a scavenger-like smile. I tried to keep my face completely expressionless. He was looking for reaction. The wattles under his chin were drooping more than ever and his face looked purple in the sodium light of the street lamps. He reminded me more of a sad old turkey left over from Christmas than the most cunning officer in the GMP, but I knew better than to underestimate him.

'No, what concerns me is why you got involved in the first place.'

'Just hold on a minute,' I interrupted angrily.

'You hold on, young David,' he snapped back. 'You might disclaim it but you've got quite a reputation with the force. What your young assistant Jay, who admires you so much, would call "street cred" . . .'

'So that's what you told DCI Jerrold, is it?' I said bitterly.

'I told Jerrold that he was barking up the wrong tree, but, believe me, he'd already heard plenty about you and your "hard man" reputation from others. I told you after your last skirmish with the law that the GMP would appreciate it if you confined your amateur activities to supermarket crime. But have you?'

'Times are hard,' I explained.

'Maybe. But I've heard that someone else is making enquiries about you. One of my officers was offered money for information on you.'

The queue of traffic behind both of us was now growing rapidly and I could hardly wait for his punch line, but knowing Sinclair there had to be one. A deputation of aggrieved drivers, mostly Muslims departing after evening prayers, were advancing on us in a body and Sinclair's driver opened his coat to show them his warrant card, casually revealing the gun in his shoulder holster. They scattered, then began making organised efforts to reverse in both directions.

'Don't look at me like that!' he said, mistaking my sullen expression for defiance. 'You always were too stubborn! Listen laddie! I've every right to be concerned if unknown parties are asking round Manchester as to whether your reputation for violence is genuine. We've enough loonies knocking about without the son of my oldest friend joining them.'

'Sorry, Mr Sinclair,' I muttered, just about managing to give him my best naughty, but repentant schoolboy's grin.

'Well, if this character gets in touch with you I want to be the first to know. And, David, be warned. You're off the Rishton case now. Stay out of it!'

He fixed me for a moment with a fierce stare and I felt a sudden chill that wasn't from the cold air.

The road in front of me was empty and I drove off at high acceleration taking a sharp left at Nell Lane, for the Parkway, and on back into town. I didn't really know where I was going. The Assistant Chief Constable interviewing me from his car in the middle of the road like a drugs baron! I fumed. Pretty high-profile way to conduct an interview if I was supposed to be in disgrace! The more I thought about Sinclair's behaviour, the less I liked it.

The idea of sitting alone in the office with a takeaway meal became even less attractive than it had seemed previously. I worked out that of the last six meals I'd eaten, chips had played a major part in five.

I drove back towards Chorlton and the car seemed to find its own way to Thornleigh Court. I needed a kitchen to do my thinking in. All my best ideas come while I'm working in the kitchen. Damn Jake Gordon for depriving me of my flat.

I sat outside in the car for some time, then went on up to the Salways. They might have arrived back from Ramsgate by now. Finbar let me in. He looked at me rather oddly, I thought.

'Fiona's not noticed anything, so I didn't tell her about you moving your furniture into the flat – least said, soonest mended, eh?' he said in a conspiratorial way. 'She's not in anyway. Gone to some sort of meeting at church. I don't think they could keep the roof on that place without her. Come in and have a drink.'

No sooner was I seated with a whisky glass in my hand, than I realised that I'd made a mistake. There was nothing I could discuss with Finbar. I could see the light of battle in his eyes and he was eager for me to launch him into action, a cruise missile waiting to be fired. But I was baffled, I didn't know who the opposition was or what to do. I looked at him, his blue cigarette smoke curling upwards. He and Fiona were in a race to see which one of them would succeed in smoking them- selves to death first and there was a yellow/brown tidemark of nicotine round the ceiling. I decided that I wouldn't ask for Finbar's help on this one.

I complimented him on his hangover cure, told him that I expected to be back in Thornleigh Court soon, and that I'd left stuff in 'my' garage. He agreed to keep an eye on it. I could see he was surprised and disappointed when I got up and left but I was too tense to make polite conversation. It might have been different if he'd given me a scouring pad and the run of his kitchen, but that's not the sort of thing you can ask.

I drove around aimlessly for some time. I hadn't felt at such a loose end for a long time. There was a brightly lit off-licence on every street corner and I was tempted to go and buy a couple of bottles of Scotch. A drink might settle me, I told myself.

Sinclair had really rattled me. Which no doubt had been his intention. Had pressure been brought to bear on him, I wondered? Was somebody in Macclesfield worried that despite the efforts to discredit my evidence I might still be able to damage the case they'd constructed against Headlam and Rishton with the help of their friends in the press? I was supposed to shut up and accept that my evidence was somehow tainted; that I was the sort of man who could easily lose a couple of hours out of his day.

The last thing I needed now was to start solitary drinking again but the night was dark and I felt very alone. I drove down to the car park at Chorlton Water Park and tried to get my thoughts straight. I looked down at the steep-sided little lake they'd made in the reclamation scheme. The choppy water was being stirred by a stiff breeze, its surface faintly illuminated by a residual glow from distant street lights. I only needed to wade out, put my head under water, fill my lungs and my troubles would be over for ever.

What was happening to me? I must be getting maudlin in my old age. I needed food and bright lights.

Chewing my way through a massive plate of fish, chips, mushy peas with tea and bread and butter at a fish restaurant on the corner of Dene Road I began to feel more human. I supposed it was better to end up looking like the Michelin man than drowning myself. Thousands of Mancunians survived on a continuous diet of chips, so why not me? There was a danger that I would neglect to feed myself properly but the loss of my own beloved kitchen rankled and I resolved to buy myself a microwave oven for the office. I could claim a tax rebate for it under work expenses.

It was a filthy night, rain lashing down in all directions and even the streets of Didsbury, usually thronged with students aimlessly mooching from pub to pub, were deserted. There were spreading pools of water on the road and pavements. I drove back into the centre of town and left the car in a small street at the back of the Atwood Building.

Suppressing a faint tremor of nervousness I let myself in. It was a cheerless place to spend the night but no one else was offering me a bed and I couldn't afford a hotel. The tiny blue safety lights on the stairs gave a spooky feel to the place, and I hurried up to my cubicle in the attic. Sinclair's talk about 'enquiries' had made me jumpy and I looked over my shoulder several times. I felt relieved when I finally reached my landing and entered the office. Here at least was light and warmth.

In my little perch on top of the building I could feel the whole place shaking as gusts of wind hit the giant glass wall that fronted the fabric buyers' rooms. Although the sleeping bag was warm and comfortable sleep wouldn't come. Flashbacks of the events of the last few days kept playing across the back of my eyeballs. I'd been crazy to think of throwing myself into the lake earlier.

10

I must have been shattered when I finally fell asleep because it was after nine when I woke up and Delise was banging on the outer office door. I remembered that I'd left the door locked from the inside. My head was banging in unison with Delise's blows; oversleeping in the cold office had given me a clanging headache. I struggled out of the bag to the door.

Delise flounced past me to her little cubby-hole and I hurriedly grabbed some clothes from the pile where I'd dumped them. I had my full wardrobe to choose from but somehow it didn't seem important any more. I felt grubby, but there was only a tiny sink in the office so I couldn't do much about it, apart from use a lot of after-shave. I peered in the mirror at my pasty-looking features; no zits yet, but I suppressed a shudder at the thought of the saturated fats accumulating in my arteries.

I decided that I might as well look good and hastily grabbed and unpacked my best suit – a heavy worsted woollen three piece in a very dark navy. As I studied myself again in the small mirror I could almost feel the depression which had settled on me yesterday lifting. The main thing on my mind was locating Rishton's and Headlam's solicitor. There must be one by now. Then I needed to get started on those files of Clarke's. The sooner we found whatever documents there were relating to Mary Wood's father, the sooner I could forget about her with a clear conscience.

'Make a cup of coffee will you, Delise?' I asked humbly enough. She looked grumpy but complied. I knew that

182

she was irritated by my loss of home-owning status. I'd been getting the vibes for the last two days and she'd left me to fend for myself last night.

'Delise, if I found a new flat and gave up all hope of getting the old one back, would you think about moving in with me?' I asked diffidently as she washed the cups out. 'You know, it could be a fresh start for both of us. You away from your mum, and me away from the memory of Elenki.' I couldn't see her face but she rocked her head from side to side to indicate that she was considering my proposal. I hoped that's what she meant. It was a somewhat ambiguous signal.

'Not get married then? Just live together?' she asked when she returned with the coffee. I nodded, perhaps a little too vigorously.

'Not a very romantic type are you, Dave? First you offer me marriage and when that's a no-no you come back at me with cohabitation. Most people would do it the other way round. Do you need a cleaning lady? Is that it?' This speech was delivered on a gradually rising note of indignation and all the danger signals were there; flashing eyes, flaring nostrils. I braced myself in case she threw the coffee at me.

'Delise, you know I love you,' I said sincerely, standing with my hands outstretched, looking like a market trader trying to flog a 24-piece pottery set. 'After the other night when your mother was away I thought you wanted me.' I tried to put my arms round her but she pushed me away.

'It's always what's most convenient for you, isn't it, Dave?' she said sarcastically. 'Well, I'm not sure it would work. Whenever I stayed with you at your flat you seemed to spend hours tidying up after me. You made me feel uncomfortable.'

I groaned loudly. 'Give me a chance and I'll turn over

183

a new leaf. I'll live in squalor, anything. God! There are worse obsessions, you know. I have a friend who chews every mouthful of food he eats fourteen times. Eating a meal with him's like waiting for the next Ice Age to start . . . you can see the glaciers forming on the hills.'

'Oh, stop feeling sorry for yourself!' she said, interrupting my tale of woe. 'I don't suppose your friend's married either, is he?' I must have looked baffled because she laughed, suddenly changing her mood in that strange way of hers.

'I'll think about it, Dave,' she said. 'I haven't had any better offers and . . . well I'm getting fed up of living at home.'

She smiled at me and suddenly my headache felt better. I was ready to face whatever the day offered, my internal elastic had snapped back into place.

'Would you phone Jake Gordon on the number he gave you and see if you can get the name of Rishton's solicitor out of him,' I asked her. 'If Gordon himself answers, tell him I'm out on another case and that we just want to close the file on Rishton and Headlam; that we don't want to prejudice any police enquiries. Tell him I decided to follow his advice. Please, Delise, you know you're better on the phone than I am.'

She considered my request in silence and then consented with a curt nod. I hurriedly drained my coffee and prepared to leave.

'Don't you dare get out of that chair,' Delise said. 'What am I supposed to do here all day, and where do you think you're going?'

Desperation led to inspiration . . . as I spotted the two filing cabinets belonging to Clarke that Jay and I had lugged up to the office.

'I want you to go through those cabinets,' I said in a serious tone. 'Clarke was so keen to guard them that
184

there must be something valuable in them, but remember you're looking for something that will satisfy our only current client, Mrs Wood. Anything else you come across is merely incidental, OK?'

I could see that Delise wasn't exactly displeased at the prospect of poring through somebody else's personal papers. But in my line of work I can hardly criticise her for being nosy. She's more of a student than I am, anyway. I prefer to glean information in the highways and byways.

When I hit the streets it was a brilliantly sunny, fresh day. The constant rain and gale-force winds had vanished, there wasn't a cloud in the sky and the air was so clear that the distant Pennine Hills were in sharp focus.

I drove down to Levenshulme to see Barney Beasley, my contact in the road-building trade who'd located Clarke for me, and asked him if he'd heard any rumours at Strachan-Dalgetty about recent events on the southbound carriageway of the M40 and the present whereabouts of Clarke. One of their vans, twin to the one I'd borrowed, was parked outside his house so I guessed he was at home, but when his wife opened the door she took one look at me and slammed it in my face. I rang the bell again. I was puzzled. I was respectably dressed with a green anorak over my dark suit. I didn't look like a Jehovah's Witness or an insurance salesman, so what had Mrs Beasley got to be afraid of?

I banged on the door with my fist and then started shouting 'Barney' at the top of my voice through the letter box. When that didn't produce a response I put my hand on the horn of my car and started honking and then shouting 'Barney Beasley, Barney Beasley' as loudly as I could. Eventually his door opened a crack and a disembodied male arm emerged and beckoned me in. I knew it was Barney because the arm was clad in the sleeve of a faded and stained suit jacket.

'You crazy bugger! What the bloody hell do you think you're doing!' was his mild greeting when I entered his narrow hallway. 'Well, shut that bloody door behind you. You've announced I'm here to the whole neighbourhood so you might as well come in.' He led me into the cramped 'parlour'. A piano and a cluttered three-piece suite took up most of the available space.

'It's all your fault,' he said in a whinging tone of voice. 'I knew I never should have told you anything. Now half the lads are on their way back to Ireland, and the other half are running around like a bunch of headless chickens. Strachan-Dalgetty operations are at a complete standstill throughout the country.'

I put a suitably mystified expression on my face and asked him what he was on about. Beasley studied my honest and guileless features intently for a long moment. He didn't look deceived, but then he knew me well.

'It was you,' he said slowly, 'who told the DSS that Jimmy Clarke was running a false-claimants racket, wasn't it? One day you're asking questions about him and the next he's raided by the heavy mob from the DSS. At least ten of them, there were!'

I breathed an inward sigh of relief. He couldn't have heard about my one-man raid on Clarke's trailer. 'That's too bad. Did they raid his house?' I asked innocently. 'Where does he live? Kilburn, I suppose?'

'I'm saying nothing to you, Cunane,' Barney muttered.

'Look Barney, since when have I worked as a grass for the Government? Do I look like a civil servant?' I asked in a very sincere way. Actually, my surprise was genuine enough. It was a pretty big coincidence.

Then it hit me like a sledge-hammer. There had been no DSS raid on Clarke. What I was hearing was a second-hand account of my own activities, with the numbers of raiders flatteringly inflated to cover up the incompetence of Clarke's mates.

I must have looked startled because I saw the expression of distrust on Barney's long, morose face slowly fade.

'You're a persistent bugger, aren't you?' he said. 'Will you have one?' He pulled out a bottle of Power's whiskey from a cupboard. I did.

'Jimmy Clarke's been running the worst labour racket in this country for years,' he said. 'Half of these poor shites that come over here from Ireland are earning more for him than for themselves. He sends the vans out to pick them up from Cricklewood Broadway, Camden Town or a garage forecourt in Manchester or wherever. They get paid £30 a day cash in hand for a ten-hour shift but Clarke and the site bosses he supplies with labour get a lot more than that.'

'What's wrong with that?' I said, ever the devil's advocate. 'Nobody's forcing them to work.'

'That's where you're wrong. He does force them to work. Most of them are claiming benefit. Clarke supplies them with papers, either to claim the benefit in the first place or to get themselves a job. It's not just the Irish. He has Poles, Bulgarians and Bosnians as well. Clarke's Foreign Legion, they call them. They all know you can't get a job off one of these bloody sub-contractors without the right papers from Clarke. Clarke gets a slice off the top from the employer, a slice off their earnings from the workers and a slice of what they spend.'

'How come?' I asked.

'They get paid with a cheque, but most of them don't have a bank account. They're here under false names anyway. The buggers have no choice but to cash their cheques in a pub at a ten per cent discount, and you

187

know who pockets some of that. It's bloody slave labour! The lads couldn't survive if they weren't getting the dole as well.'

'I don't suppose they pay a penny of tax either,' I said.

Barney looked at me as if I'd gone mad. The pity he apparently felt for his exploited countrymen didn't extend to the taxpayer. He started whistling 'The Rose of Tralee' through clenched teeth. I remembered my father's advice on handling the Irish . . . 'fierce when provoked, gentle when stroked'.

'Why is Clarke allowed to get away with it?' I asked mildly.

'The Government want the bloody roads repaired, don't they?' he said indignantly. 'Do you think they're going to get Englishmen to spread tarmac? They've been turning a blind eye for years, as long as things didn't get too obvious. Clarke kept everything nicely under wraps. Until now that is!'

I decided it was time for a bit of special pleading on my own behalf. 'I was only trying to trace a client's papers through Clarke and came round here to see if you know someone who could ask him politely if he knew of their whereabouts. And by the way, my client is one of your female compatriots.'

'I couldn't care less whether you're working for the Pope, the Tee-Shirt of Ireland or the bloody Sisters of Charity! I didn't want you meddling with Jimmy Clarke. Anyway, he's in hospital in Cork with a broken back, would you believe it?'

My heart sank. So it had been Clarke who'd hunted me down on the M40! And he'd survived the crash with only a broken back! It should have been his neck. He knew exactly who I was and where to find me. But who had it been asleep in the trailer?

Some animation crept into Barney's glum features.

'There's worse! While they were flying him over to Ireland in an air ambulance some bastard stole his bloody trailer with his missus in it! Straight into the trailer park and drove off with it, with herself asleep in the back! Tossed her out in the middle of the motorway like a sack of bad spuds. Poor old Bridie, she got a bad dose of frostbite!'

Was there just a touch of amusement at the Clarkes' plight in Barney's expression? He didn't seem to suspect me of being the author of Mrs Clarke's woes, but how long would it take Clarke himself to put two and two together?

'So you're saying all Clarke's papers have gone, including my client's, if he had them.' The genuine upset I felt at the revelation that Jimmy was still alive gave a ring of authenticity to my words. 'I don't see how all this affects you, Barney,' I continued carefully.

'No, you wouldn't,' he agreed. There was a touch less scepticism in his voice. 'Who do you think saw to it that Clarke collected what was owing to him? Only me, and dozens of other mugs like me, God help us!'

'Everything'll be all right once the dust has settled,' I said reassuringly.

'You're joking me! Do you think the Inland Revenue or the Customs and Excise are going to forget how much tax and VAT they're owed! I don't think there's one of us made a straight tax return in years. Now they've got the information they'll be through our tax returns like a nun searching for nits.'

There was a silence as Barney looked at me.

'I'll tell you if . . . we . . . ever catch the rat that dropped us in it he'll be joining the sopranos next time he sings in the church choir, that's if he's still breathing.

'Now, the wife and I are just packing for a short visit to the "Holy Land". It's a while since we've been back to

189

Kilkenny. If you'd come half an hour later you'd have found me gone,' he said, standing up and showing me to the door.

I drove swiftly away from Levenshulme, following Stockport Road back into the town centre. At least one mystery was solved. I didn't waste any pity on Clarke. He'd been trying to do more than break my bones.

I was driving past the back of Piccadilly Station when the warble of the car phone startled me. It was Jay Anderson, not Delise.

'Boss, you'd better head this way. Something's come up.' As usual, Jay was laconic to a fault.

My heart was in my mouth. Had Paddy blown himself up on some secret cache of explosive hidden in the trailer? My over-active imagination supplied all sorts of possibilities. 'Spit it out Jay! What the hell's happened?' I shouted in exasperation.

'Yo, mon! Liberty turned up here ten minutes ago. Your mother says he's got to go,' he replied.

My sigh of relief must have been audible above the loudspeaker at the station. It was only that pernicious kid! At the next roundabout I changed direction and headed for the Mancunian Way, Stretford and the motorway to Bolton. It was time Jay started earning his wages again. The no-hopers who'd tried to kneecap him had probably forgotten all about him by now.

I waited until I was past the malodorous sewage works and over the Ship Canal at Barton Bridge before phoning Delise. I liked to keep deep breathing to a minimum on that part of the M63.

'I'm finding lots of fascinating material here, Dave, but nothing about your tinker lady yet,' she said.

'Be as quick as you can with it and if you find Mary Wood's stuff we'll dump the rest in front of the DSS offices in town and let them sort it out,' I told her confidently.

'Dave, some of this stuff might be worth a fortune. There's bound to be a reward.'

'We can't touch it. Might incriminate ourselves if they knew how we got hold of it. Just have a quick flick through to see if you can find anything about Wood. Have you got in touch with Gordon yet?'

'You must be joking!' she snorted. 'I've spoken to the great man's secretary's secretary. She'll ring me back if he deigns to speak to us.'

I told her I would spend the afternoon looking for some cheap temporary accommodation while she tried to turn up some more work for the firm. I couldn't face the next few weeks dossing down on the office floor.

When I finally arrived at my parents' cottage Jay and Liberty were waiting for me. Liberty was swinging on the lintel of the kitchen door.

'What's going on?' I asked mildly enough. 'I think you'd better come back to Manchester, Jay. You've been out in the hills too long.'

'I'll have to get back there to return this relative of mine to his mother.' Jay looked as if a lot of his usual bounce had been knocked out of him. I couldn't decide whether this was the result of a stay with my father, which was certainly enough to drain anyone's self-confidence, or whether it was due to the sudden appearance in the Pennines of his long-lost relative.

'What's the story, then?' I asked. I could see he was anxious to get it off his chest.

'I was just beginning to enjoy myself up here when he turns up. Hasn't been home for two days. The silly faggot's been living in a tree house in Hulme,' Jay said angrily. The silly 'faggot' himself gave Jay a sly grin and swung himself in the air again. I studied him carefully.

He was still wearing the leprechaun outfit that I'd first seen him in but it was looking a bit the worse for wear.

'Come on Jay! We both know there are no tree houses in Hulme. There are no trees there for a start.'

At this Liberty swung from the lintel to land at my feet.

'I do have a tree house. It's at the side of the Parkway,' he said indignantly in piping Glaswegian.

'Have you any idea what the temperature was last night? It was well below freezing,' I said sceptically.

'No, it's true, it's true!' he shrilled. The pitch of his voice was so high that it was painful to listen to him. In the hope that he would moderate his voice in a more confined space I led the pair of them out to the car. There was snow on the hills and I gave an involuntary shudder. I needed to get back to Manchester. All this air and space was having a bad effect on me.

Jay pushed the kid into the back seat of the car and turned the rear-view mirror upwards. I wondered what he was doing, then I remembered Liberty's talent.

'We'll drop him off at his mother's and then you can get to work helping Delise. You'll love it, she's in a foul temper,' I told Jay.

'It might not be so easy to get rid of him,' Jay said, speaking with his hand cupped over his mouth. 'His mother's a smack-head and her boyfriend chased Liberty out.'

'This is great! Just what we need. You'll have to sort this out Jay.'

'Yuh, mon. I will. But it ain't so easy. I told you the Social Services don't want to know. He did spend the last two nights in a tree house. I've seen it. It's made of wood and he's covered it with plastic sheeting. He has a candle and a torch and a bed in there. But that's not all ... He's started dealing ... running messages for dealers.'

I looked at Jay in surprise. He fumbled in his pocket and took out a little paper bag. I thought he was offering me a mint, but the bag contained two small rocks, crack crystals. I almost swerved the car off the moorland road. Then I realised that I shouldn't have been surprised. There had obviously been more to the incident I had witnessed between Jay and the youth last week than he had cared to tell me. He might have been trying to protect Liberty.

'Throw that out of the window, right now,' I said and to his credit Jay didn't hesitate at all. He slung the package into a field. God knows what effect it might have on a sheep if consumed, but it was more likely to be dissolved by the rain than eaten.

'Is that the lot?'

Jay nodded and I believed him.

'A lot of these crack dealers are so far gone themselves that they have to involve kids as runners,' he explained, 'making the deliveries, like.'

I was still pondering the implications of all this a few minutes later when the phone rang. It was Delise again. 'Dave, stop whatever you're doing. Gordon's going to phone you in ten minutes.' There was a pause after she hit me with this news. I knew I was supposed to be impressed but all I could think was that this must be my day for unexpected news. First Barney, then Jay and now Gordon.

'He's going to make you an offer,' Delise continued in a reverential voice. 'He wants to talk to you. I know it's going to be something good, Dave. He was so friendly and nice on the phone. He apologised for blowing up last time. Dave, promise me that you'll just listen to what he has to say? It could make all the difference to us.'

'Oh, Delise. I'm *so* flattered. Jake Gordon, the take-over king, is actually sparing me a few moments,' I said sarcastically. 'Do you think he wants to buy Pimpernel Investigations?'

'At least listen to what he has to say,' she said menacingly, then hung up.

Having already been the target of Gordon's unique business methods once, I felt a lot less willing to let bygones be bygones than Delise did, but I had nothing to lose by listening to what he had to say. I pulled to the side of the road and explained to Jay and Liberty that I was expecting an important call. We seemed to have stopped in the Islamic quarter of Bolton. Most of the people on the streets were in Asian dress. There was a McDonald's back up the road where I could have left Jay and Liberty but I decided to stay where I was. Liberty seemed absorbed in the street scene so we waited in silence until the phone rang.

'Cunane, is that you?' Gordon said. 'I need a few minutes of your time. I'll make it worth your while. Your personal assistant tells me you're in Bolton. That couldn't be more convenient. I'm staying in a small hotel on the edge of the moors, the Last Drop Inn. Do you know it?'

'I do, but there's a slight complication, Mr Gordon. I'm with an employee and his young relative at the moment. I'm giving them a lift to Manchester.'

'Don't worry about that. I'm just going to pop over there in the helicopter. Let your man take the car and I'll fly you in. I've got an appointment with Lance Trevose at Alhambra TV in an hour and I can fit you in on the way.'

'Oh, I see,' I said weakly.

'Be with me in twenty minutes,' he said peremptorily, and there was a click as the line went dead.

'You'd better go then, Boss. I'll take the car into Manchester and meet you at Alhambra.' Jay looked as if a lift in a helicopter was an everyday occurrence.

It seemed as if the decision was made for me.

It didn't take long to get to the Last Drop Inn, a large complex with two big car parks. Looking at the hotel restaurant I noticed that I was salivating. A helicopter was parked in the smaller of the two car parks, flanked by two grey Mercedes. As we drove towards the helicopter grey-suited figures began to emerge from the grey cars.

Then I spotted Gordon. That big round genial face was now gazing across at me. He looked a lot bigger, fitter and tougher than I remembered him seated in Trevose's office and seemed to fill the car park by himself. His three attendants hovered around him like pilot fish around a great white shark.

I stopped some way from this scene. I was out of place in my dark suit among this convention of grey men; it looked like a meeting of Mormon bishops, or perhaps representatives for a giant soap company. Only Gordon himself cut a different figure, dressed in a chestnut-coloured leather anorak over a yellow polo-neck sweater and bright tartan trousers.

'Mon, that dude's got no dress sense at all,' whispered Jay next to me.

'He's telling the big guy with the crewcut not to get his gun out,' said Liberty. 'He's saying you don't represent a threat.'

'You want to think twice before going over there, Boss. Look at that mother with the briefcase,' Jay said, referring to the individual mentioned by Liberty.

Gordon waved me over impatiently.

We got out of the car. 'This is cool,' said Jay as we stood by our red Nissan facing the expectant party gathered round the helicopter.

195

'The fella in the leather coat's telling the others to be friendly,' whispered Liberty. However much of a nuisance the kid might be his unusual skills were coming in useful now.

I gave Jay the car keys and told him to keep an eye on Liberty and then walked briskly over to the helicopter.

'Is that your son?' Gordon said, pointing at Liberty. 'Bring him along. He'll enjoy the ride. Something I've always regretted myself, having no children.' I hastily denied parentage, but the damage was done. Although out of earshot, Liberty was already skipping over to join us. 'It's all right, Dad,' he said cheekily when he arrived, 'Mammy won't mind if I have a ride in the helicopter.' There was a grey tidemark round his neck and he obviously hadn't discovered the benefits of deodorants yet. He needed at least an hour in a hot bath.

I could see Gordon calculating as he studied Liberty closely, then looked at me again.

'Oh, it's a long story,' I said, 'and I'm sure you're not going to be interested in it, Mr Gordon.' Let him think what the hell he pleased, I thought. It was none of his business anyway.

Liberty bounded towards the Bell 47 and swung himself in ahead of Gordon and his retainers. Gordon gave an appreciative chuckle. 'That's all right son, you can sit right here next to me,' he said as I reached to pull Liberty back. 'You'll be fine here, and I can talk to your daddy without interruption.'

'Well, where's the pilot going to sit?' I asked.

'I'm the pilot. Did you think I was going to take this crew with me?' said Gordon, pointing to his bodyguards who were already heading for the two Mercedes.

'You're not windy are you, Cunane? We can talk in the hotel if you like but it would be a shame to disappoint the kid,' said Gordon.

196

Liberty turned and gave him a warm smile.

'All right, then,' I said grudgingly. I should probably have got written permission from Liberty's mum and half a dozen social workers, but what the hell? The kid deserved a treat after surviving two nights in a tree house.

'Yes, I've done nearly two hundred hours' flying time,' Gordon boasted. 'What's your name, son?'

'I'm called Liberty,' piped up the Scottish waif. I noted with irritation that he carefully omitted his surname. Gordon passed me a pair of earphones and mike and showed me how to operate it. When he moved to do the same for Liberty I explained that the boy was deaf.

'That's no handicap in one of these, Cunane,' he boomed, turning to the control console as he did so. There was a deafening clatter from the exposed engine, he pulled the lever to his left up and the one to his right forward and we were in the air. I had to admit that his methods of travel were certainly impressive. As we climbed, the country unfolded below us. It was far too noisy to talk even with the headset on, so I concentrated on the scenery.

The snow-covered hills lay around us and then the black ribbons of the M61 and of the M6 further west curled across the landscape as we headed southwestwards, towards Liverpool, the Mersey estuary and the hills of Wales.

'We're taking the scenic route,' Gordon said. The background noise had diminished as the helicopter settled into level flight, just a continuous 'whup, whup, whup' from the rotors. 'You like the black ladies, then, Cunane?' he continued in a conversational tone. I knew he was trying to wind me up, but I still hadn't worked out why.

'I don't like them any more than I like anyone else,

197

or any less,' I said carefully. 'Liberty's mother's white, a Scots girl, if that's what you're referring to. And I already told you the boy's nothing to do with me.'

'Now don't go taking offence,' he answered, patting my arm protectively. 'I know you're an independent type. I've been having a little research done into your background and I must say I'm impressed. You were married to an African medical student, weren't you?'

The last thing I wanted was this plutocrat's sympathy over my personal tragedy, but when I looked at him I realised that sympathy was the last thing on his mind. The smile on his face had a cutting edge, a smile like a hatchet falling on someone's neck.

I felt repelled, but tried not to show it. The last place in the world to quarrel with a character like Gordon is in a helicopter a thousand feet above the Mersey Valley with him at the controls.

'What do you think of all this then?' he asked, waving his arm proprietorially over the scene below.

As his wave took in most of the North West of England and a substantial chunk of Wales, I was at a loss for an answer.

Gordon put both his hands up to his face and gave his eyebrows a twist. The effect was startling, it was as if he was trying to fine tune his brain. 'They could hold the Olympic Games in Manchester, or Liverpool, every year from now until Doomsday and still not regenerate this area but I know how to. I'm going to give you a little tour.' There was a mad gleam in his eye, though I suppose some might have said it was inspiration. He peeled off his leather coat and unfastened his seat belt so he could accompany his words with gestures. I liked the coat; it was wasted on him.

'What could we export from round here that would fit an Atlantic and world economy just as we used to in
198

the old days of the textile trade?' he demanded. I stared ahead not knowing what I was expected to say.

'It's staring you in the face,' he prompted. In front of us lay Liverpool. I could see the massive derelict docks along the Mersey, the two cathedrals, even the sun gleaming on the gilded birds on top of the Liver Building. Liverpool . . . Beatles . . . entertainment, I thought. 'You mean we should export entertainment,' I began hesitantly.

He slapped his hand down on my leg, hard.

'There, I knew I was right about you. And if you can spot it others will! Britannia no longer rules the waves but I intend to see that she rules the airwaves! That's why it's so urgent that I complete my business in Manchester without a hitch.' There was a pause in his conversation while he checked the compass. 'I'm going to fly on into the Bay. I like to see what's happening to my tankers,' he continued.

'I want to make Alhambra TV the hub of a powerful entertainment media company. I've already got some of the other components lined up, but now I need the studios and expertise to start turning out product,' he said excitedly, his eyes feverish. I nodded encouragingly but he must have detected the doubts I was trying to hide.

'I'm not talking about "Slatheredge Pit" here, son! I'm talking about tailormade soaps and features and films for a worldwide English-speaking audience. What do you think the biggest export of the United States is these days? Entertainment, that's what! And there's a limitless worldwide demand for more. There are over a thousand million people for whom English is the first or second language and I'm talking about British English, not American, mind you.'

I could see that he was quite moved; he seemed carried

away by the grandeur of his vision and lapsed into silence for a while. When we were over Runcorn, at the point where the Mersey widened into an estuary, he directed my attention below. There, inside a huge rectangular compound, was the word GORDON written in yellow letters across the tarmac of a landing pad. He really had made his mark on the region.

The helicopter swept on over the Wirral, passing the vast oil refineries along the south bank of the Mersey, and on towards the Point of Ayr and Liverpool Bay. Gordon lost interest in me. He got out a pair of field glasses, from under his seat, then turned to Liberty. 'Here, son. Take hold of the cyclic stick,' he said, guiding Liberty's eager hand onto the vertical control between the two central pedals that I had guessed was the joystick. 'Hold her steady,' he ordered. There was a stomach-churning lurch forward when he took his hand off the cyclic, but Liberty quickly restored equilibrium. I should have remembered that he had probably clocked up considerably more than two hundred hours at the joystick of his computer. He held the helicopter in level flight, with an expression of intense, rapt concentration on his eager little face.

'These things don't run to an autopilot,' Gordon confided, scanning the sea with his binoculars.

Bobbing about in the cold grey waters of the Irish Sea there were several supertankers. They didn't mean anything to me until I remembered what Ted Blake had said about the foundation of Gordon's wealth. The ships seemed to be streaked with rust but I supposed that was normal. They weren't going anywhere, they were anchored off the Welsh coast.

Gordon studied each ship intently and when he was satisfied he took the cyclic from Liberty and we turned back, following the course of the Mersey towards Manchester.

Gordon of Manchester, I thought, or was he the Mad Mahdi? Either way, he had the ambitions of an empire builder. Liberty was chattering away in his high-pitched squeak and Gordon was explaining the controls to him.

Suddenly he swung his attention back to me. 'In twenty years this whole area could be as prosperous as Southern California. That's where you come in. I think you could fit into my plans very well.' He turned that fierce smile on me again and I felt a tingle of fear up and down my spine.

'I'm offering you a choice, Cunane.'

'Why me?' I asked.

'I liked the way you stood up to Lancelot Trevose, a sickening little ponce with the soul of a shopkeeper. Would you like to take his place? I'm going to need a number-two man up here.'

'I don't think I'm ready to don a grey suit yet, Mr Gordon.' I wasn't aware I'd stood up to Trevose, but I let that pass.

'Nor would I want you to. Lackeys are ten a penny, I need tough-minded individuals who will spark up my own creativity, not a flunkey. I'd like you on my team.' I looked at his face. He was studying the terrain below us. He obviously didn't know that I'd rumbled his sly trick with the Polar Building Society.

'There's just the business of Rishton and Kath Headlam,' I muttered.

'You think I'm trying to nobble you. Well, I'm not. It was Trevose who was putting the pressure on, he can't stand Rishton. But I've done the decent thing and appointed a top-flight solicitor to look after Rishton and what's her name. That's the least Alhambra could do for them. You were quite right about that. You must believe that I'm not putting the heat on you. I don't operate like that.'

If I hadn't seen that memo in Susan Attleigh's office I might almost have believed him. He was a convincing liar.

'Geoff Bartle of Bartle, Bartle and Grimshaw is acting for them and I'll have a word with him. I'm sure he'll be happy to hear your side of the story.' Gordon glanced up from his piloting, and gave me a warm smile. 'That all right then, Cunane?' he asked.

I gave a nod that he chose to interpret as agreement.

'I could start you off at somewhere around sixty K, plus double that in incentive bonuses, not to mention preferential stock options.'

I was momentarily stunned into silence by his offer and while I was collecting my thoughts Gordon pointed out a few local landmarks to Liberty. I looked out over the ravaged landscape below me: crumbling warehouses and derelict factories lined the wharf area where the two canals and rivers Irwell and Medlock ran into one another. Not much future there. I could do a lot with sixty K.

The pitch of the rotors changed as we descended towards Central Manchester and I studied Gordon's profile as he concentrated on landing the helicopter, trying to glean some clue as to his motives. I told myself that Jake Gordon was interested in one thing, and one thing only, the advancement of Jake Gordon's empire.

I knew without bothering to ask what Delise would say about his proposal.

Suddenly, we were over the Alhambra building and the heli-pad on the roof came rushing up at us. We landed with a hefty, spine jarring jolt and I saw Gordon's features crease into a frown but he quickly rearranged his face into a happy smile and gave us the thumbs-up sign with both hands.

'Heavy one there, Cunane. Rate of descent indicator doesn't seem to be working properly,' he said cheerily.

'Thanks for the ride anyway,' I said, 'it's been a unique experience.' I was grateful. The landing had jolted my brain back into gear.

'Well, have you thought it over?' Gordon asked me.

'Yes, certainly, I'll be happy to see Geoff Bartle and give him any help I can,' I replied quickly. I didn't say in so many words that I'd be working for him, but he took it that I was complying with his wishes.

'Great! I knew you'd see sense,' he said putting his arm round my shoulder as we stepped off the helicopter. 'Consider yourself on the payroll, Cunane. When you've seen Bartle, I'll give you another mission. There are some people here in Manchester that I need checking out. What do you know about this Assistant Chief Constable Sinclair? Fancies himself as another one of these high-profile Manchester coppers, doesn't he? You dig up something juicy about him and we'll see he features in the *Sun*, the *Mirror* and the *News of the World*. I need to know about anyone else round here who might prove obstructive to our plans. I've no time to waste waiting for things to fall into place by themselves.'

'About my flat,' I interrupted.

'What about your flat?' he said sharply. 'I don't provide accommodation for my employees. Sort something out for yourself.'

'But you know, the Polar Building Society?' I persisted.

'If there's some sort of problem with finance I'm sure it'll be sorted out in the next few days when news of your new status gets around.'

In other words I'd get my flat back when he was sure I was going to comply with his wishes. My train of thought was interrupted as the tall, lanky figure of Lancelot Trevose, clad in one of the ubiquitous grey suits, appeared. His face, when he saw me with Gordon, was comical; his expression changed from an ingratiating smile, to a fierce scowl, and then back to a pleasant smile, as he struggled to take the new dispensation on board. The Adam's apple was doing a war dance.

Liberty skipped round from the back of the helicopter and saved him from embarrassment by saying to Gordon, 'How much would you give me for minding your heelicopter for you, Mr Gordon?' in his most shrill Glaswegian. Gordon laughed, took out his wallet and flourished a £20 note, then changed his mind, put it back and extracted a fiver.

'You take care of your daddy, son,' he said to Liberty, stressing the last two words. 'I've got lots of men to look after my helicopter for me.' As Liberty pocketed his windfall Gordon turned to me and said, 'Smart boy of yours, that. You want to take better care of him. He knows where the main chance lies. You could learn a lesson from him, Cunane.'

'He's not my son, I've already . . .'

He cut me short with an imperious wave. 'You don't need to be embarrassed. Wish I'd had a few brats myself. We're all men of the world here, aren't we Lance? Mr Cunane and I have reached an understanding, so that's one more little problem sorted.' Trevose himself didn't look as if he could have mustered the energy to father a frozen chicken. The stuffing had been well and truly knocked out of him. His face was the same steel-grey colour as his suit.

11

Jay was waiting for us when we got out of the Alhambra
building. Our air trip had taken twenty minutes longer
than his road journey.

'You survived then, Boss?' he asked cheerily as we got
in the car.

'Yes, but I'm brassed off at you and this young man,'
I said. 'Do you know that he encouraged Gordon to
think that I was his father? It's time to call a halt to all
this crap. I want you to drive us round to his mother's
place.'

There was a silence that lasted for several minutes.
Liberty had been able to follow what I had said because
I was facing him. The corners of his mouth drooped
slightly and he began counting on his fingers. 'She'll be
up and he'll be out somewhere,' he muttered. I took this
to refer to his mother and her boyfriend.

'Come on then, Jay. What are you waiting for?' Jay
licked his lips nervously and set off. However we didn't
get far. Liberty insisted that we stop at a McDonald's and
I found myself once again consuming a Big Mac and fries.
It made me all the more determined to sort Liberty's
problems out. He was ruining my digestion. When we
were once more on the move Jay turned off into the
Brunswick district. This estate is a mixture of older
'system built' and new housing sandwiched between the
University and Ardwick Green. Liberty's mum didn't live
in one of the new houses but in a concrete box facing
the heavily barricaded health centre, which was appropriately located in the middle of the small estate. Living

205

in one of these damp chicken coops must do nothing for anybody's health. At least with a cardboard box you get fresh air. This particular block looked like something a child might have put together with Lego except that it lacked all the brightness and colour of Lego. There was damp leaking out of all the concrete joints and the wood-work infill looked rotten.

Jay stayed in the car – this wasn't the sort of district where you would leave a car unattended for long – and I walked with Liberty along the raised pavement outside the row of houses to the end segment occupied by his mother.

Liberty banged on the door with the flat of his hand and eventually it was opened by a scrawny-looking white woman of indeterminate age. I could see that she was a smack-head. She was thin, her skin was almost transparent, revealing the blue tracery of veins and arter-ies running up her puncture-marked arms. Her blue eyes were very prominent, almost thyroidal and a faint bruise on the edge of her scalp extended under her thin mousy-coloured hair.

She looked from me to Liberty and then back again.

'Are you from Social Services, then? About time you brought the little bugger back! Where's he been? I phoned your office at nine o'clock this morning to report him missing.' She spoke with the same accent as her son. I raised my eyebrows fractionally. It was hard to believe she'd been awake as early as 9 a.m. She still had sleep in her eyes.

Apparently she hadn't missed Liberty for the two days he'd spent in the tree house.

He made a move to push past her and when I gave no sign of wanting to leave she reluctantly spoke to me again. 'You'd better come in then,' she said. She was wearing a pink short-sleeved dressing gown over her
206

slip, and bedroom slippers but I didn't think my morals were in any danger as I looked at her bony ankles and skinny legs.

There was no sign of loverboy. He was no doubt engaged in larcenous activity to raise the wind for the next fix.

The living room was very hot, oppressively so, and surprisingly well furnished. Perhaps Mrs Walker had managed to retain some mementos from Liberty's father's life of crime. There was a large television and video recorder in one corner and an Amstrad PC on a table in the other. I looked with interest for a photo of Liberty's father but there were no family photos of any description. My hostess watched me scrutinising the contents of her living room. 'All bought and paid for! Cash on the nail. I can show you receipts.'

I cleared my throat. I hardly knew where to begin.

'Well what's your name? Is the regular social worker off sick then?' Mrs Walker asked.

'I'm not from Social Services . . .' I began.

'I knew it! He's in trouble with the Polis!'

'No, you've got the wrong idea. I'm Liberty's half brother's boss and I've come to return Liberty to you and to ask you to keep him away from Jay.' As soon as I started talking, Liberty himself seemed to lose interest in what was going on. He must have been frightened that I was going to grass on him for possession of crack but now he knew I was only going to have a moan at his mother, something he must have witnessed a thousand times before. He switched on the television and then the computer. His mother's face had lost the appearance of mild concern and annoyance she'd first shown. She now looked totally imperturbable.

'Well, what are you doing with him, then?' she

demanded, drawing the front of her dressing gown together and folding her skinny arms across her chest.

I explained that Liberty kept turning up where Jay was working and that he might be in danger, but I could see that I should have saved my breath to cool my porridge. All this woman thought about was her next fix. I retreated to the door.

'I can't keep the little bugger chained up to suit you, you know. He climbed out of his bedroom window and down the drainpipe. Social Services should look after him or give me more money to feed him. I've begged them to take him into a residential unit but they say there's a waiting list and he's not an urgent case,' she said in aggrieved tones. 'Phil can't stand him. They keep fighting over whose turn it is on the computer.'

'Yes, well, I'm sure you know best,' I lied, 'but if you could just try to keep him away from Jay and stop him wandering the streets on his own. Perhaps Jay could see him at the weekends.' I hurried out of the flat and towards the car before she managed to palm Liberty off on us again and she stood watching us as Jay turned the car round.

'I could have told you it wouldn't do any good, Boss,' Jay said irritatingly. 'She doesn't want to know, does Sheena. That's why my mum won't have him in the house. Once she finds somewhere to dump him we think she'll be off for keeps. It's real sad, man.'

'Your mother's got the right idea, Jay. You want to keep well away from him. He'll get you into all sorts of trouble if the police pick him up with you and he's got stuff on him. They'll say you were dealing and you can kiss any hopes of a career with the boys in blue goodbye.'

'Yeah, right on Boss. But it's a bit hard, isn't it? He's only just turned ten and he is my half brother.'

I had nothing more to say on the matter and I told

Jay to take us back to the office. When we got into town we had to cruise around looking for a parking space and finally left the car on a meter outside a gay bar in Canal Street. I felt uncomfortable walking along with Jay to the office, but from the angry glances he kept giving me I don't think anyone could have formed the wrong impression.

To make conversation I asked him who Phil was.

'He's the live-in boyfriend, Boss. He's always beating her up. Still he's an improvement on the last boyfriend.'

'How do you work that out?' I asked.

'The bloke before Phil put Liberty in hospital. Hit him on the head with a hammer. That's why Sheena moved down here.'

We walked on in silence. I sympathised but what could I do about it? There was a damp chilling rain falling on everything and the sky was purplish grey. I could feel the depression which I thought I'd shaken off this morning returning. Hell, the kid wasn't my problem!

When we finally reached the headquarters of Pimpernel Investigations my assistant and partner Delise Delaney received me with open arms. She was on Cloud Nine. Before I could ask her what had caused such rapture she told me. 'Mr Gordon's fixed you an appointment to see Rishton and Headlam's solicitor, Geoff Bartle. He'll meet you at 4.30 in the foyer of the Holiday Inn-Crowne Plaza.'

'You mean the Midland Hotel, I suppose,' I said grumpily. The change of name from Midland to Holiday Inn-Crowne Plaza was still resented by some in Manchester.

'Same place you took me the other night! What's got into you? We've got the best chance in years to take the firm into the big time and you've got a face on you like a wet weekend in Wigan!'

'You're right. I'm sorry,' I said curtly. 'Who is this

Bartle anyway and what's wrong with his office, or hasn't he got one?'

'I'll speak to you when you've finished your sulk,' Delise replied. She went out of my office and shut the door behind her. A moment later, she was back. 'If you really want to change the subject,' she said, 'these files are dynamite. They must be worth an absolute fortune to the DSS. This Clarke must have been blackmailing, or at least collecting a percentage from, hundreds of men. He has a complete record of their original identities, false names, details of their claims. Everything's photocopied and filed. He supplied them with their false passports and birth certificates. And it's not just the Irish, there were Polish names in there as well.'

'Delise, we're supposed to be finding out about Mary Wood's grandparents. That's what we've been paid to do,' I said sarcastically.

'Let me just see if I can work out some way in which we can claim the reward. If it comes off we'll be able to do a lot better than a two-bedroomed flat in Didsbury,' she wheedled. She could be very persuasive at times.

'All right, Delise. You've convinced me,' I said, 'but don't do anything yet. We've enough happening at the moment with Rishton and Headlam, Mary Wood and Jake Gordon without taking on the DSS and the Chancellor of the Exchequer as clients.'

'Oh, Rishton and Headlam! I told you to forget those pathetic losers,' she snapped.

'I will, Delise. Just as soon as I've seen this solicitor. Then I can do whatever you want with a clear conscience. How about coming for a drive round the flat agencies with me? We can leave Jay to mind the store.'

After warning Jay to put his half brother in a taxi and send him straight back home if he turned up we set off into Didsbury and parked the car opposite the library
210

while we checked out the estate and flat agencies. We collected several promising addresses and even managed to take a look at one of them in a converted Victorian house near the synagogue on Old Landsdowne Road. I didn't fancy it. There was no parking space and the road was so narrow that you would never be able to guarantee getting in and out of the place. I needed somewhere with space, somewhere that gave me access to the Mersey Valley for running and cycling and I was busy explaining all this to Delise while we waited at the end of the street trying to turn right into a continuous stream of traffic when a familiar green Mitsubishi Shogun drove past. It was definitely Ted Blake's new car but he wasn't driving it. But the youth driving looked familiar and I felt the hairs prickling on the back of my neck.

Such coincidences usually only happen in fiction, not in real life. But here was such a one. Ted Blake's car. His pride and joy, a personalised off-road vehicle which would never see mud, being driven off by Declan the tinker car thief. Without hesitation I turned out into the road, pushed into the traffic and was soon within three cars of the stolen off-roader.

'Dave, are you trying to kill us both! We're not in that much of a hurry!' shrieked Delise.

'Look at that Mitsubishi Shogun up in front. Who do you think it belongs to?' I asked her.

'It looks like Ted's, but that's not him driving it,' she confirmed.

'I know that, Delise. It's a couple of those travellers from Salford.'

She gave a shriek of horror and then turned to me. 'Oh no you don't, Dave Cunane! I can read you like a book. You think you're going to drag them out of that car into the street, don't you? Well, forget it. You've got yourself in quite enough trouble chasing missing cars and tinkers. We'll let the experts handle it.'

She picked up the car phone and dialled.

'Yes, I am sure it's Mr Blake's car,' she explained after giving the details.

'You know Ted Blake . . . he has a show called "Bang to Rights" on Alhambra TV. That's right . . . the car's being driven by two youths . . . he has no children . . . I should know, I'm a friend of his . . . What do you mean, it might not be his! . . . His name is painted on the door!'

We heard sirens start up in front of us and behind us before Delise even had a chance to replace the phone in its cradle. The Shogun was only two cars in front in the slow-moving stream and I was able to see Declan and his mate stiffen in their seats. Unluckily for them, they'd chosen to pull their stroke near one of the busiest and most policed intersections in the area. A police Range Rover whizzed past us on the inside and a panda-car converged from the front. That was enough for the twoc-cers. They were off out of the massive vehicle and darting across the six lanes of traffic towards Chorlton, but not before Declan had clocked first Delise, with the car phone in her hand and then me, seated beside her.

I looked across the wide road in the direction they were headed. On the other side of the road, across from the cemetery, I saw an overgrown football field. I must have passed it a dozen times a day without looking. I knew it had been bought up for property development some time ago but there had been an outcry and the deal had fallen through.

There was development on it now though. Even through the heavy drizzle and gathering dusk I could see the shapes of trailers. The travelling people had made the abandoned field their own. The police blocked the traffic at the lights and retrieved Ted's car but they were far too slow to pursue the lads.

I felt uneasy. Declan had certainly had a good look at my face.

We drove on into town, through Moss Side and Hulme, past the new British Council headquarters and into the underground car park at the G-Mex Centre.

When I got out Delise came round and started brushing down my suit with her hand.

'You may be a hooligan, but you don't have to look like one, David Cunane,' she said in an exasperated way, like a mother with a small child.

We hurried up the steps to the Holiday Inn-Crowne Plaza as Manchester's most historic hotel, once simply known as the Midland, had been wordily renamed.

I was eager to meet this solicitor, Bartle. Remembering that my first efforts to tell the whole truth and nothing but the truth, had resulted in a fourteen-hour grilling and bash on the head from the Cheshire Police, and that my second attempt had ended in me being thrown head first out of the Alhambra Studios I could only hope that this was going to be third time lucky.

It was Delise who spotted the solicitor sitting on his own in the coffee lounge. He seemed to be on the point of making a rapid retreat when we introduced ourselves, but agreed that he was Geoff Bartle when I pressed him.

He was a tall, well-dressed man in his early forties, wearing a dark suit, a Manchester Grammar School tie, well-polished shoes and an expensive suntan that hadn't come out of a bottle or off a sunbed. He had the weather-beaten, but fit, look of a skier and I could imagine the winter sunshine of Gstaad, or St Moritz, gleaming down on his well-combed blond hair. Looking at him, I was glad that I was in my best suit, and that for once my clothing had survived the daily toll of detection duties more or less intact. I surreptitiously polished my shoes against the upholstered side of the chair.

We exchanged small talk for a few minutes while coffee and sandwiches were served and then, over the coffee, I told him my story – that in my opinion Rishton and Headlam hadn't had the necessary time to get themselves to Prestbury to kill Gloria. He appeared totally unimpressed, a faint smile played across his sleek features and suddenly I got a strong feeling I was being fobbed off. I began to get annoyed.

After our helicopter ride Gordon had said that he would be delighted if I told my story to the solicitor Alhambra TV had selected to represent Rishton and Headlam. Uncut, unedited, word for word. He hadn't wanted me to retract or alter a detail. No wonder! The solicitor in question was a total wanker!

'Mr Bartle,' Delise said, coming to my rescue before I turned nasty, 'Dave's very concerned that Mr Rishton and Ms Headlam are being tried in the press before the case even comes to court.' As she spoke, Delise took out a folded piece of newspaper. It was the front page of the *Banner* from last week. 'SOAP LOVE PAIR IN MURDER CLAIM' read the headline. 'You may not have seen this if you were away,' Delise said politely. I wasn't aware that Delise had gone to the trouble to save the paper. She must have been taking more notice of my rantings about the raw deal Rishton and Headlam were getting than I'd thought.

Bartle frowned and pushed the paper away from him with his extended little finger. I could see that he was considering the headline. It took most people a couple of goes to work out what a *Banner* headline meant.

'This isn't germane to the issue,' he said finally. 'We know that they'll get an absolutely fair trial. My job is
214

to brief leading counsel and prepare the papers in the case.' He took a bite out of his sticky bun.

'Well, are you checking out all the evidence?' I asked, trying to keep my voice even.

He chewed his way through the mouthful of bun before replying carefully. 'Surely the police do all that. The CPS would never have allowed the charges to go through if they weren't satisfied that there was a case to answer. If counsel wants anything investigated before the trial, he will request it and we will arrange it.'

I began to wonder in which legal backwater Trevose had discovered this guy; perhaps his choice had been a deliberate one. His condescending manner was getting to me. 'Look, I don't want to be offensive, Mr Bartle, but surely it's well known that solicitors have to take a rather robust line with the police in cases like this. It's not been unheard of for them to fail to disclose some piece of evidence which might be vital for the defence case. You need to go through their pre-trial disclosure material with a microscope looking for inconsistencies.'

'I believe you were questioned extensively yourself, Cunane, yet the evidence you offer me is rather jejune,' he replied, hitting me with the dictionary.

I was obviously banging my head against a brick wall. Almost without exception, everybody I'd spoken to believed that Headlam and Rishton stood justly accused and their 'defence solicitor', Bartle, was no exception. The fact that his clients couldn't possibly have been present at the time they were supposedly killing Gloria Rishton seemed to be neither here nor there. Conceivably, he was taking his instructions from the people who were paying him but at this point, I was ready to rip the shirt off his back and carve the numbers 5.40 on his chest with a table knife. My partner stepped in.

'That's what Dave means, Mr Bartle. The police trawl

around for all kinds of evidence in cases like this where they're relying on circumstantial evidence. They put pressure on . . .'

'Miss "Whatever your name is", I'm not used to being told my business by some jumped-up secretary,' Bartle interjected.

Delise looked dangerous. 'I didn't do five years at university to be told I'm a jumped-up secretary. Just who do you think you are?' She stood up, ready to go for him. This time it was my turn to calm her down. I pulled her back into her seat.

While Delise glared at him, I attempted sweet reason and blackmail. 'Mr Gordon assured me that you would cooperate fully, Mr Bartle, and that everything was being done that could be done,' I said mildly.

'Are you referring to *the* Mr Gordon, Jake Gordon?' Bartle asked, his sticky bun forgotten.

'The very same. I was speaking to him about the case only this morning. In fact I understood it was through his good offices that this meeting was arranged.'

'Yes, I see. Well, my clerk took down the details. I was under the impression that Lance Trevose had requested that I fit you in.' Bartle was actually smiling now – dazzlingly, like the sun's rays bouncing off an Alpine glacier. 'If you think there's anything more I should be doing . . . I didn't mean to sound churlish, Miss . . . er . . .' Delise was still glaring at him. She wasn't about to let him wriggle off the hook just because he gave her a glimpse of his orthodontist's handiwork, but I needed his cooperation now that he seemed to be more amenable. There had obviously been some crossing of the wires between Trevose and Gordon over just how cooperative this solicitor was going to be.

'I was wondering if you could arrange a visit to Simon or Kath in their remand prisons for me.'

Puzzlement clouded Bartle's smooth features. 'Do you think that's necessary?

'I wasn't intending to go in normal visiting hours. I want to go as part of their defence team.' I could see Delise's expression from the corner of my eye. I ploughed on regardless. 'Mr Gordon was most anxious that he, and especially Mr Trevose of course, should not be seen to be obstructing the case for Mr Rishton and Ms Headlam in any way. You see one possible interpretation of all this might be that Alhambra have engaged an unsympathetic solicitor ... Someone who is unfamiliar with criminal practice ... Someone who'll make a mess of their defence, deliberately, thus ensuring Mr Rishton's departure from the corporate scene,' I asserted recklessly. I wasn't sure what he would want said, but I didn't care. This was the one chance I had to clear my own reputation, and I was going to make the most of it.

'Oh, I do take your point, Mr Cunane. I hadn't looked at it from that angle. We wouldn't want it to be said that Bartle, Bartle and Grimshaw had left any stone unturned. But I think you've been watching too many American detective shows on TV. We couldn't employ you on the "defence team" as you put it. Your "crucial" evidence would be ruled inadmissible if it came out that we'd paid you or were about to pay you, and I should very likely find myself being "struck off" by the Law Society.'

He joined his hands, as if in prayer, and seemed to be admiring his own perfectly trimmed fingernails. The precise way in which he had dashed my hopes impressed me. 'Tell me, Mr Cunane,' he went on, 'why are you so keen to exonerate Mr Rishton? After all, you hardly know him.'

'It's like this, Geoff. You're worried about being struck off. So am I, in a way. A private investigator states he was with two clients at 5.40 p.m. The police say he can't have been. The clients weren't there. The investigator's lying, or drunk, or suffering from Alzheimer's or whatever. Would you be likely to employ that investigator if you'd heard that?' I asked.

'I can see your point,' he said judiciously.

'Besides which, I know I'm right. The police have raked up two witnesses to buttress their phoney case and have primed the tabloid press as Delise has already shown you. The witnesses must be mistaken and, although I can't say that Kath and Simon had nothing to do with the murder, I do know for certain that they couldn't have done it in the way, or at the time, the police claim.'

'I can see that you have a strong personal interest in the case,' he murmured. 'Here's what I propose. I'll nominate Miss Delaney here as a legal executive for my firm, acting in an unpaid capacity. She can visit my clients and you can go with her to hold her bag or whatever.'

I breathed a sigh of relief.

Bartle extracted a portable phone from his briefcase and made the arrangements right away. Speaking to Delise he said, 'You'll have letters of authorisation delivered to you by courier. Meanwhile I can phone the authorities at Styal Prison and alert them to the fact that you will be coming to visit Ms Headlam. Mr Rishton's more of a problem. They've tucked him away at Haverigg Prison up in Cumbria, but I should think you'll be able to see him tomorrow.'

The expression on Delise's face was far from comical and I could see that I was in for bother. She'd gone along with this meeting in the expectation that I would just pass on my evidence and then go.

There was genuine class in the way Bartle concluded his phone call, got up and accompanied us out of the hotel. He didn't look like a man who'd just had his arm twisted. Before we parted he assured me that he would spend the evening checking the evidence on timings which was so vital to the case.

No sooner had he left us than Delise bared her claws.

'Dave, you said you were dropping all connection with Rishton and Headlam and now here we are, with me acting for their lawyer.'

'If you hadn't been so willing to blab to the police about the diary they wouldn't *be* in prison now,' I blurted out angrily.

'We're back to that, are we? You won't let it drop, will you? I suppose you'd prefer to be in jail charged with the murder in place of your precious friends? Because that's where you would be if it wasn't for me.' She was shouting as we descended on the long escalator into the caverns under the G-Mex and a couple going up turned to stare when she said murder.

When we reached the cars I realised that I hadn't phoned Ted Blake about his tanklike vehicle. I got through to him as we were driving along Deansgate. He wasn't even aware that the car had gone missing.

As we drove along Chester Road I told Delise that we were going straight out to Styal Prison. She set her lips tightly.

'I suppose I'm included whether I like it or not,' she said at last.

'Don't be like that, I've got to clear my name, Delise.'

'Don't give me that crap. I know exactly why you're doing this. You can't stand the thought that this policeman Jerrold may be right and you wrong! All that about your precious reputation was rubbish!'

They say the cruellest cuts are inflicted by those closest to us. We drove on in silence. Styal Prison lay at the end of a winding road past the National Trust centre at Styal

Mill. The prison made a big contrast with Strangeways, the male prison in Manchester. More like a fairly up-market student hall of residence, with only the high wire fence and entrance lodge indicating its real purpose, the prisoners are housed in separate accommodation blocks.

It took some time and a good deal of checking before we were allowed in but eventually we were ushered into an interview room on the ground floor of the nearest accommodation block. Delise was looking nervous, it was her first time behind the wire.

Kath Headlam was ushered in by an officer who left us on our own. An attempt had been made to humanise the interview room and it had a low table, comfortable chairs, even a couple of paintings on the wall, but it was a far cry from the Alhambra building. Headlam seemed to be holding her own. The wrap-around smile was still there but it obviously cost her an effort to wear it.

She was wearing her own clothes, an expensive-looking rose-coloured sweat top over a matching t-shirt with dark-brown jogging pants and dark trainers, and a whiff of expensive perfume followed her into the room. She must be going down a treat with all the bull dykes and prostitutes in here, I thought.

'Quite a change from our last meeting, Mr Cunane,' she said, sitting down and lighting a cigarette. There was already a stale smell of tobacco in the room and I noticed the many cigarette burns on the carpet and chairs for the first time. 'I was amazed to be told that you were now working as part of my legal defence.'

'Ms Headlam, I spent two days having my head banged against walls by the Cheshire CID after our last meeting. They wanted me to confess that you'd hired me to kill Gloria Rishton.'

She exhaled her smoke. I could see that she wasn't too interested in my troubles. 'How awful for you,' she

220

said quietly. 'I only agreed to see you because you can't possibly do a worse job defending me than that idiot Geoff Bartle.' She put her head down suddenly and seemed to be on the point of tears, but then pulled herself together. 'I see you've brought your partner with you. How are you, Ms Delaney? You're looking a lot better than I feel.'

'You can change your lawyer if you want to,' I said.

'What's the point? This whole business is so absurd that it's only a matter of time before they let us go,' Kath said dismissively.

Delise looked at me and raised her eyebrows. All at once tears began streaming down Kath's cheeks. Delise passed her a packet of tissues and she briskly mopped up her face.

'It's hopeless, isn't it?' she said, contradicting her earlier optimism. 'Everyone thinks I'm guilty. We've both already been tried and convicted in the newspapers. It won't make a scrap of difference *who* my solicitor is. We've already been tried and found guilty in the press. I'm the wicked woman who put Simon up to it. That's what everyone believes now.'

Turning to Delise, she said in a very bitter tone, 'It was the diary you know. That's what tipped the scales. Why did you tell them about it?'

Delise had the grace to blush. 'Dave thinks I shouldn't have told them about it but they would have found it sooner or later anyway. The police knew that was why you got in touch with us in the first place. They were bound to go through it in great detail.'

'But I wrote that about Gloria years ago,' Kath wailed. She'd certainly lost the cool executive look now, her face smudged by tears. She took a deep drag of her cigarette and blew the smoke in the direction of Delise, who shifted uncomfortably on her chair.

She looked like an object of pity, not a powerful figure from the world of TV.

'I'm sure that you didn't murder Gloria Rishton and I want to help you to prove it,' I said, glancing at the bristling Delise. I felt like a United Nations peacekeeping force trying to insert itself between two hostile armies. 'Now, Ms Headlam,' I continued.

'Do call me Kath,' she interjected, carefully folding her facial muscles over the prominent teeth. I watched the process, fascinated, and she gave me a very benign smile, with her lips closed this time. I felt a very faint stirring of something not unlike pleasure in a remote corner of my consciousness.

'Er . . . Yes, Kath. We both know that it was after 5.40 that I left the studios that night and that you were still there when I left. Yet Poulter, the head security man, has told the police that I left at 4.30, thus ruining your alibi. Why would Poulter have it in for you?'

'Hah! I never liked him and I imagine that he must have known that but there was no reason for him to lie like that. The police produced a log book stating that you left at 4.15 p.m. and that we followed at 4.30 p.m. Poulter only agreed with the stated times when the police threatened to charge him with conspiracy to pervert the course of justice.'

This was all news to me. Delise was taking notes furiously and Headlam frowned. 'I don't see the point of this visit, Mr Bartle has already written all this down,' she said.

'The point is that, unlike Bartle, Dave will check all this out,' Delise said firmly.

'We'll demand to see this log book. There will have to be ESDA tests done on it,' I added. 'That will help to establish whether the false times were inserted in the log after other subsequent entries.'

222

'All very mysterious,' Headlam said, puckering her lips over her teeth again, 'but I suppose you know your job.'

'He does know his job and if you ever get out of here it will be due to him, not that stuffed shirt Bartle,' was Delise's angry reply.

'I don't know what I know at the moment,' I said pleasantly. 'Can we just stick to the case. Kath, what can you tell me about this eyewitness who claims he saw you entering Gloria's house just after 6 p.m.?' I asked.

'Some eyewitness! We were in the middle of Manchester at the time.'

'Yeah, I know that,' I said patiently. 'Please believe I'm on your side.'

'He's an airline steward called William Coleman. He lives next door but one to Gloria. He was leaving for the airport and he claims to have seen a man and a woman going into her house. He didn't report it until he returned to Britain two days later. They put us in an identity parade and charged us when he picked us out. It was a total farce. Simon's been on TV so often everyone knows his face and I was the only woman wearing Chanel Number 5 in the line-up.' She sounded close to tears again.

'Do you know Coleman?' I asked.

'All I know is that he's already claimed the reward that Gloria's bank offered. I'd never seen or heard of him before the identity parade. He looked foreign, very chic. A short dark man, I thought he was an Arab at first.'

'He wasn't trying to get off with Gloria, was he? He was her neighbour,' I asked hopefully.

Kath shook her head sadly. 'I wouldn't know anything about that.'

'OK, let's try another line. How well did you know Gloria? Can you tell us anything about her?' I persevered.

'Can I ask you something?' Kath said unexpectedly. She looked angry. 'How old would you say Gloria was?'

I decided to humour her. 'Late twenties, early thirties, somewhere around there,' I hazarded.

I thought Kath was going to punch me, but then suddenly she covered her face with her hands and began to sob loudly. It looked as if she'd flipped her lid. Delise gave me a very puzzled look.

'Can you tell us why you find Gloria's age so distressing?' I asked as gently as I could. I think both Delise and I were wondering if this was guilty remorse on Kath's part.

'Don't you see? Gloria was at least thirty-nine, to my certain knowledge. She was working at Alhambra as a researcher long before I was. She was so concerned about her appearance. She wouldn't have any photographs taken unless she could have them retouched. And she was greedy too. She was always on at Simon for money. She broke up with him. She thought he wasn't keeping her in a grand enough style. She wanted a million-pound villa, not a poky little town house. But now everybody thinks she was a lovely young innocent wronged by a scheming older woman. It's so unfair.'

Delise was scribbling all this down and while we waited for her to catch up I reflected that what Kath had said was accurate as far as the reporting in the press went but would her obvious resentment against Gloria seem like a sufficient motive for murder? She was going to need a very smart brief.

'Did you hate Gloria then, Kath?' I asked, taking a chance.

'No, not at all. I was surprised and hurt when Simon married her so suddenly. After all, he'd been living with me, but being with Simon prepares you for the unexpected. Then she left Alhambra and took the job as a
224

researcher at the Northern Pioneers Bank and I didn't see very much of her again. Then one night Simon came round to my flat and asked if he could stay. They'd split up, I never found out why, but I know it was nothing to do with me.'

Kath's words held the ring of truth. Rishton had even boasted to me that he'd relegate any woman who tried to muck about with his dietary habits.

'But what about Simon? Do you think he might have had a reason to kill Gloria that you don't know about? Was she blackmailing him over something?'

Kath gave a shiver, despite the warmth of the room. She lit another cigarette and balanced the butt of the other on the arm of her chair. There was no ashtray. 'Simon's very self-centred, but he'd never kill anyone. He lives in a fantasy world – creating another character for "Slatheredge Pit" is the most important thing in his life. He can't keep a secret either; I've spent almost every minute in his company for months, so I'd know.'

'What about blackmail then?' I prompted. 'I was hired to deliver her a packet of money. I was never entirely convinced of his motives, myself.'

'That wasn't blackmail, not really . . .' she trailed off.

'Well, what was it then?' demanded Delise.

'You'll have to ask Simon,' Kath said defiantly.

'All right. Was there somebody who might have wanted to get at Simon through killing his wife?' I asked.

Kath just shook her head sullenly. I knew how she felt. She'd probably heard all my questions a thousand times already. I decided to quit before she started to come apart. We could always come back for another session and if she was hiding something I didn't want to take the questioning to the point where persistence became bullying.

'You obviously don't want to tell us everything,' I

225

said before leaving. You've given us something to go on anyway, but please get in touch if you feel you can tell us more.'

Kath gave a haggard smile in reply. I noticed that she had dark rings round her eyes.

On the way out I couldn't help spotting that security wasn't particularly tight. Each accommodation block was sealed and there was a high chain-link fence round the perimeter, with cameras on poles at regular intervals. Delise was watching me as I checked the place out but she didn't challenge me until we were passing the Styal Village war memorial about a mile beyond the prison gates.

'Thinking of springing her then, are you, Robin Hood? Going to rescue Maid Marian from the wicked Sheriff?' she said sarcastically.

'Just professional curiosity,' I replied nonchalantly.

'What the hell are we doing here? Anyone can see that she's as guilty as sin.' Delise was buzzing. I pulled the car over onto the verge.

'Thank God you're not a judge, Delise. What makes you so certain?' I asked calmly.

Delise held out her left hand and began ticking her fingers off with her right as if explaining something to an idiot.

'Firstly, they've got the timing evidence backed up by documentation and an eyewitness, that damned storm-trooper Poulter. Secondly, they've got the diary. Oh, and thanks for supporting me over that, by the way,' she said scornfully. 'Your tearful friend omitted to tell you that the police found it carefully hidden under the spare wheel in the boot of her car. Thirdly, the police have an eyewitness at the actual scene of crime. An airline steward, no less, who has his eyes tested every few months and whom no one has been able to link to either of the suspects. Fourthly, the police have a meddling private detective wandering about the scene with his pockets full of cash for which even Headlam herself can't or won't give any explanation, other than blackmail.' Delise clenched her fists and I thought she was going to hit me. Her deductive skill was certainly impressive. She hadn't finished. 'And fifthly I could see you were leching after that woman the first time you laid eyes on her. That's what this is all about.

'When are you going to get real, Dave?' she said with real contempt. 'Can't you see that Gordon was impressed by your loyalty. Gordon's giving us a break so that no one can say that he pulled strings to get those two put away and he recognises dumb loyalty when he sees it. You're giving that snidy bitch something that rich people like Gordon can't buy at any price, and yet you're giving it her for nothing.' She began to cry in frustration.

'Delise, it's not like that,' I said pleadingly. 'Gordon's a bastard all the way through. He's like an aniseed ball, it doesn't matter how many layers you suck off him, he's still a complete bastard. It's not just a surface thing with him. He's the one who put me out of my flat!

'You're wrong about Headlam. I'm only interested in you, Delise. I know she's innocent and that has nothing to do with my likes or dislikes. If you had seen the body in the garage, if you had spoken to Rishton and Headlam that same afternoon, you'd understand. The police were determined to wrap the case up as soon as possible. First I was the killer, professional hitman Cunane! Then when that wouldn't wash it suddenly became a domestic killing, the husband and mistress doing away with the wife. Simple as that, case closed.'

'But the evidence, Dave . . .'

'Evidence be damned! Nine tenths of what they've got

227

is circumstantial. There's a lot about this case that hasn't come to light yet,' I said angrily.

'So St David Cunane, patron saint of hopeless causes, is going to sort everything out. Where are you going to get the money to finance all this investigating? We can't live on air, or do you think the Lord will provide?'

'He already has. Gordon's put us on his payroll,' I reminded her.

'And how long do you think we'll stay there when Gordon finds out that you're trying to pin the killing on him? I don't know why you need to investigate anything. You *know* she's innocent, you've got psychic powers. Well, you can count me out. I'm having nothing to do with this. Now take me home and don't try getting in touch with me until Tuesday.'

We drove in silence along the winding country lane and then into Wythenshawe and Manchester. As I turned into the little street by the park where she lived in such bliss with her mother I tried one last time to coax her round.

'Delise, it's New Year . . .'

'Don't I know it just?'

'I thought we could book into a hotel somewhere,' I said in a last futile attempt at appeasement.

'Get lost, Dave!' She jumped out of the car and slammed the door before I could say anything more.

I drove slowly to the end of the street, feeling sour. Once again I had to face the problem which hits all the homeless at the end of their daily stint on the streets, where to go? I had no choice but to drive back into town to the Atwood Building, my only port in a storm.

12

Atwood Building. 8 p.m. New Year's Eve 1993

Jay was long gone when I reached the office but the stench of the fried onions on the burger that he'd eaten lingered. My stomach heaved and I tried to prop the window open with our out-of-date copy of *Who's Who*. It was typical, I thought; we could only afford a four-year-old, second-hand copy of an essential reference book and then we had to use it for air conditioning.

The cold air restored a little balance to my weary brain as I paced up and down the cramped little office. The different pieces of equipment and furnishing that we'd acquired were like sedimentary layers from different geological eras, charting the economic rise and fall of the business. The battered old desk went way back into the deeps of time, definitely into the Precambrian. I tried to draw what comfort I could from familiar surroundings but this was the last place I wanted to spend the New Year.

I gradually became irritated by Clarke's filing cabinets blocking my restless path and decided to have a look at them for myself. It might pass the time and Delise still hadn't found anything on Mary and Dermot Wood.

There was research material here to keep someone busy for years. Clarke must have spent hours trawling local newspapers for accident victims with the right ages to suit his clients. Then he'd applied for the birth certificates and passports. Some of them went back twenty years. Clarke was running a factory for supplying false identities, some of which had been used over and over again by different men. Delise was right, this could be a gold mine; Clarke had carefully kept a record of the genuine identities and addresses along with the false ones.

I assumed that the first thing she'd done was look under the Ws, but I checked anyway.

There wasn't anything there but the file jackets themselves were old and bent and the retaining rails that they were supposed to rest on were twisted. After a great deal of fiddling about I pulled all the Ws out and put them on my desk. After checking them again, I lifted all the files out and stacked them on the floor. I spotted three files that had slipped off the rails and fallen to the bottom of the cabinet. None of them was marked 'Wood'. Nor were Mary's papers filed under Windsor, Cassells, Tinker, Timber or Tree. I finally located them under 'Forest'.

The file was disappointingly thin but I felt a surge of excitement as I pulled out the crinkled old papers. Most of them related solely to Dermot Wood, the deceased tarmac spreader. Sure enough, he'd been claiming benefit under the name of Eamonn Casselly while he worked for Strachan-Dalgetty under the name of Wood. There was an Irish birth certificate and a passport, both in the name of Casselly, fakes presumably unless there was some Casselly who'd died young for whom Wood was claiming. There was also a yellowed and dog-eared envelope. I picked it up and opened it, my heart thudding.

Inside were several sepia-coloured photographs. One was of a fresh-faced young woman in full 1930s style servant's rig. It bore a stamp on the back from a photographer's shop in Buckingham Palace Road; it must be Mary's alleged grandmother. The next showed a scene on a tennis court, the same pretty young woman was holding a tray of drinks for a group of players. She was looking across at the unmistakable terrier-like mug of Edward Windsor, Prince of Wales. The background of the picture seemed to be some sort of moated fortification with real cannon mounted on the walls.

I found the books and photographs Delise had assembled in her office for 'research', put them on my desk and began trying to fit names to faces. I thought the woman the Prince had his arm round was Thelma Furness, presumably his current bedwarmer. Two of the other women in the group were Freda Dudley Ward and Wallis Simpson, past and future mistresses. A moustachioed man at the back of the group was almost certainly Ernest Simpson and one of the other men looked like Edward's younger brother, Henry, later Duke of Gloucester. The photograph certainly showed Wood's grandmother and Edward together, but not as anything more than master and servant. I took a magnifying glass out of the desk drawer and tried to study their expressions. Edward's face had the same bland and bored look which it seemed to have borne throughout life, but the servant girl was definitely looking at him with a tender and adoring gaze. Was that why the photographer, possibly Cecil Beaton, had left her in the frame ... to point out the contrast between the servant's naive worship from afar of her future King and the brittle, super-sophisticated smiles of the women from the 'smart' set?

I got really excited when I took out the two other pieces of paper. I could hardly believe my eyes. One was a birth certificate dated August 1934 from Enniskillen, Northern Ireland. It recorded the birth of Edward Arthur David George Windsor. The mother's name was Mary Montgomery (Windsor), brackets, inserted in the same hand as the entry, suggesting that the Registrar was uncertain about Mary Montgomery's claim to the surname. The column for father's name and occupation was left blank.

The other piece of paper was folded several times.

I unfolded it and held it up to the light. It was a piece of top-quality notepaper headed 'Fort Belvedere – Windsor' complete with the three feathers of the Prince of Wales crest. Written in a firm hand across the top of the page were the words:

Contract of Marriage November 1933

A contract of marriage solemnised between Edward, Prince of Wales and Mary Montgomery, spinster of this parish, and performed by one Eric St John Summersbee, clerk in Holy Orders.

A marriage service according to the rites of the Church of England, by law established, between H.R.H. Edward, Prince of Wales and Mary Montgomery was performed by one Eric St John Summersbee, (signed). The signatures of H.R.H. and Mary Montgomery are appended below, as are those of the witnesses.

Edward P.
Mary Montgomery
Thelma Furness
Ernest – illegible

I held the paper up against the desk lamp. It was water-marked and seemed genuine, but I had to admit that its discovery in the files of an arch-forger must tell against it. Whatever else, this piece of paper represented a very interesting set of newspaper headlines. It looked as if the present incumbent of the British throne might be in for another 'annus horribilis' if this delayed-action time bomb left by her uncle ever exploded.

What a spiteful pillock he must have been! Edward must have thought the secret marriage was a wonderful 'jape' to play on his parents, who, like my own parents, were constantly prodding him to find a suitable bride.

Of course, the girl he'd chosen hadn't known that he needed George V's consent, under the Royal Marriages Act, to make a legal marriage.

I found the key to the second-hand safe which stood in the corner of Delise's office. I'd bought the safe during one of our prosperous eras for next to nothing but then had to spend a fortune getting clearance from a building inspector to have it installed.

Fittingly for a relic of the Edwardian era, it opened with a big brass key. A child could probably have cracked it. I kept my automatic in there and little else. Now it would be the repository for Mary Wood's secret.

And what a grubby little secret it was. I could imagine the scene. Edward's friends must have thought the 'marriage' of the Prince and the servant girl highly amusing. The naive girl must have insisted on marriage before surrendering her little 'jewel' to the jaded Prince. There had probably been jokes about him needing to find a certified virgin to produce the royal heir. Then the joke had backfired. Montgomery had announced that she was pregnant. Edward must have been certain that he lacked the faculty to father a child but then had he ever tried it with a healthy young virgin before?

I walked across the office to the window. Down in the street throngs of people were heading towards Chinatown. It wasn't Chinese New Year but the restaurateurs of the area were willing to lay on a celebration for their 'round eye' customers. I wanted company, but I knew that if I ventured out into clubland in my present state I was likely to end up lying face down in a gutter at the end of the evening.

Self-pity is an ugly emotion and I was drowning in it. I shut my ears to the distant sounds of New Year merrymaking and spent another uncomfortable night on the camp bed.

By 7.30 a.m. I was on the road to Stretford Leisure Centre. I swam forty lengths and had a much-needed shower, and then startled myself by going for brunch at McDonald's. I might curse their calories, but they were convenient.

Back in the office, I phoned Geoff Bartle and left a message on his answer phone telling him to request that ESDA tests be done on Poulter's log book, but the possibility of establishing Kath Headlam's innocence seemed remoter than ever and I wasn't feeling so enthusiastic as yesterday. The price of her freedom seemed likely to carry a high personal cost for me. Maybe I ought to leave things alone and let the police and the Courts sort it all out. I took a slow walk around the centre of town. It was a fresh day, not too much hydrocarbon in the air, with a mild southwesterly breeze blowing. After a slow lunch in a pizza restaurant I returned to the office. There was nowhere else to go.

Late in the afternoon Miss Attleigh of the Polar Building Society rang, and was surprised to find me in the office on New Year's Day. Apparently there had been some developments in my 'case'. Mr Harrison had asked to see my file on Friday afternoon and said the case might have to be reviewed. She seemed to be lingering over the details, spinning things out a bit and I felt so chuffed by the prospect of returning to the flat that on impulse I asked her if she'd like to come out for a meal. She'd struck me as the sort of woman who could shift a decent plateful. She accepted swiftly, not to say hastily, and there was an eagerness in her tone as we discussed a location that made a pleasant contrast to recent negotiations along the same lines with Delise. She was phoning me from her own home in Poynton.

'Look I'm going for a walk in Lyme Park, why don't you come over now and join me and then I can make you

234

a meal at home?' she suggested. I paused for only a moment before agreeing. 'We could go out for a drink later,' she added. In for a penny in for a pound, I thought, and agreed.

She lived in Chuzzlewit Avenue on an estate where all the streets were named after Dickensian characters. Odd to think of the inhabitants of Micawber Avenue all waiting for something to turn up in the post. Her directions were equally puzzling when I reached the estate. Left at Cheeryble, right at Havisham and right again at Trotwood but eventually I found my way through the maze of identical semi-detached homes and was warmly received by Miss Attleigh.

'Call me Susan,' were almost her first words. She was ready for the field trip in navy-blue Barbour, jeans and boots. Lyme Park was only a short distance from her home and she worked hard at the small talk until we reached the gates of the stately home and parked. She was suitably impressed when I produced my National Trust card and got us into the Hall. I might be a mortgage defaulter but at least I was cultured. Afterwards we strolled round the huge Park and gawped at the deer along with thousands of others. Despite the warming westerly winds, everything was still frozen hard up here in the foothills of the Pennines, but I could feel myself thawing out slightly in Susan Attleigh's company. I held her hand to pull her up one or two of the steeper slopes. It was all very natural out there in the grey moorland scenery.

When we returned to Chuzzlewit Avenue the defrosting process continued. Susan had left a moussaka casserole cooking and while my ears were still tingling with cold she served it in the small dining room. Her home was cosy, with hundreds of small feminine ornaments and keepsakes on all surfaces. They were the sort of thing that I'd never accumulated. Whenever anyone gave me something for my home it stayed wrapped and I'd find it months later at the back of a cupboard. It was as if my whole domestic life had been one big preparation for eviction.

The walk in the woods and the meal left me in a mellow mood. I was ready to be entertained. Susan was a good talker with lots of anecdotes about the different ways people tried to avoid paying their mortgages. I filed some of them away in the recesses of my brain for future reference, meanwhile it was pleasant to be the recipient of these confidences. It suggested she didn't include me in the category of defaulter. Nothing too personal was said, but I managed to gain the impression that there was no man in Susan's life at present and that this was a cause for regret.

'What's this Harrison like, then?' I asked.

'Oh, he's just a typical boss. Very conceited,' she said vaguely.

'Well, what does he look like?' I prompted. The more I could find out about him the better. But she wouldn't play ball.

'Harrison's a big man, trains with weights, David,' she said, rolling her eyes upwards as if this was normal for all bosses. 'He has them right there in the office. He's done awfully well for himself, he was only a matelot in the Navy. Still has a coarse side to him. But let's talk about something pleasant. I can't stand him. He's as thick as two short planks, and he never notices my work.'

Competition was tough at the Building Society, mainly from other women, and she'd noticed that while unattached women like herself did well, it was the females who had a partner who seemed to go on to the highest levels.

'The men at the top seem to be able to relate to them better,' she said with an expression of regret as she
236

cleared away our plates. I'd eaten well. The moussaka had certainly made a change from cholesterol-laden burgers eaten against a constant backdrop of children's birthday parties in McDonald's. I volunteered to wash up while she changed and felt a real surge of pleasure as I washed the pans and plates, the first time in a week that I'd had the run of a kitchen. My thinking seemed to be clearer as I arranged the pots to drain. I must try to find out from Susan what Gordon's involvement in her Building Society was. If Gordon thought he could put pressure on me by having me unjustly evicted maybe I could return the compliment in some way. I was sure there were all sorts of regulations about the way building societies were financed, or were allowed to use their capital, so if Gordon was able to tell this Harrison what to do so easily perhaps there was something I could find out and use against him. I knew I was clutching at straws, but what else did I have to clutch at? I was soon to find out.

'You're so domesticated, David,' Susan said when she returned to her kitchen. She looked at me appraisingly. 'Are you sure you're not married?'

Suddenly I found her very attractive. Features I had considered cow-like on our first meeting now seemed pleasingly fulsome and regular. It was a bonus to be with a woman without having to worry about whether her mother was going to make a sudden descent to break things up and I realised all at once that I was tired of the whole Delaney set-up. Susan and I smiled at each other as I explained my unattached status. She was wearing a pink blouse, with the top two buttons undone, and leggings. Her outfit showed her figure off well and there was plenty of it to show.

In the lounge I moved to sit in an armchair but she indicated the sofa next to herself. 'You'll be able to see the television from here, David,' she explained as she tucked her feet under her and curled up in the corner.

'I prefer to be called Dave, Susan,' I said, 'and I thought we were going out.'

'Why bother? It's so cosy here.' She handed me a heavy crystal glass tumbler of malt whisky. 'I don't like going out in pubs much, they're so noisy and then I might meet someone we've just foreclosed on,' she explained. I had to accept that it was a cosy evening with Susan or an early return to the Atwood Building. Her company was certainly relaxing.

I sipped the whisky and we made conversation.

There was an item on the news about the Royal Family and we chatted about their troubles for a while. I had difficulty in restraining the urge to tell her my news, but Susan was such a firm loyalist that I felt telling her that the true heir to the throne was not Prince Charles, but some unknown traveller lad, might introduce the wrong note to the proceedings.

Then we talked about Susan. Her parents were dead. She had a brother and sister, both married with children. Thinking about Liberty, I was able to agree that children certainly added a load of complications to any-one's life. Susan said she'd 'always preferred her career but liked to have some fun out of life'. I detected a wistful expression on her firm and determined features and felt banked-up fires springing into life. By eleven o'clock I decided I had better leave before my life took on an added complication.

'Don't hurry off, David. We'll have another little snack. I've got a fondue set, do you like cheese?' she asked. She bustled into the kitchen and in a short time was feeding me melted cheese. She displayed great dexterity and I was impressed. However, simplicity is everything,
238

as some great Chinese philosopher is sure to have said, and I made another lurch towards the door.

'David, you've had far too much to drink to hit the road. You ought to stay,' she said, holding onto my hand.

'I haven't got any pyjamas or anything,' I said feebly.

'Do you think you're going to need them?' she asked, leaning against me and pinning my back to the door. She took a strong grip on my shoulders and kissed me strenuously. My powers of resistance were not great and it was good to be desired by someone. I let her lead me upstairs. Her bedroom was as feminine as the rest of the house, all pink chintz and little knick-knacks.

'Now we're really comfortable,' she said as I slipped into bed beside her.

'You know, I do like to be called Dave,' I reminded her, but it wasn't my name she was interested in.

In the morning I was the first to wake. I looked across at my bunk mate. She was snoring lightly, with a contented expression on her round face, her chin tucked down towards the duvet revealing a firm fold of flesh under her jaw. Her left hand was folded in the cleavage of her full breasts and I could feel heat rising from her body. I covered her up.

I hadn't got much of a hangover but I felt thirsty. I drank some orange juice I found in a fridge then took a look outside to check on my unfamiliar surroundings. There was a heavy frost over everything. My car would need a blow torch to make the windows transparent again. Just looking at the wintry scene made me feel cold despite the central heating. When I closed the curtain Susan had woken up. I slipped back under the duvet with her and she did her best to take the chill off me.

For some reason my instinct for self-preservation was switched off. The warning bells should have been ringing by now, but the food, the warmth and comfort contrasted

239

with the prospect of yet another lonely day in the Atwood Building dulled my normal responses.

When we finally got up the day seemed to pass quickly. Susan produced a succession of excellent meals, the phone didn't ring and there was a tremendous sensation of privacy. It was faintly disquieting that no one at all tried to get in touch with Susan.

I should have realised that this was a more than normally lonely, thirtyish-year-old woman on her own. I should have guessed that she was on the rebound from an intense relationship and that it wasn't just my manly profile attracting her. If only I'd been as self-reliant as Liberty Walker, who was prepared to go off and live in a tree house when things got heavy on the domestic front.

We stayed indoors, apart from a bracing walk in the afternoon.

'I don't make a habit of this, you know,' she said.

'What, going for a walk in the fields?' I asked innocently.

'You know what I mean. I felt you'd had a raw deal. You looked so sure of yourself when you came into the office, then when I told you that the repossession wasn't a mistake you looked so grim I got quite frightened for a minute. I have a panic button you know, but I'm glad I didn't press it. We'd never have had this weekend.' So that's two things I have to thank you for, I thought. A nice piece of information would be a helpful third item.

'I thought you were going to rush upstairs and strangle Harrison when I told you that he'd ordered the foreclosure. That's why I let you look at the file.'

I waited patiently for further indiscretions but none came. I stared into her innocent blue eyes and decided to plunge on.

'Susan, you remember the memo which your boss
240

Harrison placed in the records?' She nodded. 'It said that someone called Gordon had informed the Society that I was a fraudster.'

'I'm not surprised,' she replied calmly. 'I was Harrison's personal assistant for years. He's always been interested in high-profile businessmen like Jake Gordon. He's got filing cabinets stuffed with information about them. Barry's always wanted to be an entrepreneur, you know. He doesn't want to be stuck as the manager of a provincial building society for the rest of his life.'

I noticed that Harrison was now Barry. 'Got a taste for stretch limos, Turnbull & Asser shirts, and steak tartare, has he?'

'Likes a nice piece of steak, does Barry, and he has a big car, but I wouldn't know about the shirts. His wife would buy him those,' Susan said seriously. 'I don't know anything personal about him.'

'Your Barry sounds like a prime candidate for the Gordon treatment,' I told her. 'It turns strong men into jellyfish, a big mass of flab with a sting in the centre.'

'David. Don't be cruel! Barry Harrison's no jellyfish. I'll admit he was very rude to me when I questioned him about your mortgage but normally he's very sympathetic.'

'Well perhaps you'll tell me the reason he slung me out of my flat without even the briefest investigation when he got his phoney tip-off from Gordon? He may think he's covered himself by mentioning Gordon's name in that memo, but he must have broken every rule in your blessed Society's book.'

Susan gave me a thoughtful look.

When we got back to the house I sat in the kitchen with her while she prepared another little snack.

'So you think there might be some clue in the office that would show how this Gordon's managed to get

241

Barry to dance to his tune?' she enquired, as she was buttering the bread for our ham sandwiches. I controlled my impatience. Despite the impetuous way in which Susan had pulled me under her cosy duvet, I knew she would proceed with due deliberation and caution where anything concerning her precious Polar Building Society was involved.

'I thought we might have steak for our evening meal,' she offered while I ruminated on what else she could do for me. 'I hope you don't think I'm trying to turn you into an aggressive capitalist.' She smiled winsomely.

'Well, Susan, if you hear me shouting "Greed is good!" then I want you to take the steak away immediately and give me a nut cutlet. No, really, steak sounds great,' I said, giving her a warm smile in return.

Actually, my thoughts hadn't gone as far as an evening meal. I'd assumed I'd be returning to my lonely post in the office, but now I seemed to have my feet under the table. While I pondered, Susan worked up a mild sweat hammering the steaks with her tenderiser and when she'd finished we sat on the sofa.

'Would there be anything written down?' I asked mildly, returning to the topic at hand.

'Mmmm, sure to be. That or it'll be on his computer. Have one of these peppermint crèmes, they're delicious.' I was beginning to feel slightly more sympathetic to the Animal Rights movement. I now realised how a Strasbourg goose feels when it's getting close to market time.

'Any chance you might be able to dig something out, then?' I asked as I forced a peppermint down.

Her rosy cheeks dimpled winningly.

'I'll think about it, David,' she said running her hand under my chin, 'but it'll have to be tomorrow morning. Everything will be locked up today but there'll be maintenance staff there tomorrow even though it is a Bank Holiday.'

'That's fine,' I said, realising that I was committing myself to sharing her bed and board for another night, 'but I'd like to get some clothes and my razor and things. I'll only be an hour or so.'

But Susan had no intention of letting me go off on my own and insisted on accompanying me to the office. I prayed Delise wouldn't have felt an unprecedented surge of guilt at her treatment of me and be waiting there. When we arrived in the Atwood Building Susan surveyed the arrangements with disdain. 'You could do a lot better than this, you know. How will you ever attract customers stuck up here? And the district, well the streets round here aren't exactly salubrious. Office space is very cheap just now. As long as you've got cash flow you'd have no trouble finding somewhere up-market. I could handle the details.'

I threw a few clothes into a plastic bag. Unfortunately this provided her with another stimulus. She saw the unwashed underwear and shirts that I was intending to take to the launderette. 'I'll wash them and iron them for you,' she volunteered. It would have been churlish to have refused, not to say impossible, judging from the determined expression on her face as she sorted through my clothing and gathered up the soiled garments. It seemed that by chance I had landed on the one upwardly mobile career woman in the country who was yearning to do everything for the man of her choice.

On the way back to Poynton she kept returning to the theme of my office and methods of improving my business. Why do I always land up with women who want to improve me? It's as if they think I'm a development site with a great big 'Vacant Possession' sign stuck on it. Back at the cosy semi-detached we devoured our steaks while watching a video of Susan's sister's wedding, with Susan supplying the commentary. The sister was younger than Susan. Her husband was a plumber's wholesaler, doing very well for himself. Like a tiny cloud on the horizon, no bigger than a man's fist, that heralds the approaching thunderstorm, I dimly realised I was being given a glimpse of what really lay behind this unexpected cornucopia of hospitality and sex.

I wasn't feeling even semi-attached to her though, I realised, as I mopped up the last of the gravy with a chip. She'd made all the running. Sensibly enough, she hadn't made any fuss about romantic preliminaries before getting down to practicalities.

I would have preferred the chance to digest my steak but I had to do the right thing. We came to grips and then lay back on the sofa and talked through our plans for the visit to her office. She had keys to get herself in and out and to switch the alarm off, and she thought she might be able to get into Harrison's office via connecting rooms.

'He's probably got extra alarms in there. I shouldn't try it if I were you,' I said pouring cold water on her enthusiasm. 'What about the computer? Can't you access his computer from your office?'

'They're all networked but I'd have to know his code-word to get into his hard disc,' she said, 'and you only get two wrong goes before it shuts down your terminal. The girls in the office are always having to ask him to get the codes out of his safe.'

'Is there any way that you can work out his code? The name of his wife or his eldest child?' Susan's forehead wrinkled into the faintest trace of a frown.

'He'll have the key of his safe with him but he sent me a Christmas card, I'll go and find it,' she said. It turned out to be a picture of the house Harrison lived in,
244

an appropriate card from the boss of a building society. It was signed but not with the names of his wife and children, the only personal feature on it was the odd name of the house – 'Oberon'. Susan explained that Harrison had served in the Navy and this had been the name of his submarine. I was intrigued by this. She seemed to know more personal details about her boss than she'd admitted to earlier. It was strange that she should know the name of his submarine but not of his wife.

'Well, that's it, then,' I said, 'give Oberon a try and then leave it.'

'All right, David. I'll try it but you've got to promise me that anything I find is for your use alone, and that you'll see me again; that this is the start of a relationship not the end of one.'

I'm a cold-hearted bastard at times, the death of my wife three years ago has left me an emotional cripple in some ways, at least that's what I use as an excuse. I think that at bottom that's why Delise has always hesitated over tying the knot. However, cold-hearted though I may be, I have to live with myself. Lying there, tucked up next to Susan, I thought carefully before speaking. 'Look Susan, I didn't come here to seduce you or to charm information out of you. It was you who offered me information about Harrison and Gordon last week. I don't use people, or drop them like disposable handkerchiefs and it's been great being with you these two days, but as for anything else we'll have to see what develops.'

I thought she was satisfied with my temporising, but I mentally kicked myself for my stupidity. I was beginning to realise that Miss Attleigh was hoping to play Mothers and Fathers for keeps.

The next morning we got up early. I had a long shower and felt fresh and relaxed. Susan put on her business clothes, a formal navy skirt with matching jacket and an ivory-coloured blouse with a necktie.

'You'd better stay here,' she said. 'It would only raise eyebrows if anyone saw me letting you into the office.' She slipped on a long double-breasted camel overcoat.

After she'd left I felt so anxious at the thought of illegitimate offspring and the Child Support Agency closing in on me that I went upstairs, changed into my tracksuit and went out for a run. The physical exercise helped to restore my sense of balance but didn't entirely remove my fears of having my income pruned. When I got back Susan was waiting in her living room with a thick concertina folder of computer printouts.

'It wasn't "Oberon" after all. I tried it and it was rejected, so then I tried "Oberons" and it worked!'

I looked at her closely. That wouldn't have occurred to me. The use of the plural form of the vessel's name to identify the crew was an arcane piece of naval knowledge for someone who claimed to know so little about Harrison. Susan smiled triumphantly and handed me the folder. I felt a tingle of apprehension . . . Was I using her to find out about Gordon or was she using me to drop Harrison in the mire?

'A lot of this is accountancy stuff, you're going to need help going through it,' she said. I caught her drift. I would have to stay another night.

'Susan, what you said earlier . . .'

'David, stop worrying,' she interrupted soothingly. 'I can see you think I'm trying to trap you. Well, I'm not. Do you want to start looking through these while I heat up some soup?' She headed for the kitchen.

The computer files, as she had said, were mostly incomprehensible masses of numbers records of loans Harrison had authorised. Looking at them my heart sank; I was definitely searching for the proverbial needle in the haystack. I needed a squad of trained accountants from the Serious Fraud Office, or perhaps not.

When Susan returned she put two bowls of home-made French onion soup complete with croutons, a stick of bread, a large piece of Stilton cheese, biscuits, and a bottle of Bulgarian cabernet sauvignon wine on the low table in front of the sofa.

'Don't look so serious, David,' she said handing me a napkin, 'most of these files will just record normal transactions. We can go through them and eliminate them. Your Mr Gordon isn't going to be involved in a loan for someone wanting to buy a terraced house in Knutsford.'

I concentrated on eating for a few minutes. My run had left me with an appetite, but I was not confident of my ability to burn off the calories faster than Susan was shovelling them into me.

'Perhaps I'd better take these down to my office and burn the midnight oil over them,' I said, pointing to the files when we'd reached the wine and Stilton stage.

'Don't be silly. I'm involved in this as much as you. Anyway, I want to know if Harrison has been ripping off the Society, doing a bit of private speculation with investors' funds. Come on, help me with this map.' We spread a large map of Greater Manchester over the dining-room table and on her instructions I began marking those places where a transaction had been recorded by Harrison with a dot. We'd soon discarded a surprisingly large amount of paper and the map of Greater Manchester had sprouted a rash of measles. It was late in the afternoon before we hit pay dirt. Harrison had granted a firm called Extraction Enterprises a £350,000 mortgage to buy a field on the outskirts of Poynton. And another to a firm called Mineral Services Ltd, to buy an adjoining field for the same amount.

Susan eagerly got out a large-scale map of Poynton and we marked off the land indicated. It showed up as part of a large abandoned gravel pit. After another hour the pattern was beginning to emerge. Harrison had given money to firms to buy the gravel pit but they seemed to have bought the wrong side of the pit. There was no access from the sector they had bought. They were going to need planning permission to build a road through an expensive private housing estate to reach their site. It didn't make sense to me unless the firms were buying the fields as part of some elaborate tax avoidance lark.

'This kind of deal's very sweet if you can get it up and running,' Susan explained. 'With permission to reopen the site you can extract a hell of a lot of gravel which sells at premium rates to the road-building industry. Then you're left with a very large hole in the ground which you make another massive profit from by leasing it to the waste disposal people as a land-fill site. Having filled it in, you wait until the site has consolidated itself, grass it over and you've got prime building land in a very desirable area. It's what they call the "open cast three step" in the land-development game; extract, exploit and then develop, making a big profit at each turn.'

'Yes, that's fine, but all we know so far is that Harrison's been authorising some very heavy loans in the Society's own back yard. There's nothing to tie in Jake Gordon.'

'Let's drive round there,' Susan suggested. 'As an officer of the Society I'm interested to see what so much of our investors' money has been put into.'

By this time it was dusk. It was still bitter cold when we left Susan's house and drove off towards the spot where twelve thousand years ago melting glaciers had dumped millions of tons of prime building materials so that modern speculators could get rich. The road to the site was unmade and the Nissan took a jolting. On one side there was an estate of large detached houses, each of individual design, on the other side the plots which Harrison had been giving loans for companies to buy.

Susan got out the map again and studied it closely. 'That's what you might call "Harrison's Ground",' she said, indicating the area we'd just passed, 'but he doesn't own this.' She pointed out the derelict farm at the head of the lane on our right. 'Look,' she said excitedly, 'this is the access road down there. It runs between this estate of luxury homes and that public park. To get in and out you'd need the private farm road but that seems to be the one piece of property round here that Harrison *hasn't* lent anyone money to buy!'

'Right, and I'm not giving out prizes for guessing who owns it,' I said. I felt certain it must be Gordon.

'I'll be onto the Land Registry as soon as everyone gets back to work,' Susan said impatiently. 'These Bank Holidays are a waste of time.'

'I wouldn't say that. We seem to have found a use for this one, don't we?' I said. We drove back slowly, crunching and slithering over the ice-filled potholes.

'They wouldn't be allowed to use this road to take the gravel out,' Susan commented, 'it belongs to the estate over there and as you can imagine the last thing the owners of those exclusive properties want is hundreds of lorries a day passing their homes. So the only access is through the farm – Grange Farm.'

'So what do you think about Harrison now?' I asked.

'*If* Gordon owns that land, and *if* Barry Harrison has a financial interest in all these companies that the Society has loaned money to, then Barry *may* be in very deep trouble,' she said cautiously. 'I'll admit it looks suspicious but there might be a perfectly innocent explanation.'

I got lost on the way back and we toured Copperfield, Micawber and Havisham before finally finding our way back to Chuzzlewit. When we got in it was quite dark and a freezing fog was descending. Susan said, 'Are you going to stay? I was thinking of doing a prawn curry. I love a rogan gosht, don't you?' She looked at me, her eyes were very round and her expression serious.

'Sounds great,' I said, 'if food be the music of love, cook on.' These last two full days with Susan were almost certainly the longest continuous period I'd spent in a woman's company since my wife died. It was having a calming effect on my nerves and almost certainly there was going to be some effect on my waistline.

Everything now seemed much simpler. I was now certain that I didn't want to marry Delise or anyone else – certainly not Susan.

13

I left Susan the next morning and joined the commuter stream inching its way through Poynton and Cheadle towards Manchester.

Delise was already in the office when I got there. 'This arrived by courier,' she said, looking at me with bright, narrowed eyes and tight lips. It was her letter of authorisation to visit Headlam and Rishton as a legal executive on behalf of Bartle, Bartle and Grimshaw. It was only three days late, quite efficient of Bartle, really.

'You're looking glossy and well fed,' she said unpleasantly. Her antennae were as sensitive as ever. 'What have you been doing with yourself?'

I felt a pang of irrational guilt – after all, it was Delise who had initiated a split – and found that I still cared enough not to answer the question truthfully.

'I've been doing this and that. Surviving ... What do the homeless do at this time of year? ... I stayed in the office most of the time ... then I went to my friend George's last night ... you know, we had a few drinks and I stayed over,' I said vaguely.

I surreptitiously stowed away the incriminating ironed shirts and underwear provided by a loving Susan only this morning.

'Anyway enough of this personal chit-chat. We've got work to do. Do you know what I found in those files you're supposed to have checked?' I demanded. I took out the safe key, opened the safe, placed the folder of material about Mary Wood in Delise's waiting hands.

251

She turned up her lip, but went to sit at her desk meekly enough, and began reading.

I took my Beretta 92 automatic pistol from the safe and went into my office to fiddle about with it. I find that occupying my fingers gives my brain a chance to get into gear, but this time no great insights dawned. I must have a dirty cooker to scour before I can truly get direction in my thoughts.

As usual the desk top was littered with a load of junk mail and bills. I made a half-hearted effort at sorting through it. There were two offers of insurance, begging letters from charities, circulars from computer salesmen but no pressing bills. There were no cheques either. I really missed that regular cheque from Happyways Supermarkets.

I heard the lift ascending and I looked at my watch. It was 9.15, rather early for Jay to arrive for another day's endless drudgery. Perchance, he'd made a New Year's resolution to come in on time! I moved quickly to put the gun out of the way. Jay's always trying to get his hands on it, and I like to keep it out of his sight.

As I was placing it in a deep drawer on the right-hand side of the desk a loose thread from my shirt cuff snagged on the safety catch, I bent over to release it and had to put the safety off to pull the thread free. At that precise moment my door was kicked open and two burly figures wearing ski masks burst into the room, one of them dragging Delise by her throat.

'Come out Cunane, you thieving bastard!' the first intruder roared. 'We want Clarke's bloody files back, or we'll break this bitch's neck for her.' Delise screeched and I was so overcome by the sudden fright that I let the chair against which I was supporting myself slip out from behind me. I went over backwards and as I fell the gun in my hand went off.

It was like a dream, or a slow-motion sequence in a Peckinpah film. The bullet passed right through the front of the desk, spraying splinters, nicked the right ear of the man holding Delise and smacked into the wooden doorpost next to the other bastard's head. Delise was thrust to the floor and our assailants were out of the office like Olympic sprinters off their blocks. We lay still, frozen, and listened to the repeated solid shocks as the pair of them jumped down each separate flight of stairs all the way to the ground floor.

I struggled to my feet, although my legs felt like jelly, the smoking gun still in my hand, and hastily slipped the safety catch back on. Delise looked up at me from the floor, her mouth forming into a perfect O shape. I stretched out my hand to help her up, struggling to find words, but none came. How could I tell her that the shot I'd fired had been a complete accident, and that the bullet could have lodged as easily in her brain as in the doorpost?

She looked at me with a wondering expression. 'Oh, Dave! I was sure they were going to kill us both. But you were so quick, firing at them like that. Did you know they were coming? You must have known,' she gasped.

I held her in my arms until she got over the nervous reaction. I was feeling pretty shaky myself and my mouth was dry.

'Was that an Irish accent?' I asked her through parched lips.

'Do you think they were from the IRA? The one who grabbed me had huge hands,' she said holding her own up to her throat.

'No. Why would the IRA be bothered with us? They must be some of Clarke's mates come to reclaim his property. Somebody's been putting two and two together and coming up with some right answers. Probably Barney Beasley. They must know that it was us who pinched the trailer. Clarke's wife got a good look at me before she ran off screaming down the M1. We'd better offload these files and fast. As long as they know we've got them we're a target. Do you think Ted Blake would be interested in them?' I knew that Delise would jump at the chance to get back into Ted's good books. I heard a sound in the outer office and hastily picked up the pistol again but it was only Jay, arriving late as usual.

'Hey! My man! Don't point that thing at me!' he shouted. 'I saw two dudes running out of the building like the devil himself was after them. They nearly knocked me down. I should have known they'd been up here.'

'Did they have masks on?' I asked.

'No. One had red hair and the other was bald. They weren't kids, either,' he said, scanning the room with his eyes, and landing on the big hole in the front of my desk.

'Oh my God, man! Have you been doing your Clint Eastwood number? Hot shit! "Make my day ... this is the most powerful handgun ever made, it'll blow your head clean off," ' he quoted in an American accent, looking longingly at the gun.

'Shut up, Jay!' shrieked Delise. 'It's not funny. I might have been killed if it hadn't been for Dave.' She didn't know how wrong she was and I didn't rush to correct her. She stared at Jay. He was wearing a dark fleece jacket over a denim shirt and jeans. No tie, of course, but this was relatively conservative dress for Jay. But it wasn't the clothes that had caught Delise's eye. She was looking at the New York Yankees baseball cap on his head.

'Take that off!' she ordered sharply.

254

'Shaz-zam!' he said and doffed the cap.

The locks had gone. His head was closely cropped, but not entirely clean shaven. The remnants of three or four of his mini-dreds remained in the centre of his forehead, like the survivors of a rain forest after timber clearance.

'What have you done to your hair? You look like a half-chewed coconut,' Delise yelled.

'Wow, that's really shady! I mean, mon! You two's always goin' on 'bout mi locks!' Jay was now using an exaggerated Jamaican accent and I looked at him curiously. I didn't think it was our criticism that had persuaded him to part with his beloved locks. He must be getting serious about the police and that was the last thing I wanted him to do at the moment. It was all hands on deck at Pimpernel Investigations right now, and I couldn't afford to lose his services, casual though they were.

'Calm down now, Delise. Leave his haircut alone and you put your cap back on, Jay!' I ordered. They both looked at me in surprise, they weren't used to the smack of firm control.

'I've made a New Year's resolution, I'm the boss of this firm and I'm going to be obeyed,' I said sternly. 'Jay, your job for the morning is to get these files out of the building and deliver them to Ted Blake's flat in Didsbury. I don't care how you do it but don't take all day about it. I want rid of them.'

'How'm I goin' to do that little t'ing. They must weigh a ton!' he complained.

'I don't care. Get on with it! Phone Finbar Salway, tell him it's a matter of national importance. He'll be delighted to help. He'll find you a van from the British Legion Club.'

Jay saluted with two fingers.

'Now, Delise,' I said, turning to her. 'Tape up these

holes and get these splinters off the floor. I don't want the place looking like a Wild West saloon if anyone calls. Then cast your eye over the Wood file again and tell me what you reckon.'

'Yass, Massa. Don' beat me again,' she scoffed. 'Say, Massa David, what we doin' 'bout our big secret? You know, dat de Great White Mudder, Elizabeth, am not really de Queen o' Englan'?'

While Pimpernel Investigations turned itself into a hive of industry I took out the whisky bottle from the medical box in the left-hand drawer of the desk and poured two small shots. While Delise sipped she continued to look through the Wood papers.

'These could be very valuable,' she said thoughtfully. 'They're part of our history, you know. They belong to everyone. Ted Blake would give an arm and a leg to have a look at them.'

'Now Delise, they don't belong to us, remember,' I cautioned. Then seeing the glint in her eye, I added, 'Make one copy of everything for the firm's records and then put the originals in an envelope back in the safe.'

Experience told me she was an adept in all uses of the photocopier but I also knew that if I stood over her and made sure that she only made one copy she'd be bitterly offended. The shock of the last half hour had made me realise that I needed Delise. I knew I loved her for herself. Irritating though she was. I beat a retreat to my own room and closed the connecting door.

'How did you get into work this morning?' I asked her when she reappeared with the copies, moments later.

'I borrowed the 2CV. Mum's still on holiday, and anyway she thinks using petrol unnecessarily is wasting the world's non-renewable resources.'

'Fine, well I want you to drive up to Haverigg Prison in Cumbria and interview Rishton. Here's the letter of authorisation from Bartle.' I was pleased that she wasn't making any fuss. 'Take your time on the roads, the weather's not too bad. You're going to need money, so take some of this Irish stuff we found in Clarke's trailer and change it.' I passed her two hundred of the green Irish notes, then helped her into my old brown sheepskin flying jacket, suitable wear for a winter drive in the old 2CV.

'You want to get us out of the way, don't you Dave?' she asked anxiously. 'You think they're going to come back. Well, just be careful.' She gave me a warm kiss on the lips before leaving.

When I was alone again in the office I reloaded the Beretta, strapped on my shoulder holster and put the pistol in it. Then I rang Bartle and exercising whatever charm I could rally, I asked him to arrange a visit for me to the Northern Pioneers Bank, Gloria Rishton's employer.

'There might be a problem there, Cunane,' he drawled. He obviously found it easier to snub me on the phone than face to face. I knew what the main problem was, he didn't want to be bothered.

'Can't you just phone and say you're sending someone from your office over to discuss Gloria's last movements?' I asked in my sweetest tones. 'I don't want to have to trouble Mr Gordon or Mr Trevose with this.'

'Oh, all right,' he said grudgingly, 'I play golf with the Bank's MD,' and hung up.

He rang back within a few moments. He was really earning his fee today. 'Ask at reception for Alan Ashbee, and he'll come down to meet you. He was Gloria's immediate boss,' he said curtly. 'Gloria Rishton was employed in the Bank's research department.'

'Oh, really,' I said politely.

'The Bank's research department is a highly sensitive department, organises secret research into prospective clients and whatnot. They won't welcome you stamping about all over the place in your big boots, so just behave yourself . . .' He paused for breath before the final onslaught. 'All this *sleuthing*, I suppose if you must do it, you must, but don't bother me with it again.' He hung up on me without another word.

I could feel my ears burning. Bartle was 'extra', as Jay and Liberty would say.

I put on my loose-fitting brown leather jacket and a scarf to disguise the bulge of the gun under my left armpit. At one time I had been very reluctant to go out wearing it, but now I didn't give a damn. Then I picked up the envelope containing Wood's precious documents, folded it carefully and zipped it into an inside pocket. It wasn't that I didn't trust Delise but Mary Wood had paid me £2000 for those papers and she was entitled to them. Knowing her life style I might run into her anywhere in Greater Manchester.

It was only a short distance to the headquarters of the Northern Pioneers near Manchester Cathedral but I took the Nissan and left it in Long Millgate car park opposite one of the few remaining scraps of medieval architecture in Manchester, Chetham's School. I strode quickly through Fennel Street and Hanging Ditch towards the Bank. I was only dunned once by a beggar and hurriedly gave him a handful of loose change. Strange how the beggars hung about round there, almost as if they found the lingering trace of medieval atmosphere congenial to their trade.

'Mr Cunane for Mr Ashbee,' I said confidently at the reception desk of the Northern Pioneers headquarters. The pretty blonde receptionist picked up the phone and shortly afterwards Ashbee came down in the lift to meet me. A tall, thin donnish-looking man with stooped shoulders and leather patches on the elbows and cuffs of his sports jacket he looked as if he'd strayed from some university quad; definitely a backroom boy, he came blinking into the light, shook my hand diffidently and led me towards the stair.

'Can't we take the lift?' I asked.

'I'm afraid they only work one way, going down. Unfortunately, everyone coming in has to go through a security check. The times we live in.'

On the first floor we approached a metal detector behind a turnstile with a uniformed guard in attendance. There was only one exit at the end of the short corridor and this was opened by the guard operating a hidden switch. It was simple but effective security.

Before stepping through the screen I took out the Beretta and handed it, butt first, to the guard. He didn't seem at all put out, but Ashbee shied away like a frightened horse.

'No one said anything about this. Do you always go about armed?' he asked, peering at me over the top of his glasses.

'Times we live in Mr Ashbee, times we live in,' I said piously. The guard put my gun in a small safe and handed me a receipt. He was obviously used to guns and probably had one handy himself.

The Research Department was a large open-plan office on the top floor of the building, mostly taken up by microfilm readers, but there was a mainframe computer in the corner screened off in its own glass enclosure as well as the personal computers that sat on almost every desk. The staff seemed to be mainly grey-haired, bespectacled academic types, both male and female – clones of Ashbee. This assembly of silvertops hardly looked like suitable company for the late Gloria Rishton, if she really had been the busty young glamour queen portrayed in the tabloids. There wasn't a brassy-looking typist, or brain-dead dolly bird in sight and it was clear that Gloria must have been quite different from the image the press had landed her with if she had held down a job here. It was a fully electronic office, they even had an automatic machine for the coffee.

Ashbee tried to hurry me along into his section of the office as my presence was attracting attention. The cloistered inmates must be unused to visitors. One slip here and the Bank stood to lose millions.

'I'm just trying to absorb the atmosphere of the place where Gloria Rishton spent her working life. Did she have anything to do with those?' I asked, pointing to the Christmas decorations which festooned the walls and ceiling.

'Funny you should ask that. She certainly did. Most insistent she was, we all had to chip in towards the cost, of course. The Bank won't pay for anything like that,' Ashbee said.

By this time we'd reached his inner sanctum. It was fenced off from the rest of the open-plan office by a low partition, the height of which, I'm sure, was carefully calculated to allow him to watch over the rest of the staff without seeming to be too obtrusive.

'There's a very studious atmosphere in here,' I commented. 'How did a fast piece like Mrs Rishton fit in?'

His nostrils flared. 'Mrs Rishton always conducted herself with perfect decorum whilst she was here.'

'Oh, come on! She was the fourth Mrs Rishton, she did displace the third wife, and also Rishton's mistress Kath Headlam, she can't have been entirely above flashing a bit of leg or showing off her boobs now and then.'

'How dare you speak of her like that? Gloria was always a model of correct demeanour . . .' He stood up to make his point. 'The police never asked me anything like this. How dare you . . .?'

'This is nothing to what you'll face when you're in the witness box,' I said. He sat down suddenly, looking perplexed. I knew that nothing would fetch him off his high horse more quickly than the knowledge that he might have to defend his position in public and I could see that I had thoroughly shaken the walls of his ivory tower.

'Very well, Mr Cunane. What else can I do for you?' He couldn't wait to get rid of me, but I was in no hurry. I wasn't here to win friends.

'I'd like to see where Gloria worked, I'd like to see her locker or whatever, and I'd particularly like to see the staff log book. Also I'd like to interview some of her workmates.'

'I'm not sure I can allow you to do that,' he said stiffly.

'Phone your managing director then,' I invited. 'He'll give permission.' I was bluffing – Ashbee was well within his rights to show me the red card – but he looked a timid sort.

'Very well,' he said, caving in completely. 'We'll start at her workstation.'

He led me to one of the few unoccupied desks in the room. The staff pretended to be busy as we passed, but we'd been conducting our conversation at top volume and I knew everyone in the room had been listening. It was a technique I'd learned during my years of investigating supermarket fraud. If you defame one of the staff loudly enough most of their colleagues will hold their hands up in horror, but there's always the one who will come and whisper in your ear how right you were and dish the dirt.

Gloria's workstation was devoid of personal touches. The computer monitor had a few anti-pollution stickers on it of the sort favoured by Molly Delaney which caught my eye, but there was nothing in the drawers. I sat on her chair. It was on a low setting, she'd been a small person, which figured. Rishton was small, too. 'What was Mrs Rishton working on at the time of her death?' I asked blandly.

'That is entirely confidential to the Bank. You'll have to get a subpoena before we breach client confidentiality,' Ashbee snapped.

'Fine, I might just do that. Now I'd like to see her locker,' I said evenly.

Ashbee was fuming, but he led me to a row of lockers standing against the far wall. 'Here, rummage to your heart's content,' he said, handing me the pass key. 'The Cheshire Police have already seen it. I'll go and get you the staff attendance records.' I opened the locker door, there was another anti-pollution sticker on the inside. Gloria must have been very fond of the environment. Her locker was stacked to a height of four feet with reference books. 'Oh, those shouldn't still be here,' said Ashbee disapprovingly. 'They should have been returned to the library.' He retreated to his own screened-off corner of the office.

I knelt down and started checking the titles: *Commercial Abstracts – United Arab Emirates 1991–2*, was the first. I opened it. The book was a mass of statistical tables about trade in the Gulf Emirates. There were similar books going back to 1980 covering Saudi Arabia and Kuwait. Another title was *Commercial Tank Farm Management*, a massive tome about how to store crude oil. *Bunkerage Facilities of the Port of Liverpool, Rotterdam Spot Prices 1974–1990, The Secondary Oil Market, Oil Spillage Avoidance, Lloyd's Register of Shipping 1990–1991, UK Trade Statistics 1985–1990, Shipping Lanes of the World* with the pages for the Irish Sea marked. They were all specialised trade texts focusing on the oil business. I spotted one brightly coloured paperback wedged in among the weighty tomes, *The Rout of Runcorn – One Man against a Movement . . . The story of Jake Gordon and the defeat of the Drivers' Union.* It was a pamphlet written and produced locally and looked like a publicity puff for Gordon, the popular benefactor. All the titles had been supplied by a commercial lending library and I jotted down its name and address in Harrogate.

Out of the corner of my eye I saw Ashbee bearing down on me again with an expression of acute distaste on his face so I shut the locker and didn't mention the books. He handed me the staff attendance ledger. It was an antique red ruled register with a page for each day. They liked things old-fashioned at the NPB, no sign of flexitime here. The staff signed the book as they arrived in the morning and Ashbee drew a red line across the page at 9 a.m. and another at 5.30. Mrs Rishton had always been among the first to sign in the morning and the last to leave in the evening. As far as punctuality went, she was a model employee. On the day of her death she was the twelfth person to sign out after 5.30, so she hadn't been in a rush to leave.

'Satisfied?' said Ashbee.

'No. I'd like to see two of your staff in private, the youngest and the oldest employees in this department.' I might as well start somewhere, I thought.

Ashbee gave me a puzzled look as he led me back into his cubby-hole, and ushered the youngest researcher in. She was a very thin, mousy woman of about thirty, wearing spectacles. She put her hand over her mouth nervously as she sat down and introduced herself as Mrs Renfrew. Mrs Rishton had always been polite, had no worries, never flirted with male colleagues, was a regular paragon in fact, according to Mrs Renfrew. I thanked her. When her older colleague replaced her in the chair I immediately sensed that I was dealing with a very different personality. She was a solidly built person in her mid forties with shrewd little eyes set in a round, chubby face.

She licked her lips before speaking and then opened the batting straight away, without any prompting from me: 'I couldn't help overhearing what Mr Ashbee and Mrs Renfrew said to you,' she said in a quiet tone, folding her arms under her well-cantilevered bust, and settling herself in the chair with a little wriggle. 'I'm Mrs Davidson, Caroline Davidson, and I'm afraid you're being led up the garden path about Gloria. Of course Maggie Renfrew was her friend but "Ashbee the Has-been", as we all call him, knows better. He was always hanging round Gloria's workstation leaning over her. She left the top of her blouse undone, you know.' Mrs Davidson's own blouse, the strength of which was being severely tested, was buttoned right up as I couldn't help but notice.

'Gloria liked the blokes, did she?' I asked.

'I should say so, talk about vain,' Mrs Davidson confided, in the manner of one performing a public duty. 'And she lied about her age, too, and lots of other things. Of course, she was only teasing Old Has-been, keeping herself in practice. I could tell. She wasn't really interested in the men around here, they don't earn enough.'

I smiled encouragingly and she went on. I could see she was disappointed that I wasn't taking verbatim notes, but she was too anxious to get her story out to quibble. 'At the beginning of September, Gloria went away for an operation, she said it was an eye operation at this private hospital in London, the Royal Jenner. At any rate, when she came back after two weeks she had bruises on

264

her cheek-bones, they were on both sides but especially on the right. You couldn't see any other marks. She seemed to be finding it painful to talk, not that much talking goes on round here. She couldn't move her lips.'

'Just a minute,' I interrupted. 'Why don't you talk to each other? I should have thought it was essential for researchers to confer.'

'We're not supposed to discuss our work, even with a colleague. It's all supposed to be confidential.'

'So, you wouldn't have known what Gloria was working on?' I asked sorrowfully. This was a real knock-back.

'No, but I do know it was something big and that she was very excited about it.' Caroline Davidson looked at me patiently while I took this in.

'What about all those anti-pollution stickers she had? Are they recent?' I asked.

'Yes, she put them up not long before Christmas,' Caroline replied. I paused to consider the significance of this.

'You were saying Gloria had trouble speaking . . .'

'Anyway, as I was saying,' Caroline went on, 'one day shortly after her op, over by the photocopier, I saw a drop of blood appear below her right ear. It was the creepiest thing I've ever seen.' I looked at her in surprise. 'She'd pulled her stitches, that's what it was,' my inform-ant said in answer to my unspoken question.

'She'd been for plastic surgery and she had to show me. Behind each of her ears there were two sets of parallel lines, incisions, and one set was leaking. There was a mass of cuts under her hair but you couldn't see them and two cuts below each of her eyebrows each stitched up – you could hardly see those. The woman was in agony, taking massive doses of painkillers and penicillin.'

'You seem to have gone into this pretty thoroughly,' I complimented her. Caroline Davidson obviously had all the tact and charm of a human Rottweiler, but there was no denying her effectiveness. The woman was employed as a researcher, after all.

'According to her the surgeon was only charging her £8000 which is a lot less than the full price because she was so beautiful! Have you ever heard the like? Does it sound possible?' she concluded sceptically.

'Have you told anyone else about this?' I asked.

She shook her head.

'Tell me, did Gloria take anything out of here with her? You know, on the day she was killed, or at any other time. Any papers, a folder, anything like that?' I asked.

'No, our bags are always checked before we leave. Mind you, she could have tucked something under her clothes. Old Has-been doesn't strip search us, not that he wouldn't welcome the chance.'

'Is there anything else, Caroline?' I encouraged, reluctant to stem her flow.

'I'm sure Gloria was nearer to my age than thirty-five, which is what she admitted to.' Caroline brushed an invisible piece of lint off her bosom.

'And that would be?' I queried with a smile.

'Let's just say the wrong side of forty, shall we, Mr Cunane? Or can I call you David?'

I smiled gratefully at Caroline Davidson and gave her hand a squeeze but that was all. On my way out I had another look at the attendance record. It confirmed the dates Davidson had given me. The jealous old boiler wasn't telling porkies.

Ashbee was on hand to escort me out, a duty he performed in silence. 'Have you got a currency-dealing floor in here?' I asked.

'Of course,' he said, speaking out of the side of his mouth. 'We have to buy and sell large sums of foreign currency for our customers. It's a service of the Bank. But Gloria Rishton had nothing to do with that department. Why do you ask?'

'Oh, no reason,' I said, as he glared at me. 'Just interested.'

Back in the car I wasted no time in calling the library that Gloria had used.

'Hello, Detective Chief Inspector Jerrold of the Cheshire Police here. I'm making urgent enquiries. If you want to check my ID, phone this number,' I said, reading out the number of a local Asian taxi firm, 'and ask for the Chief Constable.' My luck was in. They were willing to assist a Detective Chief Inspector, and to waive the positive proof of ID.

It turned out that Gloria had been ordering books about marine matters and the oil trade only since the middle of November. Before that she'd been researching cocoa futures. The library were happy to cooperate with the police and save Inspector Jerrold a tedious trip to Harrogate.

Next I found the number of the Royal Jenner Clinic from Directory Enquiries, and followed the same procedure. There was a much longer wait this time, but again authorisation was obtained without further checking. I suppose they figured that as Gloria was dead, and her husband banged up, there'd be no one on hand to sue them. I stressed the urgency of the murder investigation . . . DCI Jerrold was trying to find out how much the late Mrs Rishton had paid off her plastic surgery bill . . . *She still owed £4000 and Mr Simon Rishton also had an outstanding bill of £3000 for the last time he'd had his tucks taken in. They were very happy to help the Cheshire*

267

Constabulary, and was there any chance of them being paid what they were owed?

When I put the phone down, for the first time since I'd started this case I felt happy. I left the car and made my way to Sinclair's in the Old Shambles, a pub in a genuine Elizabethan building stranded on a raft of concrete behind Marks & Spencer's. I pushed my way into the crowded upper floor and treated myself to a celebratory turkey sandwich washed down by a pint of bitter. The town was thronged with bargain hunters heading for the sales and I caught some of the feeling myself. The remaining Irish punts which Paddy had found in Clarke's trailer were burning a hole in my pocket, and remembering that there was a branch of the Bank of Ireland opposite M & S, I went and changed the gaudily coloured Irish notes.

Then I walked through the Barton Arcade and managed to blue £400 in forty minutes before I reminded myself that I was supposed to be investigating a brutal murder.

I drove back across town to the office. On the way, I tuned in to the local news on GMR, then braked sharply when I grasped the announcer's drift: *'It is believed that the ailing TV giant, Alhambra Television, responsible for such masterpieces of Northern culture as the soap opera "Slatheredge Pit", will shortly announce a link-up with a consortium led by the local multi-millionaire philanthropist, Jake Gordon. Gordon is reported to be the organiser of a multi-million pound rescue package which will inject much-needed finance into Alhambra. When asked to confirm the rumours, Alhambra managing director Lance Trevose simply smiled and said, "No comment". We'll give you an update on the situation every hour, on the hour.'*

The news that Gordon's plans for Alhambra were apparently on the point of success induced a short-lived
268

twinge of gloom. There were so many aspects of this case that needed unravelling, yet I could only count on the help of Jay, Delise and possibly my neighbour Finbar Salway.

And when I reached the headquarters of Pimpernel Investigations, who should I find, drinking coffee, but Jay and Finbar.

'What was of such "national importance" about those files we've justed moved, then?' Finbar asked. He was kitted out as if for an evening in the mess in a neat check sports jacket, gabardine trousers and regimental tie. Not the gear for humping filing cabinets about in. His face was flushed and I felt faintly and momentarily guilty for asking a man of sixty to help transport the cabinets.

'Did you deliver them to Ted Blake?' I countered.

'He wasn't in, Boss,' replied Jay. 'But we left them outside his flat door with a message taped to them.'

'Well, I've another job for you both, that's if you're willing, Finbar.'

Finbar raised his eyebrows, making it clear that I would have to give a full explanation before he would volunteer further unpaid assistance.

'I want you to check this William Coleman out. He's the witness who claims to have seen Kath Headlam and Rishton entering Gloria Rishton's house over an hour before Jay and I arrived. Apparently he's an airline steward. Head out to the airport, spread a bit of money around and find out what you can about him.' I took out my wallet, counted out £100 in fivers and gave them half each. 'Ask anyone you can find. You don't need to be discreet. I want to pull this guy's chain. If he hears people are asking questions he may have second thoughts about what he claims to have seen.'

They set off without further fuss, after I'd promised to pay Finbar's expenses. I watched from my high perch at the top of the building as they walked along the street below towards Finbar's van. They made an odd pair. Jay was loping along, swaying from side to side with his stereo headphones on, and Finbar marched beside him in his brown sheepskin coat, his arms and legs moving with military precision.

I phoned Alhambra to set up a meeting with John Poulter, the thuggish 'security man' who'd changed his evidence to suit the police.

'What makes you think I want to talk to you, Cunane? I wouldn't piss on you if you were dying of thirst in the desert,' he barked when I got through to him, incidentally revealing his fine grasp of coarse language.

'Don't be like that, Mr Poulter,' I said smoothly. 'I just wanted to know the reason you changed your story so drastically. We both know that it was 5.40 when I left the Alhambra.'

'What *I* know, and what you *need* to know, Cunane, is that you can get five years for trying to nobble a witness, now get off this fucking line before I call the police,' he rasped.

I hung up. Obviously my charm was wasted on him. He sounded like someone who'd had his head banged repeatedly with a coal scuttle. It struck me that I should have sent the former officer, Finbar Salway, round to interview Poulter. He might not have got more out of him than I would but Finbar had a better command of military swearwords than I did. Well, I was going to talk to Poulter, whether he liked it or not. I'd just have to go down to Dock Street and wait until he finished his shift.

The dark waters of the Rochdale Canal were covered with shimmering petrol stains as I walked along Canal Street towards my car, taking my time, wondering how

Delise was getting on with Simon Rishton. Shé'd gone off so willingly. I must be truly crazy getting myself involved with a woman like Susan Attleigh. If I kept up my affair with her I'd have to get the trousers of my suits let out by several inches and Susan might be expanding her own waistline if the coy hints she'd dropped about getting herself in the family way came to anything.

14

I had to drive round the block on which the weirdly
modernistic Alhambra building stood three times before
I found a space from which to begin my stake-out of
John Poulter. There were other exits from the building
but I'd just have to hope that Poulter came out onto
Dock Street.

Daylight gradually faded, the street lights came on and
it started to drizzle, and at about 5.45 my vigil was
suddenly rewarded. Several of the black-coated security
men came out of the building and headed up the street
towards Deansgate. I guessed that they were heading
for the Pig and Porcupine pub. About ten minutes later
Poulter himself emerged, with a self-satisfied smirk on
his face. There was an innate arrogance about the man,
I thought. He didn't cross the road to the car park, but
continued up the street towards Deansgate and the pub.

I waited until he passed and then slipped out of the car.
He was striding along confidently, without a backward
glance, and I fell in about a hundred yards behind him.
Surprisingly, he didn't go on up to Deansgate but took a
right turn down a side street. As I recalled the geography
of the area, that street led into the Bridgewater Canal
Basin, a formerly derelict area that the City Council had
recently renovated. I hesitated for a moment. It was a
dismal, grim spot, despite the best efforts of the Council.
If Poulter came out in his car, while I was still on foot,
I'd have lost him for tonight. I decided to carry on,
regardless. He'd hardly park his car all the way up here
when he could leave it outside the Alhambra building.

He must be making for a quiet pint at 'Dukes', a pub named in honour of the canal building Duke of Bridgewater, not John Wayne.

Sure enough, he went over a footbridge in the direction of 'Dukes' and disappeared round a corner. I headed after him. But as I set foot on the narrow bridge, Poulter stepped out from behind the railway viaduct with a couple of his heavies. He'd seen me coming. I turned to escape, but three more Alhambra security men were coming up close behind me. I was trapped. The security men I'd seen leaving earlier must have doubled back to set the trap.

The bulge of the Beretta 92 under my arm made me bold and I stood my ground. There didn't seem to be any other option.

'You arsehole, Cunane! You won't be told, will you?' sneered Poulter, unoriginal as ever. 'I can read your sort like a book, mate. You just go blundering in where you're not wanted. Now I'm going to teach you a lesson you bloody well won't forget!'

Right on cue, his black-suited heavies charged towards me from both directions hoping to squash me like tomato ketchup in a chip butty. I leapt the guard rail over into the canal like a mountain goat, happily landing on top of a narrowboat. I ran along its roof and then jumped again, reaching the side of the basin furthest from Poulter. The one idea in my head was to aim for lights, people, and if I was lucky, even policemen.

I hared across an open space, the auditorium prepared for the Olympic Games announcement. It led nowhere, just like that sad event itself. I didn't feel like running around in circles singing 'Always look on the bright side of life' until Poulter's groupies clobbered me. I pressed on.

There was a steep-sided ditch in front of me, with a

273

massive wall behind it. Poulter's uniformed posse were converging on me from two sides, with Poulter bringing up the rear as I scrambled down the ditch and then up the other side, slipping and sliding as I went. It dawned on me that I was standing against the wall of the reconstructed Roman fort of Mamucium.

Trying to cut me off, two of them attempted to jump right across the ditch built according to Roman Army specifications. As I rounded the fort corner towards the entrance gate I heard a yelp of pain from one of them. The 'ankle breaker' at the bottom of the ditch had scuppered yet another barbarian, but my triumph was short lived.

They closed in on me. The Roman gateway was barred, the stairway up to the top of the viaduct was blocked. The five remaining security men surrounded me. A giant Roman legionary, painted on the railway arch opposite, gazed down on me. I could have used his loricated armour now. I was grabbed from behind. Not a word was spoken, but as a signal to his men Poulter tried to break my right knee with a kick from the toe of his boot. I blocked him successfully with my foot but was rewarded with an agonising kick in the testicles from the man standing on Poulter's right. I must have screamed, but Poulter had picked the spot for his ambush well. It was well lit, but deserted. There was not likely to be anyone rushing to help me from the streets near the fort. Poulter and his men continued their work with the methodical thoroughness of professionals, taking turns to hit me. In my last moment of agonised consciousness I was aware of lying face down in a puddle while a boot thudded into my ribs.

I worked out later that it must have been at least two hours before I came round. The cliché about one seething mass of pain was certainly true in my case. My testicles felt as if they were being cooked over a slow fire and my ribs on the right side were probably broken judging by the pain breathing caused. Slowly and painfully I checked myself out. All my bits and pieces seemed to be there; in fact I had so many swollen bruises there seemed to be more of me than there had been before.

My gun was still tucked in place, for all the use it had been. I cursed myself for being a coward. Why hadn't I shot one of the bastards?

When I tried to stand up, breathing was extremely painful. My solar plexus and diaphragm felt very tender and I was frightened that a broken rib might penetrate a lung. Eventually I managed to move away, doing an imitation of Quasimodo by leaning heavily to the right as I staggered along. The Roman soldier on the wall looked down stoically. He'd seen it all before.

I limped along Dock Street to my car. Anyone noticing me would have taken me for an early evening drunk, a not unusual sight outside the Alhambra Studios. Sitting in the car caused another wave of nausea. I put my head down for a while until the street lights steadied, then I set off up Dock Street towards Oxford Road. I was weaving in and out of the bus lane but fortunately there was not much traffic. More by luck than by judgement, I found the turning to the Manchester Royal Infirmary and took the curving road to the Accident and Emergency unit. I just managed to stow my gun under the dashboard and phone Jay to tell him where I was before I passed out.

When consciousness returned once more, I was lying on a bed completely naked and a pretty young nurse was placing a bag of ice cubes on my bruised testicles. 'Back in the land of the living are you?' she asked. 'I thought

the ice would bring you round.' Mistaking my expression
of distaste for fear, she continued, 'Don't worry, everything's still there, though it looks as if somebody's been
trying to make sure it isn't. You'll have to behave yourself
for a couple of weeks until the bruising heals . . .'

As I struggled to take in what she was saying my
consciousness faded again. Lights were flashed in my
eyes and people shouted my name loudly in my ears,
then mercifully the dark waters folded over me and I
receded into a deeper level of unconsciousness. The last
thing I heard was the word 'coma' muttered from a long
way off.

There were more people around me when I surfaced
again. I blinked and tried to raise my head but my neck
seemed to be fastened to the bed. I could only twist it
sideways. I groaned.

'Shush, he's coming round.' Delise appeared in my
field of view. She lifted something off my head and I was
able to see Jay Anderson, and Finbar Salway peering
down at me anxiously. Oh, God! I'm at my own wake,
I thought. At the foot of the bed I could see the cheeky
little face of Liberty Walker grinning at me.

'They thought you were slipping into a coma. They've
had us here talking to you, but I knew you'd come
round,' Delise scolded.

I couldn't speak. It felt as if a carillon of bells was
peeling inside my head. I cautiously felt my body. I
was packed in ice all down one side. There was another
ice pack on the side of my head which Delise had moved
so I could see. My chest was tightly strapped up. There
was a surgical collar on my neck, a drip into my wrist
and someone had been using my arm as a pin cushion;
otherwise I felt fine. The throbbing pain between my
legs was greatly reduced.

'They're going to keep you in. They think you might

have a skull fracture,' Delise said comfortingly. 'The doctor was amazed that you'd managed to get here. There might be fluid in your skull.' She was a mine of information. Her voice sounded very loud. I tried to control my breathing and relax. Everything I'd been trying to do seemed much more urgent now I could hardly move.

'What about Rishton?' I croaked.

'Don't worry about him,' Delise said in a strained voice. 'Try to rest.'

'Tell me,' I croaked.

'You better tell him, Delise. He's not going to shut up,' advised Finbar.

'Simon Rishton doesn't give a damn about what's happening to him, Dave. He seems to have lost his marbles. I tried to question him but all he wanted to do was to proposition me. He was horrible . . .'

'Go on,' I whispered.

'He kept going on and on about sex, Dave, and about you. He wanted to know what we did together. I left after a short time. I couldn't stand it. You should have gone yourself,' she concluded reproachfully.

'Sorry,' I muttered. 'I'll sort the bugger out. Get my clothes. I need to get out of here.'

'You're going nowhere! Get that into your thick head!' she snapped, her gentle tone instantly cast aside.

I struggled to move but I hadn't the strength. None of my visitors volunteered to help.

'All right. It looks as if I'm staying the night,' I said.

'You'll stay for as long as they want you to,' Delise corrected me.

'Let Jay take the car,' I continued, 'but my gun's under the dashboard. Make sure Finbar looks after it for me.'

The screen round the bed was briskly folded back and a nurse elbowed her way through the crowd to shine a

277

light in each of my eyes. Then she ushered my visitors out. I descended into oblivion and sleep.

Next morning, at daybreak, a doctor came round and checked me out yet again. He insisted I provided him with a urine sample immediately. When after much fussing and struggling I managed one – it had to be midflow – he held it up to the light and examined it like a fine wine before sending it to the lab. After he'd gone I tried to doze a bit, but rest was hard to come by.

'Hello Dave, feeling sorry for yourself, man?' boomed a familiar voice. It was Ted Blake. He stood at the end of my bed scanning my records, wearing a heavy lumberjack's coat in clashing colours. My eyes ached.

'Let's have a look at you.' He cheekily gave me a quick once-over. 'I shouldn't try using that again for a while,' he said finally, replacing the sheet over my lower body. 'But if you were a cat I'd say you'd used up eight of your nine lives.' I glowered at him but he sat down on the bed. 'I guessed you had something heavy going down at New Year. I must have phoned you half a dozen times. Let's hear it then.'

I gave him a highly edited version of recent events.

'Shit, Dave! I know you're as God made you, but if you keep lying down in the road in front of the traffic, one day it's not going to be just a few bruised ribs. I don't want to be the one that has to identify you in the morgue.'

I had no answer. I hoped I might be able to spare him that chore for a long time yet.

'Are you still going after Jake Gordon?'

I shook my head feebly.

'You can't fool me, Dave. You're pretending to be on his payroll so you can try and help Headlam and Rishton.'

278

I said nothing.

'There you are! You've admitted it. Well, just remember, if you sup with the devil you need a long spoon. You've just no idea what really goes on in this town, Dave. No idea at all.'

Ted spared me another full recital of how little I knew about the local crime scene. Instead he gave me a look in which compassion and impatience were about equally mixed, shook his head and went on his way.

When he'd gone I tried to analyse my feelings but soon gave up. Whatever the engine was that was driving me along there was no way I could switch it off now.

I signed myself out at 11 a.m. The young houseman was horrified when I handed in the surgical collar. He warned that there might be fluid in my skull, that I might black out at any time, not to speak of internal damage.

I took a taxi to Moss Side. Although I felt shaky on my feet, I reasoned that activity was the best cure. My Nissan was standing outside the Andersons' house, and Jay opened the door to me.

'Delise said I should come home, Boss. Honest. I've got Liberty with me and she couldn't stand having him around the office. He keeps swinging on things.' He let me into the living room, and sure enough there was Liberty watching an Australian soap. Douglas was reading a biology textbook in the corner.

'Right, Jay. I want you to drive me to work. He'll have to go home. I thought I told you . . .'

'What are you talking to him like that for,' piped up Liberty. 'He's my big brother, Dad. I need him to look after me.'

'I'm not your dad,' I snapped. 'Will you drop that? I'm warning you. Say it again and you'll be the one waking up with men in green coats prodding you.'

'You can't speak to me like this! I'm on the "At Risk" register. Tell him, Jay!' Liberty shouted back.

'It's true, Boss.'

'I don't give a damn what register he's on. I need you to drive for me,' I said to Jay.

'I can't come without him. His mother's boyfriend's chucked him out and I talked my mum into letting him sleep on our sofa. If I leave him, he'll run off,' Jay said, helplessly twisting his wrists in frustration again.

We seemed to have reached deadlock.

We drove into town, with Jay behind the wheel and Liberty in the back seat. Delise was painting her finger-nails when we arrived at the office.

'Some woman phoned earlier. I told her you weren't available but she wouldn't leave a message. She insisted that you ring her as soon as soon as possible,' Delise said suspiciously, passing me a piece of paper with Susan Attleigh's office number written on it. One of the advantages of being so bruised was that Delise couldn't read my facial expression.

'And that snobby solicitor Bartle's secretary rang to say there's been a complaint from Northern Pioneers Bank.' She paused for breath and looked at me closely to see what kind of impact this was making.

'In fact, there's been a call from the Northern Pioneers Bank, itself. You've to phone Mr Ashbee on his private line. His secretary said you have the number. Are you sure you should be here, Dave? You look dreadful. I'll go and make you a cup of coffee.'

I took advantage of her momentary absence to phone Susan.

'It's you,' she said eagerly. 'Why didn't you phone? I was expecting a call last night.'

'I was tied up,' I mumbled. 'Did you discover anything from the Land Registry?'

'Well, I did and I didn't. The land round the gravel pit is owned by various companies, all registered offshore. The derelict farm is owned by the Runcorn Realty Agency, registered in Vaduz, Liechtenstein. All the other parcels bought with loans approved by Harrison are owned by companies registered in St Helier, Jersey, C.I. All you've got to do to prove your theory is confirm that Gordon owns Runcorn Realty and that Harrison is behind the others,' she said triumphantly. 'There is one other thing, the serial numbers of the Jersey companies are consecutive, that should tell you something.'

'We're making progress then,' I said. 'If your boss Harrison *is* behind these companies there *must* be something tangible to connect him.'

There was a few minutes' silence, then Susan said, 'I might be able to do something about that. When am I going to see you again? I've had some lovely ideas for meals.'

It was my turn to lapse into silence. 'I won't be able to get away from here until Friday or Saturday,' I said eventually. 'Can I ring you then?'

She reluctantly agreed to postpone our next tryst. I was amazed at my own powers of deception. When I put the phone down I felt my forehead. I was sweating. There had to be some way that I could put Susan off; anyway the parts of me that she was most interested in were definitely out of commission for the time being.

'Delise, do me a favour,' I called into the outer office. 'See if you can get Runcorn Realty Agency on the phone. Pretend you're doing a market survey for a computer firm and dig out what you can.'

'Back to our normal master–slave relationship, are we?' she asked with a smile, but she did as I requested. There was only an answering machine at the offices of Runcorn Realty. I decided it would be definitely worth paying them a visit. It might be useful to check out Gordon's other operations in Runcorn at the same time.

'Dave, you look as if you're going to fall off the chair.' Delise was standing over me with a frightened look on her face. I waved her away and dialled Ashbee's private number.

'Cunane!' he yelped down the phone. 'What were you up to in the Research Department yesterday? I've complained to Bartle, Bartle and Grimshaw. You had permission to ask a few questions, not to wreak havoc. I had to suspend two of the female staff for fighting. I've never seen anything like it in all my years in banking.'

'Just hold on a minute, Mr Ashbee,' I said calmly, trying to stem his flow.

'No, you hold on a minute, Cunane,' he said. 'Caroline Davidson told me that you were asking for sensitive information about clients and I want to know why you asked me about the currency dealing floor.'

I wasn't feeling well enough to be nice to him. 'Have you ever considered that Gloria Rishton might have been killed because of the work she was doing for the Bank?' I asked him. 'In my view it's at least as likely as the theory the police are operating on. She was researching the viability of a loan to Jake Gordon, wasn't she?' If I was wrong he'd soon let me know.

'*How* the hell did you know that?' Ashbee was furious, all his usual long-winded turns of phrase forgotten.

'I didn't have to be Gary Kasparov or Nigel Short to work it out once I saw the books she was using.'

'That's commercially sensitive information. I must ask you to respect the Bank's confidentiality.'

'Balls!' I said nastily. 'We're looking into a murder here, not a bad debt. Have you approved the loan? Did Gloria give it the thumbs-up?'

'Well, it wasn't just on her say-so. We don't work like

that,' he said sniffily. 'She hadn't actually finished her research, erm, before, er, she was killed. She hadn't said anything negative to me about the loan . . . She did give me regular reports of her progress. What she'd done was more or less complete so . . .'

I cut him off.

'Just suppose she was about to produce a report that wasn't merely negative, but suggested actual fraud on Gordon's part? She wouldn't be likely to broadcast that until she was sure of her facts, would she? I mean, you don't encourage too much speculative thinking in the Research Department, do you, Mr Ashbee?'

There was a sharp intake of breath from Ashbee. 'The loan application goes before the main board of the Bank tomorrow, bearing my recommendation for approval. We're playing the major role in a package which Gordon has put together with a number of banks. The first tranche of the loan is due to be paid to him tomorrow. Approval by the board is just a formality.' Ashbee's voice was shaking with suppressed emotion, much more emotion than he'd shown over the fate of his erstwhile employee.

'I wouldn't be in any hurry to approve it if I were you. I'd catch a dose of the slows, duplicate the research. Caroline Davidson is far more astute than she looks. Tell her to watch out for rats in the woodwork, and I'm sure she'd find some! You ought to reinstate her. And while you're at it, you might like to phone Bartle, Bartle and Grimshaw and withdraw your complaint,' I prompted, and put the phone down. I spent a pleasant moment imagining him feverishly recalling all copies of the document in which he'd approved the loan.

I'd burnt my boats now. Gordon would soon find out that his loan wasn't being granted. He'd tried to double-cross me with his pretended friendship while ejecting

283

me from my home; now I was repaying the favour, with interest.

'That was quite a performance from a man who looks as if someone had been trying to kick him into the middle of next week,' commented Delise, from the doorway. 'You still haven't told me what happened to you yesterday. Am I going to be privileged enough to hear about it?' She gave me an old-fashioned look.

'I'll tell you but first I want Jay to get his butt out to the airport again and improve on his recent lack of information about William Coleman.'

Jay and Finbar had failed dismally yesterday. All they'd managed to glean was that Coleman seemed to be a good father, very attached to his children, and that his wife was pregnant.

We needed material that would discredit Coleman as a witness, not prove him to be a model citizen and father. I agreed to Jay taking Liberty along as well. Liberty was better than a public address system. He'd spread the enquiries about Coleman around quicker than a dose of jalap through a sick sheep.

When they'd gone, I told Delise what had happened to me lately; everything that is, but my stay at Susan's.

'I could tell that man Poulter was a Fascist,' she said bitterly. 'How can he get away with something like that? Do you think Gordon or Trevose told him to work you over?'

'No, I think he's quite vicious enough to do it for his own amusement, or to keep his lads in trim. My theory is that he was forced to change his story by Gordon and Trevose and he'd like to deter me from asking why.'

'What are you going to do, Dave? By the way, your gun's in the safe. Finbar brought it back this morning.'

'One thing I know: I can't rest up now. There's limited time. If I'm right about Jake Gordon he'll be turning very nasty, very soon. I've got to keep this investigation moving, anyway I've had worse kickings playing rugby.'

'You scare me, Dave. You're obsessed! You want to go pursuing this Gordon, although you can hardly stand up. I can't cope with it any more.'

I didn't feel up to making a reply. I'm a private enquiry agent not a milkman – my life doesn't run on tramlines. If I get a lead I must follow it. Why Delise finds this hard to understand I can't imagine. Maybe we're better apart. A wave of weariness passed over me. 'Delise, do you think you could go and buy me a street map of Runcorn and some film for the Minox camera? I might need it tomorrow,' I told her.

As soon as she'd gone I put the two armchairs together and fell into a deep sleep. When I woke up it was shortly before 10 p.m. and there was someone knocking on the outer door of the office. I was covered up with my sleeping bag – Delise must have wrapped me up before leaving the office.

I cautiously took a look at my visitor through the glass panel to one side of the door. I couldn't believe it. It was Assistant Chief Constable Sinclair, calling on me in person accompanied by a fresh-faced, young female detective wearing a long blue raincoat. I opened the door. As she preceded Sinclair through the door he barred her path with his arm. 'You stay here, I don't want to be disturbed and I don't want you to get any closer to this gentleman than you are already. He might contaminate you.'

Sinclair looked me up and down contemptuously but made no comment about my appearance. He was looking well himself, the colour of his skin within the normal human range for once. He was wearing a neat grey double-breasted suit, obviously not for my benefit.

'I can't believe this,' I said. 'You here in person. What's wrong with the middle of a main road?'

Sinclair ignored my comment and wandered round the office picking up pieces of paper, moving things about, and generally giving the place a good ferreting through. I waited for him to make his pitch. 'What's this? Thinking of moving, are you?' he asked hopefully, when he spotted the map of Runcorn.

'It's nothing to do with you. I'm working for Bartle, Bartle and Grimshaw helping to assemble evidence on behalf of Headlam and . . .'

'Oh, that. I haven't come about that. Investigate away to your heart's content. Haven't you been listening to the news?' he asked, looking at his watch. 'Turn on your radio.'

I obediently turned on the radio and tuned it to GMR. The travel report came on almost immediately and I started to tune to another station.

'No, this is what I want you to listen to. Leave it,' Sinclair ordered.

'This is GMR from the heart of the Northwest . . . Well, is it a strike or isn't it? The motorway network is facing paralysis following a mysterious shut-down of construction and repair work throughout the country. The Department of Transport apologises for delays at over twenty-one major motorway sites and states that strenuous efforts are being made to find replacement workers. A spokesman for the leading construction firm Strachan-Dalgetty stressed that the problem is due to an unexpected labour shortfall caused by seasonal problems, and is not an official strike. The AA Roadwatch announces prolonged delays and single-line traffic on the M6 at . . .'

The announcer proceeded to list sites all over the country including the M25/M40 interchange. With some travellers trapped in their cars for up to eighteen hours on the M25 near London Airport, the police had had to

286

declare a state of emergency. An enquiry at the highest level had been promised.

I switched the radio off.

'This is all down to you, laddie. Isn't it? This mysterious flight of the Paddies. You've just single-handedly caused more economic damage to this country than the last two dock strikes put together. If I didn't know you so well, I wouldn't have believed it possible.'

'Do you mind telling me what you're doing here, Mr Sinclair?' I said with a straight face.

'Oh, come on David. You know very well what I'm doing here,' he said. 'We've got grasses in the construction industry. Have to because of the IRA connection. I see some of their reports and they're all singing just one tune ... a private investigator from Manchester has kicked over the ant hill by making off with the info on their benefits racket.'

'And I'm the only private investigator in Manchester?'

'No, David,' he said wearily. 'There are seven hundred and twenty-one detective agencies in this country. Now, tell me I'm wrong to start my investigation in the only one run by a certified crazy. I mean, look at you.'

I said nothing.

'Right, well I'll take it that I've come to the right place. Next question, what have you done with the files?'

I started laughing hysterically. The strain was beginning to tell. 'What files? What are you talking about? I haven't got any files. You're trying to trick me into incriminating myself.'

'I don't know what they're going to charge you with,' he said, shaking his head wearily. 'High treason, I hope. I don't think economic sabotage is on the statute book, so that's the next best thing. Still carries the death penalty. The Home Secretary himself was on the phone to the Chief for over half an hour this morning. He's waiting for me to report in. We want to get everybody back to work, then we can all forget about the whole thing including your part in this business. And don't say those files weren't here, I can see the marks on the carpet in this corner.'

'I haven't got them,' I admitted. 'I sent them round to Ted Blake so he can use the material on his show "Bang to Rights".'

'Damn! Damn! Damn!' Sinclair sat down and mopped at his forehead with a brightly coloured handkerchief. He rarely, if ever, uttered an expletive of any sort, or showed any sign of distress, but he seemed almost distraught now.

'I should have known that if you were involved, everything would get out of hand,' he said, looking at me with extreme bitterness. 'I suppose Blake paid you to lay on this whole stunt? It's time that man was muzzled. He's constantly fishing for information from us. The Home Secretary stressed that this has got to be kept from the media if there was to be any chance of restoring the situation. Now we'll have an international incident on our hands. The Irish Government's already involved.'

'Blake hasn't paid me a penny,' I said indignantly. 'I sent the files over to him because I wanted him to expose this racket.'

'Oh and you're so public spirited!' Sinclair said sarcastically. 'If the British Government and the Greater Manchester Police stand to be humiliated, believe me, laddie, your days as a private detective are numbered. And your fat friend Blake will find that his licence to amuse is revoked quicker than he can blink. I'll see to that.'

I'd never seen him so furious. He was going right over the top. 'I sent the files round to Blake yesterday but he didn't even mention them when he saw me this morning,' I pleaded.

With Sinclair breathing down my neck, I phoned Ted. He hadn't received any files, to his knowledge, he said, but he'd look. People were always leaving things at the wrong door.

Sinclair was out of the office before I'd put the phone down.

I looked round my poky little office with its poorly matched furniture. It looked more like a prison cell than ever with its high, barred window. I'd have to stick it for now. I made up the camp bed, poured myself a glass of whisky and resumed my interrupted slumbers.

I was up before six next morning, still stiff and sore but my ribs felt better and I could breathe easily again. With the new day some of the bounce and optimism I'd been feeling two days ago returned and I unpacked the purchases I'd made at the sales. It was all summer gear, which was why it had been cheap: a light-weight mid-blue jacket, a blue linen check shirt and a natural linen, plain waistcoat. I put two long-sleeved thermal vests on first. There wasn't a full-length mirror in the office, a deficiency I'd often lamented, but I snipped all the labels off anyway. The waistcoat hid the shape of the shoulder holster.

I was very hungry, having hardly touched any food yesterday, so I strolled over to Piccadilly Station for an early breakfast, pausing to look at my reflection in the shop windows on the way. The station was exceptionally crowded, possibly due to the chaos on the major roads.

When I got back to the office I made some calls. Finbar Salway reported some progress. He had made a contact in airport security, and dictated a report he'd been allowed to see down the phone to me: *Coleman had worked for British Airways for five years and seven years for Alitalia before that. Now aged thirty-five. Nationality, natural-*

ised British. Reason for change of airline: didn't like his previous route – Rome, Hamburg, Berlin. Employed by BA because of his fluent Italian and German. Regarded as a first-class employee, never been ill, never missed a flight, never a complaint. He'd turned down a promotion that would have put him on the groundstaff at Heathrow, training other stewards. Reason: loved the travel. He'd received help with his mortgage for the house in Prestbury and for a flat in Naples.

There didn't seem to be much grist for my mill there. Coleman sounded like a solid citizen in every respect. Except that he'd lied about Rishton and Headlam.

I rang Jay. His mother Lovena answered. 'How you feelin' boy?' she asked.

'There's nothing wrong with me that a day's work won't cure, Lovena,' I replied. She cackled away. 'Listen, can you get Jay out of bed. I want an early start.'

'You should be resting, Dave. I did some powerful prayin' for you but you can't expect to leave it all up to the Lord. You need to be careful after a beating like you had, you might have delayed concussion or a ruptured spleen or something.'

'I'm fine. Lying about only makes me worse. Is Jay on the move?' I asked.

'You just be careful. Sometimes it's days before the symptoms show,' Lovena said with professional caution. 'Jay was up early. That scamp Liberty is leading him a merry dance, but the responsibility's doin' Jay good. I'll have him comin' to church with me yet. He's just settin' off now and don't you ax me to look after that kid. I'll tell you what I told Jay. Why should I take him into my care? Social Services won't, so they must think his mother's still capable. He's her liability, and she can just haul her idle backside out of bed an' look after him herself.'

With that she rang off. I couldn't blame her for not

wanting to be lumbered with Liberty, but surely he should be at school today?

I studied the map of Runcorn. The street plan looked complicated, what with a New Town and an Old Town and a ring road.

Jay arrived just before Delise, with Liberty in tow. Liberty had thrown a wobbler and refused to go to school and Jay didn't want him to spend the day wandering round Manchester. Remembering what had happened last time, I agreed, but when I suggested we deliver him back to his mother Liberty showed me a side of his character I hadn't seen before. He lay on the office floor, drummed his heels and screamed while Jay stood beside him, twisting his wrists and writhing in embarrassment.

I decided to give Jay a break, and asked him if he'd got me any information on Coleman.

'Liberty tried to gatecrash the staff restaurant at the airport yesterday,' Jay said sullenly. 'He was going round from table to table asking for Coleman. Then when we were in the terminal this announcement came over the public address. He'd left his name everywhere, of course. Well, when we got to the phone it was Coleman. He wanted to know what we after. I thought he'd send the Dibbles after us, but when I told him we was making enquiries he just put the phone down.'

This news put me in a better mood. It sounded as if Coleman might have something to hide, after all. If Liberty Walker came chasing after me I'd want the police on hand immediately.

The three of us set off down the M56 for Runcorn with Jay driving. There was a massive traffic jam at the road works by the airport, inward bound for Manchester but that didn't affect us. The weather was fine but I had my 'Drizabone' Australian rainproof with me. I also had sandwiches and cartons of fruit juice in case this turned into a prolonged surveillance job. As we approached Runcorn we passed a big industrial estate at Rocksavage and there on the left was the Gordon compound. Military base might have been a better description. It seemed to go on for miles with a heavy chain-link fence fronting the road. Jay drove past as slowly as the traffic would allow, and then we were into Runcorn New Town with its rows and rows of neat little starter homes, all clean and fresh.

It didn't seem anything like the concrete jungle I'd been led to expect. There were no graffiti and the Lego houses with circular windows for which the place had been famous had all been pulled down.

After what seemed like hours of circling, weaving, and getting mixed up in the specially laid out bus lane, Jay managed to park in the old part of town and we found the street where Runcorn Realty claimed to have its office. Liberty's keen eyes spotted a brass plate bearing the company's name on a wall adjacent to a car insurance saleroom. It didn't seem to be adjacent to any door though.

I entered the insurance shop and enquired but the young male assistant nervously denied any connection with Runcorn Realty. He kept his mouth shut when I asked what the plaque on the wall was for.

The other two were across the narrow street and when I rejoined them Liberty was hopping from toe to toe with excitement. His eyes were fixed on the insurance shop. 'Look, the first man's just told him that you came in looking for Runcorn Realty,' he said, pointing to the lad I'd spoken to, now deep in conversation with an older man. The pair of them stood gazing out at us, then the younger man disappeared into a back room and the older picked up the phone.

I looked at Liberty.

'He's telling someone off,' Liberty explained. 'He's saying that when they agreed to be the acco . . . accommodation address they didn't think they were going to get visits from heavies trying to put the frighteners on. He means you, Boss. He wants protection. He's saying you're mob-handed and look as if you're tooled up. He means us. Oh, great! Wait a minute, now he's saying something's just not good enough.' Liberty's lip reading was better than a directional microphone.

I wondered who the insurance salesman was in touch with, probably one of Gordon's grey-suited underlings.

We drove out to the industrial estate. There was nowhere to park near the Gordon complex and we had to leave the car nearly half a mile away and walk along the grass verge until we reached the sixteen-foot high chain-link fence. I inspected Gordon's defences carefully. They made Styal Prison look like a kiddies' playpen. Behind the heavy-duty fence there was a cinder-covered area and then a second fence marking the inner perimeter made of anodised vertical steel strips, fourteen feet high, topped with spikes and razor wire. The stanchions on which the fence was mounted were massive. A tank would have had trouble smashing its way through.

Jay pointed to the cameras and infra-red sensors mounted on the inner fence. There was an enamelled sign on the outer fence. It said, 'Danger – Intruders are warned that the perimeter track is patrolled by savage dogs.' Liberty's sharp eyes spotted something else, sticking up here and there among the cinders were little white cylinders of plastic about the size of a milk bottle top bearing small horns or antennae.

'Are they mines? Has he got a minefield, mister?' Liberty asked in his high-pitched voice.

It certainly looked as if he had, but I guessed that they were in fact movement sensors.

Back in the car we drove past the entrance to the site again. There were no private cars on the site, just large numbers of tankers, tractor units and container trailers, and the entrance itself was as intimidating as the fence, with floodlights, barriers and a team of enthusiastic-looking guards. My vague plan to cast a close eye over 'Gordon's Gulag' was clearly a hopeless one: any idea of a quick lob over the fence to take a peek round the offices was out of the question.

Temporarily baffled, we left Runcorn, taking the North Wales coast road. There was no other address for Gordon, apart from the Gulag. He seemed to divide his time between there and various hotels up and down the country.

Gloria Rishton had been interested in oil tankers and Jake Gordon had taken me up in his helicopter over the Mersey for a look at his. There must be a connection. There must be. We drove in defeated silence. Even Liberty was quiet. 'The only way to get through that lot is to post yourself in as a parcel,' he eventually volunteered. Something along similar lines had crossed my mind.

He'd come up with one realistic method of entering Gordon's fortress. Another might be to stow away inside one of the lorries that went in and out, but as they were all either container lorries or tankers, getting inside one was going to be almost as difficult as breaking into the place itself.

It had been a mistake to start talking to Liberty. Once he got started, the words flowed in torrents. He wanted everything explaining; the place names, the history of Wales, why the sea was green, everything. The kid was getting far more education than he would have in school, but my mind was running through ways of getting rid of him. Social Services was apparently out; a direct appeal to his mother had failed; something more drastic was called for. Maybe, I should put him in a box and post him to Gordon, after all.

When we finally arrived at Point of Ayr on the North Welsh coast it proved to be a disappointment. There was no road down to the Bay, just a working coal mine complete with winding gear and spoil heaps in the middle of flat green fields leading to the sea. Further on, there was a construction site where a gas terminal was nearing completion. We drove as far as we could and then continued on foot. I lugged my binoculars along.

It was a clear day and I settled down to observe the tankers while Jay tried to work off some of Liberty's energy by taking him for a long walk along the foreshore. I could see the tankers, big red-stained hulks lying side by side out in the Bay, but I couldn't pick out much detail even with the binoculars. I should have done my research before setting out, like poor Gloria Rishton. I soon got bored watching them, they looked deserted and there was very little shipping moving towards Liverpool or Seaforth. My attention was drawn towards the sea-birds and the rich feeding ground of Hilbre Island.

After observing marine wildlife for nearly an hour I realised that I was wasting my time. The damp was beginning to penetrate, even two vests couldn't keep me warm in this climate.

I walked off along the beach looking for Jay and Liberty. There was a vast caravan site in the distance but rather nearer was a solitary green caravan on its own at the edge of the beach. As I walked towards it, I realised it was an RSPB recruitment point, and that it was manned, or rather womanned. Dressed as I was in my dark-coloured long coat with the binoculars round my neck I hoped the young woman inside would take me for a fellow twitcher. She was a plump, excitable-looking person in thick glasses, with her hair cut in a short cropped style that sat on her head like a tea cosy.

Laid out on her counter were various pieces of RSPB literature, which I examined cursorily. I spotted some stickers identical to the ones I'd seen on Gloria Rishton's computer monitor – 'Keep Pollution off our Beaches', 'Protect our Birds, Stop Oil Dumping at Sea' – and bought some.

'Sell a lot of these, do you?' I asked.

'Oh yes, of course we do with all the gas prospecting going on around here,' she said in the pleasant Deeside accent, a blend of pure Welsh and Merseyside twang. She went on to explain that a major gas terminal was being built a little way along the coast.

'I expect you get a lot of pollution here, with all these oil tankers parked offshore,' I prompted her.

'Funny you should mention that,' she said, 'but actually we don't. There was a bit at first, but they've been here such a long time perhaps the currents sweep it away.'

'Is it possible to hire a boat?' I asked.

'Wouldn't be for the fishing, would it?' she replied. The expression on her face made it perfectly clear that the fish ought to be left for the birds.

'No, I just wanted to make a short trip, that's all,' I explained, brandishing my binoculars.

'You'll have to go as far as Rhyl, to hire a boat.'

'One last question, did an attractive blonde lady looking about thirty-five years old stop off here a few weeks ago and ask about the tankers?'

'What is this? Jeremy Beadle or the police?' she asked suspiciously. 'Anyway, I couldn't tell you. I've only been here since Christmas myself, though the 'van's here all the time.'

296

Back at the car I found Jay and Liberty huddled inside with the radio on top volume and the heater fighting a battle against the environment. I shared out the sandwiches and turned off the ragga music. On the way back to Manchester Liberty's prattling got so bad that I borrowed Jay's headphones and listened to one of my Cajun tapes. Somewhere past Flint I must have fallen deeply asleep because the next thing I knew Jay was parking the car outside the Atwood Building. I was still clutching the anti-pollution stickers. It was three p.m., almost the whole day gone and not one piece of hard evidence to show for it.

I sent Jay to deliver Liberty into the arms of his mother, who must now be enjoying one of her first waking hours of the day. Then carried on up to headquarters, wondering if my day had been wasted.

Delise was at her desk. I couldn't fault her for industry. 'My God! You've been splashing out,' she shrieked when I took off my coat. 'You do realise that we haven't any money coming in and you've got to meet your wages bill and the rent on this place tomorrow?' she asked, bringing me down to earth with a sickening crunch.

'Trevose phoned. He wants to see you right away at his office down at the studios, you've got to get down there by four o'clock. He seems to think you're on his payroll, so why don't you ask him for some money?' Her olive-bronze skin was glowing and she never looked more beautiful than when she was angry.

'When are you going to leave your mother's company for mine?' I asked, moving round the desk towards her and changing the subject radically.

I was rewarded with a smile. 'That might be solved sooner than you think. I told her about that trailer you gave your father and she's crazy for it. She wants to buy it and take it on an extended tour of the country. She

297

has a friend who's into ley lines and sacred sites, you know, who might go with her. If you can be patient for a little while longer.'

I looked at Delise sceptically. There would always be some obstacle, I thought, but then I smiled warmly back at her. Hope springs eternal . . .

15

Delise came along to Alhambra with me as my minder
but I was wearing my automatic and had reached the
stage where I was ready to use it at the first sign of
reopening hostilities. The weight of the steel under my
left armpit gave me a feeling of security.

But Poulter must have received orders to behave himself. He grinned at me from his desk in reception as if
the last time we met had been at a hotpot supper in
some parish hall. Perhaps in his circle beating people up
was the recognised way of introducing yourself. I walked
right up to him and leaned over his counter so that my
face was almost touching his, but he continued to wear
the same self-satisfied grin. God! He thought he was
hard!

I whipped out the automatic and jammed it into his
stomach. The safety was still on but he wasn't to know.
The pupils of his eyes dilated in surprise but he didn't
back off or move an inch. He just kept staring into my
face, a cocky sneer still dominating his expression. I
pushed harder.

'Dave, there are people coming!' whispered Delise in
alarm. 'Put the gun away!'

'You're a big man with that in your hand, aren't you,
Cunane?' Poulter whispered between clenched teeth. His
jaw was sticking out firmly. It looked like an amalgam
of all the jaws ever jutted. He was a determined man
but he'd made a big mistake in reminding me that I'd
failed to use the gun to defend myself the last time we
met. It must have been the crazy gleam in my eyes which

frightened him far more than the gun because he finally pushed back his chair; beads of sweat sprouted on his forehead.

'Don't do anything foolish, I stopped the boys before they got over-excited. It was your own fault.'

'Oh yeah! You set your thugs on me and it's my own fault!' I put the gun under my coat. 'Take us up to Trevose.'

I kept the gun jammed into the small of his back. 'You can do what you bloody well please, but I'm not changing my story on the time you left the building again,' he insisted as we got into the lift. 'I told the police it was 5.40 that you left, but then they brought my own log book and showed me the time 4.15, written in there, in my own handwriting. Neat as you please. Then they told me they would charge me with conspiracy to pervert the course of justice so I just agreed with everything they said.'

He rapped on the oval-shaped door of Trevose's office. A light flashed above the curved lintel and the three of us entered.

'What's going on?' Trevose rose from behind his massive, Presidential-sized, oak desk as I pushed Poulter towards him. His gaze flickered over his executive toys, as if help might come from his cellular phone or laptop computer.

'You might start by telling Poulter that he's fired,' I said.

'I don't know what you're on about, but if you insist,' Trevose said, eyeing the gun. He obviously thought he was dealing with a maniac. 'Get out Poulter. Consider yourself on notice.'

That didn't amount to a firing, but it was more than I'd expected, and more than Poulter had, too. He started cursing, but when I waved the gun in his face he departed.

I relaxed and put the gun away.

'Well, Mr Cunane, I'd heard that your methods were somewhat direct. You certainly have a way with you,' Trevose said soothingly. 'Can I offer you and your companion a drink? No? Well, you won't mind if I do.' He poured a large brandy, then led us to the massive leather-covered seats in the corner and offered me a cigar. I put it in my top pocket.

'I'll keep this for later if you don't mind, Mr Trevose. My personal assistant here, Miss Delaney, finds that smoke upsets her.'

'My goodness, Mr Cunane, you are an unpredictable character. One moment you burst into my office and order me to sack my head of security and the next you're politely asking me if I mind you not smoking. Do as you please, I don't imagine I'll be running things round here much longer, anyway,' he concluded gloomily.

'You sound depressed,' I said happily.

'Yes, we were hoping for an injection of cash to keep the receiver at bay but there seems to have been some kind of hitch in the arrangements. I'm expecting the man from Cork, Gully to come through that door at any moment.'

I looked on unsympathetically as Trevose dabbed at his brow with a tissue.

'What was it you wanted to see us about?' Delise asked.

'Yes, well, it was at Jake Gordon's instigation, really. Suppose I owe you an apology. Naturally I'm very pleased you've been finding evidence that seems to cast doubt on the police case against our employees. Do you think Simon Rishton might be released soon? How was he when you saw him?'

'I visited Simon,' responded Delise stonily. 'He was all right but I can't tell you anything. It's confidential.'

Trevose was certainly trying hard to look pleased at the idea of Rishton's imminent release.

'I'm hoping that the judge will dismiss the prosecution case at the committal proceedings if I can garner enough evidence to show that there's no case to answer,' I said.

'If only I'd followed Rishton's advice, he might not even have been here in Manchester the week before Christmas,' Trevose said.

'Why was that?' I asked.

'He'd have been in Birmingham negotiating a merger with Heart of England Television. He was very keen, but I thought Jake Gordon's proposals seemed like too good an opportunity to miss.' Trevose took a deep gulp of his brandy. He was obviously hoping to ingratiate himself back into Simon Rishton's favour through my good offices. The wheel of fortune that controlled the never-ending power struggle at Alhambra TV seemed to have taken a turn in Rishton's favour.

'Mr Rishton might be very interested to hear what you had to say about him last week,' I said piously.

'I never believed he was guilty.' Trevose's prominent Adam's apple bobbed up and down. 'I felt it was my duty to distance Alhambra from the case.' He looked at me steadily, without a trace of embarrassment. 'And after all we did follow up your request to provide him with legal assistance. I do hope you can tell Simon and Kath that we're missing them both and look forward to having them back with us soon.'

I had to admire the smooth way in which Trevose had reversed gears. Jake Gordon claimed that he had forced Trevose to provide legal help for Rishton. Someone was lying.

'Well, there's just one little thing you could tell me

that might help Simon,' I said. 'Was the log book left unattended down in reception at all directly after Gloria's murder? Was there anyone who could have nobbled it?'

'There were a lot of people in and out. Jake Gordon was in here all day on the 24th. He and his assistants were going over the books. Ted Blake was here recording his show so there was a great deal of coming and going even though it was Christmas. Of course, the Cheshire Police were here making enquiries.'

'Would it have been possible for someone to doctor that book?' I demanded.

'I told you, there were people in and out all the time, and with the press storming the place for news about Simon and Gloria, our security might have lapsed a little. Anyone might have had the book for a few minutes. The police didn't come for it until late on Christmas Eve.'

His answer didn't help me much.

'If that's everything, Mr Trevose, we'll be on our way,' I said. 'We're going to see Simon at Haverigg Prison.'

'I was hoping you'd say that,' Trevose said. 'Don't forget to tell him that I'm thinking of him and that "Slatheredge Pit" has been in safe hands in his absence.'

There was no sign of Poulter on the way out. His position wasn't clear, but I doubted whether Trevose would dare sack him.

Delise and I were feeling more tolerant towards each other. I told her that there was still £500 of the Irish money left and it would tide us over. We'd got out of tighter holes before.

Delise is trained as an archaeologist – she knows how to erect elaborate theories on flimsy evidence – and was all for blaming Jake Gordon for the killing of Gloria Rishton and the attempt to implicate Simon Rishton and Kath Headlam.

303

'You missed your vocation, Delise,' I said, 'you should have been a journalist writing these "true crime" articles for the weekend colour magazines. We know that Gloria needed money to pay for the plastic surgery and that she *may* very likely have sniffed something out on Jake Gordon's nefarious activities, but we need hard evidence for Bartle if he's going to get them released.'

'You've no imagination, Dave Cunane. It's obvious that Jake Gordon must have hired a hitman to murder Gloria when Simon Rishton let slip whatever it was she'd found out.'

'We don't know what it was she did find out,' I interrupted. 'We'll have to go and see Rishton straight away, and this time we're going to make sure he talks. Phone the prison and tell them we're on our way,' I said imperiously.

While she phoned I tried to get the facts straight in my own head, not easy without a kitchen to clean. The police, or DCI Jerrold at least, thought they had Rishton for the killing, and that he had both motive and opportunity. Yet my brief experience of Rishton told me that he got rid of the women in his life with a decree nisi, not with a bullet. In any case, he hadn't had the opportunity.

Gloria had probably found out something to Jake Gordon's disadvantage and she needed money for her plastic surgery. Had she tried to put the bite on Gordon? Possibly, but much as I distrusted Gordon I couldn't quite see him as a cold-blooded murderer; Trevose either for that matter. Which left me more or less back where I had been on day one of this investigation.

There was something missing in this case – the killer, he, and I still thought of the killer as a 'he' at least, had been a ruthless professional. In and out in a few minutes, with no sign of hesitation. The idea that a bunch of middle-class media executives would start rubbing people out like American gangsters just didn't add up except in DCI Jerrold's imagination.

I knew there were no professional assassins for hire in Manchester, outside the pages of the press anyway. There were murders in the so-called Manchester 'Badlands', but they weren't professional hits. For a professional, you'd have to go to London and pay anything up to £50,000.

As far as I knew, the police weren't even looking for a hitman. So where should I start?

'The prison aren't very happy about such a late visit, Dave,' Delise said, breaking into my train of thought, 'but they're prepared to make an exception because of the distance.'

'All right. Let's get going. It's five now and we'll have to collect the car from Jay,' I said brusquely.

Delise pulled a face. I put some moral pressure on. 'Look Delise, I can't drive. I might have concussion and Jay will have to look after Liberty or spend a couple of hours in the barber's, so that leaves you.'

She was still grumbling twenty minutes later when Jay arrived with the car. I had to promise that we'd book into a hotel for the night before she agreed to make a return visit to the remote prison.

It was after eight when we arrived at Haverigg and were ushered in for our meeting with Rishton.

Rishton was as perky as ever, his hair still an unnatural shade of brown. The skin on his face still smooth and taut; the plastic surgery was holding its own. For a man in his seventh decade he was bearing up to prison well. There was a seraphic expression pasted across his sharp features and I'd no doubt at all that he'd managed to locate a supply of cocaine. His eyes had the same unnatural brightness he'd shown when he was gobbling raw steak back in Salford Quays. However, from the way he was eyeballing Delise it was obvious that prison hadn't been able to meet his demands for sex. I wondered why Kath Headlam had ever got herself mixed up with him.

'Have you got a decent cigar on you?' were his first words. 'I've been trying these low-tar cigarettes, but they're so short of tobacco that you give yourself a hernia trying to light one.'

I handed him the cigar Trevose had given me earlier and he immediately performed his cigar-lighting ritual and filled the small room with blue smoke. He radiated confidence. As Delise had reported, he certainly didn't look like a man facing a lifetime of imprisonment. I felt suddenly uneasy. Nobody could be this confident; what were HM Prisons coming to? I looked at him again. He was wearing a loud red plaid overshirt, buckskin trousers and Gucci shoes. Perhaps he was bribing the guards with promises of bit parts on 'Slatheredge Pit'.

'Mr Rishton,' I said in a pleasant tone, 'we know why you were sending money to Gloria – she needed money to pay for her plastic surgery.'

'Been doing a spot of detective work, have you?' he jeered. 'More than the police could be bothered to do, anyway. But why on earth should I pay for Gloria's cosmetic surgery?'

'I've come about Jake Gordon,' I said, ignoring his last point. That was what I wanted to find out. 'Had Gloria discovered something about this loan Gordon was applying for with Northern Pioneers Bank?'

His expression didn't change at first, then he did a little comic mime to indicate bewilderment . . . scratching his head, raising his eyebrows, screwing up his face.

'Gordon? . . . Loan? . . . Gloria? What are you on about? Barking up a whole forest of wrong trees? No, a random killing . . . We're looking at a random killing here . . . Sadist out testing his shiny new shooter . . .

Bang... Bye, bye Gloria... Her bad luck... Wrong place... wrong time. Pity, if only she'd known, she needn't have had all that plastic surgery... Waste of money... Was helping her out... Clever of you to spot that... Hoped the poor bitch would find herself a new meal ticket... Keep her youthful looks, you know... All done in friendship.'

This whole performance was accompanied by enough hand gestures and facial contortions to busy Desmond Morris and his team of interpreters for months.

'Mr Rishton!' I shouted, attempting to interrupt his staccato flow. 'Are you telling us that Jake Gordon had nothing to do with your wife's death?'

'Might have... ambitious plans for himself, Gordon... but so might anyone...' His attention wandered over to Delise again. 'Into S and M, is he?... Likes rough sex, does he?' He was incorrigible. I had the alternative of hitting him in the mouth or ignoring his provocation. I ignored him.

'Mr Rishton, Lance Trevose says you had a rival scheme to get Alhambra out of its mess.'

'Huh! Trevose! That little nerd. What's he been saying?' I had Rushton's attention again and for the first time I sensed that he was truly interested in what I was saying. I relayed Trevose's comments and good wishes to him and he looked disproportionately pleased. Maybe this was where his insane confidence was coming from. Did he think that 'Slatheredge Pit' was so popular that the nation would not allow its creator to languish in jail?

'I'll tell you what's worrying Trevose,' he said puffing smoke at the ceiling, and then turning to leer at Delise again. 'He knows I own most of the best shows on Alhambra. I devised them and put my own money into them when the management were too mean to risk theirs. You look at "Slatheredge Pit"... What do you see at the end of the credits? "Written and Devised by Simon Rishton".' He lapsed into silence as he contemplated his own artistic genius.

'So you think Trevose's change of heart is due to the fact that you actually own a lot of Alhambra's assets,' I prompted.

'Darn right I do, sunbeam,' he said. 'And more . . . there's not a jury in this country would convict me . . . Trevose knows that . . . Whatever the old Bill think.'

'Nice to be so confident,' I said sarcastically. Even with his hyper-confidence I felt there must be something more buoying him up. 'Did you tell Jake Gordon that your ex-wife Gloria had the goods on him?' I demanded.

'Never met the man . . . never laid eyes on him.'

'Come on, Mr Rishton. Anyone would think you wanted to do time. We know you met him. You've interviewed him on your own programme.'

'Never said anything to him . . . You just have to listen to him . . . A clear case of megalomania . . . Did you know Clive of India grew up in Salford?'

'Did you tell him about Gloria?' I shouted. I could hear the warder stirring outside and it was obvious that short of putting a pair of thumbscrews on Rishton I wasn't going to get any information concerning Gordon from him. He was hiding something. The door flew open and the prison officer stepped in.

'We're just going,' I said hastily. 'Come on, Delise. We'll be in touch, Mr Rishton.' Rishton didn't bid us farewell, just sent a cloud of blue smoke wafting after us.

We drove to our hotel in Millom, a one-horse town that looked like a set for a social-realist film about the 1930s Depression but the Victorian hotel was comfortable in an overstuffed way, and it was pleasant to be with Delise without the constant stress of expecting the

Killer Whale to loom over the horizon. There was a feeling of truce in the air and we drifted up to our shared bed as naturally as if we'd been doing it for years. Thanks to Poulter and his boot boys, I wasn't able to put any strain on my undercarriage but I felt more relaxed in Delise's company than I had for months.

In the morning we were the only people using the dining room for breakfast. Why is it that the knives and forks get bigger the further north you go? The heavy table knife I was using was at least fourteen inches long, but was still smaller than the cavalry sabres I'd seen used in Scotland. We were settled up and on the road to Manchester by nine o'clock, refreshed and ready for action.

We were on the M6 passing the Ashton Memorial Tower at Lancaster when the phone rang. It was Jay. 'Ted Blake's here and he wants to see you urgently,' he announced importantly down the line. I wasn't impressed. I had no time to spare for Ted. I wanted to spend the rest of the day checking out William Coleman, the so-called eyewitness.

Jay's stunning revelation that Coleman was very popular with all his colleagues but never went out with them for a drink or anything wasn't going to get us far. It looked as if I'd have to do everything myself, as usual.

'I suppose you've got Liberty with you?' I asked him.

'As it's Friday, he was willing to put in a day at school,' Jay said, sounding relieved.

'That's big of him. You can make up for all the time you've wasted child-minding him,' I told him harshly. 'So far you've not come up with one useful thing on this case. Get round to Finbar's and and persuade him to go back to the airport with you again. If you can't dig up anything there, go to Coleman's home and chat up the neighbours this time. The man must have some faults. Tell them you're from the press. Now put Ted on.'

There was silence for a moment, then Jay replied in a very awkward tone, 'Mr Blake says he won't speak to you on the phone, Boss. He says it's not secure. He says he'll mind the office until you get back.'

'Like hell he will!' I shouted. 'Under no circumstances is he to be left alone in my office! Put him on the phone.'

There was another buzz of explanation and then Ted Blake spoke. 'Look Dave, I can't talk over an open line. Meet me at my place as soon as possible. This really is very important.'

'It'd better be. My time's spoken for today and I'm going to send you a bill if I find you've been wasting my time.'

'Just get round to my place, pronto! You've got one hell of a lot of questions to answer if you don't want your ugly face on the front cover of the *Sun* tomorrow!' Ted slammed the phone down on me and I looked at Delise and shrugged.

Despite delays due to road works (I suppressed a twinge of guilt), Delise got us back to Manchester within an hour of Ted's call. Outside the office I decided that I wasn't going to suddenly keel over from concussion, so having dropped Delise, I took the car on to Ted's home in Spath Road, Didsbury. For years Ted had referred to the Whalley Range flat he'd moved to after his wife decamped as the 'bug hutch'. This new location, a large flat in a mansion that had been divided into four in the prosperous part of Didsbury, was distinctly up-market.

I'd no sooner driven into the grounds of the mansion, than Ted stepped into my path. He was so impatient to see me that he'd been waiting outside. His section of the house included a first-floor room with an excellent view over the golf courses that lined the Mersey in this area

310

and it was to this room he now led me. It was furnished in Scandinavian pine from IKEA but with some robustly constructed armchairs. It was a room I could be comfortable in myself, uncluttered and spacious.

He must have taken advice on his interior decor, because his personal appearance showed the effects of a high income combined with little sense. As usual, he had too many clothes on. Ted loves things with flaps, buckles and zips and today his outfit was a massive green sports jacket with buttons the size of young soccer balls, worn over a heavy check pullover and collar and tie. The jacket looked as if it had been cast for him in an iron foundry. All it needed was a few rivets at the shoulders.

'What gives, big boy?' I asked jauntily, as the bulky star of the small screen settled himself into an armchair. His face looked red, almost swollen. I glanced at my watch. It was a bit early for him to have been hitting the sauce. He narrowed his eyes and stared at me.

'You're a selfish pig, aren't you, Cunane?' he said slowly, rubbing his hands up and down on his thighs.

'Nice description from a self-serving do-gooder like you, I don't think. What's brought this on? Are you having hot flushes or something?' Ted and I go back a long way, we can speak our minds to each other, but I had rarely seen him so burnt up.

'You've only been sitting on the biggest royal story of the year, haven't you? And not one little whisper to the dear old mate who saved your neck at Alhambra the other day.' How the hell did he know about that? I stayed quiet.

'Notice that I'm not mentioning the cock-up you made over those filing cabinets someone left at my back door,' Ted went on. 'Hell! That bloody Sinclair nearly broke my arm when I tried to shift them inside.' Beneath the

311

banter, I could sense his underlying anger. The heat generated in his fat face was oppressive.

'Look, I haven't a clue what you're on about, Ted, but as you're so good at remembering things, how about me getting your Mitsubishi Shogun back for you? I haven't had a word of thanks for that.'

He shrugged his shoulders, not an easy manoeuvre under his many layers of clothing. 'Don't change the subject, Dave. I've seen the Wood file. I know you have it and I want it.'

I tried to hide my surprise but I couldn't believe what he was saying. I almost fell out of my seat. Delise must have been at it again. How could she? I felt my stomach do a somersault. I was angry.

'There is no file,' I lied. I was under no obligation to tell Ted anything. 'The only files I had were the ones that you so incompetently let slip through your fingers. They were the cause of all these road hold-ups.'

'Oh those!' he said. 'That's not much of a story. A few cones on motorways! Who cares? I managed to grab a couple of those files before Sinclair and his attractive little sergeant arrived. I couldn't have done anything with the rest anyway. I have to keep well in with the police. You know that.'

I shook my head in wonder. 'Those files were evidence for the biggest story about fraud you'll ever get your hands on, and you've passed them back to the police to be buried for ever. I can't believe it.'

'A quarter page in the *Sun* and a couple of paragraphs on an inside page in the *Guardian* at most. Social security scandals are yesterday's news.'

'And pieces about the Royal Family aren't?' I asked scornfully.

'So you've got the papers then,' he said and a smile lit up his big square face. 'You've got everything with this royal story, it's really romantic. It'll run and run and run.' He sighed, as happily as a schoolgirl being told that the entire Take That quintet had arrived to take her out on a date.

'You're not getting any help from me,' I said sourly. 'Who told you about the Wood file?'

'Come on, you know a journalist's sources are confidential,' Ted said coyly. 'I had hoped you'd be cooperative but if you won't help it doesn't matter. You'll return the papers to this new royal bag lady and then we'll see how much she'll get for them! Just don't forget that I gave you the option.'

I wondered whether to get hold of him and shake him until the buttons fell off his jacket, but looking at the complacent smile on his face I realised that it was pointless to blame him. You might as well condemn a leopard seal for feeding on cuddly little penguins. It was the nature of the beast.

I returned to the Atwood Building in a hurry, determined to sort things out. Pimpernel Investigations was getting far too leaky: first Headlam's diary, now this. I couldn't understand Delise. The last time she'd broken client confidentiality there had been the justification that I was in jail. Had Blake given her cash in return for a set of the photocopies? She'd had plenty of time to make the deal yesterday morning, when I was in Runcorn. Yet it was hard to believe. She'd had the story all last night and she hadn't said a word. Hot-tempered and change-able as water? Yes, that was Delise . . . but treacherous, no. If she hadn't tossed me a lifeline at a crucial moment of my descent into a pool of booze and self-pity I might be sitting at the back of Victoria Station with the other rumpots now. But this job was my life as well, and if she was going to toss every juicy morsel I uncovered to the gannets of the press, that was it. I'd have to make other arrangements.

The lift wasn't working and I sprinted up the stairs to the top floor, my sore ribs quite forgotten. Delise was at her desk peacefully typing up the report about the meeting with Rishton when I entered the room. I stared at her.

'Has anyone seen the Wood file apart from us?' I asked, straining to sound normal and matter-of-fact.

'I haven't shown it to anyone, if that's what you mean,' she said. She sounded short of breath. When I didn't reply she looked up at me sharply. 'That is what you mean, isn't it? Open the safe and look for yourself. I haven't touched that file since I made the copies and put them in there.'

She took the key out of the old cocoa tin under the sink and opened the safe. The duplicate file was there, and the originals were in my pocket. My face was burning.

'I'm not the only one who's seen these, you know,' she muttered angrily. I knew that I was witnessing the initial puff of smoke before a full-scale eruption commenced. With a guilty start I realised that she was correct. There was Jay, Finbar and of course Clarke and his buddies to add to my list of suspects. 'You're right. I knew it wasn't you,' I said untruthfully, 'but we're going to have to find out if it was Jay. Meanwhile, priority numero uno is to get these papers back to Mary Wood. I've had no luck since I took her money in the first place.'

'How are you going to do that exactly?' Delise dripped sarcasm.

'I don't know,' I said, 'but I don't want to pay her a visit. I'm not exactly flavour of the month with her charming relatives.'

314

'Can't you hire someone to take them round to her? You'd think it would be easier to get in touch with a woman who's just won £150,000,' Delise said.

'Oh yeah, you can just see me saying to some motor-bike courier "Take these to the fourth caravan on the left and deliver them to the rich lady who looks like Queen Victoria". No, it'll have to be me, but I'm going to need some back-up and I don't mean Jay. I'll ask Bob Lane if I can borrow his brother for a few hours,' I said angrily.

Bob Lane was the only person I could think of who might supply me with muscle in a hurry. He's in the 'bouncer business' or the supplying of club doormen as he puts it; he has any number of oversized steroid-overdose victims on tap, and a brother who'd reached giant size without artificial aid.

I left the office almost as rapidly as I'd entered it, 'Hurricane Cunane'. Doubt was gnawing at me. Jay didn't have any interest in the Royals. All that passed him by. They might have been the Flintstones for all the concern he showed. And I just couldn't see him touching Blake for a fee. It must have been Delise.

I drove through town and up Rochdale Road towards Middleton and the Langley Estate, home of the Lane family. I'd heard that Bob had prospered since the last time I had dealings with him and graduated from being a sort of 'foreman' club bouncer to running a club of his own. I hadn't heard any bad news about the club, so presumably he was working the right side of the street. Bob owes me more than one favour and I didn't think the loan of his brother Clint for a couple of hours' escort duty would cause him any grief. Clint's a great character. A giant with a giant's strength, he is slightly lacking in the intellectual area but makes up for this with his amiability. He looks frightening to anyone who doesn't know what he's really like.

The Lane house had once been council owned but now as a mark of private ownership it had been personalised by the addition of a Regency-style front door and fancy 'stone effect' covering to hide the plain brick. The Lanes were moving up in the world but their neighbours weren't. The rest of the street still looked like Hell's Kitchen with a full complement of mangy dogs, and truanting children with runny noses. Broken cars punctuated the streetscape at intervals.

Mrs Lane, the tiny mother of two oversized sons, opened the door. I'd never met her husband. She always spoke of him as if he was about to appear, but somehow he never did.

'Why, it's Mr Cunane. Come in. Bob often talks about you. He'll be glad to see you. You're lucky to have caught him in,' she said with a welcoming smile. She was as quaintly dressed as the last time I'd seen her, with her grey hair in a granny bun and a pinafore over her dress. Mrs Lane was a real rarity, the old-fashioned mum, still looking after her sons even though they were about as grown up as it was possible to be, especially Clint. I was pleased that she had recognised me immediately. 'Sit here,' she invited, pointing to one of the solidly built wooden dining chairs beside the small living-room table. 'I'll make you a cup of tea. Bob will be down in a minute. He's getting ready to go out.' She went to the foot of the stairs and howled 'Bob' in a voice that could have shattered glass at close range and then pottered off to the kitchen.

Bob 'Popeye' Lane came down a few minutes later, a pungent reek of aftershave trailing after him. His shadow wasn't getting any less and he was dressed in a petrol-blue, off-the-peg suit which didn't quite fit over the massive forearms that had earned him his nickname. He smiled when he saw me examining it. 'I know,' he said ruefully, 'it doesn't fit properly. It's me mum. She likes ordering stuff for me out of the catalogue and I haven't the heart to make her send it back. At least I've moved her onto Next, instead of Janet Fraser.'

I smiled sympathetically. He looked as if he could do with an account at the local tentmaker's shop, or maybe a visit to the same tailor as Ted Blake.

'I was wondering if I could borrow Clint for a couple of hours,' I asked. I hadn't too much time to waste on the niceties if I was going to achieve any useful work on the Rishton case today.

Popeye frowned, then looked at me closely. 'Been in the wars again, haven't you? I can see by the bruises on your face and the way you're holding your chest.' Considering that my face looked like a canvas by Jackson Pollock, this wasn't a very perceptive remark.

'I have had a spot of bother, but it was quite unrelated to the little errand I want Clint for,' I explained. 'I just need somebody to walk a couple of paces behind me and make sure no one tries to bash me over the head with a shillelagh when I pay a very brief visit to a travellers' camp. Some of the residents might not be too friendly.'

'You're carrying a gun, aren't you?' Popeye asked doubtfully. 'I'll ask Clint what he thinks, shall I?' He put his fingers to his mouth and gave a piercing whistle and there was the sound of ponderous movement from the adjoining ground-floor room. 'He's colouring in some pictures next door,' Popeye explained, 'keeps him busy for hours.'

Clint ducked under the door frame and entered the room, instantly altering the scale of everything. He stood well over seven foot, and lowered himself onto one of the strongly made dining chairs, looking like an adult in a kiddies' nursery.

'This is Mr Cunane. You remember him, don't you,

Clint?' said Popeye. His brother gave me a beatific smile and extended a hand the size of a baseball catcher's mitt. I offered my right hand carefully.

'Mr Cunane wants you to go for a walk with him. Would you like that?'

'I like walks,' said Clint, his massive face beaming like the full moon in a clear sky.

'Well, that's that, then. But I'm coming with you,' Popeye said. 'You'll need me to stop him pulling the heads off any awkward customers. He remembers you from last time, he likes you.'

'Mr Cunane's nice,' confirmed Clint.

'Once he likes you, you've got a friend for life,' added Mrs Lane, as she arrived with the tea tray.

Our journey to South Manchester was not quite what I'd had in mind. Popeye took Clint with him in his new Ford Maverick ATV, as he claimed that my car might not be able to bear the burden of Clint's thirty-two stone. We drove in convoy on the M62 and M63 to Chorlton, turned off the road past the illuminated cross on top of St Ambrose Church and straight into Derwent Avenue.

Across the street the travellers had broken down the fence to gain access to the derelict playing field. Once a soccer pitch for medical students, it was now a temporary home for at least fifty trailers. Mary's home was there, snuggling up behind the former changing room, which the travellers were using as a watering point. Mickey Joyce's chrome super-trailer was right next to Mary's.

There weren't many adults moving about on the site when Clint, Popeye and I strode boldly forwards into the encampment and we walked right across to Mary's trailer without meeting interference. I knocked politely on the door, and she opened it at once and stared at me in surprise. It took some moments before she recovered enough to invite me in. Clint tried to follow me in, but the trailer shuddered under his weight so he remained on sentry duty with his brother at the door.

Mary's appearance had changed for the better since our last encounter. I looked at her closely, it wasn't the teeth ... they still needed fixing, nor the hair. Then I guessed what it was: she'd bought herself some decent underwear, something with lots of strong elastic. Everything was well supported, all curves were firmer and flatter.

She blushed to the roots of her blonde hair. 'Do you like what you see, then?' she asked shyly. She was wearing a light-blue chambray blouse, a green body-warmer and a denim skirt; all new.

I apologised for my frank appraisal of her physical charms. She'd certainly changed. She looked less like a beaten-up bag lady and more like some well-endowed Hollywood star playing in a squalid drama set in the Deep South. All we needed was the beat of Cajun music and a hint of magnolia in the air to create the right atmosphere. I sat down and, taking the documents out of my inside pocket, laid them out beside me.

'Was this the lot?' I asked.

'You've done it!' she cried enthusiastically and gave my hand a squeeze. 'I knew you were the right man as soon as I laid eyes on you.' She clapped her hands in pleasure.

'Did you know that James Clarke is a serious criminal?' I asked. 'I had a pretty rough time finding these for you. Are they all there?'

She examined the papers closely.

'They are. God bless you!' She plunged her hand into her cleavage and rummaged about for a moment. For a second I feared that her gratitude was going one step too far, but then she withdrew her hand clutching a tightly rolled up bundle of notes which she offered to me.

'Dermot always did say that Clarke was a mean lump of shite, but I didn't know that he was any worse than some of the other whores' gets that Dermot worked with. Here, take this for your trouble,' she said, pushing the money into my hand. I pushed the money back but she stood over me and put the money into the top pocket of my jacket. I felt like a schoolboy having a treat forced on him by an impoverished maiden aunt.

'You've already paid me well,' I protested and gave it back to her but after a few more rounds of her giving and me declining I submitted gracefully. Her face was full of pleasure and joy at the return of her ancestral documents and the role of bountiful giver suited her well. I couldn't help thinking that maybe she really was a descendant of Queen Victoria.

'Have you anything which connects you to these documents?' I asked. 'You see, as they stand they could belong to anyone.'

'They're mine!' she said indignantly, sweeping the papers up and clutching them to her chest. 'Wasn't it me that sent you out looking for them?' she demanded with a fierce gleam in her eye; now she looked more like Boadicea than Victoria.

'Of course, *I* know they're yours, but other people might be doubtful. Have you anything to prove a connection between you and the people in these photographs?' I persisted.

'Why should I give a *feck* about people's doubts? Gran told me I must never do anything to harm the *fecking* Family. I only wanted these for myself. I told you that.'

With a regal wave of the hand, she crossed over to a cupboard and pulled out a battered photograph album. Of course, I told myself, it was bound to be the camera rather than the pen which the travelling folk used for record keeping.

'This is our family album . . . here's my gran,' she said pointing to a picture of the same beautiful girl who'd appeared in the photograph taken at Fort Belvedere. In this frame she was holding a baby and there was a small boy of about two at her feet. 'That's my Auntie Rosie she's holding and there's my da.' As her head came close to mine I got a strong whiff of dewberry; she must have been down to the Bodyshop as part of her programme of personal enhancement. She went through the pages with me. I saw there were plenty of photos to link her to her father, Edward Arthur David George Windsor and her grandmother, Mary Montgomery Windsor.

'Me gran was a *fecking* Protestant,' she volunteered. 'She was always too good for this life. That's why she died young. She came from Enniskillen and the job in royal service was a great honour for her family. Then when that idiot Edward put her in the club her own family wouldn't take her in! Stuck-up Orange bastards! They kicked her arse right out in the street! They wouldn't believe a word she said about the marriage. She was always bitter about that, that's why she never went back. The nuns took her in at the Magdalen Home in Galway and when she had the baby they wanted her to put it up for adoption. She was supposed to spend the rest of her life doing the laundry to show her gratitude. She wouldn't, she ran away with another girl and me da. They met up with travellers in Connemara, and they took her in.'

It sounded as if Granny Montgomery had been taken in a good many times by a wide variety of people. Nevertheless, she'd certainly been a spirited lass. She was lucky to have avoided lifetime incarceration in a home for 'wayward girls', a common enough way of dealing with single mothers in the 1930s. I had enough clues to check up on various aspects of the story, but I knew that only a DNA test might establish the royal parentage of Mary's da.

My thoughts were interrupted by Popeye banging on the door. He was shouting my name.

'It's that bloody toe rag Declan!' gasped Mary as she raced to the door. 'I'll *fecking* murder him!' But when she flung the door open there was no sign of the car thief, only his intended victim, Ted Blake, up to his heels in mud and clad in his brown leather coat. Arrayed behind him was a full television news crew, lights, camera, sound, the works. Clint was holding them all off single handed, his arms outstretched to prevent them from reaching their objective.

I yanked Mary back inside. 'It's you they're after. They want to put the story of your grandmother on the television news. You'll be famous,' I added unnecessarily. The look of disdain that crossed Mary Wood's features was enough in itself to convince me that she was a direct descendant of the Widow of Windsor. She was definitely not amused. I had to explain myself quickly.

'You can't keep these things secret; once one other person knows, the story seems to find its way out however hard you try to keep it in. If I find that the story was leaked by anyone working for me I'll sack them . . . I'm sorry.'

'*You're* sorry and they're going to put *my* face on every *fecking* television in the country and me with my teeth still not fixed! That *fecking* cousin of mine, Mickey Joyce, will have every penny off me if he finds out that I won the *fecking* National Hunt jackpot!'

I realised, with something approaching despair, that all Mary was worried about was revelation of the source of her wealth. She didn't give a damn about her 'breeding'.

'Jaysus, Mr Cunane! You don't look at all well,' Mary said. 'You've not been at the poteen again, have you? Well, don't you go worrying about me. I've been looking after myself for a very long time . . . If you can just take these and look after them for a while . . .' As she spoke she was busily packing the photo album, the documents and a very large bundle of cash into a Happyways Supermarkets bag. 'I know I can trust you, Mr Cunane. You've got an honest face.'

I looked back at her dumbly; for once the pace of events was catching up with me.

'If you take these with you, then I might be able to make an arrangement with that fat boyo out there, and with Mickey,' she explained carefully. 'I don't want to make it easy for them to get their hands on what they want.' She undid my shirt and carefully stowed the parcel under my right side. 'There, we'll make a shoplifter of you yet!' she claimed. 'No one will see what you're carrying under that loose jacket.'

I couldn't believe what was happening. Why was I still in the caravan? I'd carried out the commission, there was no need to stay and she didn't need me to help her to fend off Ted Blake.

'You're a great guy, Mr Cunane,' Mary said and then planted a warm kiss on my lips. I suddenly understood how generations of Royals had persuaded groundlings such as myself to do their bidding. 'Now, when you get out, I'm going to curse the hair off your head to put Mickey off the track. Out you go now.'

She was as good as her word. She didn't so much lead me to the door as pitch me through it.

Clint had by now equipped himself with a twelve-foot-long steel scaffolding spar which he was swinging round his head like a drum majorette twirling her baton and Ted and his crew were watching the performance in awe from a safe distance. At a signal from Popeye, Clint started forward and at that moment Mickey Joyce emerged from his trailer.

'What the *feck*'s going on?' he roared, advancing towards us with his henchman Declan and a whole gallery of craggy-faced individuals behind him. I watched Ted Blake taking in this figure from the Middle Ages dressed in his long smock-like pullover and I could almost see the wheels dropping into place in his agile brain as his lust for news overcame his fear of the menacing tinker chieftain.

He stepped up to Joyce officiously and within seconds they were talking business. 'That bloody Eddie Windsor Casselly!' Mickey shouted and then turned towards Mary's caravan, supported by Ted's crew as well as his own followers. Only Clint, Popeye and myself barred their way.

Clint might have been slightly lacking in the brains department, but his speed of reaction was terrific. He whirled his steel spar into the air, bent and seized Declan, unlucky enough to be nearest to him, by the neck with his enormous right hand and caught the descending spar in his left hand. The advancing gang stopped.

Clint gave a deep-throated chuckle of pleasure and held the struggling Declan out at arm's length. Declan fought to free himself from the enormous hand round his neck but only succeeded in encouraging Clint to tighten his grip. Declan's face began to turn puce. There was a dead silence. Clint laughed again, a real happy chuckle. 'Now put him down, Clint,' Popeye urged. Clint turned to look at his brother and sighed. He shook Declan once like a pitbull, and then contemptuously tossed him in the air.

324

As he collapsed onto the turf, arms and legs flailing, the crowd began to laugh. Clint looked so jolly. He rested the steel pole on the ground and clapped his own performance. Popeye hastily pulled the pair of us across the field and into our waiting cars before the Joyce family could regroup.

16

Temporary Travellers' Camp in Chorlton.
Early Afternoon. Friday 7th January 1994

I watched the Lane brothers weave away down the Parkway in the direction of the M63 interchange. I'd only gone to the campsite to rid myself of involvement with Mary Wood and her royal entanglements. Now I was leaving, not only with the complete documentary evidence of her claim to a royal connection, but also with the entire Wood fortune stuffed inside my shirt. I wondered how long it would take Blake to get after the first and Mickey Joyce after the second. Mary must have been certain that neither would have stayed in her possession for long.

I tried to close my mind to Mary's troubles and concentrate on my own . . . I had to find that one elusive little piece of hard, incontrovertible evidence to convince a judge that Headlam and Rishton had no case to answer. I drove up to Mauldeth Road, parked and phoned Delise.

'Dave!' she yelped as soon as she heard my voice. 'This place is buzzing! Come and rescue me!' She sounded hysterical. 'I've got two of Ted's female researchers camped in the corridor outside and the phone's not stopped ringing since you left the office. It's not just Blake, there's half a dozen papers trying to get us to confirm that this Mary Wood is Edward VIII's granddaughter. Then there's been some woman from Poynton who's phoned at least a dozen times. She says it's a matter of life and death. Finbar Salway's sister, Fiona, wants you to go round to Thornleigh Court right away. She didn't sound very thrilled with you, so God knows what's happened to Finbar.'

'Try to calm down, Delise. It'll all be the same in a hundred years,' I urged. 'Is that all?'

'Are you on Valium or something, Dave?' she asked in her most sarcastic tones. 'I've hardly begun yet. The police called to tell you that Mr Sinclair wants to see you urgently at Chester House. The message is that if you don't turn up they'll send someone round to collect you. Bartle's secretary rang for an immediate progress report from me, most insistent she was, so I told her that as they weren't paying me anything they'd have to wait their turn behind everything else. Oh and finally, just to round out another quiet day in the office, my mother's here in person to tell me that she's thinking of leaving Manchester and would I like to go with her.'

'Do you mean she's actually there in the office?' I asked incredulously. The Killer Whale had always maintained what she termed a 'complete ignoral' of the method by which Delise and I earned our living. She seemed to think private detective work was in the same category as testing cosmetics on animals, or the fur trade. I gripped the phone so tightly to my ear that it hurt. A 'call waiting' signal bleeped discreetly on the line.

'There's someone waiting to talk. Shall I put you on hold?' Delise asked.

'Bugger that!' I said fiercely. 'Look, can you get Molly to keep a firm eye on those two researchers for an hour? Run over to Piccadilly Station and take a taxi to Thornleigh Court. I need to have you with me.'

'Dave, that's the nicest thing you've said to me in weeks. I'll try it,' she said doubtfully. The 'call waiting' signal bleeped again and I hung up. It crossed my mind that I ought to try to escape to the hills and ask my parents to hide me for a couple of weeks. I was unlikely to ever be any richer than I was now. There couldn't be many people walking round Manchester with over £100,000 stuffed into their jacket.

I phoned Susan Attleigh at her home, not expecting any reply but she answered immediately. 'Oh David! It's you at last,' she wailed. It seemed to be my day for desperate females. 'I've been sacked. Harrison found out that I'd accessed his disc. I was escorted off the premises immediately. Right there in front of everybody. They didn't even let me empty my desk, just tipped all my little keepsakes into a bin-liner and marched me out. David, you'll have to do something. They'll put me out of this house. It's all your fault.' She paused to draw breath. I felt like laughing, I don't know what it was, delayed shock, or the revenge of the leprechauns but there was something amusing about Susan's plight. How many hundreds must have cursed the name of Attleigh when her dreaded final-demand letters thumped onto their doormats? Perhaps I could sell tickets to her eviction.

Call me heartless if you like, but the few days of separation had given me perspective. Susan was as nutty as they come.

'David! Are you there?' Her voice was shrill. 'What are you going to do about it? I might have to move in with you. Oh, and that secretary of yours will have to go. "Join the queue" she said, when I asked to speak to you again, the cheeky hussy!'

My brain began to slip into gear. I had to help her and quick, not only to soothe her outraged pride. The rough side of Delise Delaney's tongue might not be the only danger she faced today.

'Have you still got all those computer printouts Susan?' I asked in as calm a voice as I could muster.

'Yes,' she replied shakily, 'What do you take me for? An idiot?'

'No, of course not, darling. Did Harrison ask for them back?'

'You only want me for the printouts, don't you? That was all you ever wanted. You were just using me, weren't you? You were, I know you were. You're just like all the rest.' The hard shell she'd shown when I first met her had definitely cracked. One little extra push and she might finish the day in a strait-jacket, if not a cement overcoat.

I spoke carefully. 'Susan, we both had a wonderful time last weekend, but neither of us made any commitment. It was one of those once-in-a-lifetime encounters. We were going to see how things developed, remember?' Even as I spoke, I knew she'd been cooking with gas last weekend and long developments were exactly what she'd had in mind.

'Just listen, Susan,' I said, trying to get off the topic of our relationship. 'You may be in danger, you've got to get a grip.'

I had a sudden vision of someone putting two bullets into the back of her pretty head; blonde hair, blood and brains on a concrete floor . . . She was the only person who had a shred of proof that Gordon and Barry Harrison had been up to anything. Harrison was probably busy covering his tracks at this very moment. 'What I want you to do is to grab the printouts and drive into Manchester right away. Meet me at the White City car park near the police HQ. I'll try and get there before five. Don't bother about putting a casserole in the cooker or packing a bag. Just get yourself out of there right away.'

'David! What's going to happen?' Her voice had lost the accusing tone. She was now just plain scared.

'Nothing, if you get a move on and do what I say. Did Harrison ask about the printouts?'

'No, he didn't. He might not know I have them. There

won't be any record of the printout, just that his hard disc was used by someone else. But why am I in danger? Surely Barry wouldn't want to hurt me any more, would he?'

I reckoned that Susan deserved to know what she might be up against. 'I don't think it's Harrison you have to worry about, it's Jake Gordon. He's involved as well, isn't he? Gloria Rishton had something on him and look what happened to her.'

'You mean the woman who was shot by her husband?'

'Alleged to have been shot by her husband, Susan,' I corrected her sharply. 'We're dealing with some very nasty people. Just get your coat and the evidence and get yourself out of there now. Don't waste any more time, and don't stop for anything until you see me.'

Well, there was one chicken coming home to roost. Sad, the way she'd come unpacked so quickly. I wondered if I would go the same way if someone pulled the props out from under me. It was going to be a bit squashed in the camp bed if she did carry out her threat to move in with me. Harrison had fired her this morning, he must have passed on the good news to Gordon by now. There was no particular reason for them to connect me with the possible discovery of their lucrative scam, but once they started to compare notes it wouldn't take an operator like Gordon long to guess who'd rumbled him. This whole business was getting too much for me – the sooner old Sinclair was informed about it all the better.

I started the car and drove down into Chorlton and my rendezvous at Thornleigh Court with Delise and Fiona Salway. The Friday afternoon traffic was dense, the cold and lashing rain had brought out all the mums to pick up their kids from school and there was a queue of cars trying to get into Safeway. I was so impatient to move that I was tempted to drive on the pavement. Eventually the traffic cleared and I crossed the busy centre of Chorlton and drove into Thornleigh Court. I thought of my flat, the door boarded up by Harrison's lackeys, and still felt a jolt at arriving at the familiar address, but somehow the loss of my home didn't seem as serious a blow as it had last week.

Delise was waiting for me when I got out of the car. She came over and gave me a hug. I straightened my shoulders guiltily. 'What's that for?' I asked. Surprisingly she failed to detect the burden I was carrying under my jacket.

'Do I need a reason for giving you a hug, Dave?'

I wondered whether I should use this uncharacteristic sentimental outburst on Delise's part to break the news about Susan Attleigh's imminent descent on Manchester. My natural cowardice, and previous experience of Delise's sudden mood swings, both counselled caution. There'd be a whole cesspit full of untreated sewage hitting the turbine blades if Delise ever found out what I'd been up to at New Year and what Susan's plans were for the coming weekend. I didn't think 'three in a bed' was on the list of Delise's preferred activities, somehow. It was 'all or nothing' with her, she was a proper existentialist.

We ascended to the first floor when Fiona opened the automatic door for us and on the way up I gave Delise an economical version of events over the New Year weekend. 'This Attleigh woman has some information she wants me to take to the police with her. She's discovered something about Jake Gordon and I'll have to go with her.'

She shot me a puzzled glance but then we were at Fiona's door and she had no chance to ask questions.

'Come in, you two. You've got some explaining to do,

David Cunane. What have you been doing to that twin brother of mine? Do you realise that he's out at the airport right now searching for information for you? He's sixty years old, you know.'

Finbar was a grown man, and I certainly hadn't forced him to do anything.

Fiona's fierce stare softened. 'I worry about him. He's all I've got. He's actually a couple of minutes older than me but I've always treated him as if he was a younger brother. You know he can't do anything for himself. He was the apple of my mother's eye, and then he's lived in an army mess all his life.' We must have looked uncomprehending because she explained further. 'You know, the Officers' Mess. They do everything for them.'

I wondered what she was leading up to. I soon found out.

She spoke in a rush. 'Finbar told me what you had found out about this Wood woman. I told my cousin in confidence and she told her brother-in-law whose sister works for Ted Blake. Finbar knows and he's gone storming out. He says he won't come back until I've made it right with you. He's taken his passport with him and everything.'

Delise forced a smile and turned to me. 'Just as well you didn't sack me or Jay then, isn't it?' she said.

I was gob-smacked. I'd been so sure that Finbar would have been close-mouthed about Wood, I'd forgotten the strength of the bond between him and Fiona.

'Finbar says he thinks this air steward Coleman is really Italian,' Fiona volunteered uncertainly. Having made her confession, she'd staged a quick recovery.

'It's not against the law,' I said gruffly. I wasn't letting her get off so lightly.

'Why would he change his name? He must be hiding something,' Fiona insisted.

332

'Perhaps he had one of those complicated Italian names like Bergnococcioni or Sbzegutti. Perhaps his wife insisted. The police must have made some enquiries into his background or they wouldn't be resting their entire case on his evidence,' I said dismissively. I was annoyed at myself as much as at Fiona. I should have trusted Jay and Delise. Thanks to Fiona I might have fired Jay and lost Delise at the same time.

'Is this all you called us over for?' I asked brusquely. I was anxious to leave. 'We don't need local radio when you're around, Fiona. Just tell you and you'll tell the world,' I said curtly.

'Oh dear! I suppose I deserve that.' She looked crestfallen. 'Actually, there was something else. Have you been upstairs? They've taken the "For Sale" sign down outside so either someone's bought it, or they've withdrawn it from sale.'

'Go and have a look, Dave,' Delise urged.

I let myself out of Fiona's flat and took the familiar stairs to the room above. There was a padded envelope sellotaped to the door with my name on it. I opened it and two keys fell out. They fitted the new door lock. I let myself in. There was a pile of mail behind the door but the letter which caught my eye bore the familiar logo of the Polar Building Society. It was a brief note of apology from Harrison for foreclosing the mortgage 'prematurely' and repossessing of the flat, due to an 'administrative error'. Typically of the Polar Building Society there was no promise of compensation. I walked round the rooms. The carpets and curtains and light fittings were all still there. All I had to do was move my furniture back in.

But somehow it didn't feel the same. This flat had been the only 'home' I'd known as an adult. I'd bought it after marrying Elenki. We'd only known each other three months when we married, and had faced the fierce opposition of both families. Then she'd died from sickle cell anaemia.

Maybe I do have traveller's blood. With a trailer you can always go when the spirit moves you. I realised I'd been slowly stifling here among my suburban bricks and mortar.

The break had done me good. I'd been in a rut. Being put out of the flat had been just the stimulus I needed. What did I need a stable home for? I'd no wife and children (yet). Having nowhere settled to live made every day an adventure.

I took a last look in the bedroom. Whatever else the Building Society had done for me, they had laid the ghost of my wife. I left the flat, determined never to return.

When I went back downstairs, Delise and Fiona were chatting.

'Well?' said Delise expectantly.

'I can move back into the flat, it was all a mistake. But I don't want to. I just realised that I'd been making that place into a shrine and that it's time I moved on.'

Delise gave me a sympathetic look. It was too much. We'd all be blubbering in a moment.

'Right, well that's enough of that!' I snapped. 'I've got to go and meet the woman who put me out of here in the first place, and you've got to dig out John Poulter and try to make him give us a truthful statement about what went on with that log book at Alhambra. You'll have to ring Trevose and get Poulter's home address, go round and offer him money, or his job back, or a pound of my flesh, or whatever else you need to get him to retract the story the police squeezed out of him. I don't care about the legal niceties. We'll let the lawyers argue about them.'

Fiona bustled back into the room with tea on a tray.
334

We drank it down and left. Fiona's a wonderful person, she'll do anything for you, except keep her mouth shut.

In the car I showed Delise the money that Mary Wood had stowed round my waistline and we decided to head back into town and to leave the money and documents in a left-luggage locker in Piccadilly Station. Delise could hire a car at the same time and head out after Poulter while I returned to GMP HQ to meet Susan Attleigh and answer the urgent summons from Sinclair. I hoped Susan would be safe enough in the car park opposite the police headquarters until I arrived. I decided to leave my gun in the locker as well. If I needed it I could always retrieve it.

I had some trouble sorting myself out at Piccadilly – Delise was too skinny to make an effective shield against the public gaze – but eventually we got everything stowed away and hired a Ford Escort at the Avis office. Returning to Pimpernel Investigations was out of the question. Blake knew for certain that I had something to hide and the place was probably still being staked out by his researchers.

Delise and I went our separate ways. 'Is this Susan a blonde, Dave? Just you be careful,' were her parting words. I wasn't sure how much she'd guessed from the very abbreviated account of my dealings with Susan Attleigh that I'd given her, but she seemed to be in a tolerant mood, and we arranged to meet later at her mother's house. The rush-hour traffic was very heavy along Deansgate, it took me twenty minutes to go past Kendal's, and when I finally arrived at the White City retail park, adjacent to GMP headquarters, I was nearly half an hour late for my appointment with Susan.

I drove slowly over the sleeping policemen at the entrance to the park, scanning the area for Susan's car. Children were streaming out of the big Bowling Alley and the Pizza Palace was doing a roaring trade. Then I spotted her sitting primly in her neat little white VW Golf. She waved. I drove over but there was no space to park alongside her, so I parked some way off and started to walk towards her.

I never reached her car. I was about ten feet away from it when I heard someone shout, 'Grab the bastard!' and a bulky shape shot straight at me in a classic rugby tackle. My reaction was instinctive and I felt the bones in his face crunch on my knee as he went down. Suddenly assailants seemed to be coming at me from all directions and I had no intention of standing still for another clogging such as I'd received from Poulter and his mates. I was away like a hare, weaving and dodging among the parked vehicles.

I ran madly towards the Bowling Alley, startled children were dragged out of my way by angry parents as I ran. I was aware of pursuit, of hoarse shouting and gasping behind me but I just kept my head down and ran. When I reached the narrow doorway of the Bowling Alley a hand gripped my shoulder, I stopped and took a wild swing at its owner. My fist made a lucky connection with the top of his head, he went down.

Then I was into the brightly lit Alley. I ran across the lanes and a heavy bowling ball flashed at my feet. I fielded it, whirled round and hurled it with both hands at the nearest of my pursuers and it hit him with a solid thump in the chest. I heard the breath whistle out of his lungs as he slammed into the polished wooden floor. There were five more of them. They seemed to have coshes in their hands. Fear made me desperate. I raced on, reaching the end of the lanes, and scooped up a couple of the heavy skittles but then they were all on me at once and dragged me, bent double, back along the way that I'd come. The sound level in the arena seemed to reach a crescendo and it was just as well I'd left my gun behind because given the chance I'd have certainly shot the lot of them. I was conscious of a large crowd of onlookers forming a circle round us as I was pulled out into the open air and towards the open doors of a van. This looked like the end of the road.

What happened next was like a nightmare. They were dragging me into the van, I was struggling furiously, when suddenly, there were men in blue uniforms everywhere, screaming 'Halt, armed police,' at my captors. I could feel them hesitating, then I was pitched forward, face down onto the tarmac and all the breath was knocked out of my body. I lay there gasping. Then the police were all over us.

My arms were pinioned behind me with plastic handcuffs. The men alongside me without exception were cursing foully and violently, and gradually my confused mind grasped the fact that they were police themselves, from the Cheshire Serious Crime Squad. This fact apparently made not a scrap of difference to the uniformed officers, the GMP Armed Intervention Team, who had rounded them up. We were all bundled into the cages in the back of marked police vans which had made the short journey across the road from the GMP HQ. As I was hoisted up I caught a glimpse of Susan Attleigh's Golf winding its way out of the car park.

'Wankers' was among the politer expressions I heard Cheshire detectives use about the armed and uniformed Greater Manchester Police officers when, after warrant cards had been produced and identities checked, they unloaded us in the secure car park between the Communications Centre and Chester House, and Sinclair, with a uniformed Chief Inspector at his side, arrived. He wove his way among his own officers, beaming like a football manager whose team has just emerged victorious from a particularly physical cup tie. He seemed delighted when DCI Jerrold from the Cheshire side, blood streaming from his nose, protested that two of his men needed hospitalisation. He then demanded that I be released into his custody and returned to Macclesfield in his charge immediately. 'I'm taking this man back with me,' he raved. 'He's involved in a major attempt to swindle a building society and we're still not satisfied with his story over the Rishton killing.'

Sinclair gave him an enigmatic stare.

'On what charge, DCI Jerrold? Where's your warrant?' he asked.

There was a speck of foam on Jerrold's lips. 'We want to question him, sir. We're not sure what the charge is yet,' he insisted argumentatively. 'We think he's been impersonating an officer over the phone, among other things.'

'I want to question him myself,' Sinclair insisted firmly. 'He was on his way here when you waylaid him. The least you could have done was inform us of your plans. I'd have told you not to waste your journey.' Sinclair's tone was mild and friendly but he clearly didn't intend to give an inch. He turned on his heel, indicating to his own officers that I should accompany him.

I seemed to be causing a fracas. Everybody wanted me and push turned to shove, generally. The Cheshire Constabulary couldn't be faulted for determination. They intended that I should return to Macclesfield with them, come what may, and formed a solid phalanx about me, trying to fight their way out past the Communications Centre and across the road towards their own waiting van. Blows whistled through the air and I saw one man rip the collar off Jerrold's jacket. The silent struggle was ended by a single word from Sinclair.

'Enough,' he barked. Then, 'You.' He pointed to me. 'Over here.' He turned to the defeated Cestrians. 'You lot, out. Now!' Led by their battered leaders, and nursing their bruises, the Cheshire detectives left the area. We watched as, helping their wounded brethren along, they collected their van from over the road and drove away in silence.

'Never again, come fire or flood, is this man David Cunane to be admitted to this building,' said Sinclair ringingly, once again extending his bony finger in my direction. 'Regardless of his crime, he is to be taken elsewhere. Disaster follows in his wake like a stormy night after a sunny day.'

Sinclair's audience of tough policemen and women looked at me wonderingly. Turning to his own sleeveless Chief Inspector, Sinclair concluded, 'Take him upstairs, and get those ridiculous plastic cuffs off him.'

I wasn't feeling too bad myself. Apart from a momentary loss of breath, I'd not come off badly. I was anxious about Susan Attleigh, all she had seen was a bunch of thugs trying to kidnap me and then being foiled by the police. She was bound to be thinking that it was her turn next and she might well be right.

The Chief Inspector pushed me into Sinclair's office on the top floor and went over to draw the blinds.

'Well, what is it this time, David?' asked Sinclair as he followed us into the room. He looked well pleased with himself. Nobody had ripped his suit.

'*You* summoned *me*, Mr Sinclair, and I don't think it was very fair of you to blame everything that DCI Jerrold did on me,' I said sullenly.

'So I did, so I did,' he replied pleasantly enough, and then whistled through his teeth. 'I wanted to tell you that your large chum Ted Blake has agreed to forget about those filing cabinets you dropped in his lap and I advise you to do the same if you know what's good for you.'

'What filing cabinets, Mr Sinclair?' I said.

'Very droll, Davie. I presume you have something you'd like to tell me?'

'About Jake Gordon, I was bringing someone in to prove he was involved in . . .'

He interrupted. 'Before you start, let me tell you that your evidence against him had better be more than just hunches and suppositions. He's one of the most powerful men in the country.' He gave me a searching look.

'I was bringing Susan Attleigh, a Building Society executive, to see you here with hard evidence but she cleared off when Jerrold and his cohorts assaulted me,' I explained reproachfully.

'What evidence would that be, then?' he asked.

I explained about the printout, without going into much detail about how I'd come by it.

'The trouble with a computer printout, Davie, is that a computer can be altered so easily. You can't do an ESDA test on a computer. I'm not saying that your man might not have been up to something but we'd look silly if we went in there and all we came up with was a few innocent property loans. You'll have to do better.'

'Perhaps you'd like someone to get rid of Susan in the same way as Gloria Rishton?' I asked scornfully. 'She's the only one who can put Gordon and Harrison, the boss of the Polar Building Society, in the frame.'

'This is all to do with the Rishton killing, isn't it? Davie, the Cheshire Police are already satisfied that they've caught Gloria Rishton's killer,' he said. 'You should be more careful with your allegations.'

He loaded his pipe and lit up. Clouds of dense blue smoke began to drift in my direction. 'Manchester's already lost the Olympic Games, not that you had anything to do with that, had you?' he said, eyeing me speculatively. 'It can ill afford to lose one of the three major television companies it still has. Have you any idea how many people are employed at Alhambra? The situation there is delicate enough as it is. The last thing they need is the GMP barging in.'

I was disappointed that he wasn't going to arrest Gordon right away.

'Look Davie, as soon as you leave this office I'll start discreet enquiries, but that's all, and if I find even a shred of evidence the decision to proceed will have to be taken at a high level.'

So there it was. The police had their killers and Jake Gordon was to be regarded as squeaky clean until someone actually found him standing over a corpse with a smoking gun in his hand. At least, while there was still a chance that Alhambra and two thousand jobs might be saved. I didn't tell Sinclair I'd already put the skids under Gordon's rescue deal.

'Listen, Davie, bring in this star witness of yours and the Chief Inspector and I will talk to her. You're not giving us much to go on without her, are you?' Sinclair shook his head, as if amazed at his own rashness.

As I groped for an answer the phone on his desk rang. Sinclair's tattered Chief Inspector picked it up and then handed it to Sinclair. 'The Chief Constable of Cheshire,' he said reverentially.

'Yes, sir,' Sinclair said. 'He's right here with me now . . . Your lads seem to have got hold of the wrong idea entirely. No, Cunane is one of our best informants. He was actually bringing in one of the chief witnesses to make a statement when your boys jumped him . . . Oh yes, sir. I was right here in my office talking to my Chief Constable and Chief Inspector Everett here . . . Yes, they tried to make a surprise arrest in the car park across the road from Chester House . . . I saw it myself. I thought it was one of these infernal drug gangs . . . Fortunately, the Armed Response Team were here for a briefing . . . Nice training for them . . . Shall we put it down as a realistic training exercise then . . . Yes sir, just a touch of high spirits . . . so we'll say no more about it . . . Nice to hear from you, Jack. Remember me to Ethel.'

When he put the phone down, Sinclair's face was deadpan. Then he put the tip of his little finger to his right eye and pulled it down. Clearly, that was all the explanation he intended to give.

'It looks like you're going to have to find this mystery witness of yours, then, if only to back up the wee story I was just telling,' he said finally. 'Chief Inspector Everett here will have to go with you. I can't run the risk of leaving you unsupervised at the moment.'

I eyed the burly uniformed copper, who was giving me an unfriendly glance. 'What about that female detective you had with you when you came round to my office?' I asked hopefully.

'That's enough. Fred here will go with.'

Fortunately I was spared the pleasure of an evening with 'Fred' Everett by the fax machine in the corner, which began to buzz. Everett went over and ripped off the flimsy.

White male, forty-seven years old, identified as John B. Poulter, head of special security at Alhambra TV, was admitted to Wythenshawe Hospital with gunshot wounds. 18.45hrs. Pronounced DOA by the A&E Department. A major crime investigation unit headed by DCI Stradley is responding. Witness Delise C. Delaney of Chorlton, M21 is assisting. First report of the incident logged at 18.31hrs. Suspect, a motorcyclist described as slightly built male, wearing black leathers and helmet and riding a Yamaha scrambler, registration unknown . . .

I felt as if someone had kicked me in the stomach.

'That's your lady friend, isn't it?' asked Sinclair. His eyes were like two small dead pools. 'I suppose you think you're going to run over there to hold Miss Delaney's hand, don't you? Well, you're not! You'll find this Attleigh woman or spend the night in the cells. Your choice.' He continued, addressing Chief Inspector Everett, 'Fred, you'll have to go down and liaise with Stradley in Sale. Take a back seat, leave everything to him, but find out what's going on. Let me know at once if there's the slightest evidence that Cunane's wild allegations about Gordon are true.'

Sinclair's accent was much closer to the Scottish vernacular now than his usual, 'refeened', Edinburgh tones. The sudden news about Poulter, an Alhambra employee, had thrown him. I'd never known him get this frantic. His cool was legendary throughout the British police force. He gave lectures on Stress Management to other senior officers. A trace of a smile may have appeared on my face because his adjutant, Everett, grabbed me by the shoulders and projected me through the door before I could say another word.

It wasn't the first time that I'd left the GMP HQ after a hostile interview but on this occasion there was a special charge in the air. I walked across the road to where I'd left my car, got in and tried to work out my next move. There was nothing I could do to help Delise, she wouldn't be in any danger now. I switched the car radio on. News about Poulter wasn't long in coming on. He had been shot down in the street while walking to the pub with a female companion. The assassin had coolly ridden up to the couple, shot Poulter twice in the head and then driven off. There was no clear description of him and no motive was suggested.

I looked at my hands and then held them out in front of me. They were trembling. I felt odd. It wouldn't help anyone if I fainted in the street, so I left the car, walked over to the Pizza Palace and ordered a deep-dish pizza and a pint of Coors. I drained it in one draught. It was well-spent time. When I drove away from White City I felt ready for anything.

Eating had given me time to think about the next move, and I decided that my first stop had to be the Alhambra Studios. Either Gordon or Trevose must be behind Poulter's murder. Somehow I had to pin it on one or other. I phoned ahead to let Trevose know that I was on my way. He was about to leave the building when I got through. I was at the roundabout at the end of Deansgate when he spoke so I asked to him to hang on for a few minutes. His answer was indistinct. I raced down Dock Street to the surrealistic studio building which looked more like a wrecked aircraft carrier than ever in the dusk and parked outside on the double yellow line.

The doorman came bustling down to shoo me away and I asked him if Trevose had left. He pointed towards the car park across the street. I abandoned the car and sprinted across, leaving the engine running in the Nissan. The rough, poorly lit condition of the Alhambra car park was the factor that saved Trevose's life.

He was about fifty yards away from me at the other end of the enclosure when I spotted the motorcyclist racing towards us from the opposite direction. I yelled at Trevose to get down, as I saw the assassin aim a long-barrelled pistol at Trevose and fire. His bike was jolting up and down over the ruts and both shots hit Trevose's car. Trevose stood like a frozen rabbit as the second bullet thumped into his car, then the biker spotted me closing on his intended victim and sheered off without going in for another shot.

He roared off up Dock Street towards Deansgate. Trevose, slow to react when first threatened, had now rolled right under his big Range Rover and was refusing to emerge. I had to get hold of his ankles and threaten to drag him out. He was covered in filth, there was a puddle right under his car and he'd succeeded in mopping most of it up with his cashmere overcoat. When he saw the two big holes in the side of his car he bent over and vomited.

I took him forcibly by the arm and hurried him across the road. Several of the stalwart doormen who'd used me as a punch bag a few days previously relieved me of my shivering burden. They looked shocked and frightened too. They must have heard the news about Poulter.

'Get him up into his office and phone the police,' I ordered.

'You're not going to leave me, are you?' Trevose said pleadingly as his guards stood about woodenly. 'I'll pay for protection. You saved my life.' That was true in a way, if the hitman hadn't seen me hurrying towards his victim he would have taken his time and closed in on his kill, but I had no intention of nursemaiding Trevose.

We crossed the glittering loggia into a ground-floor reception room and Trevose immediately picked up a bottle of brandy from the tray in the corner and poured himself a stiff belt.

'Where's Jake Gordon now?' I asked.

'I don't know, he never seems to be in one place for long. He's always on the move. Do you think he's responsible for this?' If he had anything to do with what was going on he was giving a convincing performance in the role of innocent victim.

'I don't know. It seems logical to blame him, but for all we know our friend on the Yamaha has him down as the next target.' This was the wrong thing to say. It launched Trevose off into another bout of hand wringing and lip flapping. I took pity on him. There was an old blue raincoat in a wardrobe so I stripped the filthy over-coat off him and thrust it at him.

'You've got to lose yourself for a few days,' I said.

'Please stay with me,' he begged.

'You'll be all right,' I said unconvincingly. 'You've got all these guards to protect you.' It was unfortunate for Trevose that the elaborate building plan hadn't included an impregnable bunker for the chief executive.

When I stepped outside, there was not one of the black-suited security men to be seen. They'd all vanished like smoke. In the end I bundled Trevose into my Nissan, still waiting on the double yellow line with its engine running, and after impressing on him that his survival depended on secrecy I dropped him at an obscure hotel in the suburbs. I drove off towards the Atwood Building. I still had to locate Susan Attleigh and I needed help.

More information was coming in about the Poulter shooting. There was a statement claiming that the assassin might have mistaken Poulter, who had been wearing his security uniform, for a policeman and trying to make out that the killing could have been drugs related.

Certainly, Sinclair would clutch anxiously at any straw that suggested Poulter's connections with Alhambra and with the Rishton case were just incidental details. A mistaken-identity case would suit him down to the ground.

The news-reader droned on. The killing had taken place in Marsland Road, Sale, fifty yards from the victim's home, on the steps of a pub. Calls for police to be routinely armed were voiced by a local Police Federation spokesman.

It had to be Gordon who was behind all this.

When I reached the salubrious neighbourhood I'd chosen for the headquarters of Pimpernel Investigations things were already hotting up for an evening's entertainment. The prostitutes, male and female, were at their stations as I cruised along Aytoun Street and Chorlton Street looking for a parking space. There were crowds of lightly clad young people making their way towards the spurious massage parlours and less spurious restaurants situated on the narrow web of streets around Chinatown and Piccadilly. I finally parked in a space opposite the bus station and made my way towards the Atwood Building on foot. I resolved that if I found Susan Attleigh alive I'd take her advice about relocating the office.

The first thing I saw was Attleigh's white VW but she wasn't in it. There seemed to be hundreds of people milling about the entrance to the office. I groaned to myself. It had been a sorry day when I took the commission from Mary Wood. The hyenas of the tabloid press had gathered with the scent of royal blood in their nostrils. Nothing less than a small nuclear explosion would put them off my trail now.

I made my way back to the car and phoned the office number but the line was engaged. Who the hell was in my office, I wondered? I had nothing else to do and nowhere else to go. I knew that Susan wouldn't have gone back to her home and the only other place we'd been together was my shabby little office. After ten minutes of listening to the engaged signal the dulcet tones of the BT telephone voice advised me that my waiting call could not be accepted at this time. I cursed the day I'd had 'Call Waiting' installed and redialled. Half an hour later, having checked that Susan wasn't in Poynton, I finally got through to the office.

Liberty Walker answered the phone. I told him to put me through to Jay but he just went on repeating that Pimpernel Investigations was not giving out any information about the royal claim at this time. I tried shouting my name very loudly but Liberty just went on with his spiel. In desperation I yelled the word 'McDonald's' as loudly as I could. The sound must have reached his better ear. He stopped speaking and put Jay on the line.

'Boss, is that you? Where have you been? It's a real sad scene here. We can't get out of the office,' he said plaintively. 'They want a statement from you. You've got to tell them something, I'm supposed to be going to the Hass tonight.' Jay was losing his cool. His voice had lost its usual tone of ironic detachment.

'That really breaks me up, Jay. You can't miss an evening at the Hacienda. I'm heartbroken about interfering with your plans,' I said.

'Sack it, man! I'm doin' the best I can,' he replied angrily.

'Is Susan Attleigh with you?' I asked.

'If you mean the snidy white woman who says she's going to be running things round here soon and keeps threatening to put my ass on the street every five minutes, then she is. And she's a right bum clart if you's axin'.'

'OK Jay, that's enough. Cool it. What are you doing in the office anyway?'

'Oh man! It's that Finbar Salway! He only trailed Coleman to Italy, didn't he? He'll be in Naples by now. He thinks he's SuperDibble. Got right on the plane with Coleman, an' he got real hard with me. Told me to go with him, or come back here, so here I am.'

'God!' I groaned. 'As if life isn't complicated enough.'

'Yeah, that's what I thought, Boss. I told him he's going to end up "sleeping wit' de fishes" in the Bay of Naples.'

'What a little Job's comforter you are. You should have stopped him.'

'Now you're joking me, Boss. He's one mean mother
348

when he wants to be. I wasn't going to mess wit' him . . .
And Boss, there's another little t'ing.'

'Hit me with it,' I said fatalistically.

'When Liberty and me were coming in the building,
this big mother came up and served us a writ.'

'Oh God! Have you read it? What is it?'

'It's from Bartle, Bartle and Grimshaw. It's a restraining
order. It says somting 'bout they will lock you up if you
claim to be working for them or to have any connection
with them.'

'Is that all?' I asked with a real sense of relief. I'd been
expecting this. Gordon must know what I was up to.

'Forget the writ. What's Susan doing now?'

'That t'ing's holding the door shut with her big fat
behind, that's what she doin', and I ain't takin' no more
earache from her.' Jay was laying the Caribbean on by
the trowel load. He must be really stressed out.

I asked him if he had any ideas for getting the three
of them out of there.

'Liberty wants us to crawl along the parapet to the
next office . . .'

'That's out. It's broken in several places.'

'Then he wants to start a fire under the smoke detector
and set the sprinklers off. We're s'posed to rush out in
the confusion . . .'

'You're going to have to work on that one. I don't
want the office flooded or set fire to,' I said cautiously.

'Wait a minute, Boss. Liberty's sayin' what if we light
a fire in the bin? Then blow smoke under the door and
just set the alarm off by breaking the glass. That way the
sprinklers won't start up.'

We both paused to consider this for a minute.

'I need to get out of here, Boss. I'm going to go mad
with agoraphobia,' he urged.

'Claustrophobia, Jay,' I corrected automatically. 'OK,
349

go for it. Make sure that Susan has the computer print-out. You drive her car yourself and meet me at Delise's but don't let anyone from the press follow you. Take them for a tour of Salford Quays, anywhere, but lose them. There'll be a bonus in it.'

I sat in the car until the sound of fire sirens could be heard coming from the direction of the Atwood Building, then I set off. As I pulled out onto the main road, traffic was held up as two more fire engines raced past in the direction of the office.

I drove to Chorlton by way of Rusholme and Fallowfield.

17

Chorlton. Friday Evening. January 7th 1994

It looked as if the others had dodged the press when I arrived at the narrow little street alongside the handkerchief-sized park where Delise lived. Attleigh's white VW was already parked in front of the house. It was impossible to be certain with so many cars jammed onto the pavements round the fashionable little restaurant near the end of Delise's street, but Jay appeared to have shaken off unwanted attention. For how long, was anyone's guess.

When I knocked, the door was opened by a tall young policewoman. 'The boyfriend, are you?' she asked in a nasal North Manchester accent. 'You'd best come in, then. She's been expecting you for a while.' I didn't like the way she said that, but I knew better than to complain.

When I entered the long living room there was a heavy atmosphere. Delise was sitting on her own at the end of the sofa, a slight figure in her dark sweater. She managed a feeble smile in my direction, but the long expressions on the faces of Jay, Liberty and Susan Attleigh suggested that there'd been some tension. The sight of Susan in the same room with Delise was like a knife in the guts and I resisted the urge for a quick getaway. I went and sat next to Delise, and put my arm round her. The only noise in the room was the radio chatter on the officer's communicator.

'You'll be all right now then, Delise? Your friend looks big enough to take care of you,' the policewoman commented cheekily, speaking in the louder-than-normal

351

voice reserved for conversations with children. 'You won't forget to phone us if you remember anything.'

No sooner had she donned her coat and exited from the room than a babble of noise erupted. It was Susan who broke through the din to express herself forcefully. 'Just what is going on, David? I thought you were supposed to be rescuing me but it turns out you're involved with all these other people.' She looked pointedly at Delise. Her voice had entirely lost the beseeching tone which had blighted our earlier conversation and she looked mean and predatory in her turtleneck sweater, long denim shirt and black leggings.

All my old aggression against Building Society employees came flooding back. If it hadn't been for her and her Society, I'd never have been so eager to take the commissions that had landed me where I was now. Susan must have seen the fierce gleam in my eye because she took a step back. I leapt up from the sofa and grabbed her by the arm.

'You're going to tell me exactly what the hell has been going on,' I shouted. My head was throbbing. 'You think I'm a soft touch, don't you? You think you can spin me any old yarn and I'll believe you.' I moved to grab her by the shoulders and shake the truth out of her. I'd lost my rag completely. She thought I was going to hit her and flinched away. I was conscious of Delise trying to pull me back.

'Dave! Leave her alone!' She took a grip on my hair and jerked my head, as Liberty and Jay looked on with eyes like saucers. I backed away from the frightened comfort-eater, but my fists were still clenched. She put her hands up to her face like a little girl and fell back into the armchair sobbing her heart out. Life on the wild side in Chorlton was too much for her, after all. I felt bitterly angry with myself for losing control but at the same time nettled that I'd kept enough control to stop myself shaking the truth out of her. She spared me the need for explanations as she began to speak again, but in a barely audible whisper this time.

'You're right. It's all my fault. I should never have tried to involve you, David. I was desperate.'

I could feel the hair standing up on the back of my neck. Delise went and sat on the arm of the chair beside Susan and put her arm round her. She looked up at me. 'If we're going to have a row in here we'd better do it in comfort. I've no idea what you've been doing to upset this woman but I can guess.' She gave me a contemptuous look. 'Go and make some tea,' she said turning to Jay and Liberty, 'and take your time about it.'

'You've got the wrong idea,' I started to justify myself but Susan interrupted me.

'It's my fault. I wanted to use David to get revenge on Barry but I never thought it would turn out like this.'

'Barry? What do you mean *Barry*?' I said, like an idiot. Delise looked from Susan to me with a puzzled frown.

'Barry Bloody Harrison, who else?' Susan replied bitterly. 'I'm having his child. I thought he'd leave his wife, but when I told him, he wanted me to go and get an abortion. He gave me the name of a good clinic in Stockport. He said he'd pay.' She began sobbing again.

Delise scowled at me and then patted her on the shoulder. 'Men are bastards, aren't they,' she said comfortingly.

'Hold on!' I interjected angrily. 'Let her tell her story. I think I've a right to hear it.'

'He's right. I'll feel better if I tell someone,' Susan volunteered. She dried her eyes on a tissue. 'When David came to see me about his mortgage problems I thought he was just another punter with a hard-luck story but . . .' she paused and looked at me anxiously, 'I sensed that

353

he was capable of violence. It was the day after Barry told me he wasn't going to leave Madge, that's his wife. What Barry had done was irregular . . . I mean about David's mortgage. I thought we could work together.'

'Susan, you're not making much sense,' Delise interrupted impatiently.

'Yes, she is. Just let her get on with it,' I said.

'Well, even before we went through those printouts I knew that Barry was up to his neck in all kinds of "get rich quick" schemes. There was a lot more than I ever told you, David. His salary of £120,000 has never been enough for him, the greedy bastard.' Susan was getting into her stride now, she leant back on the sofa and made herself comfortable. 'He'd been involved with a ring of bent solicitors and estate agents. They used to buy up properties at a special low price and then they'd overvalue them and the Society would grant some punter a mortgage. The profits went straight into their own pockets. 'They used to meet at the golf club for a share-out every other Saturday. He used to joke about it. "Going for his dibs," he called it. He was just a branch manager then and I was a counter clerk. But when the bottom fell out of the property market there weren't the same number of suckers queuing up for houses.

'Then he met this Jake Gordon at some business lunch. I told you he worshipped successful businessmen. Well, that was true. After that I hardly used to see him. He was always trailing round after the wonderful Jake Gordon. He spent more time in that man's helicopter than he spent in my bed.' She had another little weep and got to work with the tissues again.

'He said Gordon's contacts were good, and so they were. Barry was summoned to head office and given a job supervising the really important loans. He never looked back after that.

'When they made Barry chief executive at Polar everything was wonderful, we had a marvellous time. But Barry just couldn't resist trying to make more money than he was earning. A lot more money. He said no successful entrepreneur lived on a salary. That was just pin money. He used his own money at first ... I mean the money he'd made before. There were disused railway lines round Wigan, he bought them up hoping to opencast mine the coal underneath, no one had ever touched that land before. But he lost money. There isn't the market for coal any more.' She paused to mop her face with the tissue. Her mascara had run, giving her a ghoulish look.

'What about Jake Gordon? Where does he come into it?' I prompted.

Susan gave an involuntary shudder. 'I was hoping that Barry would give up hope of becoming a multi-millionaire and settle down with me. We could have been ever so comfortable. I'd have made a lovely home for him. He hadn't had a proper marriage with Madge for years, she's years older than he is.' She dissolved into tears again.

A glance at Delise confirmed that she was putting two and two together and making four about what had been going on between me and Susan. Her jaw was set at a very firm angle and her expression had lost the sympathetic smile but in her self-absorption Susan didn't notice that her female audience was now distinctly less sympathetic.

'But she's like a limpet is Madge, always threatening him with losing the children, and back he'd run, just like a big soft kid himself.' Susan was oblivious to the increasingly hostile atmosphere surrounding her. 'I thought if I got pregnant he'd make the break, but he didn't!' she said fiercely.

'No, tell us about Gordon,' Delise insisted firmly, 'not about Barry and Madge.' She took hold of Susan's hand tightly, I could see the whiteness of her knuckles as she gripped Susan's chubby hand.

'Well, it was Gordon who showed Barry how to set up the dummy companies. He was the man on the outside, you see. He showed Barry how to set up companies in Liechtenstein and Jersey. Like I said, this deal they're into now is only the latest in a series. The Building Society doesn't always lose money because Barry has to pay back the loans, at the lowest possible interest mind you . . . Whatever happens, he and Gordon always make a fat profit for themselves and naturally while the Society's lending money to them there's less to go into home loans. We've become much less tolerant of people who get behind with their mortgages. You know all about that, don't you, David?' She started sobbing again. 'Oh God, I'm sorry,' she wailed.

Delise made no move to comfort her this time. Susan rubbed the mascara-stained tissue into her eyes again. Her face now looked as if she was wearing a black mask.

'Well, we'll have a cup of tea and then we'll go down to police headquarters and tell all this to Assistant Chief Constable Sinclair,' I said gruffly. 'I've no doubt Barry and Jake will be able to spend a lot of time reminiscing in some nice cosy jail.'

'No, no! I can't do that. I love him. I'm having his baby,' Susan squawked, folding her arms across her abdomen like some Henry Moore sculpture.

'Yes you will!' I shouted back at her. 'You and Barry are not the only people that Jake Gordon has messed with. Who the hell do you think's behind all this shooting?' But I could see that my words were wasted on Susan. It was like arguing with a lump of suet.

356

'Do you think it was Gordon who had Poulter killed?'
Delise asked breathlessly. She looked very pale.

'He's the only one I can think of with a strong enough
motive. Poulter could have fingered him for doctoring
the log book. Gordon must have got to know that we
were pressuring Poulter. The same motorcycle assassin
who killed Poulter has already tried to kill Trevose, the
only other person who can prove Gordon's involvement.
He fired at him twice and missed.'

'Do you think the killer will come round here after
us?' Delise sounded nervous. 'Gordon must know that
you're onto him.'

'He'll not come here,' I said with a confidence I didn't
feel. 'How would Gordon know where you live? No, I
should think he's trying to make himself scarce now. If
anything, he'll think we're round at Chester House,
telling all we know to Mr Sinclair. That's where we
should be.'

'I'm not going,' said Susan. 'Can I use your phone? I
want to phone Barry. I'll not tell him where I'm calling
from.'

'Oh, you great stupid cow!' Delise yelled. 'Don't you
realise that he'll have you killed? You're the only one
who can tie him in with Gordon. What does it take to
make you see sense? He's made you pregnant, sacked
you, threatened you, and now he'll kill you.'

'I don't think so. Barry's not like that,' Susan said
uncertainly. 'If I phone him, I can tell him I'm going to
the police unless he takes me back. Oh, I wish I'd put
something in the oven, but you told me not to, David. He
loves his casseroles, does Barry, especially a nice goulash.'

Delise gave me a despairing look. The woman was
clearly deranged as I should have realised long ago.
'Look, Susan, you'll have to do what you think is best.
I'm not a policeman, I can't arrest you or force you to

grass on Barry, but at least leave all the printouts here. Then if he does threaten you, you'll have something to come back at him with,' I said.

'Thanks Dave!' exploded Delise. 'Thanks for offering to turn my mother's home into a shooting gallery. As if I hadn't seen enough violence for one day with that horrible man Poulter having his head blown off right in front of me. You want to make us into a sitting target by protecting this crazy woman's papers. As soon as she tells her precious Barry where the papers are, they'll have their hitman round here straight away.'

Susan Attleigh gave a little smile. 'No, David's right. I don't think Barry will try anything nasty. He's more like a mischievous schoolboy than a real villain. As long as he knows I have the printouts hidden somewhere it'll keep him in line.'

She went over to the phone to give Barry the glad tidings. Delise hovered beside her to prevent any untoward indiscretion. Jay and Liberty, sensing that the drama was over, came in with the long-delayed tea on a tray, then Jay went out to Susan's VW and collected the heavy bundle of printouts while she went to wash her face. Returning with the mascara removed, she hastily made her way to the door, all efficiency and calm again, but I blocked her path. Before I released her I had one last question for her. There was something bugging me, 'How old is Barry, then?' I demanded.

'He's fifty-one, in the prime of life,' she said haughtily and then made a rapid departure, tossing her hair back and muttering to herself.

When she had left Delise said gloomily, 'You know that's the last anyone will ever see of her. You're totally irresponsible, Dave.'

'No, I can't stop her doing what she wants to do. She had this whole thing worked out, probably all she ever wanted to do was to give me the printouts so she could blackmail her blessed Barry with them. Anyway both she and Barry are going to be lucky to keep out of prison if there's any sort of official investigation into Jake Gordon. I can't see him keeping his mouth shut to protect small fry like Barry.'

I sat beside her and she put her arm round me, so maybe I wasn't in such bad trouble after all. We turned to Jay.

'Will you be mother, Jay?' I asked.

'Wicked, man!' he muttered as he poured.

Jay knew a lot about herbs and weeds, but brewing tea wasn't one of his skills. I didn't say anything, but carefully removed the tea leaves from my mouth with a handkerchief so that he couldn't see. He'd done well in getting Susan out of the Atwood Building and I felt guilty about my earlier threats to sack him. He must have been able to sense that I was in a good humour towards him.

'Any chance of me borrowing the Nissan, Boss?' he asked hopefully. 'I've got this girl in Chorlton that I was taking to the Hass, but all this messing has made me late and I'll have to take Liberty home before I pick her up.'

'Jay, you know I don't like lending the car for your nocturnal excursions,' I replied sarcastically. The last time he'd had it for this purpose it came back with mud up to the axles, the seats pushed back and a used condom in the ashtray.

'Go on, Boss, don't be snidy. You promised me a bonus for rescuing your lady friend!'

'Just watch it, Jay! Zip your lip! She was no friend of mine,' I said quickly. I scrabbled through my pockets. 'Here's £40, and think yourself lucky that I don't dock your wages for cheeking your employer.'

'Aw, go on, Boss,' he persisted, unsatisfied with this bounty. 'At least let me have the car tomorrow. I might end up here in Chorlton tonight and I could take it down to the office for you.'

In the end I gave him the keys of the Ford Fiesta that Delise had hired yesterday and of my own car. He could use the hire car, return it tomorrow morning, and then pick my car up from Chorlton. I was feeling generous. At any rate, it was a relief to get back to normal problems, such as sorting out Jay's private life. All I had to worry about now, on the personal front, was whether Delise had forgiven me and if Finbar Salway had managed to avoid having his throat cut in some Neapolitan back alley. Jake Gordon was probably already on a flight to Brazil.

'You're too generous to him,' Delise said when Jay had left, towing his half brother behind him. Liberty looked weary and ready for sleep. I'd given him £10 as well. To fend off the press he'd put the phone to his deaf ear, like Nelson with his telescope, and he had come up with the idea for the escape.

'Dave, what do you mean about getting killed? I thought you said there was going to be a police patrol outside,' she said nervously.

I described my encounter with the assassin in the Alhambra car park. I knew that failure to kill Trevose would probably make it too hot for Gordon to hang around Manchester.

'Why would someone want to kill Trevose? Or even Poulter, come to that? It was horrible, Dave. There was blood all over my clothes. That's why they let me home so early. The policewoman helped me to change. I've got to go in and look through photos and make a statement tomorrow.' Delise was on the verge of tears, I could feel her trembling. I hated to see her down, she was normally so buoyant.

'I think there's something really big going down. There

are hundreds of millions involved somehow. I'm sure that's why Gloria got herself killed; she lifted up a tiny corner of the carpet and saw a little bit of what had been carefully swept away by someone who didn't want it revealed. Perhaps Finbar will find something on his Italian expedition.'

This wasn't much comfort to Delise but it was the truth. I wasn't much closer to 'solving' the case than I'd been the day she'd got me out of Macclesfield police station. Apart from those printouts, I still had no 'proof', in Sinclair's sense, that Gordon was involved. Delise got up and found a half-filled bottle of Bushmills in a cupboard. I looked at her in surprise.

'Well Dave, you're going to stay the night, aren't you? And after everything that's happened I don't feel like making love, so I think we both need a sedative.'

When I surfaced from my alcohol-induced slumbers the sun was shining full in my face through the bedroom window and we were cosily tucked up in the Killer Whale's brass bed with its folksy patchwork quilt.

I lurched out of bed in search of paracetamol but there was nothing in the bathroom cabinet or in the medicine chest downstairs.

'Mum doesn't believe in chemical cure-alls,' Delise explained – my noisy search had woken her. 'She only keeps homoeopathic stuff in the house.'

After a hastily snatched breakfast in which she offered me muesli and natural yoghurt and I settled for toast and black coffee, we set out. Delise insisted on me inhaling some of the Killer Whale's peppermint oil. It didn't have much effect but I was anxious to please her and told her my headache had gone. When I put my head out of the door I knew that walking was the wrong choice, but there were no cars available. The old 2CV which Delise often borrowed was in the garage for repair, Jay had the hired car and I'd foolishly promised him the use of the Nissan, so there was no alternative to the fresh air. Although it was bright and sunny, the wind came straight from the Arctic and we walked at a fair pace to keep warm.

We took the footpath along the Manchester bank of the Mersey at Jackson's Boat. There were a few brave early morning cyclists taking advantage of the weekend for a spot of exercise and I realised that it was those early morning solitary excursions through the reed beds that I missed. Three cormorants were perched up on an electricity pylon looking over towards the lake at Sale Water Park, enjoying the chilly conditions and each other's company. The wind was making the huddled birch trees bend and tremble. The Mersey was bowling along too, not quite at flood levels but near enough to have flattened all the grass and bushes along its steep embankments.

The Met deposited us at St Peter's Square and we joined the affluent Saturday morning shoppers in King Street for a slow trawl through the fashion shops, starting at King Street and taking in Kendal's, and St Ann's Square. I thought Delise deserved something to keep her mind off her troubles.

It was lunch-time before we finished, and she managed to spend half of Mary Wood's 'tip'. We staggered into the restaurant in the Royal Exchange, Delise had a salad while I slaked a raging thirst with a pint of lager. When we came out we headed across St Ann's Square for a taxi to the Atwood Building. There was a news-stand at the corner of the Square and written on the yellow poster I saw the words 'BOMB KILLS TWO IN CHORLTON'. I felt an invisible hand gripping my throat. Jay was supposed to be picking my car up in

Chorlton, almost certainly with Liberty in tow. The tension headache that I'd had last night came back with a vengeance. I was getting paranoid. Why should I assume a bomb had anything to do with me? I loosened my collar and looked at Delise. She hadn't seen the poster.

'Why don't I drop you off at GMP headquarters now, and you can make your statement and then you go on to Bolton and stay with my parents for the rest of the weekend? You can go on the tram to Bury and my father will pick you up. Or better still you phone him when they let you go, and he can set off to meet you. I'll join you later this evening and we can see how far Paddy's got with renovating that trailer.'

Delise gave me a peck on the cheek. 'We could both do with a change of scene. I'll have to go home to pick up my toothbrush and a few things though.'

'Look Delise, you've already bought enough for your own car-boot sale. By the time you go home and pack a cabin trunk the day will be over. Just ask the police to drop you at Trafford Bar when they've done with you and go straight to Bury on the tram. I'll get Paddy to pick you up.'

In the back of the taxi we repacked Delise's purchases into one large bag. I dropped her off at Chester House and went on to Chorlton. I don't know what I expected to find there, but I had a premonition, and I didn't want Delise involved. I hadn't really thought it all through. If it was her house that had been blown up the police would be sure to question her about it anyway. All I knew was that she'd been through enough yesterday.

My worst fears were realised when we reached Willows Road. The whole street was blocked off and the taxi had to let me out on the main road. When I joined the sightseers pressing along the street I could see that the explosion had taken place in the centre of the road at the corner of the park diagonally across from Delise's home. Her house was undamaged. A car had blown up in the middle of the road. A red car. My car.

And Jay was the only one who had a key.

Bits of it were strewn about the street, each in its own enclosure fenced off with blue and white tape and there was a hole in the road, still steaming, which showed how far the car had moved since exploding. Police were trying to erect large hessian screens to fence off the site, a difficult task against the stiff breeze, while others were on their hands and knees in the street picking up fragments of metal and dumping them in dustbins. There were soldiers from an Army bomb disposal team lounging about near the twisted railings of the little park, chatting and laughing; obviously their services weren't required. A BBC TV news team was filming a reporter against the background of devastation.

I felt numb. I just stood there in the crowd, staring open-mouthed at the spectacle. A heavy arm fell on my shoulder and I almost jumped out of my shoes in fright.

'So Manchester's very own harbinger of disaster finally made it to the scene. I was wondering how long it would take you to get here,' said ACC Sinclair. He wasn't in uniform.

I had to struggle to bring words to my lips. 'It's nothing to do with me,' I croaked. He slapped me on the shoulder heartily. We might have been at a football match instead of at the site of a fatal explosion. 'I know that. Not quite your scene, is it? We haven't identified the car or the victims yet, two youths by the look of it. But there's not that much left of either of them. At first they thought it was a gas explosion but now it looks like high explosive, and whoever did it used one hell of a lot. They might have been carrying a bomb for the IRA and got careless with their detonators. Anyway, Davie, I can't stand here gassing to you. Had any more fantasies about Jake Gordon?'

As he turned to go I grabbed his arm. 'I wanted to talk to you about Delise Delaney, she's down at Chester House making her statement and I'd be grateful if no one told her about this. She's been through enough.'

He looked at me and shook his head. 'Want favours from the police now, do you?' He stood looking at me for a moment. 'All right, Davie. I'll call it in from the car.'

He pushed his way through the crowd and disappeared.

I managed to put one foot in front of the other and move myself away from the area. What was I going to say to Lovena Anderson? She'd already lost one son, now to have another blown to pieces in an explosion intended for me . . . How would she bear it? How could I bear it? I leant against a garden wall and vomited into the privet hedge. Two youths heading for the disaster area walked into the road to avoid me, eyeing me suspiciously. I thought about Liberty Walker and all the efforts I'd made to dispose of him. He was gone for good now.

I just walked and walked in a complete circle right round Chorlton, totally oblivious to my surroundings, until I came to a halt in front of Thornleigh Court. Like homing pigeons, my feet had carried me back to my former flat. I felt sick and dizzy and sat on the low perimeter wall to recover. I didn't get the chance.

'Dave, is that really you?' came the familiar tones of Finbar Salway. I lifted my head up and gazed at him. He looked as green as I felt. To my surprise he leant down and touched my arm. 'It *is* you! Thank God! When I heard about that explosion near Delise's house I was sure it must have been you and her.'

'I wish it had been me. It should have been me. They got Jay and Liberty instead,' I replied.

He continued to touch my arm, as if to reassure himself that I wasn't a ghost, and I pushed his arm away, more roughly than I had intended.

He stepped back quickly. 'Look, man, you're suffering from shock. I've seen it before. You'd better come in before you step into the road in front of a bus.'

I felt no inclination to move from where I was, least of all into my former home, but Finbar wasn't to be resisted. He half dragged me up the stairs to his sister's flat. Fiona was there, tight-lipped for once. She said nothing but directed me towards an armchair. While Finbar lifted my feet up, she pushed a stool under my legs and then wrapped me in a blanket. We sat in silence for a few minutes. I was dry-eyed, but I felt like weeping.

Fiona pushed a mug of tea into my hands. 'Drink this. I know the first-aid books say you shouldn't give shock victims drinks, but in my experience there's nothing much in life that a good cup of tea won't improve.' I drank it slowly. I did feel better, although I would have preferred whisky to tea.

'Dave, there's something you should know. This may not be the best time but I might not get another chance to tell you,' Finbar said anxiously. A cigarette burned away in his hand, its ash ready to drop onto the carpet. My old 'Good Housekeeping' instincts awakened, possibly due to the proximity of my former home, I picked up an ashtray and held it out for him.

'You know the airline steward, William Coleman, who you sent me and er . . . Jay . . . after,' he said, speaking with maddening slowness and lack of direction.

'Spit it out, Finbar,' I said wearily.

'You wanted me to find some little thing which would

help to discredit him as a witness, only I found something rather big.'

Finbar's drawn-out method of dispensing information was a wonderful cure for shock. He ran his hand through his hair, combing the tight, curly, faded locks with his fingers, then nervously lit up again. Curbing my desire to scream, I drummed my fingers on the arm of the chair.

'Put him out of his misery, Finbar!' snapped Fiona, also lighting a cigarette. I fanned the smoke away irritably.

'Right. I'm almost one hundred per cent certain that Coleman is er . . . a bigamist!' he rounded off apologetically and looked at me expectantly.

I was like a mountaineer who thinks he's reached the summit only to find himself back in the foothills. What were we going to uncover next? I wanted to laugh hysterically. Finbar's idea of a really big crime was bigamy, and Jay and Liberty had been blown to pieces instead of me.

Fiona spoke. 'You'd better tell the lot, Finny. Tell him how you discovered all this.'

Finbar looked down at his shoes and then at me again. 'The thing is Dave, I have a mate from Army days, Jack Schofield, and he lives in Naples. Er . . . Jack's got a bit of a reputation. Actually, he was cashiered for smuggling. When er . . . Jay and I couldn't find out anything at the airport about Coleman I phoned Jack. He invited me over to Naples to check things out at that end . . .'

'Playing at detectives at his age!' Fiona burst out. 'And he didn't let anyone know where he was going except . . . poor Jay.' Fiona took out a handkerchief and wiped her eyes. 'Oh, get on with it then, Finny!' she said.

Her brother paused to light another of the inevitable cigarettes before continuing, 'Jack met me at the airport and we followed Coleman to an apartment. A lot of children went in. We waited for a while. Then Jack went to make enquiries and he was told that Coleman lived there with his wife Maria and five children. According to the people who live in the apartment block his name is Gennaro Scaccaro. But he already has a wife, Margaret Coleman, and two children in Prestbury.'

'Finbar, are you sure this was the same man?' I didn't want to end up with egg on my face again.

'We had a photo. We followed him again. Jack went and got him chatting. There's no doubt it's him. He has two wives and two families.'

With my own very recent experience of trying to satisfy two women so fresh in my mind I couldn't help but sympathise with Coleman/Scaccaro. He must be a glutton for punishment. But the news was good as far as Rishton and Headlam were concerned. The guy must have seen the offer of a £20,000 reward for information about the murder of his next-door-but-one neighbour as a great chance to pay for all those Christmas presents. Then when he got in front of the police line-ups he picked out the only two people he'd ever seen before, Rishton and Headlam.

'Rather puts the kibosh on him as a witness in the Rishton/Headlam trial, doesn't it?' asked Finbar, as if reading my thoughts.

'Yeah, it does. It's great news for them, but it doesn't help me very much. There wasn't anything to link him to Gordon was there?' I asked.

Finbar shook his head.

'I was hoping when you said he was so strongly linked to Italy that he might have been the hitman, or at least one of the hitmen, and that he'd be connected to Jake Gordon in some way. Blowing up people with car bombs used to be a national sport in Italy, didn't it?' I asked.

'Well,' Finbar replied eagerly, 'I could phone Jack

Schofield and ask him to check out Scaccaro again. If you think there might be something there. He could have some criminal connections. It's awful what the Camorra have done in Naples, you know . . .'

'I'm only clutching at straws, Finbar. With a wife at every airport the man would hardly have much energy to spare, would he?'

'Will you tell the police, Dave?' Fiona asked. 'The sooner they know, the sooner your friends can be released.'

'I'm afraid it doesn't work that way. DCI Jerrold would only think we'd nobbled Coleman. There's no way that man would admit he's wrong,' I told her. 'Finbar will have to go and see Coleman and tell him that we know why he's claimed the reward and then Coleman himself will have to withdraw his identification evidence. You know, say he's no longer sure.'

'Do you want me to go right away?' Finbar asked, as always ready for action.

'I don't know,' I said indecisively. 'Did Fiona tell you that someone shot Poulter, the other witness who Jerrold was relying on to prove his case?'

Finbar looked from me to his talkative sister, now sitting quietly smoking. She'd told him all right. I realised that it wasn't just me who'd got in out of his depth. The twins might be in danger as well. I knew I was supposed to come up with a magic plan, but all I could think about was how I was going to tell Lovena Anderson about Jay. I felt very weary, the desire to sleep was overwhelming. I put my hands to my face. Fortunately Fiona came to my rescue. 'Why don't you go and have a sleep on Finbar's bed, Dave? You look shattered.'

I just managed to reach Finbar's bed before I blanked out.

*

It was dark when I woke and Finbar was shaking me. 'Your father's on the phone,' he said putting the receiver in my hand.

'David? I've rung round half of Manchester trying to find you,' came the familiar slightly aggrieved tones. 'I've got Delise here. She doesn't seem too pleased with herself. Any road, she tells me that you're on your way, and stopping the night. Do you mind informing me and your mother what's up?'

'That was the plan, but something has come up. You know that Delise witnessed an assassination yesterday?'

'Yes, she told us.'

'There's more bad news, I'm afraid.' I didn't know how to break this to him except directly. He'd taken a liking to Jay during their brief acquaintance. 'Someone put a bomb in my car and Jay Anderson and his half brother Liberty have been blown up.'

There was a long pause before Paddy spoke but his voice was as firm as ever. 'Are you sure, David? The news has been on GMR but it just said two youths, nothing about a young man and a kid.'

'From the state of that car I'm surprised they knew even that much . . .'

'I see,' Paddy said. 'He was a promising lad, was that Jay. What do you want me to do? Do you want me to break the news to Delise?'

'No. I will.'

'What the bloody hell have you got yourself into this time?' he asked angrily. 'Do you want me to come and give you a hand?'

'Sorry Dad, the less people involved the better. That's why things have turned out so badly. Just keep Delise safe.'

'Why don't you come here yourself? No one will come looking for you.' There was a barely detectable pleading note in his voice. I didn't answer. 'Like that, is it?' he continued after a moment. 'Well, make sure you come at the buggers from a direction they're not expecting. Take care. Now I'd best put Delise on. You'll want to tell her the news right away. No sense putting it off.' He put the phone down, and there was a pause while he brought Delise to the phone.

Paddy's advice was nothing if not pithy. I suspected that he'd have liked to say a lot more, but he would never allow himself to display emotion.

'Dave, what's going on?' Delise demanded. 'Your father's acting very oddly.'

I told her about Jay and Liberty. There was a long pause. I could hear sobbing.

'I was always telling him off . . .' she wailed. 'I want my mother . . . trust her to be away.'

'Delise, we seem to have underestimated Gordon and Harrison. They probably know where my parents live. It might be best if your mother came to fetch you. Where's she staying? . . . No, don't tell me. Just go with her to her commune, wherever that is, and stay put until everything gets sorted.' Finbar hadn't left the room while I was on the phone. He looked at me expectantly. 'What are we going to do?'

'You're going to do what you should have done hours ago,' I said brusquely. 'You're going to get yourself and Fiona out of here.'

'What! You need me! I'm quite used to coping with danger and I've had a lot more experience with bombs than you,' Finbar said huffily.

'And I suppose you're an expert in booby traps and so on?' I asked.

'Well, since you ask, I did do a course on booby traps, standard part of training.'

'And doing what you were told wasn't?' I asked nastily.

371

I was tired, and I didn't want the deaths of any more of my friends on my conscience.

I could see that Finbar was ready for more argument but the expression on my face must have persuaded him otherwise. He was bitterly disappointed to be missing the 'action'. I went out to let him start packing. He had his sister's safety to think of. I don't think he'd have given in but for that.

It didn't take them long to pack and we didn't spend much time on mutual farewells, there didn't seem to be any point. Finbar promised to track down Coleman/Scaccaro as soon as he'd seen Fiona safely to their cousin's home in Preston. Fiona gave me a warm hug and then they were gone.

Finbar was right about one thing, I thought bitterly. I did need him. He was the only person connected with Pimpernel Investigations who'd come up with a definite lead in the case.

I caught a bus into town. The weather had turned bitter again, there was hail and sleet in the air but that didn't stop plenty of young people from travelling into town for their Saturday night fun. I got off the bus at Piccadilly and walked down Sackville Street to the Atwood Building.

I needed time on my own to work out what I was going to say to Lovena Anderson. The police ought to have identified Jay by now, he must have been carrying his driving licence and other papers.

When I got to my office there were surprisingly few signs of the siege, just a few burnt papers in the bin. Jay had assured me that there was no damage, but there was always a little doubt where he was concerned. I sat for a while. I didn't want to face Lovena. I left the office and headed for Piccadilly railway station to retrieve my gun. When I opened the locker everything was there,

Mary Wood's winnings in the bag, the documents proving her royal ancestry, the gun. It had all seemed so important but now I didn't give a damn. In the end I felt the money was probably safer in the luggage locker than in my office. I took my gun and shoved everything else back into the bag and left it where it was. On the way back I screwed up my courage. When I got back to the office I phoned Lovena. There was a long delay before she answered the phone. I found it hard to speak.

'Hello, who is it?' she demanded impatiently in her musical accent.

'It's me, Dave,' I managed to croak.

'Dave? You sound like you've got a bad throat coming on. You want to look after yourself, you'll be gettin' a bad chest especially after that beating you had.'

'About Jay,' I started to say. She sounded cheerful enough, perhaps she hadn't yet been informed by the police.

'I tell him the same, you want to stay indoors in this weather. But will he? No! He's out chasing some girl. Did you want him?'

My ears felt as if they were about to burst into flame and my knees felt weak, but I recovered quickly. 'Have you seen anything of Liberty?' I asked.

'That pest has been round here all day. He's making Jay's life a misery. Jay was late getting out this morning. He went to Chorlton with Liberty for your car but the police had the whole road blocked off and he couldn't see it anyway. Shall I ax Jay to give you a ring? It'll be tomorrow now,' she said obligingly.

'That'll be fine,' I said as I put the phone down. I felt a surge of joy. If I'd been able I'd have had all the church bells in Manchester rung. But who had the two unfortunate youths in my car been?

I decided to phone Delise and my parents with the news at once. It was Delise who answered.

'We've all been having a good cry here, even your father. He's not so hard-hearted as I thought . . .'

I gave her the good news.

Her reaction was sharper than I'd expected. 'You're not playing one of your little games with my emotions, are you? Because if you are . . . Listen, Dave I've been thinking about that Susan Attleigh.'

'Oh yes,' I said.

'Yes. I never saw a man look so relieved as you did when she said she was expecting Barry what's his name's baby.'

'Well, er . . .' I muttered, struggling for words.

'You spent last weekend in her bed, didn't you?' she asked directly.

I cleared my throat, but the words wouldn't come.

'Right, so you've admitted it,' she said coldly. 'And I expect you had it off with that tinker woman before Christmas as well. Fine. My mother's on her way. It's good news about Jay and Liberty. I'm over the moon about that but it doesn't change anything. I'm going to stay with my mother at her commune at . . . in the Pennines, and you needn't expect to hear from me for a long while.' She cut me off. Two-timing in the line of duty wasn't in Delise's book of rules.

I felt nothing. I tried to think what my next move should be. Sadly, there was no next move.

I struggled into my sleeping bag again, thinking I would never manage to sleep. I descended into blackness.

18

The next thing I knew, I was being picked up bodily, still
inside the sleeping bag, and hauled onto the shoulders
of at least four burly men. As I struggled to free myself
from the bag, my arms were pinioned. I fought furiously
but my head was shoved back into the bag which was
zipped up over me. Then someone must have belted me
over the head because there was an explosion of light
and pain, followed by unconsciousness.

When I regained consciousness I was still trussed up
inside the bag. It was stifling, but there must have been
some air percolating through to me, or I would have
suffocated already. I could hear the voices of several men
around me, and although muffled by the bag, they had
a curious clanging quality about them, not quite an echo.
Their tone was excitable and angry and I didn't want to
make the acquaintance of their owners just yet. My head
was throbbing painfully, so I was content to lie dazedly
where I was. The debate, whatever it was about, rumbled
on over my head. Gradually, as my hearing adjusted, I
was able to make out something of what was being said.
The word 'kill' seemed to recur rather too repeatedly for
my liking.

Sweat trickled down my face. Just as the heat was
becoming unbearable someone unzipped the bag. The
relief of being able to breathe was quickly replaced by
fear as I took in the circle of hostile faces looming over
me. As I scanned the faces in the dim light, straining to
make sense of what was happening to me, my eyes met
those of Mickey Joyce. His flattened and battered pan of

375

a face held an expression of the deepest loathing and malevolence.

'Back in the land of the living, are you? You murdering bastard! It won't be for long.' Then he launched a heavy kick at my head, but fortunately the man to his left swung him to one side and the kick missed.

'Leave it, Mickey. He isn't worth it. We'll sort him out for you,' he cajoled while struggling with the giant.

'He's killed my boy. He owes me for that.' Joyce was still howling and grinding his teeth in a way that suggested he favoured swift execution. He'd been at his medicine again, and it was hard to make out what he was saying.

Then things rapidly got more serious as Joyce pulled a large old-fashioned Webley revolver out of the poacher's pocket of his Barbour coat and flourished it in my face. I wriggled back into the sleeping bag.

'I'll give you a chance to make your peace with your Maker, and that's more than you gave Declan. Then it's a bullet in the back of the head, fair and square,' he said venomously.

To my relief his mates intervened. 'Don't forget that he killed Sean as well as your lad. You'll have to wait until Sean's father gets here from Wrexham and then you can toss for it,' one of them said. I'd already worked it out. The car thieves Declan and his sandy-haired mate must have been the youths blown to pieces and I'd been tried and found guilty of their murder.

'Am I allowed to speak?' I asked, licking my lips nervously. By way of reply, one of the men leant over and cuffed me mildly across the face. 'No, let him speak, I want to hear what he has to say,' said Mickey, replacing the pistol and taking out his poteen bottle again. 'We've nothing to do until Kieran arrives from Wrexham. Let's hear what sort of a yarn he can spin.'

376

'Am I supposed to have left a bomb in my car on the off chance that a couple of car thieves would come and take it? Any normal individual would know that the bomb was meant for me, but you're retarded. Your brain's addled with poteen . . .'

Mickey's three remaining followers stirred uncomfortably. The short, heavily built man who had slapped me, a man whose brow would have been crawling on the floor if it'd got any lower, turned to his leader. 'Now, Mickey,' he said, 'we don't want any comeback from this job. You've got to be *fecking* sure that he did for Declan and Sean, or I'm out of here, now. Cousin or no cousin, I'm not risking it otherwise.'

'Well, of course he did,' said Mickey. 'And isn't he trying to get his hands on Mary, and on her money?'

'What money are you talking about?' I said. It was a mistake.

'There you are!' Mickey crowed. 'Listen to his old blarney. He's trying to kid us that he doesn't know that Mary won a hundred and fifty grand!'

'I'm looking after it for her, but none of you will ever see a penny of it if you kill me. It's safely stowed away where you'll never lay your thieving hands on it.'

This had the desired effect. Mickey kicked me hard on the leg again. I winced, but made no sound. Then the four of them, by unspoken mutual agreement, left the 'van. The light went off.

I started struggling and straining to get free. I didn't mind if they heard me, I was driven by sheer blind fury and a sense of outrage. I rolled about in the sleeping bag but they'd lashed ropes round the bag so I was trussed up like an Egyptian mummy. When I broke free, I stood up and stretched my arms. Apart from a lump on my head and a dull ache, I was in good shape, but I had no intention of becoming a pretty corpse. I ran from corner to corner of the tin can I was imprisoned in, looking for a way out. I guessed I was inside the camouflaged trailer Joyce used for hiding his stolen cars. It was an effective little prison but I had no intention of staying in it a moment longer than necessary.

What faint light there was, entered through two very small ventilators in the roof, and they were secured on the outside by bars which showed up as faint lines against the comparatively lighter shade of the night sky.

The back wall, through which Mickey's helpers presumably let in the stolen cars, was secured by a pair of massive inch-thick steel bolts, fastened on the outside. I had no chance of making an impression on them without a hacksaw and a good supply of blades. There were no windows, the floor had been reinforced by having sheet metal welded over it, so that left the door by which my captors had left. I carefully tried the handle but it had been secured from the outside.

I charged the door with as much force as I could muster, shouting wildly as I ran. I tried again and again until the whole van began rocking. The din must have been heard from one end of the camp to the other. I'd no intention of waiting placidly for my own execution. Let the pillocks do it in front of every man, woman and child in the camp if they wished, but I wasn't going quietly.

Finally, the door gave, and I managed to crash my way out. I stood, clad only in my boxer shorts, shivering from my exertions. In front of me, in a waiting semicircle, stood every living soul in the campsite from old people to babes in arms.

It was the children who saved me. Mickey, swaying dangerously, had his Webley approximately levelled at my chest and several of his friends had shotguns at the ready, but the children began to laugh; quietly at first, then loudly and derisively. Adults joined in the laughter. A man clad only in boxer shorts is hardly a threat. Mickey and his friends exchanged uneasy looks. They didn't know what to do.

Mary Wood did. She pushed through the circle, strode forward boldly, grabbed me by the arm and yanked me down from my perch. 'Get out of the way, you idiots!' she screeched in a high-pitched voice which cut the night air like breaking glass. 'Have you never seen a man in his smalls before?' She towed me through the crowd to the door of her 'van. 'Get in quick before they change their minds,' she muttered. I hastily obeyed and she slammed the door behind her.

I peered through the dirty window of Mary's trailer. The crowd dispersed, leaving Mickey and his friends out in the cold like a discussion group of Marxist philosophers at a Tory Party conference. They stood shaking their heads, fidgeting with their weapons and looking angrily in my direction.

'Calm down,' Mary instructed. 'They won't get you in here. You'll be all right as long as you don't go outside. You know what that bastard Joyce is really after, don't you? Fine lot a *fecking* mourning he's done! I've had him in here searching this trailer on his hands and knees since Friday.'

'But how did he know about your winnings?' I asked.

'It's that fat friend of yours, the TV man, Blake. He's been boasting about it. He even had a piece from a newspaper . . . "Anonymous Country Woman wins Tote Jackpot", it said.'

I groaned and put my head in my hands. Ted must have planted a bug when he made his personal visit to Pimpernel Investigations on Friday. I'd been a fool, I should have known that he'd try something. The way he'd turned up at the tinker campsite in Chorlton should have tipped me off. Bugs were part of his stock in trade in 'Bang to Rights'. He'd be bang to rights when I got hold of him.

Mary mistook my groan for distress at letting her down and at my situation. She put her arm round me comfortingly. 'Oh, go on with you, Mr Cunane, it's not so bad,' she said stroking my shoulders. 'I don't think Mickey ever really meant to hurt you. They want you to tell them where the money is. That's what all this caper is about. He's had his tongue hanging out for that money since Friday. The news about Declan only made him greedier. He says he's entitled to my money as compensation.'

'Mary, your relatives have the timeless charm of a collection of broken alarm clocks. I'm going to have to get out of here,' I said.

'Well, look at you, you'll not get far in your running pants,' she said with a laugh. She took a peek outside. 'It's freezing out and see what they're up to,' she continued, beckoning me to the window.

Mickey and his friends had banked up a fire at a vantage spot from where they could keep watch on both sides of the trailer. It looked like a scene from the Crimean War out there, with angry men pacing up and down in the firelight, cradling their shotguns, stamping their feet against the cold. She was right, I wouldn't get far.

'I'll see if I can find you something,' my hostess offered. I thought she meant clothes. She was wearing a new Marks & Spencer's dressing gown over a black thin-strapped lace nightdress. She rooted about for several minutes while I watched the scene outside, then shoved a rusty old BSA double-barrelled shotgun into my hands. It was coated with dust. In her own hands she held a modern-looking crossbow with a couple of bolts.

'There now,' she said, 'one of my lads liked shooting cats with this and the gun was Dermot's. You can do as much harm to them now as ever they try to do to you. But don't worry, Mickey's doing all this for show. He has to pretend to the lads that he's really heartbroken but money's what he's after.'

The shotgun was certainly a morale booster. I checked the shells, it was loaded but you can never be sure with old ammo. I made sure the safety was on. It didn't seem to work.

I heard a rustle of cloth behind me. The dressing gown and black nightie were on the floor and Mary was in the bed. She folded the covers back invitingly.

'Come on, Dave. You might as well be comfortable, *a gra.*'

She was right. I was freezing.

'Come on, now,' she coaxed. 'You can tell me where you've got me money hid, it isn't in your shoe and that's for sure.'

I slipped in beside her. According to Delise I was a free man again. Thoughts of a healing night's sleep quickly disappeared when she skilfully relieved me of my one remaining garment. 'It's not in them either,' she said with a laugh.

'That was great, Dave,' she said afterwards, demonstrating the same inclinations as her reputed forebear Queen Victoria, who according to one account had worn down poor Prince Albert with her constant demands for physical affection. 'I've been aching to do that since I saw you stretched out on my bed that morning, drunk as a *fecking* lord you were, but I could see you were a well-made man. You know, we could make a go of it. I'm not so old as I look.'

This offer was made so sincerely that I felt like a killjoy as I pointed out that her friends and relations had already decided that they were going to shoot me as soon as the father of one of my alleged victims arrived.

'Ach, they're only having you on,' Mary said unconvincingly. 'It's the money that's keeping them out of their beds on a cold night. Besides they'll not let you go until I tell them where the money is,' she continued in a matter-of-fact tone, 'and you haven't told *me* that yet.'

'It's at Piccadilly Station in a left-luggage locker. Here's the key,' I said slipping it off my neck and giving it to her.

Mary began laughing hysterically. 'Mickey took the safe out of your office and they've spent hours pulling the back off it. Mickey's uncle, John-Joe, has half knackered himself.'

'Tell me, Mary,' I said, 'are you really descended from King Edward VIII? Or was it all an elaborate hoax?'

'Of course I am!' she spluttered indignantly. 'You're not going to let that put you off me, are you?' she asked, clutching me anxiously. 'It's not fair! I can't help who my grandfather was. They say he had a good side to him! He wanted to help the unemployed, and all.' She tried to distract me by making the preparatory moves for more love in a cold climate. I realised then how mankind had survived the ravages of the Ice Age in all those chilly caves . . . the evolutionary pressures towards reproduction must have been intense.

Faint traces of light became visible in the openings above us and I roused myself sufficiently to disentangle myself from Mary. Crawling over to the curtains the early morning light illuminated a drab scene. There was a massive derelict power station in the distance and the trailers were parked on the edge of a heavily wooded area near playing fields. It was Agecroft in Salford.

My movement had roused Mary and as if anxious to

prove what a useful partner she would be she set to work. She lit the gas fire and began straightening things out but not before she'd found us both something to wear. I noticed that her lip was split and that she had a fine black eye. Within a short time I was dressed in a pair of trousers that were too short and a long Aran sweater reaching to my knees. The sweater looked as if it had been used as a mop, it had turned a dirty oatmeal shade. None of Mary's late husband Dermot's underwear, if he'd ever worn any, or socks either, had survived but she did search out a pair of boots that were only two sizes too small for me. Nothing fitted but I wasn't complaining.

Optimism and buoyancy began to return as I helped Mary restore her living quarters to normality. The activity also helped to take my mind off my troubles. I noticed that her wardrobe had improved and that she had invested in an impressive range of concoctions from The Body Shop.

When the place was back in some sort of order and we were drinking a cup of tea, she gave me a shy smile and said, 'You're a nice man, Dave. I could get used to you very quickly. At least you've got red blood in your veins. Most of the men round here won't look at a woman twice, except to ask us to darn their socks or patch their britches. And they need at least one bottle of poteen in them before they'll perform. They think of me as part of the furniture.'

'You're an attractive woman,' I assured her truthfully. She held my hand for a minute, then we decided to face the world. She went and opened the door.

Mickey was there levelling the massive old Webley at my chest. The gun seemed to have grown and he seemed to have shrunk, but he was standing straight enough. He seemed to be immune to the side-effects of his poteen. I pointed Mary's antique shotgun at his head.

'Like that, is it? You'll never get out of here with a whole skin,' Mickey said.

'Neither will you, if you fire that gun,' said Mary, aiming the crossbow at him.

'I'll bet you've been at it like knives, all night long. You've nearly had the trailer tipped up between you.'

I started to tell him to mind his own business but Mary piped up, 'He's not told me where it is, Mickey. So if we all start shooting now, you'll get no satisfaction. Shame, isn't it? Was it a cold night?' She laughed again and speaking to me said, 'Look at him. Doesn't he just look like a bladder of wind that someone's let the air out of?'

'Don't think of leaving, we'll shoot you at once.' His glum-looking friends had arrived to back him up, and even with Mary behind me I didn't feel that I had enough firepower to shoot my way out.

It looked like I'd finally arrived as a permanent resident on the traveller scene. We had no portable phone and no way to get in touch with Delise or Jay. Mary spent most of the day telling me about her life as a traveller. I felt indolent and lethargic.

So next morning it came as all the more of a surprise when we listened to the local news on Mary's tinny little radio and learned that Delise Delaney had been arrested at an address on the West Pennine Moors as a suspect in the killing of John Poulter and that I was also being sought in connection. Even worse followed. Police were investigating a possible link between the disappearance of Lance Trevose, last seen in my company, and the killing of Gloria Rishton. Alhambra security guards had found the bullet holes in Trevose's car.

A casual listener would conclude that Delise and I were the most dangerous couple since Bonny and Clyde. Mary was looking at me with an unfathomable expression on her face, her eyes were very wide. A crowd

384

of people was forming outside her trailer. It looked like the lynch mob forming up again. But I had a suspicion that things weren't as bad as they looked. Centuries of persecution at the hands of society have given the travellers an automatic sympathy for the man on the run. They looked to their leaders for guidance. Mickey Joyce emerged from his trailer, diverting attention from me. The crowd gathered round him and he led them across to Mary's trailer. I saved him the trouble of opening the door and stood on the top step, giving myself a slight height advantage.

'The same man killed Gloria Rishton, John Poulter and Sean and Declan, and that man wasn't me. I can prove it if you'll give me half a chance,' I said. Joyce looked grey and weary in the light of day. His face seemed to have shrunk inwards. 'All right, tell us your story. We've got all day. We don't owe the police any favours, and we'd rather hear it from you than from the radio.'

I told them the story from Kath Headlam's initial commission right down to the explosion in Willows Road.

There was a profound silence when I finished.

The silence was broken by a familiar voice shouting from the back. 'He's right. I've known Dave for years. He couldn't knock the top off a cold rice pudding, still less blow up one of your lads. The police are completely up the chute, this is like the Guildford Four or the Birmingham Six.' Ted Blake shouldered his way through the crowd right up to the door of the caravan. 'I'll help you, you crazy bugger, if you'll let me have the royal story,' he said quietly.

Mary stared down at Ted angrily but he didn't seem upset. 'I'm not after your money,' he assured her.

'But they are,' Mary replied, pointing to Mickey and his followers, who were having an urgent conference in the middle of the crowd. I was in two minds about whether to thump Ted in the face or to pat him on the back.

Finally Mickey stepped forward as the meeting's spokesman. 'Mr Cunane, you said you could prove you were innocent?' he demanded.

I felt a strong spurt of hope. 'Simple,' I said brashly. 'This killer has tried to do for me once but he got poor Declan instead. All you need to do is tell him where I am, and he's sure to try again. Then you'll have your real killer and we can find out what's behind all this.'

Mickey nodded once. 'OK, say we go along with that, there's something else. I'm entitled to compensation. I want £50,000 to cover the funeral expenses for my boy.' He folded his arms and waited for our response.

'What does he want to do? Build a bloody pyramid?' whispered Ted.

'Shut up, you,' hissed Mary venomously, 'haven't you done enough damage telling them I had the money? Trust Mickey to want to turn a profit out of his own son's death.' She turned to the crowd and said in a loud voice, 'We'll accept if you'll agree to see that no harm comes to Mr Cunane.'

Mickey paused and then nodded his head again.

'Done,' he said, holding out his hand.

The next four days were the longest days in my life. I remained incarcerated in Mary's trailer, while she moved out to share with a friend; a two-night stand was as much as her community would allow without me actually being married to her. They didn't want their young people corrupted by my example. Separated from me, she spent a lot of time in Ted Blake's company. I was as carefully watched as before, not that I'd any desire to go anywhere.

The numbers at the site grew as more and more of

Mickey's relatives arrived for Declan's funeral. There was no shortage of modern communications equipment either, most of the older men seemed to own mobile phones and were constantly doing deals for livestock, scrap iron, tarmac and concrete.

The subject of how to communicate with the anonymous killer and let him know of my whereabouts caused much head scratching. It was Ted Blake who solved the problem. He said he'd drop a few hints into the rumour mill at Alhambra. Alhambra TV seemed to be the one common factor in the whole thing.

After much persuasion Mickey allowed me to use his portable phone for a small fee. He was very wary, but he let me put in a call to Jay Anderson at his home address.

It was Liberty who answered. He was wearing his hearing aid for once. 'The police have sealed up your office, they won't let us use the computer,' he squeaked. 'I can show you where my tree house is, if you need a hiding place.'

When he eventually brought his half brother to the phone Jay gave a sigh of relief that must have been audible at the end of his street.

'Boss, it's really you! Where are you, man? That fool man Jerrold is saying you're a killer, but Mr Sinclair thinks you're dead. I had to spend hours at the office with him going over everything. He thinks that whoever is bumping all these people off must have kidnapped you. And they've taken Delise off to Macclesfield. Man! It's a real bad scene. I thought they were going to take me in again.'

'Have you heard any more from Finbar about Coleman?' I asked.

'Coleman! Boss, are you off your rocker? You should

have other things on your mind now, like how're you going to get out of this mess.'

'Listen, Jay. I want you to find Finbar and ask him if he's managed to contact Coleman. Tell him to get in touch with that lawyer Bartle. Do you understand?'

'I understand you're crazy, Boss. Bartle doesn't want nothing to do with us.'

'Jay, once Coleman admits to the police that he didn't really see Headlam and Rishton at Prestbury that night, Jerrold will have to release them and the whole case against me will be dropped. Jerrold will be back to square one. So do it.'

Jay didn't sound too convinced, but promised to start right away.

Ted Blake was at the travellers' camp most of the time and gave me a wide berth, as if fearful of me. I asked him how long he'd had the bug in my office but 'Trade secret, old man' was all I could get out of him.

Mary obviously trusted him more than I did. She let Ted take her to retrieve the contents of the left-luggage locker in Piccadilly Station. Mickey got his £50,000 and Ted got the Wood documents. He spent a lot of time closeted with Mary, preparing for what he said would be the scoop of the century. Supplies of all kinds began arriving at the camp, particularly large amounts of booze of both the legal and illegal varieties. It looked as if Mickey was sparing no expense to provide his son with the funeral of the century. I felt like a minor bit player in some mammoth film production. Things were happening all around but I was no longer at the centre.

I spent most of my time watching the telly and listening to local radio. The first crack in the police case against me came on the Wednesday afternoon. It seemed that Lance Trevose had phoned the police from his hiding place to tell them that he was alive. It was also announced that Poulter had been killed with the same gun that killed Gloria Rishton. That seemed to let me out as the hitman – even if Jerrold was convinced that I'd shot Gloria, I'd been in police headquarters when Poulter was shot. I had a cast-iron alibi. I hoped Delise wasn't being put through hell.

Late on Wednesday evening the bodies of Declan and Sean arrived back at the site. They were each brought in a separate hearse pulled by two black horses complete with plumes. A huge crowd formed at the entrance to the camp. The attendants on the hearses, tall men wearing black frock coats, black gloves and black top hats with streamers tied round them, carefully unloaded and shouldered the ornate coffins containing whatever remained of the deceased. Appropriately enough, their destination was the empty car-theft trailer that had been the scene of so much of their criminal activity.

The families of Sean and Declan attended the trailer on their own. 'You'd better not show your face, I don't think it'll be welcome, nor mine either for that matter, although I'm paying for everything,' Mary said bitterly.

That night I managed to get in touch with Finbar. He'd returned from Preston with Fiona.

'Oh, it's you,' he said. 'Jay told me you were still with us. Lying low, are you?'

'Finbar, have you managed to find Coleman/Scaccaro and force him to admit to the police that he was lying?' I asked urgently.

'I have and he won't,' the old soldier replied.

'Didn't you threaten to expose his bigamy?'

'He says he doesn't care, that I'd be doing him a favour anyway. He insists that he *did* see two people going into Gloria Rishton's house at six that night, only I don't think it was Rishton and Headlam. Coleman's now saying he saw two *men*, one big and heavy set, the other small and

389

slightly built. I believe him this time. He says it was too dark for him to say who they were and that he only identified Simon Rishton and Kath Headlam because he saw them in custody twenty minutes before the police line-up and knew that it would please DCI Jerrold.'

There was a pause while I took this in. 'You don't think I was one of those two men, do you, Finbar?'

'Of course not. I know you, Dave. I'm sure it'll all get sorted out in the end,' he said. He didn't sound overwhelmingly convinced.

Declan and Sean were buried the next day. Travellers who had attended the funeral at a nearby church, returned much the worse for the odd dram of poteen. Camp fires burned as they began their wake. I stayed in Mary's trailer out of harm's way, and was rewarded with dramatic developments on the local radio news. '*Mr Lance Trevose, Alhambra's chief executive, has today praised the role of wanted fugitive David Cunane, and, in contradiction of the police scenario in which the local private detective is cast as the demon prince, has stated that but for Cunane he would have been assassinated in the same way as John Poulter, the head of Special Security at Alhambra TV.*

'*Asked for comments, the Cheshire Police refused to make any statement but a spokesman at GMP headquarters in Manchester admitted that the search for Cunane had been scaled down and that they were seeking him for "information purposes only". He also said that David Cunane's partner, Miss Delise Delaney, had been released from police custody early yesterday. Meanwhile the whereabouts of Cunane are still unknown.*

'*In a further and probably related development Kath Headlam and Simon Rishton who have been in custody since Christmas in connection with the murder of Gloria Rishton were released today at committal proceedings at Chester Crown Court*
390

when the prosecution stated that it had no evidence to offer. Cheshire Police confirmed that the case is still open and that they are pursuing several further lines of enquiry... The Cheshire Police spokesman did not deny that a senior officer involved in the case, DCI Jerrold, has applied for early retirement.'

I was in the clear, all I had to worry about now was the assassin who knew exactly where I was and who might be waiting on his chance to shoot me even now. My mission on behalf of Kath Headlam and Simon Rishton was accomplished but whether I'd live long enough to enjoy the plaudits, if any, was problematical.

I sent Mary to find Mickey.

When he arrived it was plain that he had been consoling himself with winter preserver.

'Have you heard the news?' I asked triumphantly. 'I'm in the clear with the police.'

'You're not in the clear with me.' He was slurring his words. 'A bargain's a bargain. You said you'd deliver the real killer to us. Well, where is he? There's plenty here say you should wait until this mysterious so-called killer appears, if he ever does. So don't get the idea that you're going to walk away from what happened to Declan and Sean.'

'At least let me use the phone again,' I pleaded. 'I need a change of clothes.' He relented to the extent of lending me his mobile phone.

'Is that really you, Boss?' Jay asked when I got through to Pimpernel Investigations. 'Have you heard the news? You and Delise are in the clear.'

'Yeah, put her on,' I said impatiently

'There's a slight problem there, Boss. She's here but she refuses to speak to you. She says all enquiries have to come through me.'

'What's the matter with her?' I asked.

'She says that's private, but you know. Look, Boss, you'll have to come in and sort it out face to face.'

'I'd love to but I can't get away from here at the moment,' I said. I explained the circumstances and asked him to come at once with clothes, razor and shoes. He was willing but Pimpernel Investigations now had no transport apart from Delise's mother's 2CV and Delise had rounded up all the cash I'd left in the office and was 'looking after it'. In the end Jay persuaded her to relent enough to lend him the money to hire a car.

The first surprise when Jay arrived was his appearance. He was wearing a formal navy-blue suit, a cream shirt and dark tie. His hair was neatly trimmed back, the surviving locks on the front of his head reduced to mere roots. He looked like a keen young executive type, only a slight nervousness and twisting of the wrists reminded me of the Jay I had once been so familiar with. Even the way he spoke now had a certain snappy crispness. The second surprise came when he handed in his notice. Paddy had arranged an interview for him with the police and he'd been provisionally accepted as a recruit. As soon as the word came through for him to start he'd be leaving my employ.

'The rats are leaving the sinking ship, eh?' I asked.

'No, no it's not like that, Boss,' he said hurriedly. 'Delise is making lots of money for the firm. She's ringing all the papers that suggested you were a killer and believe me they're paying plenty, settling out of court before you sue them.'

While I gaped at him in surprise he continued, 'I'll stay with you until they get whoever's trying to knock you off. Mind your back, like. I mean it's the least I can do after all you've done for me.'

I was torn by conflicting emotions. I didn't want him to get in the way of a bullet, but judging from the reaction my well-meant concern for her safety had produced in Delise, I would be foolish to turn down his offer of help. I didn't have so many friends that I could afford to lose another.

I shaved, and then dressed in the fresh clothes he'd brought for me from the office. There was only about half a pint of water available for washing purposes, so I liberally applied eau de cologne to remedy my personal freshness problem. As I was fixing the gold cuff-links into my shirt Jay casually passed me a box of .38 ammunition. I let him reload my automatic before putting on the shoulder holster.

Mary arrived back with a whole York ham and half a turkey she'd collared from the wake, as well as a bottle of Walker's Black Label.

'We might as well enjoy this as I'm paying for it,' she said.

Outside, things were hotting up. The mourners were split into three separate groups: the Joyce relatives, Sean's relatives and a large neutral contingent waiting for developments. The hours passed slowly, several of the mourners tried to start up dancing and singing, but their hearts weren't in it. The oppressive atmosphere was clearly producing feelings of strain.

As we watched from Mary's trailer window, Mickey rose to his feet. He was now about as well oiled as it's possible to get and remain standing, and even by the flickering glow of the camp fires his face was the colour of a ripe tomato. He disappeared round the back of his trailer and then re-emerged with a large can of petrol. He started splashing this onto the sides of the camouflaged trailer, silent witness to his family's criminal activities, and recently my prison. Some of the petrol washed back over his own superb chromium-plated home which stood alongside.

This was all too much for Mary. She went out to get a better view, urging Jay and me to follow her. Ted Blake had joined us, and added his voice to Mary's in encouraging me to leave the shelter of the trailer. I didn't want to be taken for a wimp so I went. I felt it unlikely that the phantom motorcyclist would put in an appearance at this late stage.

All eyes were now on Mickey. He continued trying to get petrol onto the trailer, but most of it ended up on the ground or on his own 'van. I expected that some sensible person would now step forward to restrain him, but there was no such individual available.

Finally, he seized the unburned end of a branch from the fire and hurled it onto the trailer. It went up with a roar and the flames spread down the side of the trailer into the open door in no time. There was a heavy thud as the petrol-laden air inside ignited and the back door flew off, just missing several revellers. Flames licked along the ground and up the side of Mickey's own trailer. He stood by drunkenly uncomprehending for a while, then he gave a roar and rushed to get into it.

'For God's sake, do something,' yelled Mary. 'Don't just stand there gawping.' She ran to get hold of the tow bar of Mickey's 'van to pull it away from the other fiercely blazing trailer. Other women were running for extinguishers. Ted, Jay and I joined her, but the van was immovable. Finally, it rocked forwards and we managed to move it away from the burning wreck. Its tyres were burning and it looked as if it and its owner were about to go the same way as the first 'van.

Suddenly Mickey emerged, blackened but still on his feet, waving two slightly singed parcels at the crowd. A tremendous cheer went up from the Joyce family. Mary advanced on Mickey and snatched the smaller of the two parcels out of his hand. 'My change, I reckon,' she yelled

394

and brandished it above her head. An even louder cheer from the neutral onlookers greeted this.

I didn't get the chance to enjoy much of the spectacle because at that moment a tremendous blow struck me in the left side and knocked me to the ground. There was a roar from a high-pitched engine and I realised with a sickened shock that a black-suited motorcyclist was riding towards me to finish me off.

'It's him,' shouted Mickey, who stood behind me, in the clear line of sight of the gunman. He hauled his massive Webley out and fired into the air. I was on the ground, a fatal casualty for all my assassin knew and he didn't wait for another shot. He heaved the bike round and revved his way across the site, aiming for the open playing fields beyond. His path took him between two trailers and from my position on the ground I was able to see what happened next very plainly. The bike veered off to the right and its rider was thrust into the air as a clear thrumming musical note rang out like a chord from a steel-string guitar. The bike crashed to the ground against the nearest of the two trailers.

I felt as if a horse had kicked my shoulder. I cautiously examined my chest for the bullet hole, but there was none. His slug had struck the butt of my Beretta 92, which was now bent at a sad angle. Ted Blake helped me to my feet. Nobody was in a hurry to approach the now-still figure of the motorcyclist; his bike engine was still turning over. I realised he had driven right into one of the steel wires the travellers had strung up between trailers to stop the Council from towing them away.

Mickey was waving his pistol in the air. 'Did you ever see a shot like that?' he gloated.

'Will you get that gun off him before he really does blow someone's head off?' Mary asked Ted in an exasperated tone. To his credit Ted boldly strode up and relieved

Mickey of the gun. Mickey staggered off into the darkness beyond the camp fires and returned a few moments later, carrying something that looked like a football.

'That's done for the murdering bastard then,' he said, dropping the severed head of the motorcyclist, still encased in its helmet, on the ground. It rolled to my feet.

All the spirit and fun went out of the travellers after Mickey's revelation. Hasty preparations for departure began on all sides. I phoned Sinclair on the mobile and it wasn't long before the side of the campsite was flanked by the flashing blue lights of a dozen police cars parked along the road. At first the police tried to prevent the travellers' departure, but they soon realised that they faced an impossible task, in the darkness.

I remained standing by the flickering remains of the destroyed trailer and it was there that Sinclair joined me. He was in his full Assistant Chief Constable's uniform.

'Seems to have had a bad accident shaving,' he commented, gingerly touching the severed head with the well-polished toe of his shoe.

I explained the circumstances and he listened without comment. Ted Blake corroborated my story. We strolled over to where photographers were recording the position of the motorcyclist's body. Sinclair's Chief Inspector recovered the pistol from the man's clenched fist. It was a Mateba, an eight-shot revolver of unusual design, made in Italy. He held it in his hand. 'It's a very well-balanced gun, sir. Very handy for firing from a motorbike,' he commented to Sinclair.

To my surprise, Sinclair linked arms with me in a great show of geniality. 'You're wasted as a private detective, Davie,' he said. 'Your talent for destruction deserves a much broader field. Yes, you need more scope, well away from Manchester. Did you tell your friends here to string these wires up between the caravans?' He fingered the lethal strand. 'Just the right thickness to cut like a razor, too. Any thicker and you'd just have had a nasty mess on your hands.'

I knew it was useless to refuse the credit while Sinclair was in this mood, so I kept quiet. He led me towards the parked cars. 'Now, it may be irregular, but under no circumstances am I taking your statement at police head-quarters. We'll all go to your wee office, your young man can drive us.' All the time he'd been speaking Jay had been ducking and weaving along behind me. He now bobbed forward and opened the door of the white hire car for Sinclair like a practised chauffeur.

'Well, young man, you've got a lot of unlearning to do when you join us, but you seem to be making the right start,' Sinclair complimented him.

19

The night of interrogation which followed, mild though it was by Sinclair's standards, left me feeling weak and light headed. The name of Jake Gordon was hardly mentioned. The anonymous biker, I knew, had been nothing but somebody else's pawn; a hired gun. His name, I was told, was Sidgwick, and he was a dishonourably discharged ex-marine. All attempts to link him to anyone were failing dismally. It seemed the man was a complete social isolate. 'Patient police work, laddie! It's going to take weeks of patient police work to establish that.'

Eventually everyone left; Sinclair, his Chief Inspector and the police stenographer to Chester House, Jay Anderson to Moss Side and Ted Blake and Mary Wood to Ted's flat in Didsbury. I had no doubt what Mary had on her mind and I wished her well. Ted was as serious as she was about the issue of 'royal descent' and they were truly suited to each other with their matching body forms and equivalent dress senses. They'd make a fine couple. Ted looked happier than he'd been for years; he had the story of the year on his arm and the prospect of a genuinely exclusive deal.

Left to my own devices I decided to get some sleep and see what the day would bring. Somehow I didn't think Gloria's killer would be after me again for a while. My sleeping bag was still on the bed in Mary's trailer and when I awoke from four hours' uncomfortable slumber in a chair I didn't feel any more refreshed than when I'd started. I also noticed some nasty-looking insect bites across my back. The travellers lived too close to nature. I needed a bath. It was now just after 9 a.m. and if Delise had been coming she'd have already arrived. I phoned her.

It was Molly Delaney who answered. 'Yes!' she snapped aggressively.

I wasn't prepared to be snubbed again so I faked an exaggerated 'female' voice. *'Manchester University Archaeology Department here, may I speak to Miss Delise Delaney?'*

I heard her heavy footsteps receding and then Delise replied in a very expectant voice. 'It's you Dave!' she said in a bitterly disappointed tone when she realised she wasn't about to be invited to some exciting excavation.

'Why haven't you come in to work, Delise?'

'Look Dave, I think it's better if we give it a rest for a while. I'm glad you're back, but I need to get my head together. I'm not too enchanted at the way you replace me as soon as we have a disagreement. Don't try to deny that you've been living with that sweaty Princess No-Knickers Wood, or whatever her name is, for the past week.' She put the phone down before I could come up with a reply.

Strange how Delise was able to sense when I was being led astray, even when she was a long way off. It proved that there was real rapport between us, or maybe that I'd given her plenty of grounds for not trusting me. I knew I didn't have a leg to stand on. 'She'll get over it in a day or two,' I thought optimistically.

That left me sitting cold, hungry and fleabitten in an empty office with nothing to do. Fine! I packed up all my remaining wardrobe and personal tackle, loaded it in the hire car and drove to Chorlton. I let myself into the old flat I'd vowed never to return to, ran a bath and fell asleep. When I came to again it was midday, the long soak had done wonders for me. I went down to the garage and got out my bike and took the first decent bit of exercise I'd had in weeks. Whatever else changed, the Mersey still ran in its bed. On the way back I stopped at Jackson's Boat for a snack and a couple of pints.

I was feeling about ninety per cent normal when I returned to the flat. I arranged for a furniture remover to pick up my possessions from the basement of the Atwood Building and move them back in. They agreed to do it at once for a premium and I spent the weekend arranging the flat to my satisfaction. The Salways were in but they seemed to be keeping to themselves.

Apart from a brief conversation with Paddy I didn't speak to anyone. 'Got yourself out of another scrape, have you, David?' he asked. His tone wasn't as sarcastic as usual.

'Well, you could say that.'

'And have they come running round to your door, these fancy TV people? Delise told us all about them. Have they shown their gratitude to you for nearly getting yourself killed on their behalf?'

'I think Kath's probably busy . . .'

'Oh aye, she'll be too busy to see you, lad. And as for that Simon Rishton, bet he's forgotten your name already.' He sounded quite angry on my behalf.

'I'm sure they'll get in touch,' I said. Deep down, I was sure they wouldn't.

When Monday morning came round I decided to indulge in the luxury of a morning off. There was money in the bank. It would be a while before the Polar Building Society tried to evict me again and I needed some space for myself. I still felt strangely immune from recent events, and sure that – once he had failed to remove me so categorically – Gloria's killer would wait a while and then approach me in a subtler way. When the post arrived there was a short thank-you note from Kath Headlam, saying she'd gone for a holiday in Bermuda.

Simon Rishton wasn't mentioned. It wasn't exactly a personal visit but it proved Paddy wrong.

Jay phoned from Pimpernel Investigations at ten o'clock. 'Something bad's going down, Boss,' he informed me in a whisper, his tones flat and urgent. I resisted the impulse to tell him not to call me 'Boss' now that he was planning to desert me for the police force. 'Liberty's missing,' he continued.

'So, tell me something new!' I said curtly.

'No, he's been *taken*. It's that Jake Gordon. He phoned. He said that unless you give him all the papers you collected from the Polar Building Society in Poynton, he's going to take the kid up in his helicopter for a ride and not bring him back!'

'Are you sure Liberty's missing?'

'He's missing all right. I dropped him at school this morning, but they say he's gone now. His "uncle" called for him. Gordon must have promised him another helicopter ride.'

'Jay, we'll get Liberty back,' I said quietly, 'but you know those printouts went up in flames with the Nissan. I'd have given them to Sinclair by now if I'd had them.'

'I know, but Gordon still thinks you've got them. He's serious, Boss. He says you should bring the papers on your own to his headquarters, and that I should speak only to you about this. Shall I phone the police?'

I thought hard for a moment.

'Listen Jay, get a big slab of computer paper and put it in a carrier bag. I'll be with you in twenty minutes.'

If Gordon wanted my head on a stick I was prepared to give him a run for his money as long as he released Liberty. I'd been trying for weeks to get rid of the Glaswegian midget and, now I had the chance, I was determined to get him back.

I collected Jay and we drove out to Runcorn. Sitting

with the new-look Jay I felt as if I was under police escort. Neither of us spoke much. I thought it strange that Gordon should want those printouts back after all this time. Perhaps Sinclair had been gently nibbling at the edges of his empire and he was getting nervous.

When we reached Runcorn, Gordon's helicopter was sitting on its pad in his industrial-estate-like fortress. There was only one elderly guard on duty, nor could I see many lorries or tankers about. It seemed very quiet for a Monday morning. No sign of the machine-gun-toting 'mothers' we'd seen on our last visit.

When the guard notified him, Gordon told him to send me up on my own, with the parcel. I got out of the car and told Jay to leave without me as soon as he had Liberty in the car. The old security guard in the entrance lodge looked nervous and didn't seem to be registering what was happening. He gave me directions to Gordon's living quarters.

I was amused to detect traces of Liberty's passage on the way up. His fingerprints were on the lintels of several door frames. He was here all right. He couldn't have left a plainer trail if he'd been trying. No one impeded my passage, there were no 'big mothers' with machine-guns, not even any locked doors. Hope began to stir.

I found Gordon seated at a desk in his study. He showed no surprise or resentment at my presence when I entered. He was alone. He didn't even put down the whisky glass he was drinking from. I thought that by arriving so promptly I'd called his bluff and that he'd hand Liberty over straight away. I was wrong, something I was getting used to. His eyes were puffy and his black eyebrows had their usual twisted look. He stood up behind his desk when I entered, in his shirt sleeves, the waistcoat from a three-piece suit straining to cover his belly.

402

'You stupid, stupid little man!' he railed. 'I could have made you into a merchant prince! Now look at you! You think small and you'll stay small.' I'd never had any ambition to become a major financial player anyway, so I told him exactly where he could stuff his ideas.

Having vented his spleen, he shook his head and assumed a 'more in sorrow than in anger' expression. Whatever else was wrong with him, the old charisma was working full blast. 'Where's Liberty?' I demanded.

'Where are the printouts then?' he countered. I dumped the parcel on a chair. He was in a confiding mood. 'I don't care about those papers, it's you I want. Tell me why you did it? Why did you ruin my deal? I did everything you asked, I let you play at setting that sex maniac Rishton free – he did shoot his wife by the way.'

'Rubbish! Don't you read the papers? The police have *got* the killer, or rather his headless corpse. They've matched his gun to the bullets. They haven't been able to establish who sent him after Gloria, Poulter, Trevose and me, but we both know that's only a matter of time, don't we?' I said.

He raised his hands in the air theatrically as if cradling a child. 'I don't know what you're talking about.'

'Gloria discovered that your oil wealth is just a scam, your tankers are empty. She told her ex, Rishton, and he was going to use it to ruin the deal you had over Alhambra with Trevose. You knew Simon Rishton was having problems with her and you hoped to frame him for the killing. When Poulter was going to blab about the forged log book you had him killed, and you decided to get rid of Trevose too, to be on the safe side.'

Gordon sat down, put his dome-like head in his hands, and started laughing loudly, banging his head against the table top so vigorously that the heavy Waterford crystal whisky decanter rattled. There was a strangely shaped bronze sculpture on the desk as well. I was worried it was going to fall on him and save the police a visit. It was a convincing display of disbelief, but I wasn't taken in.

'Your method of solving a mystery is direct, I'll give you that, Cunane. You've got to understand Harrison and I were only doing what lots of others have done before. We just cut a few corners. I want those printouts because they're capable of misinterpretation in the wrong hands, but the police won't be interested. It was Rishton who had Gloria killed, I tell you. The Northern Pioneers Bank isn't the only bank in the country, you know, even if they'd turned me down for a loan I could have gone elsewhere.'

Come to think of it, it did strike me as odd that Gloria hadn't told her boss, Old Has-been Ashbee, what she'd discovered about Jake Gordon. Why should she save the information for Simon Rishton to use? I had a twinge of doubt.

'You'd better hand Liberty over now,' I told him. He looked at me blankly. I thought he might have been using amphetamines and was on his way down. There were heavy dark rings round his eyes. I realised that I was looking at a beaten man. He must have been relying on the loan from the Northern Pioneers Bank to shore up his own crumbling empire as well as to buy up Alhambra. Perhaps Gloria had tried to blackmail him. 'Will you drink with me, Cunane?' he asked pouring himself another generous whisky. He splashed a healthy shot out for me. I decided it was wise to continue humouring him and accepted.

He noticed me looking at the oddly shaped bronze sculpture on his desk. 'It's a model of my former wife Sandra's chest,' he said sadly. 'I had a cast taken of it so I can give her a fondle at any time of the day.' I restrained myself from laughing out loud with difficulty. Here was a similarity between us. The only thing he had from a broken relationship was a metal replica of his wife's boobs. It was more than Delise had left me with. Brought to bay in his lair, Gordon was more of a lap dog than a running dog of capitalism.

A moment later Liberty came bounding in, swinging from the door frame as usual. The lad's knuckles would be trailing on the floor if we didn't cure him of his habit soon. 'I've been playing this game,' he piped up in his squeaky Glaswegian. 'They've got a belting computer outwith Boss, er Dad,' he corrected himself when he remembered the part he was playing. 'Mr Gordon let me use it. He says we're all going on another helicopter ride. Great innit!'

Gordon gave me a meaningful look.

'You've got it all wrong about Rishton, you know,' Gordon remarked sadly. 'He wasn't trying to stop me taking over Alhambra. He was playing both ends against the middle, seeing how high he could push the share price up to make himself a fortune. Lance and I always knew there was someone in the background trying to arrange a rival deal. That's why Lance had you thrown out of his office in such an amusing way. We thought the people who were playing Rishton off against us had sent you!'

What he was saying was interesting, but my main interest was in giving Liberty and Jay time to get clear. I can't have been concentrating, because the next thing I knew Gordon had an automatic levelled at me. 'Why don't we take a walk down to the helicopter pad?' he suggested. I told Liberty that Jay was waiting for him at the entrance and he left quietly, obedient for once in his life, without even swinging on the door frame on his way out.

'Here, take this coat. I saw you fancying it on the day we had our little heart-to-heart chat. Go on, take it! Keep it! One less thing for the receivers to worry about.' Gordon draped the chestnut-coloured leather anorak he'd worn during our previous helicopter ride over me. He kept the gun in my back with one hand and picked up the bronze cast from his desk with the other. 'Let's give the archaeologists something to puzzle over in a few hundred years!'

I let him push me down the stairs. In the office where Liberty had been playing on the computer a harassed-looking middle-aged woman was feeding papers into a shredder. She didn't look up as we passed.

'There's only old Billy at the entrance who knows you're here and he couldn't tell anyone how many beans make ten to save his life,' Gordon commented with a low rumbling laugh. 'He's turned up for work because he doesn't understand that he's now unemployed.'

He led me through the building until we stood on the step of the exit looking out at the gleaming Bell helicopter.

It was surprisingly warm inside the bubble dome as if somebody had been running the motor and Gordon strapped me firmly into the passenger seat fastening the safety harness webbing as tight as it would go.

'This is the only place I feel free, you know. I love it. Sometimes I wish I'd been a bird.' I looked at him oddly and he laughed again. 'Only joking Cunane, but honestly most people who I do business with are so pedestrian. They have their feet so firmly on the ground they're getting rising damp. All they ever think about is their percentage, their point. That's why it was fun dealing with you. You were so different from them.'

His use of the past tense warned me.

'Rishton's a dreadful little shit, you know,' Gordon

went on almost conversationally. 'He only exists as an image on a TV screen. Precisely one tenth of a centimetre thick, he is. That's his definition of reality. They're all the same these TV executives, shallow as hell, electronic ghosts the lot of them. That Lance Trevose needs a personal assistant to help him fasten his shoe laces. Lance Trevose, he couldn't lance a boil!' He gave a cackle at his own joke before continuing, 'The only one of them I ever met that could cut the mustard was Ted Blake, but he's too greedy. None of them came up the hard way like I did. Hasn't it crossed the withered faculty that passes for your mind, that Rishton might have been trying to buy those papers from his wife to suppress them? If she blew the Bank deal, then whoever else was trying to buy the company would get it for a song and his shares and stock options would have been worthless. There aren't too many people willing to pay over the odds for a bankrupt TV company, particularly when it's only the third and smallest company in the North West of England with a massive white elephant of a studio hanging round its neck. Have you any idea what the daily running costs of that place are? First thing I'd have done would have been to sell it and put them all in prefabricated huts out at Salford Quays. Get a nice government grant for that.'

All the time he was speaking Gordon was twiddling about with the cyclic stick and the throttle. He didn't seem to be starting anything, just fidgeting. I realised I was sweating.

'Yes, now your pal Ted Blake. There's a real goer,' Gordon continued tantalisingly. 'Did he tell you that he put together a bid for the company? An absurdly low one too. More or less offered to take it off Lance's hands for nothing, cheeky young swine!'

'Really?' I said, genuinely surprised. I had no idea of Ted's meteoric ambitions.

'Oh yes, he'll go far will Ted Blake, but not at Alhambra. He was told his contract was about to be terminated right after he made the bid.'

'When was that?'

'A couple of weeks before Christmas,' Gordon replied, but I wasn't able to continue the conversation because all at once he heaved the collective lever on his left-hand side up and the helicopter shot into the air so suddenly that my ears popped.

'The old Bell 47, up in the air like a performing flea. Always takes them by surprise that does! Goes up like a rocket.'

He laughed crazily. The man was a loony.

'Now we'll see just how clever you are, Cunane,' he shouted over the roar of the exterior mounted engine.

He grabbed the bronze cast of Sandra Torkington's chest and swung it at me. I moved slightly and the left breast caught me a glancing blow on the temple. He hadn't put his strength into it. It was an awkward weapon for him to wield.

'I'm going to do a Stonehouse,' he bragged. 'Only I'm not leaving *my* sandals on the shore. They're going to find your perfectly formed body at the controls of this helicopter sixty feet under the Irish Sea. If anyone ever went out of his way to ask for it it's you, you bastard. Tell me the name of one person who'll miss you?'

I was in no state to answer his question, I was barely semi-conscious. I looked out of the window. We were already at least a thousand feet up, heading due west over the Mersey Estuary. Fear and panic triggered a surge of adrenalin, and aggressive hatred shot through me. Throughout this case I'd been the passive victim. I'd been shot at, beaten, imprisoned, sentenced to death and now this fat pig had selected me as the stand-in for his corpse. I had nothing to lose now.

I struggled desperately to get my hand on the spring release of the safety harness. He clamped his own hand over it, trying to fly the helicopter with his left hand on the cyclic while he beat me with his right. His gun, along with Sandra Torkington's heavy bosom, slipped to the floor as the blows rained down. I saw stars, coloured lights; pain and dizziness washed over me but I was sustained by my rage. I leant over and smashed my forehead into him.

He abandoned the controls completely and roaring like a bear heaved his body on top of me, crushing me down into the seat. I think he hoped to throttle me into submission. He had tremendous strength in his upper arms and I could do nothing. I could feel the breath being squeezed out of my body as he shifted slightly to bring more force to bear and for a second his head came within range. I fastened my teeth into his right eyebrow and pulled. He screamed and jerked away leaving me with a mouthful of hair.

I managed to squirm round and pressed my feet into his belly, forcing him out of his seat and right up against the flimsy door. At the same time I got my hands free. The helicopter had swung right round, one hundred and eighty degrees, and I dimly realised we were now flying a crazy path towards land. Gordon began fumbling along the floor for the gun. I could see it just out of reach of his fingers. He was stretching and straining for it. His fingers curled round the full right breast of Sandra Torkington's bronze cast but he couldn't quite pick it up and he jerked free of the seat belt that was restraining him. I started flailing at the cyclic, trying to divert his attention.

'Stop it, you maniac,' he screamed. 'You'll kill us both!' The door flew open just as I pulled the cyclic back

409

towards me, and Gordon shot through it like a champagne cork, clutching his bronze. I could see him turning over and over and then plunging straight down, head first. Then I lost sight of him.

I managed to struggle out of my webbing restraints and slid over towards the controls without the least idea of what to do. I gingerly pushed the cyclic forward again and forward motion was restored, but the helicopter was spinning like a top. Freed from control of the foot pedals by the disappearance of the pilot, the torque of the rotor blades was no longer being neutralised by the tail rotor. I was so dazed from the battering that Gordon had given me that I was almost past caring. The helicopter was see-sawing through the air, the ground below rushing past.

I experimented with my feet on the pedals and turned the throttle on the collective lever back as far as it would go. The engine cut out, but the rotors continued to spin. The whole machine began to turn round like a sycamore seed gyrating gently to earth. I was heading for the ground fast, the area I was plunging towards was a deep, almost artificial-looking green-coloured stretch of farmland. There were few houses, only faint lines traced across the virescent surface. The land began to twist rapidly in front of my already dazed eyes, rushing up at me like the end of a roller-coaster ride. I was facing death, but I felt strangely calm and must have blacked out before the moment of impact.

When I came to, I was looking at a wintry sky through the cracked bubble dome of the helicopter. I was tilted at an angle of forty-five degrees, still strapped into my seat. The pull of gravity holding me into the seat felt abnormally heavy. I awkwardly unfastened all the belts with which Gordon had intended to immobilise me. My hands were badly bruised and I couldn't move my left

410

arm. The door on my right was open and I managed to scramble out. I was only just in time – the helicopter was slowly sinking into a green swamp. I realised I was standing on the quaking surface of one of the remnants of Chat Moss, the huge peat bog which had once covered the whole of South Lancashire. It had saved my life. I staggered away and it was like walking on the surface of a trampoline. The ground was quite firm enough to support my weight although every step took effort and left a deep impression in the vegetation. The descending helicopter was slowly disappearing in the bog.

Far away, I could hear the distant wail of a fire engine. My impression that I was crashing into a complete waste land must have been mistaken. There aren't many places in England which are really deserted. Someone must have seen the aircraft crashing and summoned the emergency services. Whether it was the effect of shock, or just my natural stupidity I don't know but I decided that I didn't want to be rescued, I might face too many awkward questions, so I looked round for a refuge. The locale was completely flat and featureless and I seemed to have gone for miles, my arm in agony, before the going got slightly firmer and I tumbled into a steep-sided drainage ditch. I slithered right down the bank, coming to rest in a peaty-coloured trickle of water at the bottom. I pulled myself up out of the water and lay where I was. When I got my breath back I cautiously looked over the edge of the channel back at the way I'd come. Five hundred yards behind me I could see the nose of the helicopter still visible above the surface. On the horizon there were several fire engines and there was the clatter of a diesel engine from a point closer to my position. A tractor with huge jumbo wheels was grinding its way across the Moss towards the waiting firemen.

I stayed where I was, and improvised a sling from the

411

belt of Gordon's leather anorak which I was still wearing. There was a cold wind sweeping the Moss but the anorak was warm and I found myself dozing off as I watched the tiny figures cautiously approach the sunken helicopter across the livid green carpet. They were fastening cables to the downed machine. It was like a rescue at sea but with fire engines in the place of tugs. I must have fallen asleep because when I came round it was quite dark. I looked at my watch. It had stopped at 1.30, presumably the time of the crash. The movement had caused pain to shoot up my arm. It was definitely broken but not badly, there were no bones sticking out. I got ready for a move.

I finally emerged on a single-track road leading to a place called Moss Farm – there were posters advertising riding stables. I trudged along with no idea in what direction I was heading. From time to time cars swept past, but whether they couldn't see me in the dark, or didn't care to offer a lift I couldn't tell. None stopped. The lane was lined with scraggy overgrown hedges and hawthorn bushes at irregular intervals and I was tempted to stop and hide for the night. Far from being a deserted waste, as I'd thought from the air-view, this place was a rich farming district with vegetables growing in fertile dark soil on either side of the track.

I kept on walking and it started to rain. Eventually I saw the steep cutting of the M62 motorway and came out on the main road, the A57. It was lined with Lombardy poplars. I plodded past a large factory belonging to the Cooperative Wholesale Society and terraced houses, until finally I arrived in the centre of the small town of Irlam, an industrial settlement which had grown up around a steelworks. Of course they had closed the works 'like everything else round here' I thought crossly as I searched the streets for a working telephone. There was

412

heavy commuter traffic in the narrow main street coming from Manchester towards Warrington.

I phoned Jay at home and he agreed to come and pick me up once he got over his surprise at hearing my voice. I was pleased that he hadn't alerted the police yet. He might be on the point of joining the boys in blue himself but ingrained habits of secrecy died hard. I alerted him to look for the distinctive chestnut-coloured anorak and slumped against the wall outside a chip shop to wait for him. I realised the anorak in question was quite heavy and, feeling in the pockets with my right hand, I thought there seemed to be flat bricks weighing down the coat at both sides.

I pulled one of the bricks out. It was a tightly compressed bundle of £50 notes wrapped in plastic film. In his cunning, Gordon had sought to still any doubts about whose body was in his wrecked helicopter by stuffing the corpse with money. I supposed it was the one little detail which would convince searchers that they'd recovered Jake Gordon's corpse. I also found a steel bracelet with his name on, a passport, his lighter likewise engraved with his name, and some of his distinctive brand of cigars.

One-handed and with difficulty I lit a cigar and worked out what I had. The packets were each about as thick as a paperback book, but they felt compressed so there might be five hundred notes in each; there were six packets so that made £150,000. I knew that I couldn't touch his money, well, not much of it anyway.

Jay eventually arrived and deposited me at a private hospital in Cheadle. 'It's very expensive in here, Boss. Are you sure you don't want me to run you to Withington Hospital?' he asked anxiously. I was touched by his concern and gave him one of Gordon's cigars. He looked dubious. 'Go on Jay, now you're joining the police you'd better get used to legitimate smokes,' I urged. When I deposited my cash in the hospital safe I had no trouble at all in getting the best of attention. Before Jay left I impressed on him the importance of keeping shtum about what had happened. 'Liberty'll soon forget about it if you let the subject drop,' I suggested.

'Yeah Boss, but what about this helicopter ride he was promised? He keeps whinging on about it.'

'Jay, why don't you and Liberty take a little holiday for a few days?' I suggested. 'Perhaps even a week or two. I'm sure the school wouldn't mind. You could leave the answer phone on in the office, or try and get Finbar to go in every day to collect any messages. Why don't you take him for a few days to Center Parcs? The one in Sherwood Forest is quite near.'

'I see, Boss,' he said slowly. The old Jay, and the new future policeman Jay, were at odds with each other. 'What really did happen in that helicopter then?' he asked tentatively.

'You'd never believe it if I told you, Jay. Least said, soonest mended.' When he saw that he wasn't going to get any more out of me, he gave a broad smile, and a shake of his head. Jay was all right. He'd make a good copper, I thought. He knows how to take people the right way. I told him to tell anyone who asked that I'd broken my arm in a traffic accident and gave him plenty of money to spend on the outdoor pursuits at Center Parcs. Liberty deserved something better to swing on than a door frame.

They put my arm in plaster and I stayed there for three days, receiving physiotherapy, and eating my way through a succession of sumptuous meals. The nurses were quite attractive too, but I kept myself in check. Delise didn't show her face once, but Finbar Salway

414

turned up with a bunch of grapes on the last morning I was there.

'Dave, I hope you didn't think I was being cool with you,' he said.

'No, that's all right, Finbar,' I said sympathetically. 'You were entitled to your suspicions. You thought the heavy-set man going into Gloria Rishton's flat on the night of the murder might have been me, didn't you?'

I could see he was unhappy at having suspected me. 'So it looks like it was Jake Gordon and this Sidgwick lad then, that Coleman saw?' he asked. I didn't say anything. 'Did you see what they said in the paper about Gordon committing suicide? *"Love-lorn tycoon takes a long jump with ex-wife's cleavage"*, it said in the *Sun*.'

I smiled at Finbar's sense of outrage but it was true enough. I hoped Gordon had had the time for one last fondle on his way down.

Finbar gave me a lift back into town. He talked incessantly about the Royal Family on the way.

20

April 1994

It took me weeks to settle down to a normal routine. I was in a constant state of low-key excitement, expecting the real killer of Gloria Rishton to pay me a visit at any minute.

Delise didn't visit and I didn't call her again. I figured that she'd take her own time to forgive my many errors and I was resigned to a temporary separation. Curiously, in her absence, business picked up. The exposure of my name to the press hadn't done me any harm at all. Among other things, I was called to act as a consultant in installing alarms and security equipment at the Metropolitan University halls of residence, something I was able to cope with despite having my arm in plaster. My taxi bill got so big that I went on contract.

Jay returned from Center Parcs looking leaner and fitter than ever. Liberty had benefited too. When I saw him he was in a smart-looking green padded jacket, with a pullover, purple jeans and new boots. He was wearing his hearing aid too. He'd lost a bit of his wild look, though he still swung on the door frames.

After working out his notice with me, Jay departed for the police. I made no attempt to replace him. I was out a lot of the time and Finbar called in to look after the office occasionally. I experimented with one-handed bike riding, but gave it up after cracking the plaster on my broken arm.

The killer still hadn't turned up, but I knew that he would. It was just a matter of how long his pride would keep him away from my door.

Jake Gordon's sudden departure from this life had

been a sensation for the obligatory nine days. His landing in Risley Moss Nature Conservation Area near Warrington had been even more spectacular than my own fall to earth. The conservation area is a former munitions testing range which is being encouraged to revert to nature. There are numerous hides, including one on a tower from which the twitchers can peer out at the winter birdlife. Great, blue and coal tits, chaffinches, greenfinches, robins and blackbirds all bob about among the ferns, fritillaries and sedge. Diving with far greater speed than any sparrow hawk, Gordon had splashed down into the largest pond. Birds, and birdwatchers alike, had fled in terror.

They'd dragged his body up with grappling hooks. He'd plunged through the pond into a layer of semi-liquid mud. Apart from being dead, there wasn't much damage to him, or to Sandra Torkington's equally lifeless bust. In a way, I'd have preferred him to land on concrete, perhaps on top of the Alhambra Studios, but as it was, the question of identification didn't arise. I wondered when it was that he'd hatched the scheme to use my dead body as a substitute for his own. Was it when I first met him, or later? Had that first helicopter ride with Liberty been a trial run?

After the funeral, attended by Lance Trevose and Simon Rishton, but not by me, speculation started in the press about his motive for suicide. There'd already been complaints by the RSPB about his choice of location. They didn't want suicide over nature reserves to become a fashion. I was amused at the clever way all the TV pundits assumed that the suicide and the nature reserve were congruent: that he'd deliberately chosen to jump out of his helicopter at just that spot.

It was also assumed that he'd killed himself because of the imminent collapse of his financial empire. Diagrams were produced on the TV news to illustrate the flow of Middle East oil to the Rotterdam Spot Market and hence to independent retailers like Gordon, and graphs showed how he'd been gradually squeezed out of business when the majors managed to stabilise the oil price after the Gulf War.

But generally the press interest was in the strange manner of his departure rather than its cause. Leaping from a helicopter being considered a rather more irresponsible way to go, than jumping off a yacht in mid-Atlantic. Few expressed regret at his passing. His firm passed into receivership.

It was while browsing through the financial pages that I noticed a small paragraph stating that Barry Harrison was taking early retirement from the Polar Building Society in order to devote more time to his family. He wasn't receiving a golden handshake, either. I wasn't sure if that meant that the disappearance of Gordon had freed Harrison from whatever hold Susan Attleigh had been able to establish over him with my help. One thing was certain, I wasn't going to get in touch with Susan to find out.

Alhambra TV was under new management. The new chief executive, Simon Rishton, promised a complete revamp of all programmes. As a first step he was putting out the channel's popular soap 'Slatheredge Pit' four nights a week instead of two, with a two-hour repeat on Sundays. There was also to be a 'hive-off' from 'Slatheredge Pit', 'Cromlech Crescent', which included many of the same characters, and a private detective, to go out on five mornings a week. 'Building on established success' was how the new chief executive described his agenda. 'More of the same', is what the critics said. He also had ideas for a late-night programme called 'Viewers' Wives' where attractive, and not so attractive, ladies
418

were encouraged to reveal all on videos shot by their nearest and dearest. There'd already been a good response to the trial run. Plans were afoot to sell the expensive Alhambra headquarters building to the Metropolitan University as a college of art and design.

A big surprise for me was the failure of Ted Blake's 'scoop'. The tabloids showed little interest in his announcement of Mary Wood's royal claims, treating it all as a huge joke. As for the serious papers, they remembered the fiasco over 'Hitler's Diaries' and turned Ted down flat when he tried to peddle Mary's perfectly genuine documents around London. I heard that he'd been thrown out of Wapping by no less than the editor of the *Sunday Times*, in person. In the end he was glad enough to sell the story to the *Sunday Sport*, which ran a front-page picture of Mary coming out of a low-cut dress. The main excitement caused by the piece was that the Chinese news media picked it up and ran it as a serious item, until corrected by the British ambassador.

There seemed to be a general unspoken agreement that Britain had quite enough up-to-date royal scandals already without raking up more from the 1930s. It was as if Burger King had tried to set up shop between two McDonald's outlets. The market for royal infamy was already over-supplied.

The papers were, however, filled with the story of the cover-up of the 'DSS Fake Claimants Scandal' for several days. There'd been a bitter row in Parliament about who had attempted to cover up the fact that hundreds of building workers were in receipt of two incomes. The story rumbled on and on and I was in a state of mild dread that a Royal Commission would be appointed and uncover my own role.

With that in mind I paid a visit to my parents to tell Paddy to get rid of the trailer.

When I arrived in mid February he was just putting the finishing touches to it. He'd painted it in glowing psychedelic colours like a Van Gogh landscape. I looked at him in amazement, 'All done to order,' he explained. 'Delise has put in a bid for it, quite a respectable sum, too. Waltzed up here with all the plans and everything. I shouldn't think your friend Clarke will mind. I was going to talk to you about that. Any road, she and her mother are going to live in it for six months every year. They want to get in touch with nature, she says. I don't know what some of these folk are *mithering* on about. A good dose of castor oil now and then is all your mother and me need to keep us in touch with nature.'

It was in March that I started seeing Kath Headlam regularly. I can't say I was entirely flattered by the reason for our reunion. She was out of work and her contacts in the old Filofax had been of no avail. 'Dear Simon' had made her redundant as part of his cost-cutting drive.

She wasn't taking to enforced unemployment very well and I took her out for a meal to talk things over. She wasn't resentful about Simon, she'd long ceased to expect anything except unreasonable demands from that quarter. I still found her face as fascinating as ever. As well as the wrap-around smile she had another little gimmick when I said anything she thought was too 'laddish' or crass. She'd do the smile, cheeks folding and everything, then she'd tuck her chin in, and give just the faintest imitation of a blush.

She took to hanging about round my office and gradually drifted into answering the phone when I wasn't there and fixing up appointments for me. She certainly had the right telephone manner as far as business went, but I was very reluctant to take things any further with her although there were more than enough hints that I'd be pushing against an open door as far as that went.

420

I realised then that I've always been strongly attracted to upper-class women with fruity accents. There's a lecherous gamekeeper lurking somewhere deep among the tangle of my working-class roots who longs to run riot with the daughters of the upper classes. He's hidden away behind all those highly respectable policemen in my family tree but I know he's there. That may account for the episode with Mary Wood, she is of royal blood after all.

But with Kath I was determined to keep things on a celibate, friendship-only basis until I could see what the complete agenda was. I'd learned from my mistakes. It was when I was in this phase of self-denial that I heard the news about Delise.

I was coming down Brundretts Road in Chorlton one afternoon on my way back from the bank when I spotted the Killer Whale, Molly Delaney, bearing down on me. I tried to dodge her but she waved at me and crossed the narrow street. Her face had an unusually gleeful expression. I stood poised to run while she spoke to me. I had one broken arm already. But I needn't have worried, I wasn't required to speak. 'You're looking well, apart from the arm,' she said. 'Would you like me to sign it for you? You must be sure to watch the television tonight, tune in to Alhambra.' With that and a swish of her denim overall she departed. I wondered if someone had volunteered to do a video recording of her for 'Viewers' Wives'.

I didn't have long to wait. No sooner had the regional news credits faded than there was Delise, acting as continuity announcer and generally managing to give Simon Rishton's flashy little channel a touch of class. So she'd managed to square Rishton after all. But success has its price. It was only later that I heard the full story from

Kath Headlam. Delise had moved in with Rishton, and was well on the way to becoming the fifth Mrs Rishton.

I was bitter, but I sent her a good-luck card.

I'd been expecting a visit from Ted Blake ever since Gordon had taken his dive into the swamp. He called at the flat unexpectedly one evening, looking pretty sorry for himself, as well he might. Simon Rishton had carried out Trevose's previous edict and axed Ted's show. 'In the present climate of stringency "Bang to Rights" got the company involved in too many law suits and claims for damages.' I thought that was rich coming from Simon Rishton. Ted was coming unzipped literally, as well. He'd put on weight and his clothes appeared to have given up the struggle to contain his ever-expanding body mass. His fat neck bulged over the top of his shirt. He looked red in the face and sweaty.

'I thought I'd have heard from you before now, Dave,' he said plaintively, as he picked up the whisky I'd poured him. 'It's not like you to turn your back on a friend. Mary's been quite upset, too.'

'No, you're right. I don't turn my back on my friends. I let you do that, Ted,' I said.

He didn't reply.

'How's the story going?' Twisting the knife.

'Oh, not too bad. Mary's been asked to give a lecture tour . . .' I looked at him in surprise. 'Well, it's like a tour of the Irish clubs really, round London. She starts at the Blarney Stone in Acton next Thursday,' he admitted. 'She has a ten-minute spot after the interval.'

'Are you playing the banjo for her, then?' I said spitefully.

'Don't say you've still got the hump about that little bug in your office.' He drained his drink rather more quickly than he used to. I noticed that his hand was shaking slightly.

'Sincerely now, Dave. Are you upset that I took Mary off you, or is it about Delise, or what?' he asked.

'We both know why I'm upset, Ted, and you needn't worry that I'm taping this conversation. No one but us is interested in what we've got to say to each other.'

He cradled his drink, and then gulped it down in one go.

'Why did you kill Gloria, Ted? What had Gloria Rishton ever done to you?' I asked.

'It wasn't my fault, old son, seriously,' he said with a grimace. He knew what I was talking about all right. 'Sheer bloody incompetence on the part of the Northern Pioneers Bank, that's what it was. A bloody shame, the whole thing.'

I said nothing to prompt him, but he went on, 'Can you believe the stupidity of a bank putting someone's estranged wife on to researching a loan involving millions? Poor little bitch couldn't resist the temptation of trying to put the squeeze on the lot of us . . . well, me and Simon anyway.'

'But why *you*, Ted? What was she to you?'

'I picked her up last July after a party at Alhambra. It was just a quick grope and a spot of "how's your father?" in the car park at first, but then when Simon moved in with Kath, things got more serious. Gloria started talking about marriage. She thought I was going places, and by God I was!' He gave me a bitter look. 'I didn't kill her myself you know, nor Poulter, though it was me who altered the log book.'

'And I suppose it wasn't you who tipped the biker assassin off that I was outside by the camp fire so that he could roar up and get a good shot at me, was it?' I asked resentfully.

'Well, what was I to do? I knew you'd rumble me eventually, by process of elimination, if nothing else. It would have been quick, you wouldn't have felt a thing.'

'But why kill Gloria in the first place? Have you any idea what your little friend did to her? I still wake up at night thinking about it.'

'Of course I have. I was there, you fool! Do you think I'm pleased with what happened? Gloria had the papers that showed Gordon was on the edge of bankruptcy. The profit margin on his oil business had been brilliant at the time of the Iran–Iraq war, but he'd over-expanded. He thought he was J. Paul Getty. He ended up buying oil at greater prices than he could sell it for . . . Most people thought he was still worth untold millions. You only have to mention "oil" to a banker and his eyes turn red. The deal was that he'd use his credit to save Alhambra, and refloat his own company. Trevose knew all about it, but it was in his interest to keep quiet. Then Gloria found out. If she'd reported it she'd be alive today and Gordon, Trevose and Rishton would all have been ruined. I *wanted* her to spill the beans at first.'

'That was when you offered to take the company off Trevose and they sacked you for your pains,' I said.

'Seriously, I could have picked the company up off its feet. But Gloria didn't like it when my programme got the boot: she began to get cold feet about life as the next Mrs Blake. She thought if she suppressed the information and told Simon about what she'd done he'd boot Kath Headlam's bony arse out of his bed and put her own picture back on the mantelpiece. Women, I ask you? Who can make them out? By the way, Dave, how are you getting on with Headlam?' He had a nasty leer on his flushed face.

'Just stick to the story, Blake,' I growled. 'What do you care about Kath? You nearly landed her in prison for life. No wonder you were so keen to get Delise to reveal all about her diaries. I bet it was you who fed the press with all those stories about the jealous mistress.'

'Not on my own mate, I had help from DCI Jerrold. Wonderful copper that,' he sneered.

'Get on with it, or get out!' I snapped.

'When I scented which way the wind was blowing I left a little bug in Gloria's bedroom and another by the phone. I heard her making her plans for a reunion with Rishton. I heard him promising to send her a nice little Christmas bonus to keep her sweet until he could disentangle himself from Headlam. That didn't suit me at all. I decided that if she wouldn't help me she wouldn't help anyone. Her information was worth at least ten million to Gordon! Enough for me to start up my own production company!'

'You mean you were going to blackmail Gordon?' I asked bluntly.

'Yeah, why not? The silly little bitch Gloria had hidden the papers in a plastic bag in the cold-water tank in her loft. I spilled about a gallon of water fishing them out. When I heard that you were on your way down there, I rang Gloria up at work, had one last try at getting her to come in with me, but she told me it was too late. Simon was sending someone to collect the papers.'

'What about the assassin . . . Sidgwick?'

'I met him through a contact on the programme and took him with me to Gloria's to throw a scare into her . . .'

Come off it Ted, you knew what would happen,' I said.

'No, seriously now . . . well, you can't believe it's going to happen until the very last minute. I thought she'd change her mind. We'd just got the papers out of the tank when she came in and hung her coat up. She never

425

saw me. She said "Mr Cunane?" when she saw Sidgwick and then he bounced her out into the garage and did the job before she could say anything else. He was out of control – ex-marines – supposed to be on medication but he never took it. Then he said, "Let's leave two more cartridges here as a warning." Put the wind up me, I can tell you. After that, all I had to do was point him in the right direction. I could have offed the lot of you, I'm telling you.'

We sat in silence for a while, then Ted left without another word. He never could resist an audience.

I couldn't get to sleep after he'd gone. There was no point in phoning the police. Even if Mr Sinclair had been prepared to listen there wasn't a scrap of evidence that would stand up in court against Ted. Besides Sinclair had his hands full fending off enquiries about the DSS Fake Claimants Scandal. I rang Kath and she came round right away, which was flattering I suppose. She moved in with me soon after.

It was on Kath's advice that I set up the trust fund for Liberty Walker with Gordon's tainted money. It would pay for his boarding fees at the Royal School for Hearing Impaired Children and for the operations he needed to repair the damage to his skull and hearing.

Ted Blake died in a road accident two weeks later. His Shogun hit a motorway bridge at 90. He wasn't strapped in, and the Coroner said there was evidence that he'd been drinking poteen, so it might not have been suicide. I preferred to think that it was. Mary Wood stayed on in his Didsbury flat, and continued with her 'lecture tours'.

I didn't go to the funeral.